SIMON & GARFUNKEL
Together Alone

Spencer Leigh

M^CNIDDER | &
GRACE

Published by McNidder & Grace
16A Bridge Street
Carmarthen
SA31 3JS
www.mcnidderandgrace.co.uk

First published in 2016
©Spencer Leigh
www.spencerleigh.co.uk

Every effort has been made to obtain necessary permission with reference
to copyright material. The publisher apologises if, inadvertently, any sources
remain unacknowledged and will be glad to make the necessary arrangements at
the earliest opportunity.

A catalogue record for this work is available from the British Library.
ISBN: 9780857161505

Designed by Obsidian Design

Printed and bound in the United Kingdom by
Short Run Press Ltd, Exeter, UK

*'Simon and Garfunkel were a team.
I always knew that.
I'm not so sure Paul did.'*

Art Garfunkel, 1998

About the Author

The journalist, author and broadcaster Spencer Leigh was born in Liverpool, England, and is an acknowledged authority on the Beatles. He has been broadcasting his weekly show, *On the Beat*, on BBC Radio Merseyside for more than thirty years and over that time has conducted more interviews about the band – all captured on tape – than anyone in the world. He has written over twenty-five books, hundreds of album sleeve notes and he writes obituaries of musicians for the *Independent* and the *Oxford Dictionary of National Biography*. He is an Honoured Friend at the Liverpool Institute of Performing Arts (LIPA), co-founded by Sir Paul McCartney, and he has a Gold Badge of Merit from the British Academy of Songwriters, Composers and Authors. Spencer will always live on Merseyside.

Spencer Leigh is also the author of *Frank Sinatra: An Extraordinary Life*, *Best of the Beatles: The Sacking of Pete Best*, *The Cavern Club: Rise of the Beatles and Merseybeat* and *Love Me Do to Love Me Don't: The Beatles on Record*, published by McNidder & Grace.

Acknowlegments

My thanks to Ben Coker, David Charters, Fred Dellar, Andrew Doble, Peter Grant, Patrick Humphries, Mick O'Toole and Sue Place. Thanks to the various music magazines of the day including *Disc*, *Melody Maker*, *New Musical Express* (*NME*) and *Record Mirror*. I'm very grateful to Andy Peden Smith for suggesting that my 1973 book *Paul Simon: Now and Then* should be updated – and here it is, eventually rewritten. Love as always to my wife, Anne – we met through the first edition of this book in 1973 and are still together.

Contents

Suzi Quatro

Foreword

Simon & Garfunkel, wow... Immediate vivid memories of being fourteen, trying to find out who I am, and discovering this wonderfully unique duo who somehow spoke to me. I was hooked with 'The Sound of Silence', but the one that really reached in and spoke to me was 'I Am a Rock'. I had just started my own career in my first all-girl band, and was feeling like a misunderstood artist. Funny, I still feel like that now even after fifty-two years in the business! Simon & Garfunkel gave me a lifeline.

Being a singer/songwriter/musician, I dive deep into the artists that I like, so that I know every single breath on every single record. As I did with Dylan, another big love of mine. For me, Simon & Garfunkel are the melodious part of the same genre.

For some years after the Everly Brothers happened, there was not another harmony match that was so perfect, and then along came these two guys. Their voices fit perfectly together, and Art's high notes made some of the poignant messages in the songs a little bit easier for me to take, being a highly sensitive teenager.

Their version of 'Silent Night' crossed with a news bulletin was a brilliant idea... Say no more!

Simon & Garfunkel have been a huge part of the soundtrack of my life. Thank you for the music, boys, and I have enjoyed reading about you. Your story here has been told with sensitivity and accuracy, as is Spencer's book I am reading on Frank Sinatra.

With love and respect,

Suzi Quatro

Preface

New Books For Old

In 1973 I wrote *Paul Simon: Now and Then*, published by a small Liverpool-based company, Raven Books. It sold 8,000 copies but was not reprinted or kept up-to-date. Copies of it now are sold at silly prices, possibly because Paul Simon completists want it and because it is an early example of rock biography.

As I kept getting emails about it, I wondered if it could be reissued as an eBook. When I read the text for the first time in thirty years, it wasn't as bad as I suspected but it contained some dodgy opinions. Writing about 'Mother and Child Reunion', I dismissed the whole of reggae music, which surprised me as I thought I had loved reggae from the word go. There were mistakes – I had followed an item in the *New Musical Express* which said that Paul Simon and Carly Simon were related when they weren't. There was little first-hand research and outside of a few British folkies, I hadn't spoken to anyone.

Its big plus was that I had gone through the British musical press and found numerous interviews with Simon and Garfunkel and so I had their thoughts on most matters.

So, yes, this is the reissued *Paul Simon: Now and Then*, but only marginally so. *Simon & Garfunkel: Together Alone* is much more a new book than an old one. Mostly this is a chronological telling of the story of Simon and Garfunkel, both together and alone. As I was writing (or rewriting) it, it did strike me that there are themes that could be separate studies. I've done my best with their early years around the Brill Building but it would need their commitment to sort out their full involvement with the pop singles of the late 50s and early 60s; then there is their deep affection for the Everly Brothers and the fact they have sung so much of *Songs Our Daddy Taught Us*; there is Simon's on-off relationship with Bob Dylan which is far more 'on' than most people imagine; the strong Christian imagery in Simon & Garfunkel's songs and choice of material throughout the whole fifty years, much more than references to Judaism. A book could be written on the artists who have covered Paul Simon's songs and how they have treated them.

It has been great to spend time with their recordings. Phrases from their songs pop into my head all the time and 'American Tune' seems to be on repeat in my head. Their songs work on so many levels and even when the meanings are not clear, they still sound stunning.

Early on, Simon and Garfunkel realised two things. Firstly, the world liked them working together. Secondly, they didn't.

Spencer Leigh
July 2016

CHAPTER 1

Born at the Right Time

Although this book is largely propelled by the differences between Paul Simon and Art Garfunkel, and it would be a weaker story without that tension, they do have much in common.

They were born within a few miles and a few weeks of each other. Paul Frederic Simon was born on 13 October 1941 in Newark, New Jersey. The family tree goes back to Romania and includes tailors and shopkeepers, hence Simon's reference to a previous lifetime in his song, 'Fakin' It'.

Simon's grandfather was a cantor and his mother regularly attended services, ensuring that her son had a bar mitzvah. Simon's parents nicknamed him 'Cardozo' after a Supreme Court judge, Benjamin Cardozo, who never smiled. Indeed, Art Garfunkel recalls that his stern persona made him a great poker player at school.

Paul McCartney once said to Paul Simon, 'How come there are so many Christian references in your songs when you were brought up Jewish?' It was a good observation: you can tell from Bob Dylan's songs that he is Jewish but Simon's songs are more likely to include Christian imagery.

Arthur Ira Garfunkel was born on 5 November 1941 in New York City, so they had Ellis Island and the Statue of Liberty between them. Right from the start, he looked distinctive. Look at the childhood photo of him playing baseball on his *Lefty* LP and you'll know it couldn't be anybody else.

The two families did not know each other but Simon's family was to move east to Forest Hills, part of the Queens district. The area is famed for its tennis club and concert stadium complex and playing at Forest Hills would be Simon and Garfunkel's homecoming gig. The horseshoe stadium, designed that way for major tennis tournaments, could seat 16,000 so homecoming gigs were lavish affairs. The Beatles

1

played there in August 1964.

Paul's father, Lou, was 'the family bass man' as he played in various dance bands, while Paul's mother, Belle, was a schoolteacher. Lou played on *The Garry Moore Show* and *Arthur Godfrey and His Friends*. He was a bandleader too, but during the 1970s he switched to teaching and obtained a doctorate in linguistics.

Paul's brother, Eddie, was born on 14 December 1945. He now administers Paul's publishing and is his co-manager but he is a competent musician in his own right, and in both stature and looks he resembles his brother. In their publishing office in the Brill Building, they display their father's double bass.

Garfunkel was raised in Kew Gardens, known then as the Jewish section of Queens. His father, Jack, sold containers and packaging, sometimes marketing his own products. His mother, Rose, was a secretary. They had three sons – Jules, Arthur and Jerry – with a total of seven years between them. Garfunkel's earliest musical memory is hearing Enrico Caruso and Mario Ancona sing the duet from *The Pearl Fishers*: 'I was five years old and already I knew that I loved melody and the drama of high notes.'

Forest Hills and Kew Gardens were neighbouring sections, both reasonably affluent, and Paul and Art lived within walking distance of each other. They both attended Public School 164 in Queens, where Belle Simon was teaching. They moved on to Forest Hills High School. They were good students and Simon was a promising right fielder on the baseball pitch.

When Paul saw Art singing 'Too Young' at a school assembly, he realised that performing in public was a key to popularity. Art's repertoire included 'I Dream of Jeannie with the Light Brown Hair' and 'Winter Wonderland' and he had dreams of being a cantor, the lead singer in a synagogue.

In view of many UK connections in this book, it is apt that their first appearance together, back in 1953, was in something quintessentially British, a school production of *Alice in Wonderland* with Art as the Cheshire Cat and Paul, most appropriately, as the White Rabbit, the animal who is always running late. Fifty years later, Paul told stadium audiences on their reunion tour, 'I was the White Rabbit, a leading role, and Artie was the Cheshire Cat, a supporting role.' The implication didn't need spelling out.

Garfunkel once remarked that George Harrison had said to him,

'My Paul is to me what your Paul is to you.' Garfunkel commented, 'He meant that psychologically they had the same effect on us. The Pauls sidelined us.'

At school, Paul and Art became friends with Paul liking Art's sense of humour but being wary of his fastidiousness. Every step is neatly planned with Art Garfunkel making lists of things to do and crossing them off as they are completed.

Art told *The New Yorker* about their schooldays: 'Neither of us were the group types, except maybe in athletics. I guess we were drawn together. Being outsiders, in a sense, was one reason. Mutual interests, music among them, was another.' In 2015, Garfunkel said that he had felt sorry for Paul because he was small.

In 1953, when Paul Simon was twelve, he and his father were listening to the radio, waiting for the commentary on a New York Yankees game. The current show, *Make Believe Ballroom*, featured middle-of-the-road music but the host, Martin Block, was about to play the worst thing he said he had ever heard. The record was 'Gee' by the Crows, a lively doo-wop record which, fair enough, would be nonsensical to the unconverted. Paul Simon recalled, 'This was the first thing I had heard on the *Make Believe Ballroom* that I liked.'

There's no definitive answer to the question, 'What was the first rock'n'roll record?' but 'Gee' is a contender. Soon Paul was trying to find the new music on the stations he could pick up in New York. Although Jewish, he thought there was nothing incongruous about listening to gospel music on Sundays and he acquired a taste for southern country music, loving the wit of 'In the Jailhouse Now', a country hit for Webb Pierce in 1955. Artie felt the same way and, once homework was done, they would listen to Alan Freed's nightly shows on WINS. He was the DJ who had named the new music, rock'n'roll.

In 1955 Paul and Artie teamed up for a high school dance where they sang a rhythm and blues hit, Big Joe Turner's 'Flip, Flop and Fly'. Paul knew Al Kooper, a musician who features in Bob Dylan's career, and Paul and Al ambitiously tackled 'Stardust' as well as rock'n'roll favourites.

Garfunkel became obsessed with the *Billboard* Hot 100. He'd watch how the records climbed and fell out of favour. Paul preferred playing the new music. He has often said, 'I started playing the guitar at thirteen because of Elvis Presley', and Elvis Presley is a recurring motif in his life.

Simon discovered that a young schoolboy could not mimic Elvis

Presley's sexuality without derision. He loved the backbeat in Chuck Berry's songs and his constant theme of what would happen when school was out. He said, 'I single out Chuck Berry because it was the first time that I heard words flowing in an absolutely effortless way. He had very powerful imagery in his songs and "Maybelline" is one of my favourites.'

Paul Simon loved the Penguins' 'Earth Angel': he had learnt about oxymorons in English class and he had found one in a rock'n'roll song title. On one level he is right, but angels on earth pop up (or down) all the time in the Bible.

Although Simon acknowledged his debt to Chuck Berry and Elvis Presley, he teamed up with Garfunkel to produce a sound more akin to the Everly Brothers. Paul recalled first hearing 'Bye Bye Love': 'I called up Artie and I said, "I've just heard this great record. Let's go out and buy it." Artie and I used to practise singing like the Everly Brothers. To me, it was weird that a group would have that name. There was nobody named Everly in Forest Hills. Everybody's name was Steinberg, Schwartz or Weinstein. I can imagine how odd it was for the rest of the country when a group came along called Simon & Garfunkel.'

Art Garfunkel said, 'Don and Phil are not praised enough. As much as we think they're gods, they're higher than gods. To me they beat Elvis. We learned from them and we outstripped them, but then they didn't have the songs of Paul Simon.'

The Everly Brothers sounded new but their sound emanated from Kentucky and Tennessee. The Everlys took their lead from southern country groups like the Delmore Brothers and the Blue Sky Boys, but they sang faster and addressed teenage preoccupations. Nearly all the Everly Brothers records of the 1950s are wonderful: even when the song is lightweight, it is rescued by magical harmonies.

During 1957, the fledgling duo sang at neighbourhood dances and Paul recalled that 'New York was a great rock'n'roll place in those days.' Even at this level, they knew that Simon & Garfunkel was not a cool name. They adopted the cat-and-mouse pseudonym of Tom and Jerry, marginally better than Tweety and Sylvester. Art was Tom Graph, so named because he studied mathematics, and Paul was Jerry Landis, simply because he was dating Sue Landis.

Paul said, 'My dad was a bandleader and by the time I could play a bit of rock'n'roll he would take me out with him if he was playing to a younger audience. I saw how he worked as a bandleader and you can't learn something like that in school. He taught me how to plan a set, how to interact with other musicians and how to get the best from them. My dad did it effortlessly though and I thought it was effortless until I started getting into fights with Artie. As soon as we met, we were the kind of best friends who would fight.'

The first song they wrote was 'The Girl for Me' which Paul wanted Artie to sing. He formed a doo-wop group around him and they were influenced by a hit band from nearby Jamaica, Queens, the Cleftones. Their demo got nowhere but the song was granted copyright by the Library of Congress.

Paul's father, who was playing with the Lee Simms Orchestra at the Roseland Ballroom, would write down Paul's chords. His father would tell him that his tune was in 4/4 and he'd suddenly gone to 9/8. 'You can't do that,' Lou would say. 'I just did,' said Paul, thereby discovering one of his songwriting traits.

A commercialised form of folk music was popular in the 1950s. The Weavers, who included Pete Seeger, had successes with 'Goodnight Irene', 'Michael Row the Boat Ashore' and 'Wimoweh'. The Everly Brothers took the Appalachian folk songs they had heard from their father, Ike, to make a wonderful acoustic album, *Songs Our Daddy Taught Us*, miles from rock'n'roll but an influential album for many musicians. Paul Simon called this 1958 record his favourite LP.

The Clovers had recorded a cheerful R&B novelty written by Titus Turner, 'Hey Doll Baby', in 1955. It was released as the B-side to their doo-wop favourite 'Devil or Angel'. In August 1957, the Everly Brothers gave 'Hey Doll Baby' a neat choppy rhythm which they duplicated the following day for their million-selling 'Wake Up Little Susie'. The lyrics weren't easy to grasp: for years I thought the Evs were rhyming 'lovesick' and 'mystics' but it is 'for love's sake' and 'mistakes', so Paul and Art could be forgiven for getting the words wrong. As they attempted to put the song into their repertoire, a new song emerged.

They now had 'Hey Schoolgirl' with a hook of nonsense syllables ('Wu-bop-a-lu-chi-bop') that owes something to Little Richard's 'Tutti Frutti'. They considered it sufficiently different from 'Hey Doll Baby' to be a song in its own right and thought it had commercial potential. If they made a demo and sent it to the Everly Brothers, maybe, just maybe, they would record it.

There were many small recording studios in New York and they cut 'Hey Schoolgirl' for a few dollars at the Sanders Recording Studio on

Seventh Avenue, not far from Columbia's studios. Did they dream that they might go there one day? Although their thoughts about Columbia would be mixed: 'Just a come on from the whores on Seventh Avenue', wrote Simon in 'The Boxer'.

By chance, Paul and Art met Sid Prosen of Big Records at the Sanders studio, and he liked what they were doing, or at least said he did. In time-honoured fashion, he was going to make them stars. He saw their parents, secured a contract and released 'Hey Schoolgirl' on his small but Big label. The B-side, 'Dancin' Wild', sounded like a continuation of 'Hey Schoolgirl' and should have been held back for the follow-up. They promoted it in red jackets and white bucks. With a little payola, it was played by Alan Freed, sold well locally and was released nationally through the King label.

Somehow, and again it could be payola, they found themselves on the Thanksgiving edition of Dick Clark's *American Bandstand*, the teenage TV show of the day. This live programme for the ABC network, broadcast on 22 November 1957, starred Jerry Lee Lewis with his classic rave-up, 'Great Balls of Fire'. Paul said, 'I watched *American Bandstand* and here I was playing the show. It made me a neighbourhood hero.'

How Artie must have loved watching 'Hey Schoolgirl' climb his beloved *Billboard* chart, reaching a respectable No. 49. It sold 100,000 copies in the face of stiff opposition, not least from the Everlys' new single, who in years to come would have welcomed a hit that size.

Tom and Jerry played few concerts outside their own area, although they were booked for an otherwise black show at the Hertford State Theatre. The show starred LaVern Baker ('Jim Dandy') and Thurston Harris ('Little Bitty Pretty One') – 'and Artie and I came out running in white bucks'. Still, they had enough stagecraft to survive.

Unlike many record company owners, Sid Prosen wasn't a rogue and they each made $2,000 from 'Hey Schoolgirl'. Paul bought an electric guitar and a red Impala convertible. He crashed it a few times and its carburettor burned out near Art's house: 'I ended up watching my share of the record money getting burned up.' Not to worry, as he regained the cost many times over as his exploits inspired his song, 'Baby Driver'.

Sid Prosen promised bigger things next time, but as Simon said, 'The next one was a flop and the next one a flop and the company went broke and we went back to school.'

As simple as that.

Only it wasn't. Paul Simon had the bug.

Paul Simon may make glib remarks to throw researchers off the track. He may not want his efforts from the late 50s and early 60s to be remembered, but he is mistaken. You can't change history and anyway, many of his earlier 45s are both telling and enjoyable.

Some readers may think that I should cut to the chase and get on to Simon & Garfunkel's albums, but it would be omitting their development. The tracks show Paul Simon singing and playing, working in studios and learning his craft, including how to produce himself and other artists. He was discovering how to avoid mistakes and even before he had a hit single of any consequence, he had formed his own company, Landis Publishing. How far-sighted and confident is that? He was the first major rock musician to own his own catalogue and John Lennon praised him for his insight. There was a precedent as Irving Berlin controlled his songs through Irving Berlin Music.

Simon and Garfunkel have nursed a soft spot for 'Hey Schoolgirl'. In 1967 they opened for the Mothers of Invention as Tom and Jerry and when they were called back for an encore, they sang 'The Sound of Silence', so hopefully everybody got the joke. In 2004 they went on tour with the Everly Brothers and brazenly sang 'Hey Schoolgirl' before introducing them.

'Hey Schoolgirl' had a catalogue number of Big 613. Big 614 was an echo-drenched ballad à la Paul Anka, 'Teenage Fool' coupled with the Elvis-lite rockabilly of 'True or False' and attributed to True Taylor aka Paul Simon. 'True or False' was written by his father, Lou Simon. His father was always supportive and would transport Tom and Jerry before they could drive.

But Artie was not supportive of True Taylor. Paul hadn't told him what he was doing. Even now, Art cites this as typical of Paul's behaviour, their first big argument and one that has been repeated several times. In 1980, Paul Simon told *Playboy*, 'Artie looked upon my solo record as a betrayal. That solo record has coloured our relationship. I said, "Artie, I was 15 years old. How can you carry that betrayal for 25 years? Even if I was wrong, I was just a 15-year-old kid who wanted to be Elvis Presley for one moment instead of being in the Everly Brothers with you. Even if you were hurt, let's drop it." But he won't. He said, "You're still the same guy."'

Paul Simon was sixteen, not fifteen, and he was feeling the pangs of not being able to follow up a hit record. He told the *New York World-*

Telegram in 1957, 'Once you're down, it can be terrible.'

The True Taylor single didn't make the charts and the follow-up to 'Hey Schoolgirl' was 'Our Song'/'Two Teenagers' (Big 616). 'Our Song' is a break-up song in which the jukebox makes the singer cry; again heavily Everly with a bridge taken from 'Wake Up Little Susie'. Long before it was fashionable, Paul and Art were into recycling. The B-side, 'Two Teenagers', written by Rose Marie McCoy, who wrote for Elvis, was a cheerful novelty with irritating female back-up singers. They sneaked in the riff from 'Hey Schoolgirl'.

The new single didn't sell but Tom and Jerry tried again with the plaintive 'That's My Story', which has a brassy arrangement similar to Billy Vaughn, and 'Don't Say Goodbye' (Big 618). For Big 621, they did a cover of 'Baby Talk' backed by a reissue of 'Two Teenagers'. Jan and Dean made the US Top 10 with 'Baby Talk' but this is okay. Curiously, Tom and Jerry's version was released in the UK by Gala as one side of a single which sold for four shillings (twenty pence).

That is not quite the end of Tom and Jerry as there is a further single, the quirky novelty 'Lookin' at You' and country ballad 'I'm Lonesome', an Ember single, issued by Pye International in the UK but not until 1963. *Record Mirror* said that 'showed promise', not knowing that they were assessing a single made four years earlier.

Another Tom and Jerry single, 'Surrender, Please Surrender' and 'Fightin' Mad', features nondescript songs written by Sid Prosen, but I think Prosen invited other wannabes to perform them. I hope it is not Simon singing about the quest 'to find a girlie just like you'.

There are two Tom and Jerry singles on Mercury ('South'/'Golden Wildwood Flower' and 'I'll Drown In My Tears'/'The French Twist'), but they were the Nashville instrumentalists, Tom Tomlinson and Jerry Kennedy, not to mention some novelty singles from the cartoon cat and mouse themselves.

In 1967 the UK label Allegro released an album of their singles as Tom and Jerry, attributing them to Simon & Garfunkel and slapping a contemporary photograph on the cover. The sleeve note said, 'We are very fortunate to have captured on this recording the exciting sounds of these two brilliant young men. Contained in this album is a generous sampling of two stars of tomorrow who are the talk of the record world today.'

Paul was indignant, telling *Record Mirror*, 'What annoyed me most about the record is that it implied that this was new Simon & Garfunkel material. They used a recent photograph on the cover. If they'd released it saying, "This is Simon & Garfunkel at 15", it might have been interesting and I would have said, "Okay, that's me at 15 and I'm not ashamed of it." I made a record at 15 and everybody wanted to at that age. I just wanted to be Frankie Lymon.' Later he became more critical, calling the record 'fodder for mental eunuchs... I'm ashamed of it.'

Simon and Garfunkel took legal action and the album was withdrawn on both sides of the Atlantic. Strangely, Woolworths immediately started selling copies for just five shillings (twenty-five pence) and I recall seeing hundreds in their Liverpool branch. I bought one and I'd have been rich if I'd bought the lot.

The Allegro album has ten tracks, two of them previously unheard instrumentals, the mournful 'Tijuana Blues' and the jazzy 'Simon Says'. 'Simon Says' has the songwriting credit of Louis Simon and Sid Prosen.

Paul and Art's singles as Tom and Jerry are competent and they could have been lucky and had a chart career. Paul summarised it thus: 'We didn't plan to go on with music as a career but it wasn't just for fun. We were deadly serious about everything we did. We wanted to sing and we wanted to play. It wasn't like we said, "Let's make one record and that would be it", and then we'd travel off to university. We loved making records.'

This isn't wholly true. Paul felt that way but Art's heart wasn't in it. He enjoyed making records but he was giving private lessons in mathematics and was planning to study architecture at Columbia, though he switched to maths (sorry, math). Simon would go to Queens College to study English literature but he was less committed and wanted to make music. 'I was going to be a political science major at one time,' Paul told journalist Lon Goddard, 'but the professor used to fart a lot – and so I said, "That's disgusting – I won't be that."'

Paul loved the atmosphere surrounding the music publishing companies in the Brill Building and as well as solo singles, he made demos for songwriters. He would sing a lead vocal for fifteen dollars and he was so proficient that he could make the whole demo, playing instruments and overdubbing where necessary. He explained, 'After "Hey, Schoolgirl", I got to know studios and record labels. I'd leave my name with them and they'd call me to cut demos. I learned how to overdub and for $25, I could sound like a full group. I'd play bass, drums, piano in the key of C, and sing oo-ah-ooh in four different voices.'

At Queens College, Paul met Carole Klein who became Carole King. They both wrote songs and made demos calling themselves the Cosines with Paul playing guitar and bass and Carole piano and drums. They'd add their voices and the records would be sent to artists who were currently hot like Frankie Avalon and the Fleetwoods.

Carole wanted to be a professional songwriter, working with her boyfriend, soon her husband, Gerry Goffin. Paul shared the advice his father had given him. 'She wanted to quit Queens and be a songwriter. I said "Don't, you'll ruin your career". And she quit and had ten hits that year.' 'Will You Love Me Tomorrow' ensured her an income for life. Goffin and King were signed by Aldon Music, run by Don Kirshner, but he turned Paul Simon down.

Paul recorded solo as Jerry Landis, the first single for MGM in 1959 featuring two of his compositions. The mawkish 'Loneliness' is a typical teenage-wallowing-in-misery song from the late 50s. The B-side, 'Annabelle', is the worst song he ever wrote, his vocal competing with a squawking sax.

Also in 1959, Jerry Landis recorded two Marv Kaplin songs for Chance, 'Just to Be with You' and 'Ask Me Why'. He and Carole King worked on the arrangement of 'Just to Be with You' together. The song was picked up by the Brooklyn doo-wop group, the Passions, and their single made No. 69.

Paul Simon knew the management and the acts at Laurie Records, but he was never able to place his songs with their top artist, Dion. Mostly Paul's songs remained demos but sometimes they were released in their own right. 'Cry, Little Boy, Cry' was a carbon copy of 'Runaround Sue', while 'Noise' emulated the party feel of 'The Majestic'. Simon sounded like Dion singing 'I Wonder Why' on 'Cards of Love', a clever song about how the Jack steps in between the King and Queen. Most significant of all was 'Wildflower' from 1962 – the lyric 'She was a wanderer through and through' was aimed at Dion, and its Bo Diddley/Buddy Holly beat would have suited him. Oddly, the song suddenly changed to an African chant. Unlikely of course, but was this the starting block for *Graceland*?

Paul was mostly working at Associated Studios, again on Seventh Avenue and close to the Brill Building. He played lead guitar on Johnny Restivo's rock'n'roll chart single, 'The Shape I'm In' (US 80) and its B-side 'Ya Ya'. Restivo was a poster boy, a veritable Adonis, but the single had rock'n'roll credibility and is heard on oldies shows.

Another single was a wimpish ballad with a light beat, 'Shy', inspired by Frankie Avalon's 'Why'. The playful vocal suggests that Simon wasn't taking it seriously. The B-side was the saccharine 'Just A Boy', which would have suited Avalon, but the bridge steals from 'Secret Love'.

Paul worked, somewhat unsuccessfully, in music publishing, although one song he promoted, 'Broken Hearted Melody' by Sarah Vaughan became a huge hit. It was written by Hal David and Sherman Edwards, who passed him a teen song they had written 'I'd Like to Be (The Lipstick on Your Lips)'. This was a sugary teen ballad, typical of Frankie Avalon and Fabian. The B-side was a reprise of 'Just A Boy', so somebody liked it.

Paul recorded about ten demos for the up-and-coming songwriter Burt Bacharach. Knowing Bacharach's fastidiousness, this illustrates that Paul had his chops even at this young age.

The third Warwick single was the best track from the early years, 'Play Me a Sad Song', with the songwriting credit (Landis-Simon) indicating that he wrote it with his brother Eddie. The theme is familiar: Simon wants the radio DJ to play him a sad song as he is feeling lonely and the song borrows from Tab Hunter's 'Young Love', Sam Cooke's 'You Send Me' and Ben E King's 'Don't Play That Song'. The biographer Patrick Humphries has likened this track to 'I Am a Rock'. Paul is singing well and this could have been a hit. Indeed if it had had the distribution, what DJ could have resisted the title? The B-side, 'It Means a Lot to Them', is an unlikely song about the importance of getting the consent of his girlfriend's parents. It was not Paul's song and was as awkward as its title.

In 1963 Jerry Landis arranged and produced an excellent single for the soul singer Dotty Daniels. He didn't write 'I Wrote You a Letter', which is a strong soul ballad written by Dickie Goodman, but the other side is an impassioned deep soul version of 'Play Me a Sad Song' with an orchestral arrangement.

Another Jerry Landis single was released on Canadian-American Records; Simon wrote both sides. 'I Wish I Weren't in Love' sounds like a demo for Dion and the Belmonts, and is the first track that is recognisably Paul Simon. The B-side, 'I'm Lonely', is a plea for a girlfriend; a 'Lord above, won't you hear my plea' song.

Simon formed studio band Tico & the Triumphs and, in line with their name, he sang lead and wrote 'Motorcycle' for Madison in 1961.

He called himself after Tico because it was one of George Goldner's labels and the Triumphs because he wanted a motorbike. It was a nonsense song like 'Barbara Ann' and 'Rama Lama Ding Dong'. Simon is recognisable and the song has a good sax break but the record is disjointed. It crept into the *Billboard* Hot 100 at No. 99. The B-side is another song, teen ballad 'I Don't Believe Them', in which he mimics Dion. How he must have enjoyed himself in 2009 singing back-up for Dion who was being inducted into the Rock and Roll Hall of Fame.

The second Tico single, this time on Amy Records, was 'Wildflower', another Simon song, this time crossing 'His Latest Flame' with world music. He was trying something different that didn't come off. 'Express Train' is a train song, based on 'The Wanderer' and although a rough-voiced vocal didn't suit Simon, the session sounds fun.

With the advent of the twist, the mashed potato, the watusi and the fly, Simon created his own dance song, 'Get Up & Do the Wobble'. He rhymed 'potatoes' with 'later', something that would not have passed his Quality Control in later years.

In 1962 Simon revived Jerry Landis for a single on Amy, 'The Lone Teen Ranger', inspired by the Coasters' 'Along Came Jones' and the Olympics' 'Western Movies'. There are rudimentary sound effects and a very playful vocal from Paul Simon. It's his song but it does incorporate Rossini's *William Tell Overture*. His girl will fall for him if he wears a mask – kinky stuff. The B-side, 'Lisa', features Paul singing lead on a teen ballad. It means little more than a few radio plays but 'The Lone Teen Ranger' was on the Hot 100 for three weeks, peaking at No. 97, thereby being Paul Simon's first chart record as a solo artist.

The final Tico & the Triumphs single in January 1963 combined a fast doo-wop song, which Simon didn't write, 'Cards of Love', and a revival of his own 'Noise', which is party time in the Curtis Lee vein.

Just as Paul Simon wanted to write for Dion, the Mystics were about to record Doc Pomus and Mort Shuman's 'A Teenager In Love' for Laurie when the label's owner, Bob Schwartz, thought it was too good for them and gave it to Dion. Simon helped with arrangements for the Mystics. He sang second tenor on their doo-wop interpretation of the Welsh lullaby 'All Through the Night'. Jim Gribble, their manager, offered him a royalty or $100. Wisely, he took the money as the record only had airplay on the east coast, but who knows, it might have given him the idea for modernising old folk tunes such as 'Scarborough Fair'. He also sang on the B-side, '(I Begin) To Think Again of You'.

By comparison, Art Garfunkel was studying hard and had done little recording, but he also recorded for Warwick. As Artie Garr, he wrote the teen ballad 'Beat Love' which opens with his solo voice. He says he is proud to be part of 'the age of the beatniks', so this is an unusual record and a good one. He wrote the B-side 'Dream Alone', a decent teen lullaby.

In 1962 and inspired by the Brothers Four folk hit, 'Greenfields', Art wrote the romantic 'Private World', which he recorded for Octavia. Garfunkel is double-tracked to resemble a group and it is good work. The B-side, 'Forgive Me', written by Jeff Raphael, is about a man awaiting death.

Just two singles from Garfunkel then, but it is odd that no one picked up on his exceptional voice. He recalled, 'I wrote some banal rock'n'roll songs in the mid-50s, and then I wrote things of a more folky, sensitive nature, but I rated myself as weak. I never felt comfortable with it.'

Several of Paul Simon's demos from around this time have come to light. Sung with Garfunkel, 'Bingo' is a children's rhyme about a farmer's dog – a variant of 'Ol' MacDonald' really. If Simon & Garfunkel had ever made a kids' album, this would have been ideal.

'Dreams Can Come True' is a Simon & Garfunkel demo, purloining a little of 'All I Have to Do Is Dream' but mostly sounding like Donovan in the mid-60s. They are edging towards the Simon & Garfunkel sound here.

The romantic ballad about a girl called Flame ('Being with Flame set me on fire') has a nice combination of Paul's voice and flute. The other songs include the jazzy 'Lighthouse Point' (slow and fast versions, but the song's construction is similar to 'The Green Door' and 'At the Hop'), a song about a lethargic schoolboy, 'Up and Down the Stairs', a touch of social commentary in the folky 'A Charmed Life', while 'Sleepy Sleepy Baby' is a reflective song, which turns into a calypso – two takes have surfaced.

There is the fun of 'Back Seat Driver' with Paul sounding like the Big Bopper, and the self-pitying 'Educated Fool' where Paul has graduated in misery. There is a song about wanting to be a bachelor ,'That Forever Kind of Love', a Ricky Nelson-styled song about a marital breakdown. It's a long way from 'The Dangling Conversation' but it is the same writer.

Paul made a demo of his fast-moving doo-wop song 'Tick Tock', which he produced as a single for Ritchie Cordell on the Rori label. The song was picked by the Boppers from Finland in 1979, a record well in line with revivalist groups of the day like Darts and Showaddywaddy.

Taken together, the demos and singles find Paul Simon copying every commercial sound around. If they were parodies (but they weren't), some would be on a par with the Rutles. How could Neil Innes have improved on 'Wow Cha Cha Cha', a 1961 demo by Paul Simon?

In the late 70s, when Paul Simon fell out with Columbia, he owed them one more album. When he suggested an album of covers, he was told that this was unacceptable and Columbia insisted on original work. After weeks of negotiation, Simon bought himself out of the contract – a pity as an album of covers would have been good. His performances and arrangements would have been immaculate.

There could have been another solution. When Van Morrison wanted to leave Bang Records, he gave Bert Berns some new songs all right, but they were composed on the spot and amounted to nothing of value. He was risking his own career as they could have been promoted as the new album and purchasers would think they had been swindled.

But what if Paul Simon had decided to revisit his early songs and pick the best of them for an album called *Play Me a Sad Song*? There are good melodies and good lyrics and he could have made an homage to the early 60s with classy remakes and then taken his new songs to Warner Brothers.

CHAPTER 2

Hello Darkness, My Old Friend

Art Garfunkel completed his master's degree in mathematics from Columbia College and moved onto postgrad studies. Although Paul Simon studied English literature at Queens College, his mind was on music. He loved making records.

The enthusiasm had gone from rock'n'roll – for the most part, the rebellious stars had been replaced by inconsequential pop singers. Don McLean called 3 February 1959 the day the music died, but it was one of a chain of events. It was the day that Buddy Holly died and around the same time, Elvis had been drafted into the army, Little Richard was studying for the church, Gene Vincent had been blacklisted by the union, Carl Perkins had been injured in a car crash, and Chuck Berry was doing time. In their place was something blander, although there were considerable talents around such as Roy Orbison, Del Shannon and Bobby Darin. There were no rebellious figures and the industry hierarchy had control.

Paul Simon disliked Bobby Vee's records, which paradoxically were often written by Carole King. He felt that something new was needed, telling Lon Goddard at *Record Mirror* in 1971, 'Age made me change my style of music: age and the folk-boom. Rock'n'roll got very bad in the early 60s, very mushy. I used to go down to Washington Square on Sundays and listen to people playing folk songs and when I heard that picking – Merle Travis picking the guitar, Earl Scruggs picking on the banjo – I liked that a whole lot better than Bobby Vee.'

The performers in Washington Square largely came from Greenwich Village. A bohemian enclave of folk music had emerged from the coffee houses, young performers inspired by social commentators like Woody Guthrie and Pete Seeger. Dave Van Ronk's memoir, *The Mayor of MacDougal Street*, paints a vivid picture of the scene and, in 2013, it was the basis for a fictional film, *Inside Llewyn Davis*, which soaked up the atmosphere of those times, admittedly with little of its humour.

Ralph McTell contrasts the London scene he knew with that of Greenwich Village. 'It wasn't like Greenwich Village for us unfortunately as they had lots of places where you could stay all night and could talk and chew the fat. I go green with envy reading *The Mayor of MacDougal Street*, which is a fantastic book. We didn't have those long, languid discussions. I did get to play there which was fantastic. I did the Main Point and the Bitter End with Patti LaBelle and the Bluebelles. The audiences were kind to me but I could have had an easier start.'

Although Paul Simon had loved the Everly Brothers' album, *Songs Our Daddy Taught Us*, he had not wanted to follow through on its material. He liked the way the Everlys performed those old folk songs but 'those mountain songs didn't say anything to kids in the 22-storey apartments.'

What captured his attention was the new breed of folk songwriters, who felt passionately about the world around them and said so in their songs. Tom Paxton was one. Phil Ochs was another. The diamond in the rough was Bob Dylan, who performed literate diatribes against modern society in an intense, nasal drone that was, nevertheless, highly effective. It was very different from the cotton-wool world portrayed by Bobby Vee; although Dylan had once, briefly, been Vee's pianist.

These songs provided the stimulus that Paul Simon needed and the first song for the new-look Simon was 'He Was My Brother'. Simon and others have said that this song is about the death of a freedom worker he knew at the hands of the Ku Klux Klan, but there is difficulty here. We can date the song to June 1963 and it was recorded in March 1964. However, his friend Andrew Goodman was not killed until 21 June 1964 when he died with his fellow workers, James Chaney and Mickey Schwerner. This horrendous act changed public opinion and it has been sung about by Pete Seeger, Phil Ochs, Tom Paxton and Richard Fariña, all with different songs. In 1988, their deaths were the subject of the film, *Mississippi Burning*. The likelihood is that Simon wrote his song – and another one about the KKK, 'A Church Is Burning', in 1963 and over time he has come to believe that he wrote it for Goodman's death as it fit the circumstances.

Art Garfunkel was very impressed. 'I first heard the song in June 1963,' he recalled on a sleeve note, 'a week after Paul wrote it. Cast in the Bob Dylan mould of that time there was no subtlety in the song, no sophistication in the lyric; rather the innocent voice of uncomfortable youth. The ending is joyously optimistic. I was happy the way the song made me feel. It was clearly the product of a considerable talent.'

Although somewhat neglected, not least by Simon himself, his next song for the folk world, 'Sparrow', was better. It is an allegory along the lines of 'Who Killed Cock Robin?' and when it first appeared Garfunkel kindly provided us with a key to its symbolism. The song stands without it and the composition displays a lighter touch than most of his earlier work.

The third song was 'Bleecker Street', a favourite location in Greenwich Village for folk songwriters, among them Tom Paxton ('Cindy's Crying') and Joni Mitchell ('Tin Angel').

Paul Simon took tentative steps by performing his new material in Greenwich Village, but he felt uneasy: 'There was nothing exotic about me, coming from Queens. They were taken with Bob Dylan because he came from the Midwest, the kid who rode the rails. I was not accepted.' We now know that Dylan exaggerated his adventures but good luck to him.

Nevertheless, Paul recorded two new songs, 'He Was My Brother' and 'Carlos Dominguez' for the small Tribute label where it was issued under the name of Paul Kane. In 1964 it came out on Oriole Records in the UK, this time under the name of Jerry Landis.

'Carlos Dominguez' was never revived by Simon and/or Garfunkel but it was covered by the Irish singer, Val Doonican, who told me, 'Alan Paramor, who used to look after my publishing, asked me to listen to this young American lad. I listened to "Carlos Dominguez" and while I was there, this American chap turned up. He introduced himself as Paul Kane, but he later changed it to Paul Simon. If you mentioned it to him today, he probably wouldn't remember me or the song at all, but it was a very nice little thing.' For a time too, the comedian Tom O'Connor included it in performances.

In September 1963 Simon and Garfunkel began performing the new songs in Greenwich Village, this time billed as Kane and Garr, but they didn't fool anyone. Dave Van Ronk has much to say about Bob Dylan, Joan Baez, Phil Ochs and Tom Paxton in his memoir but very little about Simon and Garfunkel. Van Ronk saw them perform but everyone knew that they had had a hit with 'Hey Schoolgirl' and 'the mouldy fig wing of the folk world despised them as pop singers. I remember hearing them down at the Gaslight, and nobody would listen. I thought they were damn good but the people who wanted to hear Mississippi

John Hurt and Dock Boggs wanted no part of Simon and Garfunkel.'

They had started performing 'The Sound of Silence'. Simon said, 'I used to go into the bathroom because the tiles acted as an echo chamber. I'd often play in the dark, "Hello darkness, my old friend". The first line came from that and then it drifted off into other things.'

Indeed, Simon is the king of great first lines. He said, 'I've always believed that you need a truthful first line to kick you off into a song. You have to say something emotionally true before you can let your imagination wander.'

I would have thought that anyone would have recognised 'Hello darkness, my old friend' as a brilliant opening line, but not so. Dave Van Ronk described how it became a running joke. 'It was only necessary for someone to start singing "Hello darkness, my old friend…" and everybody would crack up. It was a complete failure.'

'I was trying to prove something,' Simon admitted. 'I'd think, "Gee, I'm good. Why doesn't anybody see that?" So naturally I was resentful that nobody did see that.'

'The Sound of Silence' was influenced by Bob Dylan but Paul told *MOJO* in 2000 that he never wanted to be compared to him. He said, 'I tried very hard not to be influenced by him, but I know I would never have written "The Sound of Silence" were in it not for Bob Dylan. Never. He was the first guy to come along in a serious way and not write teen-language songs. I saw him as a major guy whose work I didn't want to imitate because I didn't see any way out of being in his shadow if I did.'

'The Sound of Silence' touches on many of Simon's themes – alienation, conformity and the role of the media. The lyrics are sober and scholarly and they sound poetic ('Silence like a cancer grows'). Every line is almost a song in its own right.

Simon was working as a part-time plugger for the music publisher, E. B. Marks, and if the opportunity arose, he would slide in one of his own. He knew Tom Wilson, a jazz producer for Columbia Records (CBS in the UK), who had been assigned to Bob Dylan.

A black guy, Tom Wilson was born in 1931, raised in Waco, Texas, graduated from Harvard in 1954 and founded a jazz label, Transition, in 1955. He had worked for the jazz label Savoy, being assigned to Herbie Mann, and then moved to Columbia, where he recorded folk artists, Bob Dylan and Pete Seeger.

Paul Simon played Tom Wilson 'He Was My Brother', and Wilson

18

wanted to cut it with a promising folk group, the Pilgrims. Ever the opportunist, Simon said that he often sang it with his friend and could they have an audition. Wilson was intrigued by Garfunkel's hair as he had never seen a white man with an Afro before (so that's what you call it). Wilson told the president of Columbia Records, Goddard Lieberson (known, for good reason, as 'God'), about them. God agreed that a two man, one guitar album could be made quickly at little cost, but he questioned the name, as Simon & Garfunkel sounded like a department store.

Simon never liked being told what to do and he argued that they had to have real names for folk music. He said, 'Our name is honest. I always thought it was a big shock to people when Bob Dylan's name turned out to be Bobby Zimmerman. It was so important that he should be true.' The implication was that if you had an honest name, your songs were *ipso facto* honest.

The album, *Wednesday Morning 3am*, was made in four sessions in March 1964. It's a simple production, showcasing the songs and the voices, and an important component was the engineer, Roy Halee, who became a permanent member of their team.

Roy Halee's father had been the singing voice for Mighty Mouse and his mother had worked with Al Jolson. Roy, who was born in Long Island in 1934, played trumpet but did not consider himself good enough for professional work. He became a technician for CBS television and then an engineer for their recording division.

The byline (or buyline) of their first LP was 'Exciting new songs in the folk tradition'. The sound was good but unexciting. The strumming which begins the opening cut could easily have been the Seekers. By and large, Simon and Garfunkel are singing too sweetly and some of the outside songs were unnecessary, especially a bland run-through of Bob Dylan's heated 'The Times They Are A-Changin''. The album falls between the commercial folk of the Kingston Trio and the albums later made for lonely bedsits. Simon and Garfunkel were often pictured with college scarves as if to stress their student background.

No matter what, Simon and Garfunkel together would never make a good picture, unlike the Beatles, who always looked right. Paul was small (five foot two), Art was tall (over six foot), and you would always be drawn to Art's hair. Some bands such as Pink Floyd, the Moody Blues and Genesis did not put photos on the covers of their albums, which is sometimes a wise decision.

Simon and Garfunkel always looked wrong. What induced Garfunkel in 1975 to attend the Grammy awards, of all places, sporting a T-shirt with a painted bowtie? Simon with his long hair and moustache has his own problems – and then this pair are photographed alongside the coolest guys in rock, John Lennon and David Bowie.

The album includes two gospel songs, 'You Can Tell the World' and 'Go Tell It On the Mountain', but the performances are bland. The Weavers or the Clancy Brothers would have belted these out. Indeed, Peter, Paul and Mary were climbing the US charts with a spirited 'Go Tell It on the Mountain'.

'Benedictus' is an experiment which comes off well. It is based on a sixteenth-century setting which Art found in a library. There is a delicate cello in the background and the duo displays control and harmonic sophistication.

Simon and Garfunkel knew Ed McCurdy as the host from the Bitter End and he was a folk singer and writer with a long and varied career. In 1957 he recorded some bawdy folk songs later packaged as *A Box of Dalliance*. His plea for world peace, 'Last Night I Had the Strangest Dream', written in 1950, is among the greatest songs ever written and was performed when the Berlin Wall was demolished. In 1964 it was recorded by both the Kingston Trio and Simon & Garfunkel and although the Trio have the edge and a fuller sound, Paul and Artie's version is a good one.

The Scottish folk song, 'Peggy-O', is about an army captain whose advances are shunned so he plans to destroy the village of Fennario in retaliation. The song, originally known as 'The Bonnie Lass of Fyvie', exists in many versions and was recorded around the same time by Bob Dylan and Joan Baez. It became a mainstay of the Grateful Dead's concerts. Again, it is a saccharine performance from Simon & Garfunkel, which goes against the grain of the lyrics.

There is a song, 'The Sun Is Burning', from the Scottish folk singer, Ian Campbell, who will come into our story. It's a round robin with each verse reflecting on the position of the sun, but it could be about a nuclear holocaust. The song was regularly performed by Luke Kelly of the Dubliners.

Simon's five songs are 'Bleecker Street', 'Sparrow', 'The Sound of Silence', 'He Was My Brother' and 'Wednesday Morning 3am'. Although the last song gives the album its name, it is not the strongest. It begins as a gentle travelling song but the singer is a criminal on the run for robbing a liquor store.

Rather like 'The Sound of Silence', 'Bleecker Street' is a song of alienation. It is not saying how wonderful Greenwich Village is and how great these little clubs are. No, the fog is rolling round the street like a shroud and the performers are juggling art with commerce. It's a very good song indeed but it is unusual to find Simon retaining his false rhyme of 'sustaining' and 'Canaan'. It is a pity that they didn't return to this song as it could have worked with a full arrangement.

The album was issued within a month, but who could tell how the album would sell? President Kennedy had been assassinated in November 1963 and the public wanted uplifting, non-demanding music. How else can you explain the Singing Nun going to No. 1? But the music industry had dramatically changed at the start of 1964 and by April, the Beatles were holding the top five places on the US chart. There might have been a cult following for reflective folk songs, but the real demand was for beat music, preferably from the UK.

By including popular songs like 'Go Tell It on the Mountain' and 'The Times They Are A-Changin'', Columbia may have hoped for big sales, but as Simon put it, 'it was a real stiff'. They couldn't even get bookings to promote it. 'We couldn't get a job. Artie and I auditioned at a lot of clubs in the States, but nobody showed any interest in our music.' The initial sales of the album, prior to any hit singles, were 1,500 copies and it wasn't released in the UK until 1968, although an EP of four songs was put out at the end of 1965.

Wednesday Morning 3am was a reasonable start, but no one would call it a classic album. Well, Garfunkel perhaps. He supplies some informative, if pretentious, liner notes. You wonder what Simon really thought of them but it all helped in pushing the merits of his compositions.

CHAPTER 3

To England Where My Heart Lies

Because there were few engagements resulting from the release of *Wednesday Morning 3am* in the States, Paul Simon thought he would make his first trip to Europe and for thirteen of the next twenty months, he would be there, mostly in England. Art meanwhile would be studying in New York.

Paul Simon liked to think of himself as a troubadour, wandering from place to place like Woody Guthrie or the writer Jack Kerouac, collecting stories, amassing experiences, carrying a guitar, writing songs, and singing for his supper. But he was also deeply aligned with the great songwriters of New York, assiduously composing highly crafted songs in their cubicles. And Garfunkel? Well, go back to the song 'Earth Angel'; Garfunkel was his shadow, possessing the angel voice that he wished had been his own. An Everly Brother with wings, as it were.

Paul started in Paris, busking by the Seine and sometimes sleeping under the Pont Neuf. He said, 'I did some busking. I sang whatever was popular that had a loud high ending. I was particularly good at loud high endings. If you sang the note for a long time, you tended to get paid for it.' Paul lived in a convent for a week, which suggests he could have written a 'Sisters of Mercy' before Leonard Cohen.

While in Paris, he saw Los Incas, who performed music from the Andes using charangos and pan flutes, at the Théâtre de l'Est Parisien. They gave Paul an album which contained the highly melodic 'El Condor Pasa' with its quickened ending.

Simon met many English and French beatniks and he befriended David McLausland who ran a folk club in Brentford, Essex. David was impressed and invited him to the club. Indeed, when Simon came to the UK, he stayed with David's parents. David had attended the Campion School in Hornchurch and somehow the school scarves found their way onto the cover of Simon & Garfunkel's 1966 album, *Sounds of Silence*.

On the first night at his club, Paul met Kathy Chitty, a quiet girl taking tickets on the door. They became an item and at least three songs are dedicated to her – 'Kathy's Song', 'Homeward Bound' and 'America'.

The music writer Mike Ledgerwood recalled, 'Paul Simon sang for his supper for a paltry three quid a night in crowded, smoke-filled Essex clubs, frequented by bearded, beer-swilling folk fanatics.' Paul was good and appealed not only to bearded beer-swillers in Essex but to folk clubs throughout the country. He'd stop at a city, find a folk club and ask if he could perform. He said, 'It was a great way to spend my time. I was roaming around a small country where everything was new and exciting.'

With a broad simplification, there were two types of clubs in the UK. Ewan MacColl and Peggy Seeger favoured a traditional approach, the finger-in-your-ear clubs, where you could only perform songs relating to your region. The other, more flexible, approach related to the growing interest in writing your own songs.

MacColl was suspicious of songwriters. Even the term jarred with him as that implied individual endeavour. He regarded song-making as being an on-going conversation with what had gone on before; a collective experience, if you like. He was rigid and inflexible and in 1961 he formed the Singers' Club in London, not, you note, the Songwriters' Club. Songwriting to him was self-indulgence, although he wrote some beautiful compositions, famously 'The First Time Ever I Saw Your Face'.

The UK folk song revival came about in the 1950s, and by 1958 there were hundreds of folk clubs. They were loosely associated with left-wing politics especially CND and with beatniks and poetry.

Simon met several up-and-coming and highly influential musicians around Soho. Davey Graham had been born in Leicester in 1940 and he was turned onto the guitar and folk music by Lonnie Donegan in the mid-50s. He was a fast picker but he mellowed after lounging in Morocco. You can see him on YouTube playing 'Cry Me a River' in a 1959 TV documentary made by Ken Russell. The comedian Bob Monkhouse was a strong advocate of his work and in April 1962 Davey made an EP, *3/4 A.D.*, with his friend the blues singer Alexis Korner. It included the instrumental, 'Anji'.

Davey Graham set the scene: 'I was in Menton which is a small village noted for its lemons and its fresh mountain air. A lot of people with bronchial trouble go there and it is on the coast between Italy and France. Anji was there and we slept in Napoleon's bedroom, but most of the time five of us lived in the same room which was part of a cobbler's shop. We were arrested when four of us went riding on the same motorcycle and we found ourselves in jail. The fifth one of us, Alex Campbell, put on his best denims and carried a novel under his arm to look respectable and went to the police station to get us out.'

Davey continued, 'I wrote "Anji" in Menton. It is a simple soleares which is found in Spanish music. It's a little like "Hit the Road Jack" and it's a good way to start a tune. If you are sitting down for a jam with some musicians you don't know, they often say, 'Do you play "Pennies from Heaven" in F or B flat?' which is anathema to a fingerstyle guitarist like myself. If I suggest a soleares chord sequence, we can get a Latin rhythm going, especially with a drummer. I had taped "Anji" so that Bert Jansch could learn it and I had thrown in a quote from "Work Song" by Cannonball Adderley. Paul learnt it from that and he made a happy enough job of it. I made some good money from it but I wish I had done something else with that money.'

And who was Anji? 'Anji was a half-Czech girl who used to bottle for me when I was busking. Why did I call it that? Well you would if you had deflowered a girl like that.' With that track, Graham had created DADGAD tuning and he appeared in the cult film, *The Servant*, written by Harold Pinter and starring James Fox and Dirk Bogarde.

In January 1965, Davey released the LP *Folk, Blues & Beyond*, which had a spirit of adventure about it, and not content with that, in April, he put out *Folk Roots, New Routes*, which he made with Shirley Collins. In 1966 Simon recorded 'Anji' for the *Sounds of Silence* LP.

Paul Simon was taken with his work but Davey Graham was an erratic performer, openly known for heavy drug use: 'I did a couple of sessions with Paul but they were never released because he wasn't satisfied. He asked me to join him sometime in the 70s. I don't remember why I turned it down but not doing that was one of the biggest mistakes of my life.'

No to Paul Simon but yes to the American folk/blues guitarist Stefan Grossman. Grossman says, 'When I came to England, Martin Carthy took me to meet Davey Graham. I knew that he had problems with substance abuse and we got him back on his feet. We toured with him and soon he was starting to play really well. We did some very nice albums together.'

Another fine guitarist, Bert Jansch, born in Glasgow in 1943, heard

'Anji' when he was in St Tropez and adapted it, recording his version in 1965. Jansch was much more approachable than Graham and was often seen around Soho. He became part of Pentangle. When I met Bert Jansch and tried to sort out the timeline for 'Anji', it only added to the confusion. 'I got "Anji" from Jill Doyle, who is Davey's sister and I think I recorded it about two months before he did. We were both recording for Bill Leader at the time and Davey was working with Shirley Collins.'

And how would the listener distinguish between the two versions? 'Well, Davey's is right and mine's wrong! Mine's much faster and I think I nicked a bit from another tune and stuck it in the middle and Davey doesn't play that.'

In short, I think Davey recorded 'Anji' in 1962 and then did a tape for Bert Jansch early in 1965 where he added some of 'Work Song'. This was what Bert recorded on *Bert Jansch,* released April 1965, which is what Paul Simon followed.

Al Stewart said, 'Bert Jansch was a great influence on the guitar players on the English folk scene at the time. Everybody wanted to be Bert Jansch or John Renbourn or a combination of the two. I had never seen anyone play acoustic fingerstyle until I saw them and it was "Wow, what is this?" On an average night at Les Cousins which is where everybody went to see Bert, the whole of the front row could all play "Anji" on the guitar.'

Paul Simon had several bookings around London, and Wally Whyton saw how his charisma was taking shape. 'At places like the Railway Inn at Brentwood, Paul was the biggest thing going. He had an incredible way with the birds. He sat there wearing a polo-neck sweater and black cord jacket doing Dylan numbers and things like "The Sound of Silence" and "I Am a Rock" and the girls used to go mad.' Simon's performances at the Railway Inn were recorded by a BBC engineer, Dennis Rookard, and they can now be heard at Essex Record Office.

Wally Whyton did a booking with him and Redd Sullivan and he recalled that 'Paul liked a lot of the good old rock'n'roll numbers. I am sure it was only Art's influence which stopped him from doing more of that. He started off with "Teddy Bear" one night and I came back with "Peggy Sue". Once we got going, we went on like that for the whole session.'

Alan Bell of the Blackpool Taverners recalls, 'I remember Paul Simon playing at Accrington Stanley's football club, the old supporters' club, which was the venue for a folk night. We were top of the bill and

The sheet music cover for 'The Sound of Silence' has been changed over the years to match Simon's current look, this one is from 1975. Nice tash, Paul. If things don't work out, you can always join the Village People

he was the supporting artist. The organiser had booked him for £5 but because he had a really good night, he gave him an extra £2 10 shillings so he got £7 10 shillings (£7.50) for the gig.'

Harvey Andrews said, 'Paul was supposed to come to the Jug O'Punch in Birmingham but he got his dates mixed up and came the following week. Ian Campbell was furious. How could this little guy turn up on the wrong night? He said, 'Well, as you've driven all this way, we will let you do four songs.' He stood up, all in black, which was his trademark, and he sang "A Church Is Burning", "He Was My Brother", "A Most Peculiar Man" and "The Sound of Silence". By the time he'd finished, I was hanging from the rafters as I'd never seen or heard anything like it. He was an astonishing guitarist and I got to know him very well. I was the first person in Britain to record a Paul Simon song, which was "A Most Peculiar Man" for my first EP, and I got a letter from Paul saying "Thank you", which was rather nice.'

Performing to great acclaim in the folk clubs gave Simon increasing confidence in his material and he was determined to break into the US market. Wally Whyton of UK skiffle group the Vipers recalled, 'Paul always believed he'd make it big. He kept telling us he would.'

Paul performed at the Edinburgh Folk Festival in 1964, but his record of 'He Was My Brother' had meant little – it had been released on a minor UK label with negligible publicity and the name Jerry Landis on the label.

When Art's term finished, Paul asked him to come over. They attended the Flamingo in Wardour Street to hear the Ian Campbell Folk Group. In a neat twist of fate, the group didn't turn up. The social worker Judith Piepe takes up the story, 'There wasn't anyone around to entertain the large audience. Then suddenly we noticed a young kid with a guitar sitting on the floor. Curly Goss the promoter asked him his name. He said he was Paul Simon and he was American. Anyway, this unknown kid from New York was dragged on stage and he started with "A Church Is Burning" and he followed it with "Leaves That Are Green" and "The Sound of Silence". Just then he waved to a tall fair-haired kid at the back of the club and together they sang "Benedictus". Everyone was flabbergasted. They'd knocked the audience out. We soon learnt to our disappointment that both were returning to New York the next day.'

A former refugee and now a social worker in the East End of London, Judith realised that the themes of Paul's songs were relevant to her own work. She invited him to use her flat as a base when he returned, an offer she extended to several folk musicians. Back in New York, Simon graduated from Queens in English literature and he enrolled at Brooklyn Law School to please his parents. He soon lost interest and completed little more than a term.

While he was away, Piepe was planning bigger and better things for him. She bombarded the BBC with requests to broadcast his material. She was persuasive and they agreed to record his songs, but in an unusual way. One of Paul Simon's songs would be broadcast every day for two weeks in the *Five to Ten* slot. The song would be played and Judith would introduce each one with a short introduction about its relevance to modern living. The gist of what she said can be read on her liner notes for *The Paul Simon Songbook* or in the essay accompanying the songs in sheet music form.

This was not the first time that the BBC had used contemporary songs in religious broadcasting, but in the past it had been in a derogatory way. An example that affected me was the morning a vicar on *Lift Up Your Hearts* cited the lines about scratching your partner's back in Elvis Presley's 'Treat Me Nice' as the ultimate in depravity. My mother was horrified that her young son owned this record. This time the music was treated more sympathetically. Simon's songs were polished and pertinent and even if they were hardly religious, they did exhibit considerable understanding of the way we behave.

There was an unintended consequence as it made the songs seem ripe for sociological discussion, which continues on the internet to this day. I have a BBC script for *Jesus Christ – A Most Peculiar Man* in which Peter Baldwin sang Simon's songs and Dr John Vincent, a Methodist minister, supplied the commentary. He said, 'Many of Paul Simon's songs abound in scriptural echoes and even more take up the theme of contemporary Christian searching.'

Judith Piepe received many letters praising the series and asking whether the songs had been recorded. She found that Oriole had been taken over by CBS and she recommended that the Jerry Landis single be reissued with a new label bearing Simon's own name. This was not cost effective but because he was signed to the parent company they agreed to record an album of Simon's songs. Judith informed Paul, who was still frustrated by his lack of success in America. It was easy to build up a reputation on the UK folk club circuit but it was more difficult in the States as the clubs were so far apart and he had been greeted with some scepticism in Greenwich Village.

Meanwhile, Tom Wilson had been working with Bob Dylan on new tracks with rock musicians for the album *Bringing It All Back Home*. He proposed a similar trial with Simon and Garfunkel, which was no hardship as they had often worked with session musicians. The plan was to make a single and Wilson favoured the wistful 'Wednesday Morning 3am', but thought that the song needed more edge as the singer was on the run after a robbery. Simon reworked it, dropping a verse, adding a chorus and renaming it 'Somewhere They Can't Find Me'. For the B-side, he wrote an upbeat song pleading with a girl not to leave him, 'We Got a Groovey [sic] Thing Goin'', a lyric he omits from his published collection. The tracks were recorded on 5 April 1965 but the single didn't sound commercial and the idea was shelved. Odd that nobody realised that 'The Sound of Silence' was the song to go for.

In May 1965 Paul Simon went into the CBS studios in New Bond Street, London and made *The Paul Simon Songbook*. It was recorded over three afternoons and the studio rate was eight pounds an hour. The engineer was Mike Ross-Trevor (later called Dr Rossi by the Stooges) and Reg Warburton was the producer, although Simon virtually produced himself. It was a simple affair with Simon singing to his own guitar accompaniment. It worked very well and several songs have not made a greater impact with more lavish arrangements. This is largely because the songs are often straight reporting and their matter-of-fact nature suited uncomplicated presentations. Unlike the mediocre *Wednesday Morning 3am*, I would describe this album as a classic.

The album is based around his *Five to Ten* performances. Despite this, a bootleg album of the original broadcasts appeared, so religious broadcasts were being sold under the counter.

Both 'The Sound of Silence' and 'He Was My Brother' are reprised from *Wednesday Morning 3am*, and when combined with 'A Church is Burning', 'I Am a Rock' and 'A Most Peculiar Man', we have an album of intense, literate and thoughtful songs. The anti-war song 'The Side of a Hill' is about the plight of a dead child.

But there is lighter material – 'Kathy's Song', 'April Come She Will', 'Leaves That Are Green' and 'Flowers Never Bend With the Rainfall'. 'Patterns' is a song about how life continues.

Simon is always aware that he is engaged in the process of writing while he is working. In 'Kathy's Song', he explains how forced the process can be and the opening line of 'Leaves That Are Green' is about the very song he is writing. The conundrum starts 'I was 21 years when I wrote this song', a line that found a new home in Billy Bragg's 'A New England'. In 'Homeward Bound', Simon writes about performing his songs, while in 'The Sound of Silence', he is concerned that they may be ignored.

Although often regarded as a British Springsteen, Ian Prowse of Amsterdam highly rates 'Kathy's Song': 'That has always been a touchstone for me. Love songs that are done well work best for me and I've returned to this one many times for inspiration. It is also a song about writing songs, which is a very difficult thing to get right.'

Paul Simon said, 'I tend to think of that period as late adolescence. Suicides and people who are very sad or very lonely make a big impact on an adolescent mind. You tend to dramatise these things. It was easier to write because I wasn't known. I didn't have set standards and so I wrote about anything I saw.'

The only song from the BBC series that is omitted on the LP is 'Bad News Feeling', a ballad about drug addicts in the same vein as 'A Most Peculiar Man'. In its place we have the engaging oddity 'A Simple Desultory Philippic (Or How I Was Lyndon Johnson'd Into Submission)'. As might be expected from the title, this witty tirade is full of in-jokes. It works extremely well and the bridge includes Simon's impersonation of Bob Dylan. Perhaps he should have used that voice when he recorded their insipid version of 'The Times They Are A-Changin''.

Although Dylan's writing was influencing Simon, the results were very different. Dylan's vocals were loaded with marked mannerisms: 'At its very best,' said *Time* magazine, 'it sounds as if it is drifting over the walls of a TB sanatorium.' That's a compliment? On the other hand, Simon's voice is clear and precise with perfect enunciation. Dylan sounds bitter and resentful, while Simon is sorrowful. Dylan castigates his listeners while Simon simply tells his tales.

The sheer force of Dylan's songs and their interplay with his own personality bulldozed their way into our minds and led to him being hailed as the new pop messiah. Simon knew he didn't have this sort of personality and he wanted his songs to speak for themselves.

Dylan's outbursts and rudeness were reported in the press and, in contrast, Simon was restrained and polite. You can hear the difference in the songs themselves if you compare Simon's song 'The Side of a Hill' with Dylan's 'With God on Our Side'. Simon could never have written that remarkable putdown, 'Like a Rolling Stone'. As the rock critic Robert Christgau put it, 'Paul Simon has in abundance the very quality that Dylan lacks: taste.'

Also, Paul Simon didn't have the grounding in folk music that many of the other performers had. Dylan soaked up everything he could find about Woody Guthrie and even visited him in hospital. Paul Simon was one of the omissions from the big-name artists appearing on the *Tribute to Woody Guthrie* at Carnegie Hall. This lack of knowledge has worked to Simon's advantage as he has cleverly expanded the way songs could be written. He has given us imaginative melodies from the get-go. Relatively few of his songs follow the folk route of verse-chorus-verse-chorus. He favoured using the title as the refrain at the end of the verse.

Over a year earlier than Paul Simon, Bob Dylan had found some stimulus in the UK folk scene. A BBC Television production, *Madhouse on Castle Street*, called for an American folk singer. Although unknown, Dylan was flown over and booked into the May Fair hotel, BBC expenses being more lavish than today. He performed at three folk clubs in London – the Troubadour, the King & Queen, and the Pindar of Wakefield, the last being the Singers' Club hosted by Ewan MacColl and Peggy Seeger. In a photograph, the famed folklorist Bert Lloyd can be seen frowning at Dylan, no doubt horrified by what he was hearing. Just as Paul Simon was to do, Bob Dylan befriended the British singer, guitarist and song collector, Martin Carthy.

In 2007 Charles Ford in the academic publication *Popular Music Studies* wrote a feature on the rhythms in Martin Carthy's work and said that 'A relatively large number of popular songs in the late 60s are metrically irregular probably because of the popularity of pre-war blues and UK folk songs at the time.' He cites Robert Johnson and other bluesmen as being very irregular which was carried through onto Bob Dylan's first four albums. The most irregular of bands was the Incredible String Band.

Martin Carthy (1965) and *Martin Carthy's Second Album* (1966) are both very irregular, which was probably helped by the lack of a drummer. You can hear that in 'Scarborough Fair', where Carthy has several pauses, possibly because the singer is thinking of the response to the questions. Carthy was a compelling performer, always wanting to do justice to the songs he loved. According to Ford, his approach helped to 'fund the anti-commercial weirdness of middle-class British hippies'.

In the liner notes for *The Freewheelin' Bob Dylan* (1963), Dylan recalled Carthy singing the traditional 'Lord Franklin', to which Dylan wrote a new lyric, 'Bob Dylan's Dream'. Dylan was taken with Carthy's version of 'Scarborough Fair' and he was to adapt the tune for his own lyric, 'Girl from the North Country', again recorded for *Freewheelin'*, although the liner note said he had been working on it for three years.

The topics that Dylan and Simon wrote about were often similar. Dylan is famed for his anti-war tracts and his jeremiads about man's inhumanity to man. Simon is in similar territory with 'A Church Is Burning', 'The Side of a Hill' and 'He Was My Brother', but his intention is different. He said, 'There's no point in commenting on what's going on because everybody knows that. I just write the way I feel and the way I feel reflects the part of society I'm living in.'

Many of the songs on *The Paul Simon Songbook* bear this out. His technique is best seen in 'A Most Peculiar Man', which is based on a newspaper story. Judith Piepe explains, 'It was just three lines and included the item that the woman who lived above him thought he was a most peculiar man. Paul said it wasn't enough and so he sat down and wrote an epitaph for a stranger and for all suicides.'

'I Am a Rock' is a companion piece. The protagonist offers his own story as he tells of his preference for books and poetry. Although remote, his isolation has come from a broken love affair. In 'A Most Peculiar Man', we never learn why the character is so inaccessible, but the character stands tall in 'I Am a Rock'. He lives in self-assurance and the song forms a justification for his actions. Even so, I can appreciate what a minister meant when he likened the song to the scriptures, 'He who tries to save his life shall lose it.' Simon sometimes tells interviewers that he particularly dislikes 'I Am a Rock' and 'The Dangling Conversation' from his early songs. He has said, 'If they would go away, I would be happy, but to be kinder to myself, I should just say that I wrote them when I was young.'

Despite such topics, *The Paul Simon Songbook* is not depressing. The songs are certainly disturbing and Simon told *Rolling Stone* in 1972 that 'a lot of the pain that comes in some of these songs is due to the exaggeration of being high'. More than drug or alcohol use, however, the songs stem from living in over-crowded cities and the problems that can cause. Simon fully understands the sense of feeling lonely in a crowd, and so do we after hearing this album.

It can be argued that Paul Simon's main theme is the lack of communication between people. It's ironic that Simon himself has been so careful about what he communicates. His chief song on this theme is

'The Sound of Silence' where each line is meticulously crafted. The lyric brilliantly exposes the problem.

To think that *The Paul Simon Songbook* is all about social conscience would be wrong. 'Kathy's Song' is a fine love song, although Judith Piepe's assessment doesn't ring true: 'quite romantic but intensely emotional, brutally honest yet terribly gentle'. Kathy is shown with Paul on the cover of the album, holding novelty toys, and sitting on the cobbles outside Piepe's home.

The bootleg album, *Chez*, is taken from a tape sent to Kathy. It was recorded in New York and is a pleasant, light-hearted affair, the sort of home tape that anyone with a bit of talent might have sent to his girlfriend. Paul performs on his own and later is joined by Art Garfunkel, who has had a frustrating time obtaining a licence for his scooter. The only new tune was a guitar piece, 'Charlotte', and there is an extended version of 'Anji'. The tape ends with Paul singing Tom Paxton's 'Goin' to the Zoo' with Debbie, a little girl who lives nearby. The sound is poor but it's an intriguing curio.

The printed songbook for the album contains a short story by Simon entitled *On Drums and Other Hollow Objects*. In his early years, Simon often said that he would write a book, telling the *NME* in 1966, 'In between performances, I'm always writing, trying to develop characters, so that I can write the Great American Novel.' An ambitious task and two years on, the same periodical asked him how he was faring: 'See, I'm attacking it by doing short stories and developing character studies in the short stories. By developing these character studies, I'll incorporate them eventually into this novel.' The novel idea was abandoned along the way but the short story falls into line with Paul's musical output as it is about visiting his grandfather in a care home.

In the liner notes to the album, Paul Simon analyses his songwriting, 'I want ME to think that I'm something I'm not. I want me to think I'm something.' His capitals, by the way.

After thoughts on poppy tenders and his alter ego, he concludes, 'This LP contains 12 of the songs that I have written over the past two years. There are some here that I wouldn't write today. I don't believe in them as I once did. I have included them because they played an important part in the transition. It's discomforting, almost painful, to look back over something that someone else has done and realise that someone else is you. I'm not ashamed of where I've been or what I've thought. It's just not me anymore. It's perfectly clear to me that the songs I write today will not be mine tomorrow. I don't regret the loss.' This is strange thinking about songs that are less than two years old, but it illustrates that Simon's skills were quickly growing.

Based in Judith Piepe's flat, Simon was to meet many folk musicians socially including Al Stewart, Roy Harper, Sandy Denny and another American singer/songwriter in the UK, Jackson C. Frank. Paul was there for some weeks and then took over Martin Carthy's flat in Hampstead. While he was staying in Hampstead, a passenger was killed on the underground and this prompted his song 'The Northern Line'. A tape of Simon performing at the Jolly Porter in Exeter in 1965 has surfaced and both the song and its lengthy introduction can be heard. Curiously both Simon and the audience are making light of the death, although this is surely not the intention.

Paul wrote songs with Bruce Woodley of the Seekers including 'Red Rubber Ball' (soon to be recorded by the Cyrkle and Cilla Black) and 'I Wish You Could Be Here' (again recorded by the Cyrkle).

Showing more initiative than the parent company, CBS arranged some solid promotion for *The Paul Simon Songbook*. They released a single of 'I Am a Rock' and Simon performed it on the ITV pop show *Ready Steady Go!* on 23 July 1965. This was a live show, which was over-running. It was to close with P J Proby and his new single, 'Let the Water Run Down', and Simon, who was on directly before him with just his voice and guitar, was told to sing only the first two verses. Simon decided that Proby, a major star, would get other chances to promote his work and so he continued singing as normal. Surprisingly the cameras remained on him and Proby's song was faded out during the credits.

While Simon was in the UK, he befriended another American singer/ songwriter based there, Jackson C. Frank. He produced his first and only album and the extraordinary background to this album is discussed in the next chapter.

In July 1965, Simon did well at the first Cambridge Folk Festival, where he accepted an ad in the programme in lieu of a fee for a thirty-minute set. It was a good calling card as he was touring the UK folk clubs. He had established a reputation on his previous impromptu tour and was now with an agent for around fifteen pounds a night. There were hundreds of folk clubs in the UK with eighty being a decent attendance.

Ralph McTell recalls a gig at the end of August: 'I did a gig with

Paul Simon at Bexhill-on-Sea under my original name of Ralph May, but nobody was there. It was at Bexhill-on-Sea which is the clue really. They weren't ready for white lads singing the blues. When I finished the promoter couldn't pay me but he insisted that I took an album that he had just had sent over from the States. He insisted that I took it in lieu of payment as Paul had insisted on the full fee of £20 and there wasn't anything left to pay me my £6.10s. I took the album and it was better than a £6.10s fee. It was *King of the Delta Blues Singers* by Robert Johnson and it was one of those life-changing records that seeped into my soul. I listen to Robert Johnson's complete recordings at least once a year and I love them.'

And what did Ralph make of Paul Simon on stage: 'I don't remember him on stage, so maybe I had gone for a drink. I was 20 and I did see him around Soho and he soaked up everything. He was very earnest but you have to admire him for traipsing around England with a guitar on his own. He was a long way from home. I could get home from Les Cousins in Greek Street in 45 minutes.'

Simon played the Hough in Widnes, Lancashire on 13 September 1965 and the organiser Geoff Speed has the account book which shows he was paid twelve pounds. Geoff says, 'At the time there was a definite chasm between the lovers of traditional folk music and the then-emerging contemporary songwriters. Paul was visiting clubs in certain instances that were full of lovers of traditional music, but he was usually able to get through with his songs.'

Geoff enjoyed having Paul Simon as his houseguest and Simon repeated his desire to write the Great American Novel. He told Geoff that his IQ was 155 and he was surprised that Geoff hadn't read anything by Sigmund Freud. On the other hand, he took great delight in *Help!*, the Beatles' new album. Simon's confidence was shown on a visit to the Peppermint Lounge in Liverpool. There Geoff met a friend who had lost five pounds on the gaming tables. Simon requested ten shillings (fifty pence) and within minutes, he was presenting the loser with his lost sum.

Tony Wilson from the shanty singers Stormalong John did not book him for the Bothy Folk Club in Southport because he was 'into a purist thing at the time', but he did catch his act at the Cross Keys close to Liverpool Stadium. He remembered Simon as a shy, serious artist who was received very well, although Tony was taken aback by his arrogance. The British are traditionally modest and it may be that

Simon simply had pride in his work. He recalled, 'I saw him at a place behind the Stadium, some horrible Tetley's pub, and I thought he was conceited. It came over in his songs and in his performance. We had a chance to book him for the Bothy Folk Club in Southport but I didn't think he was worth it. I still think I would turn him down today.'

The playwright Willy Russell was in the audience. 'I remember a mate of mine taking me to the Cross Keys opposite Liverpool Stadium and seeing Paul Simon. It was strange because he was in this very casual, determinedly amateur environment. He was very sophisticated and professional and was doing the kind of act which was shunned in English folk clubs, where it was all shamble on, do your bit and get off. He had worked out routines, which he repeated night after night at different gigs. We thought that he was letting the side down by doing that but the music was terrific and the songs were great.'

Hughie Jones of the Spinners, who ran a weekly club in Liverpool, remembers, 'We had met Paul Simon at the Troubadour in Earl's Court and he was offered to our club but we refused. We didn't think he was very folky and we were very, very folky in those days and into British folk music. However, I did go and see him when he played Widnes. He was a beautiful guitar player and singer but he was nothing whatsoever to do with folk music.'

A visiting American folk singer might have to suffer other indignities while travelling around. Phil Ochs toured the UK after Joan Baez had taken his song, 'There But for Fortune' into the Top 10. When he came to Liverpool, the folk-singing duo who rang the folk club, Jacqui and Bridie, said that they would join him when he sang 'There But for Fortune'. The good people of Liverpool perhaps saw Phil Ochs' only performance where he didn't sing 'There But for Fortune'.

Geoff recorded his performance in Widnes and gave Paul the tape. Paul promised to have a copy sent to him but it never arrived. Paul told *Rolling Stone* in 1970, 'I like listening to early tapes of me. I have this tape that I did while I was in England. It gives me a lot of pleasure to listen to that.' Paul has never released this tape, although it sounds perfect for a retrospective.

Although Paul had remembered his time in Widnes, he wanted to forget the town. He told Roy Carr of the *New Musical Express* in 1971, 'If you know Widnes, then you'll understand how I was desperately trying to get back to London as quickly as possible. "Homeward Bound" came out of that feeling.'

HOMEWARD BOUND

Words and Music by PAUL SIMON

Recorded on
C.B.S. 202045 by
SIMON & GARFUNKEL

Recorded on
PARLOPHONE R. 5421 by
THE QUIET FIVE

LORNA MUSIC CO., LTD.,
5, DENMARK STREET, LONDON, W.C.2
SOLE SELLING AGENTS:
Southern Music Publishing Co. Ltd.
8 DENMARK STREET, W.C.2.

3/.

According to Geoff Speed, 'He is said to have written "Homeward Bound" while he was staying in Widnes with me and that is sure to raise the hackles of everyone from Widnes. Yes, he did complete the song while staying with me in Widnes, but I know he had been in Birkenhead the night before and I think he was really writing about Birkenhead.' There is a plaque at Widnes station commemorating the event although it does get stolen and has to be replaced from time to time.

For the record, Paul Simon played the Central Hotel in Birkenhead, opposite the train station, and the quaintly named Barnacle Bill's at the King's Hotel, Bebington, so he covered the Wirral pretty well,

Al Stewart recalled, 'I lived in the same flat as Paul Simon in London. I was in the room next door. I heard him writing songs through the wall, (Sings) "Homeward bound, I wish I was homeward bound", and after about three hours, he came out and said, "What do you think of this?" When he played me "Homeward Bound", I thought it was okay, I didn't think it was great. The next day he came out and played "Richard Cory" and I thought that was great. I remember saying, "This is the one; that thing you wrote yesterday can be thrown away. 'Richard Cory' is the hit," which began a long and undistinguished career of mine of being unable to pick hit singles (Laughs).' Colin Green, who was the lead guitarist with London club band the Blue Flames, recalls a session with Paul Simon in which they did 'Richard Cory'. This has never surfaced.

Simon had his regular partner Art Garfunkel on hand during Art's summer vacation. Together they appeared on Granada TV's *Scene at 6.30* singing 'Wednesday Morning 3am' Through her social work contacts, Judith Piepe set up some performances at prisons and Paul appeared after Sunday mass at Brixton.

That summer of 1965 was noted for the release of *Bringing It All Back Home*, which became Dylan's biggest seller to date. With the Byrds' version of 'Mr Tambourine Man', everyone was talking about folk-rock and many performers were busy rearranging their material. Simon & Garfunkel had it done for them.

Their album, *Wednesday Morning 3am*, was still not selling but a couple of radio stations in Florida loved 'The Sound of Silence'. Tom Wilson added twelve-string electric guitar, bass and drums, and issued it as a single. He told Garfunkel what he was doing. Garfunkel wrote to Paul, and a few weeks later, Paul was in Holland and bought *Billboard,* the music trade paper. Much to his surprise, 'The Sound of Silence' was 'bubbling under' the US Hot 100. Art Garfunkel no doubt approved, as he would have seen *The Paul Simon Songbook* as a recurrence of True Taylor.

Oddly enough, Tom Wilson had done a similar job with Bob Dylan's solo version of 'The House of the Rising Sun' from 1962. Once it was a hit for the Animals, he thought it would be interesting to turn Dylan's recording into a rock record and added backing. This lay in the vaults until a CD of Bob Dylan was issued over thirty years later.

Although Tom Wilson worked with Bob Dylan, he quit after recording 'Like a Rolling Stone', commenting that 'The technical standards of recording were low and you had to be drunk.' On the other hand, he said of Simon & Garfunkel, 'It was soft and very melodic – just a beautiful sound.' He left Dylan and Simon & Garfunkel behind as he moved to the jazz label Verve, but he also worked with Frank Zappa and ventured into the unknown.

Paul had no objection to going electric. He played a private party with Pink Floyd in October 1965. He performed 'Where Have All the Flowers Gone' and then sang 'Johnny B. Goode' with Pink Floyd. Acoustically, you can see Paul sing 'The Sound of Silence' at Vient de Paraître in Paris on 27 November 1965 on YouTube. It's a very clear film too but a cold night as Simon is wrapped in a thick scarf.

The heat was about to be turned on, but first, a brief but sorry interlude.

CHAPTER 4

Blues Run the Game

In the mid-60s, the artists who would be involved in the British folk revival were coming together in London. They included Martin Carthy, Donovan, Davey Graham, Bert Jansch, Ralph McTell, John Renbourn, Al Stewart and the various musicians who were to make up Fairport Convention and Steeleye Span. Visiting Americans gained much from this community: both Big Bill Broonzy and Ramblin' Jack Elliott had toured in the 50s and now the visitors included Bob Dylan, Joan Baez, Pete Seeger, Phil Ochs and Paul Simon. Any American who came to Britain sang its praises and found it changed them in some way. Dylan for example was no longer singing the blues.

In return, the British musicians were impressed by the sense of purpose and the confidence of the Americans. One visitor was the troubled Jackson C. Frank, whose 1965 album was produced in London by Paul Simon. *Jackson C. Frank* is a fine album, untarnished by time, but it was not recognised outside the folk circle on release and Frank's own career is among the most distressing in music history.

Jim Abbott has written a finely detailed biography of Frank, *The Clear, Hard Light of Genius*, the book being let down by its title: there is no evidence to call him a genius and if you do call him that, what word is going to describe Bob Dylan or Paul Simon? It is a story that is well worth telling: considering all the problems of just being Jackson C. Frank, it is remarkable that he made such a fine album in 1965. For a few short weeks, his personality and his album fit perfectly with the mushrooming folk scene.

Jackson Carey Jones, the son of Jack and Marilyn Jones, was born into a Catholic household in Buffalo, New York on 2 March 1943. Jack was a test pilot but he was also a womaniser and the marriage fell apart. Marilyn took Jackson (Jack's son) to Elyria, Ohio and she met Elmer Frank, a serviceman who had been at the Nuremberg trials and then worked as a chemist. He adopted Jackson and raised him as his own son, although they had no children of their own. It was a musical household and in the light of events, it is ironic that Marilyn was often singing 'You Are My Sunshine' to Jackson.

Marilyn wanted to return to her friends and family in Buffalo, and Elmer agreed. The city is on the shores of Lake Erie and there were long, icy winters where the snow could be two feet thick. Jackson attended the Cleveland Hill Elementary School and in March 1954, the winter was not yet over.

The school had an annexe with a wooden corridor that led to a timbered music room, where Jackson was on 31 March. A furnace in the basement was working hard to heat the school. It was an old furnace and the weaknesses in its structure had been badly repaired. The flames suddenly escaped and shot into the annexe, making their way to the music room. There was one door with no easy means of escape.

The teachers broke the windows in a frantic effort to get the children free but many were lost in the cauldron. There were some outstanding acts of bravery and self-sacrifice. Fifteen children were killed and another twenty-three injured. Jackson was among them and he recalled, 'Someone managed to throw me out of the window and into the snow. The snow helped to put out the flames that were on my back.' Nearly sixty per cent of Jackson's body was covered in burns and he was close to death.

Jackson, who was eleven years old, spent the rest of the year in hospital. His temperature soared to 108 degrees and he was placed on an ice bed to bring it down. A metal plate was inserted in his skull and calcium deposits built up in the wrong places, limiting his mobility and increasing his pain. He had a tracheotomy to help him speak. It was a long and painful recovery, although it was never complete. Far from it. He was badly scarred, he would walk with an ungainly limp, and he had limited movement in his arms.

When Jackson had some personal tuition in his sick bed, his tutor brought along a guitar and sang him folk songs from American history. Jackson wanted his own guitar and although he had limited movement, he taught himself to play. He listened to Burl Ives' records and learnt his songs.

Life magazine was criticised for showing photographs of the injured children but the horror of the event did force authorities to change working practices. Safety precautions were upgraded and many schools had to install sprinklers.

Because the tragedy was global news, celebrities, hopefully for the best reasons, offered their sympathies. Kirk Douglas visited the injured children and there is a photograph of Jackson smiling, the only picture in which I have seen him smile. Elvis Presley sent Jackson a personal letter and, in 1957, when Marilyn took him to Memphis, they called at Graceland, just like that, and Jackson had his picture taken with the King.

Jackson struggled through college, having to cope with his physical disfigurement and incapacities as well as his mental torment, with flashbacks to the fire. He wanted to be a writer and study journalism but he also liked the musical scene around Buffalo with such promising musicians as Paul Siebel, Eric Andersen and Joachim Krauledat, later John Kay of Steppenwolf. He sang in coffee houses with a Kingston Trio-like group, the Grosvenor Singers.

His compensation was $80,000 (over $500,000 today), a considerable sum which became payable when he was twenty-one. He was able to drive and instead of setting the money aside, he wanted a small fleet of expensive cars.

In February 1965 Jackson sailed to the UK on the RMS *Queen Elizabeth* with his girlfriend, Kathy Henry. He wrote his first song, 'Don't Look Back', a protest song about a racial murder in Alabama where the killer went free. This led to the melancholy 'Blues Run the Game' with its opening line, 'Catch a boat to England, baby'. The songs flowed quickly. Shortly after arrival, Kathy found herself pregnant and they returned home for an abortion. Then they split up.

Jackson returned on his own in June 1965. He was a floor singer in the city's folk clubs, notably in the basement of a Greek restaurant in Soho, Les Cousins. Jackson helped the owner's son, Andy Matheou, to arrange evenings and book guests. Ralph McTell recalls, 'I didn't know Jackson C. Frank but I saw him play. Sandy Denny was his girlfriend and I saw him at Les Cousins or Bunjies but everyone sang "Blues Run the Game". It has a mystery about it and when you are young, you understand your mortality for the first time, and so it seemed quite advanced to me. The song mentions "room service" and I didn't even know what that meant.'

Jackson was popular; he had a strong voice and he was good at fingerpicking, having developed a style similar to Paul Simon's. Ralph McTell attributed this to being in London: 'Because we couldn't see what the great masters were doing, we could only hear it on vinyl, a guitar style evolved. We listened to Elizabeth Cotton who was left-handed and played the guitar upside down and so she was playing the melody with her thumb but we didn't know that. Just think of Archie Fisher and Martin Carthy. We evolved a style that Paul really liked and Jackson C. Frank was doing the same thing and absorbed stuff from us as well. It is that British style that Paul then took back to America.'

Judith Piepe introduced Jackson to Paul Simon. Through his publishing company, Paul secured a deal to produce a similar album to *The Paul Simon Songbook* with Jackson for the Columbia label, which was part of EMI and not related to the American label.

Two three-hour sessions were booked at Levy's in New Bond Street. Bob Dylan had been there in May to record promotional messages and to put down a ragged, drunken version of 'If You Gotta Go, Go Now'.

The recording should have been straightforward but Jackson was suddenly overcome with nerves. He insisted that baffles were put around him so that Simon could not see him. Simon pressed 'Start' and eventually Jackson began singing – and singing well. Garfunkel was around but neither added backing vocals. The album featured just Jackson and his guitar but Al Stewart added a second guitar to 'Yellow Walls', which marked Al's recording debut.

Ten of the songs found their way onto the album. Nine were written by Jackson and the other was a traditional song, 'Kimbie', a prison song he had heard in Canada.

'Yellow Walls' is a song of torture with Jackson reliving his experiences. He is trapped in himself, having to view his body as his eyelids are burned away. The album often alludes to the fire and the luck, or otherwise, of survival. 'Here Comes the Blues' has the line, 'No bottle of pills, babe, can kill this pain'. Nick Drake made a home recording of this song and it is easy to see why this appealed to the troubled singer, who also put down 'Here Comes The Blues', 'Milk and Honey' and 'Kimbie'.

One of the best melodies is 'My Name Is Carnival' but the bad rhymes and mispronounced words make this track irritating. You can imagine Frank in an amusement arcade, thinking, 'I'll write a song about this.' Bert Jansch performed it better, partly because it showcased his guitar.

The album was simply called *Jackson C. Frank* and is best known for its opening track, 'Blues Run the Game'. Simon & Garfunkel recorded their own version of this, ending with a very typical Simon guitar chord, but it was not released until the 1990s when it appeared as a bonus track.

It is easy to see why the songs and the singer appealed to Paul Simon but the only potential single was 'Blues Run the Game'. As it happens, 'Blues Run the Game' was remade and released as a single with a new song, 'Can't Get Away From My Love', on the reverse.

The album has an impenetrable sleeve note from Jackson C. Frank himself – shades of Kerouac, and perhaps Art wasn't available – and it would have been far better if it had simply printed Paul Simon's assessment, '"Blues Run the Game" is a jewel of a song.' If they had released their version at the time, it would have improved Jackson C. Frank's fast-depleting funds and his status.

He was still buying cars and during his time in the UK he had a Bentley, a Land Rover and an Aston Martin, so there was little cash left. Maybe he was banking on the album doing well.

With little promotion, the album only sold 1,000 copies, but since then it has been reissued, invariably with additional songs from the session. In 'Marlene', he writes of his young girlfriend who died in the explosion, about his scars and about being 'a crippled singer'. I would have taken a chance and put this on the album.

Jackson's new girlfriend, eighteen-year-old nurse Sandy Denny, played him her own new songs, which may have included 'Who Knows Where the Time Goes', a song that would top anything Jackson C. Frank ever wrote. Possibly he wrote 'You Never Wanted Me' about their relationship. She included it on her first album and wrote a cryptic song about him, 'Next Time Around'. Roy Harper wrote about him in 'My Friend' on the album *Sophisticated Beggar*.

After Sandy, Jackson took up with a society girl, Caroline, and for a time he favoured the city-gent look of a pinstripe suit and bowler, albeit still with long hair, and would turn up to dates in an Aston Martin. He had a more substantial relationship with the model Elaine Sedgwick, who was based in England and was a cousin of Edie Sedgwick, a mainstay of Andy Warhol's Factory and the subject of Bob Dylan's 'Just like a Woman'. They were married in 1967 and moved to Woodstock. After a miscarriage, they had a son and daughter, but their son died of cystic fibrosis.

In 1968 he was back in the UK for *An Evening of Contemporary Song* at the Royal Festival Hall with Fairport Convention and Al Stewart.

He recorded a five-song session for John Peel's *Night Ride*, four of the songs coming from the first album and the other 'Jimmy Clay'. The full session can be heard on the 3CD set, *Complete Recordings*, released in 2015. His angry new songs, full of thrashing guitar, found few takers. Jackson was uncomfortable when he was back in London. He was disillusioned and would hide behind furniture rather than meet people.

Now a star, Paul Simon lent Jackson $3,000 to open a boutique and, as surety, he wanted the publishing rights to his songs, which suggests that it wasn't wholly an act of friendship. They opened Bell Bows Boutique in Woodstock with Elaine designing and making the stock but it did not do well, and so Simon had the songs.

Jackson and Elaine moved in with her parents and their daughter, Angeline, was born in 1969. She left him after he had an affair and although they reconciled, they were soon divorced. His behaviour became more erratic. He sometimes dressed as a Viking and would wave a ceremonial sword. Other times, he would spend hours watching traffic lights change.

When Art Garfunkel was making his first album in 1971, he invited Jackson to submit new material. There was a new song, 'Juliette', that might suit Art and so Art went to Woodstock to meet him. He showed up with some hippies who mocked Art for his wealth and he never recorded the song, although he did give him a new Martin guitar.

Although Jackson's album was reissued in1978, he was in no state to promote it. He had no money and he sold his letter from Elvis to buy food and cigarettes.

Paul Simon owned his publishing and in 1984 Jackson went to New York to get it back. He didn't see Simon and he slept on the street, cursing at passers-by. Sometimes he didn't take his medication, which made him worse.

In 1993 a student and a fan, Jim Abbott, befriended him and helped him straighten out his life. He was in and out of hospital and hearing voices in his head. But worse was to follow. Some callous youths said, 'Let's shoot the homeless guy,' and shot out his left eye. In 1997 he went into a care home and Simon returned his songs to him the following year. Jackson C. Frank died from pneumonia and cardiac arrest. His game had been run on 3 March 1999, the day after his fifty-sixth birthday.

Jackson C. Frank was unlucky in so many ways. Just one song can set you up for life – 'Where Do You Go To My Lovely', 'Streets of

London', 'American Pie', 'The Sound of Silence'. Jackson C. Frank had a song, 'Blues Run the Game', that could have had that status, but although it has been much recorded (Sandy Denny, John Renbourn, Simon & Garfunkel, Eddi Reader, Counting Crows), it has never been a hit single or used in a major film.

Extract showing Paul Simon (13 September) from the accounts of Geoff Speed's Widnes Folk Club, 1965

CHAPTER 5

1966 and All That...

Tom Graph, Artie Garr, Jerry Landis, True Taylor, Tico and Paul Kane had served their purpose, not to mention Tom and Jerry. The world was ready for Simon & Garfunkel. Simon said with some surprise, 'People thought 'Garfunkel' was an English name like Clive or Colin – one of those names that Americans didn't have.' Maybe, but I doubt that anyone in England thought that Garfunkel was an English name.

Although 'The Sound of Silence' was climbing the American charts, it was out of character for Paul Simon not to hotfoot back home. He remained in Europe and watched the record sell with a certain detachment. Questioned by the *New Musical Express*, he said, 'I don't even feel it at all. You see, here I am in London and this record is supposed to be selling well. I'm not even over there and so I don't know the excitement that's going on. I'm here in England and I'm going to folk clubs and I'm working like I was always working. It hasn't changed me at all. Oh, I'm happy about it, man. I've got to say that I'm very pleased. It's a very nice gift.'

So why was Simon like this? After all this time, he was about to have a major hit, so why didn't he (and Garfunkel, for that matter) pursue it? It can't have been the obligation to play a few club dates. No, they were waiting for Columbia to come up with a decent offer to make it worth their while.

That could have been the prospect of making a new album to capitalise on the hit single. Art wanted to continue with his studies but he'd welcome quick cash through an album and some concerts. In mid-December 1965, Simon and Garfunkel teamed up for sessions, this time produced by Bob Johnston, who had been working with Bob Dylan.

They already had three tracks, that is, both sides of the single and 'Somewhere They Can't Find Me'. As *The Paul Simon Songbook* had not been released in the US, the intention was to keep it that way

Simon and Garfunkel, 1966 (Camera Press, E. Taylor)

Paul Simon (Harry Goodwin)

and record some of those songs with new arrangements for Simon & Garfunkel.

The starkness of 'A Most Peculiar Man' is better suited to one man, one guitar, but 'Kathy's Song' is just as attractive and I like Garfunkel taking 'April Come She Will' as a solo. 'Leaves That Are Green' has a jaunty accompaniment reminiscent of a fairground. The most marked difference is with 'I Am a Rock', which is given a fashionable folk-rock treatment that drains the defiance from the song.

'Richard Cory' is presented with 'apologies to E. A. Robinson'. Like 'A Most Peculiar Man', this song can be traced back to a newspaper cutting, in this instance from April 1897. The American poet E. A. Robinson had read how Frank Avery had killed himself with a shotgun. Three months later he told a friend that he had written 'a nice little thing called "Richard Cory". There isn't any idealism in it, but there's a lot of something else – humanity, maybe. I opine that it will go.'

E. A. Robinson opined right and the poem became well known after being included in his collection, *The Children of the Night*. The poem itself ran to four verses of four lines each and told how the workers looked up to their wealthy employer, Richard Cory. In the poem's last line, Robinson uses Cory's suicide as a surprise ending. It runs,

So on we worked and waited for the light,

And went without the meat and cursed the bread;

And Richard Cory, one calm summer night,

Went home and put a bullet through his head.

Simon retains the surprise but in neither version is there any explanation as to why Richard Cory should have done this. Robinson dwells on his material success and Simon includes orgies and yachts. Simon adds a subtlety to Robinson's poem by repeating the chorus after his death, thereby implying that the workers envy Cory's ability in being able to do away with himself.

It is easy to see why this poem appealed to Paul Simon. They both understood being lonely in a crowd, and such songs as 'A Most Peculiar Man' and 'I Am a Rock' mark out Simon as a latter-day Mr Robinson. Indeed, Simon emphasises the link by placing 'A Most Peculiar Man' next to 'Richard Cory' on the LP. There is a sudden jolt in the arrangement for the suicide in 'Richard Cory', whereas the death comes with understated delivery in 'A Most Peculiar Man'. The sweetness of the duo's harmonies on 'A Most Peculiar Man' weakens the overall impact while the version on *The Paul Simon Songbook* is unsettling.

Like 'Richard Cory', 'Blessed' was also written in London. Simon wrote it while sheltering from a downpour in St Anne's Church in Soho. He updates the Sermon on the Mount for pot sellers and meths drinkers, while the backing duplicates the jingle-jangle of the Byrds.

In January 1966 'The Sound of Silence' replaced the Dave Clark Five's 'Over and Over' at the top of the US charts, which suggests that competition wasn't very strong, but for the next month their record and the Beatles' 'We Can Work It Out' criss-crossed with each other at No. 1, an extraordinary achievement. The Beatles and their publicity machine were being held back by two singers who hadn't done any promotion.

Indeed, they were both at home with their families. They remember smoking joints and listening to the car radio. 'It's No. 1, it's Simon & Garfunkel,' said the DJ. Artie responded dryly, 'That Simon & Garfunkel act must be having a wonderful time.'

Simon & Garfunkel needed a good manager. They picked Mort Lewis, who was handling the Brothers Four and had been involved with Lenny Bruce, Stan Kenton and Dave Brubeck. He had seen action in World War II, which was good training for dealing with Simon and Garfunkel.

Lewis could secure $10,000 a week in concert earnings, and they agreed provided the contract could be terminated in six months. The first shows were okay but they needed to work on their introductions and not sound like schoolteachers.

With bad hairdos, bad hats and the appearance of a comedy duo with the little dark-haired guy and the tall gangly one, Simon & Garfunkel didn't look hip and never would. Art's unruly hair was more of an identifying feature than a fashion statement, yet Tim Buckley with a similar style looked as hip as they come. Similarly, look at Bob Dylan with his iconic hair on the gatefold for *Blonde on Blonde*. I suppose it is all down to who is wearing the hair. Simon and Garfunkel never looked like rock stars and they were stopped by one guard at the entrance to a venue in Detroit. 'We work here,' snapped Simon.

From Nashville, Tennessee, Peggy Ann Harper, Lewis's wife, was a true life 'Pretty Peggy-O', fifteen years younger than him and two years older than Simon. She had dated one of the Brothers Four and then married Lewis in 1965. They proved incompatible and soon divorced.

At first the bookings were wrong. They were booked for dances alongside the Yardbirds and the Four Seasons. They resolved the issue and found their niche on student campuses. 'Art and I play the university dates,' Paul told Keith Altham of the *New Musical Express* in April 1966, 'We do about three every weekend all over the States. Do you know how much we earned last night in a concert in America? $4,300. I can't grasp it. It means nothing to me. Art might say after a couple of concerts, "We earned $13,000 this weekend." I kinda shrug and say, "That's a good two days' work." Their homecoming concert at Forest Hills was a double-header with the Mamas & the Papas, another harmony group full of disharmony who were climbing the charts.

Simon and Garfunkel wanted to promote 'The Sound of Silence' when it was released in the UK, but this was not possible as legislation prevented aliens working more than six months in the year in the UK. Paul had only worked in small folk clubs and even though that had been on a limited scale, the law was the law, and they'd have to wait.

Bizarrely, their 45 never made the UK charts, but a cover version from the Irish balladeers, the Bachelors, did. They had had spectacular success with 'I Believe' and other oldies – and now they took 'The Sound of Silence' to No. 3. Maybe it polarised their audience as they never made the Top 10 again.

The album was released in both territories as *Sounds of Silence*, but the British and American versions are different. The UK LP included their new single, the Widnes epic 'Homeward Bound', which was held back for their next US album, *Parsley, Sage, Rosemary and Thyme*. 'Homeward Bound' is a world-weary account of life on the road for a poet and a one-man band (Simon at the time seeing himself as both) and in a few lines it describes the monotony of touring. A dull thump from a drum accentuates this feeling. The chorus contains an element of hope, and 'home' in this instance was London and his girlfriend Kathy, not America.

More recently Paul Simon has said of 'Homeward Bound', 'It is like a snapshot, a photograph of a very long time ago. I like that about it but I don't like the song too much. I wish it had an original title instead of one that has been around forever, but it is naïve and sweet-natured. It's not angry. It was an idyllic time for me.'

'Homeward Bound' was given a folk-rock setting, and the record

Talk show host Simon Dee, Paul Simon and journalist Keith Altham, 1966 (New Musical Express)

made the US Top 10, but stopped at No. 5. The *NME* carried a *New to the Charts* feature and Simon and Garfunkel were the subject on 22 April 1966. It was headlined *Enter the Intellectual Simon and Garfunkel*. To justify this tag, the first paragraph ran, 'Life is like a game. Everyone keeps trying to find out how to win. If you stopped trying to discover this, life would be nothing. The average rock'n'roll star does not give out similes like this. But then Paul Simon is not average. Simon and Garfunkel are not average.'

This 'intellectual' slant has been prominent from that day to this in newspaper articles about the duo, and they have encouraged it. There are many pictures of them looking studious and a typical pose was used on that ill-fated Allegro album which showed Garfunkel with the book *Papa Hemingway*. They felt aloof from their fellow artists. 'We didn't have anything to say to them,' Paul Simon told *Melody Maker* in 1971. 'We'd be on planes and getting into these long discussions about whatever – some offshoot of existentialism, some bullshitty college thing – but nobody else was doing that. So, in a way, although we were real good at making pop music, we weren't of pop music.'

Nevertheless, other performers were becoming interested in their songs. On 22 April, the Bachelors were at No. 5 with 'The Sound of Silence'; the Australian folk band the Seekers were at No.16 with Paul Simon's 'Someday, One Day' (a competent but unexciting song and performance); and Simon & Garfunkel were No. 20 with 'Homeward Bound'. Three Paul Simon songs were in the Top 20. The Seekers took their song to No. 14 (No. 11 in *Record Retailer*), while 'Homeward Bound' climbed to No. 11 (No. 9 in *Record Retailer*). Apologies for the complexity over the chart placings, but the *Guinness Book of Hit Singles* follows the trade paper, *Record Retailer*, which at the time was also printed in *Record Mirror*. Regardless, the point I want to make is that 'Homeward Bound' was to be Simon and Garfunkel's highest chart single in the UK until 'Mrs Robinson' in 1968.

In addition, a cover version of 'Homeward Bound' by the Quiet Five on Parlophone made the UK Top 50, reaching No. 44. Richard Barnes, who later made 'Take to the Mountains' and was part of the Quiet Five, says, 'We had not heard of Simon and Garfunkel but we liked the song and knew we would be competing with them. We both got into the charts but theirs went up as we went down. Theirs was the best version and Paul Simon had written it, so fair enough.'

The Bachelors had broken Paul Simon's songs in the UK and made him around £5,000, but the press reported that he disliked their version of 'The Sound of Silence'. Whether he made the remarks or not, I can't say, but he was apologetic to the Bachelors and their fans in the *NME*: 'I've never said that their version of my song is "disgusting" as one paper reported. I don't sit in judgment over them. They've pleased an awful lot of people with that disc.'

Even if Paul had never said what was reported, he still felt strongly about their version, as he told Norman Jopling of *Record Mirror*: 'Like the Seekers and the Bachelors, what sort of image are we getting with our songs being recorded by groups like that? Our version of "The Sound of Silence" was far superior to the Bachelors', but we didn't even make the charts here.'

Simon was right. Any good intentions that the Bachelors may have had about his songs were lost in sentimentality, an effect magnified by sugary strings. You can't blame them. They had their own following to cater for and Simon was simply mystified as to why they had chosen his song in the first place. He said, 'I think it strange the Bachelors should choose to record a very hip song when their style is so conflicting.'

Perhaps Simon was being too sensitive about his work but if he felt bad about the Bachelors singing his songs he must have been catatonic when he heard Frank Sinatra do 'Mrs Robinson', but more of that later. Garfunkel best summarised their attitude to their craft: 'I care that what we do is good. A lot of people in the pop world are influenced by the fact that you don't have to be good but I can't do that. I can't help but take it seriously.'

Such integrity is rare in the music business and it continued with their second album, *Sounds of Silence*. The critics praised their work and a typical critique came from *Audio Review* (June 1966): 'urban folk at its very best and the effect is disturbing.' This comment was all the more poignant when you consider that Bob Dylan's 'Love Minus Zero/ No Limit' had been described as 'a work of incomparable triteness' on the previous page.

Simon & Garfunkel did have their detractors though. Nik Cohn, the author of the famed rock rant, *Awopbopaloobop Alopbamboom*, was more vehement than most. He debunked the album in his column for *Queen* saying that they were 'painful in their goo-eyed sincerity and their self-satisfaction goes beyond a joke'.

The argument is over authenticity and artificiality. Simon and Garfunkel knew they appealed to college folkies and so the album cover decks them out as students, scarves and all. But fair enough. They were only slightly older than those on the campus and indeed, Garfunkel was still studying. They prided themselves on their honesty and this image was more in line with their own personalities rather than a deliberate attempt to become the darlings of the campus.

It was something new for rock'n'roll. Whatever anybody thought of Elvis, nobody thought he was the sharpest pencil in the box. None of the major rock'n'roll stars had been well educated: most had left school early. Rock'n'roll fans dismiss Pat Boone and he stood apart from the other performers in another sense as he had a degree. This was marketed as something unusual. When it came to the British beat boom, the lead singer who was best educated (Mick Jagger) did his best to disguise it with his image as a working class yob. Conversely, Simon and Garfunkel paraded their academic leanings but their harmonies were derived from the Everly Brothers. Indeed – Simon and Garfunkel were the Everly Brothers gone to university

In June 1967 Art received a degree in mathematics from Columbia University and then moved onto a PhD. By that time the automatic deferment for going to grad school had been abolished but if someone was doing graduate work in mathematics, he could claim that this work was essential. If Art were simply in Simon & Garfunkel, this could never have been called essential. Of course, it was pot luck as to whether or not somebody was conscripted to fight in Vietnam. We have never heard of Dylan receiving his papers, but his wife Sara had a child from her first marriage and so possibly he could have claimed exemption as a married man with a child.

In 1966, *Rave* magazine said that Eddie Simon was as talented as his famous brother. I don't know how they knew this, but he was involved with the duo Crib and Ben, and the group the Guild Light Gauge.

The third Simon & Garfunkel single was 'I Am a Rock'. I didn't feel that this worked too well but it reached No. 3 in America. The Hollies, who had had a string of hits, had picked it for their next UK single. Fearing such competition CBS put the song instead onto an EP. Then the Hollies encountered trouble with EMI who objected to the word 'womb' in a pop song. The company felt that the BBC might ban it, so it was pulled. How times have changed.

The Simon & Garfunkel version of 'I Am a Rock' was released in the UK and made a respectable No. 17. By then, 'I Am a Rock' had appeared on two singles, one EP and two albums by the duo or by

Simon on his own. They made a brief promotional visit to the UK, appearing with the Walker Brothers and the Troggs on *Ready Steady Go!* on 8 July and *Top of the Pops* on 14 July.

Sounds of Silence made No. 21 on the US album charts and No. 13 in the UK, not a staggeringly good performance but it was on those charts for thirty-four and 104 weeks respectively and it has been certified double platinum, that is, two million sales in the US.

Their engineer, Roy Halee, who would become their producer, had worked out the best way to record their voices. 'I always insisted that they do their vocals together. The two of them on one mic is what gave them their vocal sound. It was very magical when they sang together. It created some tensions as if something went wrong, they both had to do vocals over again. Sometimes their voices were doubled as when they both come in on "Bridge"'.'

As well as 'I Am a Rock' being more successful in America, Paul Simon wrote another major hit. When he was in London, he had written 'Red Rubber Ball' with Bruce Woodley of the Seekers. There was nothing special about it and the Seekers had, at first, turned it down. A group from Pennsylvania, the Rondells, was looking for new material. John Lennon suggested that they changed their name to the Cyrkle, following the success of the misspelt Byrds. They did this and they recorded 'Red Rubber Ball'. It bounced up the American charts and reached No. 2. Its chief selling factor was some punchy brass riffs that showed someone had been listening to 'It's Not Unusual'.

'Red Rubber Ball' was far more successful than Simon & Garfunkel's next single, 'The Dangling Conversation', which illustrates that quality and quantity sold are not the same thing. Once again, the theme is alienation and lack of communication, but it is far more personal than 'The Sound of Silence'. The singer realises that his relationship is going stale and he displays powerful sarcasm in the third verse.

The song irritated the rock critic Robert Christgau. We have previously quoted from his article, *Rock Lyrics Are Poetry (Maybe)*, and he continues, 'Melodies, harmonies, arrangements are scrupulously fitted. Each song is perfect and says nothing... This kind of mindless craft reaches a peak in Simon's supposed masterpiece, "The Dangling Conversation", which uses all the devices you learn about in English class – alliteration, alternating concretion and abstraction – to mourn wistfully about the classic plight of self-conscious man, his inability to communicate. To me, Simon's voice drips self-pity from every syllable (and not only in this song either). The Mantovani strings that reinforce the lyric capture its toughness perfectly.'

Although I disagree with most of that, I sympathise with the Mantovani strings. It is an attempt to dress the song as another 'Sound of Silence', but the words, and to some extent the melody, are lost in schmaltz. The single did make the US Top 40, peaking at No. 25, good going for a song that namechecks Emily Dickinson and Robert Frost.

The other side of the single is 'The Big Bright Green Pleasure Machine'. Here some dull rhythms and a lack of melody obscure a shrewd lyric. The lyric is a clever list of advertising slogans and they urge the listener to buy a big bright green pleasure machine, which could be a vibrator. The duo's breathing is noticeable, perhaps to emphasise the jerking motions. It doesn't make for repeated listening but it is superior to the covers from the Carnival and Gerry & the Pacemakers.

These songs gave a taste of the duo's next album, *Parsley, Sage, Rosemary and Thyme*. This was stronger and considerably better than their previous UK album, although we were short-changed in playing time. However, hold the sleeve up to the light and look above 'The Dangling Conversation'. You will see that 'Homeward Bound' has been blacked out. The song had been placed on their first UK album and so it had to come off.

The album's title comes from a line in 'Scarborough Fair/Canticle', a track which proved sentimental dynamite. It is their adaptation of an old English folk song, which Simon had learnt from Martin Carthy.

There was an annual Scarborough fair and so the posters now said, 'Are you going to Scarborough Fair?' In 1972 a cross was erected to commemorate the site of the original fair, which had ended, after 600 years, in 1788. The song lists impossible tasks for the lover to perform. It is a sweet, delicate performance but under the layers of harmonies you hear lines from Simon's anti-war song 'The Side of a Hill', which had been on *Wednesday Morning 3*am.

This undercurrent is largely background as the main song is dominant. If we now switch from the first track of the album to the last, '7 O'Clock News/Silent Night', we find that Simon is again exploring duality but now we accept the dark conclusion.

This track starts with them angelically singing 'Silent Night'; there's a rumble in the background and you wonder what it is. As it gets louder, you can pick out phrases and then whole sentences. It is a newscaster intoning a gloom-ridden bulletin: the war in Vietnam and a killer of

Simon and Garfunkel, 1966 (New Musical Express)

student nurses. The newsman gets progressively louder until it is on a par with the carollers. Point made. End of track. End of album.

Judith Piepe said that the song was intended as a tribute to the American comedian Lenny Bruce, and Bruce's death is included in the bulletin: 'In Los Angeles today comedian Lenny Bruce died of what was believed to be an overdose of narcotics. Bruce was forty-two years old.'

More aptly, Phil Spector attributed his death to 'an overdose of police' and indeed, the comedian had been busted many times for obscenity. His appeal to Simon probably lay in his honesty. There was no compromise about Lenny Bruce – he said what he felt.

This is the only track on a Simon & Garfunkel album where Garfunkel plays an instrument – piano. Later it was planned to include just the carol on a compilation but only the mixed version has survived.

Simon revived a novelty song which had been given a new treatment, some new lyrics and a new subtitle. Now it was 'A Simple Desultory Philippic (Or How I Was Robert McNamara'd into Submission)'. It ended with Simon saying, 'Folk-rock' and then 'I dropped my harmonica, Albert', a reference to Dylan's manager, Albert Grossman, but there was no intention to put Dylan down. Paul Simon said, 'I liked protest music. I thought that *The Freewheelin' Bob Dylan* was fantastic. It was very moving and very exciting. There was a lot of bad protest because "Protest" became a thing. You knew it was over when "Eve of Destruction" happened.'

In contrast to Simon's admiration for Lenny Bruce comes his love of the American poetess Emily Dickinson. She is mentioned in 'The Dangling Conversation' and she is the ideal companion in 'For Emily, Whenever I May Find Her'. Her bittersweet love poems were often little more than fragments and, to some extent, her reputation lay in her legend. She lived in seclusion and always dressed in white. Very few of her poems were printed during her lifetime and indeed, scarcely anyone knew that she wrote at all. The discovery of the poems after her death has led to her acceptance at the front of American poetry.

Simon's whimsy has a distinctive nineteenth-century feel – it could be a centuries-old folk song, both with its stilted title and the vocabulary employed. The song is complemented by a stunning, high-tenor performance from Art Garfunkel. The track ends with Garfunkel in full flow saying 'I love you' and we are returned to the present with 'A Poem On the Underground Wall'. The song is about those midnight scribblers with their magic markers and Simon calls them 'the prophets of today', an echo of a line in 'The Sound of Silence'.

'The Sound of Silence' implies that theirs is the only voice that is heard at all, but the Banksy in the new song is only using his freedom to spread bad language. There is not the same justification as with Lenny Bruce and using the word 'Poem' in the title is part of Simon's humour.

'A Poem On the Underground Wall' was written about the London underground when Simon was living in the East End. 'I wrote it about Whitechapel tube station where I had to change every time for that little Metropolitan line to Shadwell. I never saw anything like that in New York.'

Among the lighter moments are two travelling songs, 'Cloudy' and 'The 59th Street Bridge Song (Feelin' Groovy)'. 'Cloudy' is heavy-handed with its literary references to *War and Peace* and *Peter Pan*, but Simon deftly controls the music. I prefer the lightness of 'Feelin' Groovy', despite the pretentious title. Paul Simon said, 'I wasn't satisfied with the original title. I mean, us recording a song called "Feelin' Groovy"? So, I thought, well, give it a more intellectual title – I thought of "The 59th Street Bridge Song" which was okay.'

The song's buoyancy can be attributed to Simon writing it at 6 a.m. He began it on the New York bridge itself and *Rolling Stone* pointed out that although the bridge had no cobblestones, the approach had. There's poetic license for you. If he'd wished, he could have called it 'The Queensboro Bridge Song', its alternative name. It connects Long Island to Queens and passes over Roosevelt Island.

The result is a delightful piece of fluff which contrasts sharply with Simon's other work. He realised this himself and told *The New Yorker*, 'Sometimes I make a song purely an impression, like "Feelin' Groovy". I think: yellow... pink... bubbles... gurgle... happy. The line, "I'm dappled and drowsy" doesn't make sense, but I just felt dappled. Sleepy, contented, it's a happy song, and that's what it was. There's the other kind of song like "The Dangling Conversation". It's intricately worked out. Every word is picked on purpose. Maybe it's English major stuff, but it you haven't caught the symbolism, you haven't missed anything really.' 'Dappled' normally refers to spotty colouring so Simon has given the word a new meaning.

Parsley, Sage, Rosemary and Thyme was the first album that Columbia made on 8-track machines and because Simon and Garfunkel were so meticulous, it took time to make and was an expensive production, albeit one where the costs would soon be recouped. It had a quality which could hardly be ignored and it still sells well. It climbed to No. 4 on the US album charts and No. 13 in the UK. As with Bob Dylan's first album, the back cover reprinted a review of the duo from Robert Shelton; it is very complimentary about their music but describes Garfunkel's hair in terms of an electric shock.

Although 'Scarborough Fair/Canticle' was an obvious single, it was snubbed for 'The Dangling Conversation' and then came a new song for the winter of 1966, 'A Hazy Shade of Winter'. There is nothing wrong with those songs but it is odd that a potential No. 1 was bypassed. Still, we all know what is around the corner.

'A Hazy Shade of Winter' was a commercial single with a powerful sound from the organ, cymbals and drums. The duo's individuality was buried in the production but it is a fine song. A disgruntled Simon combines the theme of growing old with the difficulty of writing. It reached No. 13 on the US chart but was only in the Hot 100 for nine weeks. In 1987 the song was revived by the Bangles for the film *Less Than Zero*, starring Robert Downey Jr as a drug addict at the very time he was a drug addict. The Bangles' single went to No. 2 in the US and No. 11 in the UK.

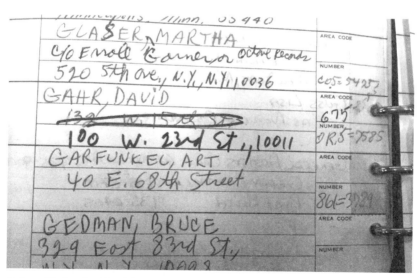

Robert Shelton's old address book with a certain Garfunkel, Art in it. (Institute of Popular Music, University of Liverpool)

CHAPTER 6

Graduation Day

Although Simon and Garfunkel had expanded their sound with *Parsley, Sage, Rosemary and Thyme*, they didn't replicate their records on stage. They still worked as two voices, one guitar, and although there were good economic reasons for this, some of the audience felt short-changed. When they appeared with the Mamas & the Papas at Forest Hills in August 1966, the Mamas & the Papas with a full band took top billing.

Still, they had a highly professional act and a New York performance was recorded for a live album on 22 January 1967. The album was not issued until 2002, when it appeared as the nineteen-track *Live from New York City, 1967*, recorded in the Lincoln Center. It was held back because there would have been too many versions of some songs on the market.

Live from New York City, 1967 is a very good CD with Artie on left and Paul on the right. Their singing and harmonies are spot on and there is little to criticise. It was drawing towards the farewell outing for some of these songs as they were being replaced by new ones. Only six of the nineteen songs are retained for their *Live 1969* album. Unusually, Simon and Garfunkel give us a work in progress, albeit not a very good one, as 'You Don't Know Where Your Interest Lies' would not appear for another seven months. They perform the earlier 'Wednesday Morning 3am' as opposed to the rewrite 'Somewhere They Can't Find Me'. The between-songs banter is amusing and not as tetchy as it was with Don and Phil Everly.

Some performances from the night before at the Lincoln Centre appear on the *Old Friends* box set including the only issued recording of Simon & Garfunkel singing 'Red Rubber Ball'.

In March 1967 Simon & Garfunkel came to the UK for concert dates at the Royal Albert Hall and in Birmingham and Manchester. They recorded an 'in concert' special for Granada TV at their studios in Manchester. That concert went well although when Simon was introducing 'Feelin' Groovy', a string snapped and he remarked, 'Wow, there's a ghost on the stage, man.'

Their introductions fell in line with their image. Art Garfunkel described how he had researched 'Benedictus' in the library and the show contains my all-time favourite Paul Simon quote: 'I returned to the States in December 1965 and I went because "The Sound of Silence" had become a hit. I had to make this transition from being relatively unknown in England to the semi-famous type scene in the States.'

At the time, Simon and Garfunkel needed something or someone to take them one step further to the 'famous type scene'. That something or someone would be the film director Mike Nichols.

Whether writing or performing, Simon is committed to integrity and he often questions what he does. The theme runs through Simon and Garfunkel's work from 'Homeward Bound' to 'The Only Living Boy in New York'. However, he is not above gentle ribbing and on their next single, 'At the Zoo', the monkeys stood for honesty.

The single 'At the Zoo' was released for the tour, along with 'Feelin' Groovy'. Simon wanted to concentrate on 'At the Zoo' in view of a cover of the other song by Harper's Bizarre, which was arranged by Leon Russell and made the US Top 20 as well as UK charts. The press release for 'At the Zoo' said, 'Abounding in aural colour patterns which intrigue and interest the listener the more with each hearing. The disc has a brilliant lyric speaking of the logical zoo inmates who play the human game!'

With the opposite of its intention, this press release makes the single sound unappealing but 'At the Zoo' had much going for it. It begins as a gentle travelling song but builds into something more substantial. By the time Simon arrives at the zoo he is ready for some bizarre comparisons, but the song lacked a chorus, which told against it. This was a drawback in the UK, although it reached No. 16 in the US. It was the third successive single by Simon & Garfunkel to miss the UK chart.

'I can do nothing to make the charts here,' mused Simon to Norman Jopling of *Record Mirror* in 1967. 'I think I write the wrong material for Britain. I make mistakes regarding the singles which are put out there. Take "The Dangling Conversation". It wasn't suitable for the British market. It was way above the kids. Then there was "A Hazy Shade of Winter". As soon as I released that, I knew the flip was better, "For Emily". I should have put strings on it and it could have been another "Sound of Silence". It was Art singing on that one. His voice is just great. I knew that "Feelin' Groovy" was a hit as soon as I wrote it. The other version is all right but I put our version on the back of "At the Zoo". Another mistake.'

Still, 'At the Zoo' has had a life of its own. Simon said, 'If it weren't for the fact that they used that song as a commercial for the zoo which makes me happy, and the fact that children like it – there's a children's book based on it – I wouldn't like the song.'

This reveals that Simon regarded himself as the dominant force in the duo, that he was arrogant (How does he know 'The Dangling Conversation' was too difficult for 'the kids'?), that he had control over their releases, and that he thought 'For Emily' was a potential hit. It has never been a chart record for anyone, but maybe its imagery was too outmoded.

It also highlights the different approaches to the media by Dylan and Simon. Paul Simon explains, almost like a schoolteacher, while Dylan is flippant and contemptuous, often giving absurd answers to questions.

A simple example: Dylan in 1964 said, 'I'm just as good a singer as Caruso.' What did he mean by that? He can't possibly have meant that his singing voice was as good but maybe he meant that he could communicate just as well. Dylan never explains so you don't know if he is being playful or ironic. If Simon had made such a remark, it would have been taken straight and he would have been mocked for it.

The year of 1967 is known for the Summer of Love, but the events of that summer had been planned some months earlier. There had been jazz and folk festivals before, notably at Newport, and now the first great rock festival was planned for three days in June in Monterey, California. The executive board included the record producer, Lou Adler, and the leader of the Mamas & the Papas, John Phillips. Paul Simon joined the organising committee and he secured the Grateful Dead, who had fallen out with Phillips.

It was decided that, with the exception of Ravi Shankar, the participants would not be paid and that the money raised would go to good causes. Although the festival took place in June, the month that *Sgt Pepper* was released, none of the Beatles took part, but there were thirty-two acts from the rock world including the Who, the Byrds, Jimi Hendrix and Otis Redding.

Backstage, Jimi Hendrix and Paul Simon had a jam session, although Simon says he was only playing rhythm, feeling somewhat intimidated. 'If he'd say to me, "Take it, Paul", I wouldn't have been able to take it anywhere.'

Over 70,000 hippies descended on Monterey, a sleepy costal village with a population of 25,000. Despite the preponderance of drugs, there were few arrests and the crowd was well behaved. I write this knowing that David Crosby in a wild stage rant said, 'I believe that if we gave LSD to all the statesmen and politicians in the world, we might have a chance of stopping a war.' This was a reference to the six-day Arab-Israeli war, which was contemporaneously being fought.

Simon & Garfunkel closed the first night but you wouldn't know that from D. A. Pennebaker's film or the 4CD set. According to Simon's memories, Lou Adler and John Phillips were in control and 'history is written by whoever writes it'. Still, they scored well with the crowd who clapped along to 'Feelin' Groovy'. Following the festival, Simon was given $50,000 to supervise the buying of instruments and tuition for teenagers in the ghettoes.

California dreaming was becoming a reality with Monterey, and then two years later there was Woodstock, although some negative vibes are attached to that. At the end of 1969, there was the disaster of Altamont but Simon & Garfunkel were not involved in either festival.

The next Simon & Garfunkel single combined 'Fakin' It' with 'You Don't Know Where Your Interest Lies'. Even though 'Fakin' It' was a US hit, reaching No. 23, 'You Don't Know Where Your Interest Lies' was the A-side in the UK. This might have been Simon's instruction, but the decision was quickly reversed. Either way, neither side made the UK charts. 'You Don't Know Where Your Interest Lies' has been ignored ever since except for a disco version in 1977 from Dana Valery sounding like Gloria Gaynor.

'You Don't Know Where Your Interest Lies' had a biting rhythm and tough-sounding vocals but it was not as inspired, nor as original, as 'Fakin' It'. There was a peaceful bridge amidst the rocking verses and some impressive lines. The track sounds like a good idea that hadn't been fully explored.

'Fakin' It' was different, indeed strikingly different, from anything that Simon & Garfunkel had done before, but this was 1967 and the Beach Boys, the Beatles and the Byrds were coming up with new ideas, one after another.

With 'Fakin' It,' Simon had written a rock song to go with a rock setting. The lyric does not sound mystifying on first hearing. The language is simple and the title is repeated over and over. Ah yes, the honesty theme again, but strange things are happening. A shop door opens and a girl, Beverley Kutner, asks Mr Leitch if he has been busy. That is Donovan's surname and it sounds like a personal reference, but that doesn't explain what it's doing there. Beverley Kutner was a folk singer that Simon knew in England. He had invited her to Monterey and in 1969 she met and married John Martyn. 'Fakin' It' was improved when it appeared on *Bookends*. The recording was slightly sped up and remixed for stereo.

The key line is when Simon compares himself to a tailor, alluding to his family history. The critic Robert Christgau called this 'extremely subtle' as Simon goes from a clever metaphor to personal identification. Simon related it to his Judaism, and he said, 'Sometimes I'm American, sometimes I'm Jewish, but mostly I'm Jewish', an intriguing quote given to the teenage girls' magazine *Petticoat*.

In the early 60s, Mike Nichols and Elaine May had a popular comedy act in the States. They were riding high on the satire boom. They appeared in the UK on a David Frost show where they did a spoof interview with Albert Schweitzer. There was a marvellous single, 'A Little More Gauze', where a doctor refuses to continue with an operation unless the nurse dates him.

After a while, Mike Nichols found success directing plays on Broadway. His debut as a film director was with Elizabeth Taylor and Richard Burton in *Who's Afraid of Virginia Woolf?* which would have been a challenge for anybody. It was both an artistic and a commercial success and his second film was *The Graduate*, which was about a young man's initiation into the adult world.

Suitable music was needed and Mike Nichols loved Simon & Garfunkel's album *Parsley, Sage, Rosemary and Thyme*. It was something that his central character, Ben, would enjoy. He contacted the duo and gave them the novel, *The Graduate*, by Charles Webb, on which the script by Buck Henry would be based. Paul Simon dismissed the book as 'bad Salinger' and added, 'I didn't like anything about the film at first. I was only impressed with Mike Nichols who asked us to do it.' Yet this was enough to persuade Simon to write the score. He told *Melody Maker* in 1971, 'We had nothing to lose and we didn't think that we had much to gain either. We weren't paid an enormous amount. We didn't think it was a big job. Dustin Hoffman was unknown.'

Thirty-year-old Dustin Hoffman played the title role, looking way too old for a graduate, but he was convincing as the shy Benjamin Braddock who has no idea what do with his life. Nichols and the producers were unsure about Hoffman as he looked Jewish and this was a WASP story.

Benjamin is told that the future is in plastics. He is seduced by the wife of his father's business partner, Mrs Robinson (Anne Bancroft, wife of Mel Brooks) and then falls for her daughter, Elaine (Katharine

Ross). When Elaine finds out what has happened, she ditches Benjamin and marries someone vacuous on the rebound. Benjamin arrives at the church too late to stop the wedding but fights off the congregation with the cross from the altar. Elaine leaves the church with him and they board a bus together and look at each other and realise what they have done. End of story. The imagery of the Christian cross had nothing to do with Simon, but it makes an interesting association with his work.

The Graduate is social satire which still works today and has many comic scenes, especially when Benjamin is getting a hotel room for himself and Mrs Robinson. He encounters Buck Henry as a niggling desk clerk. The film does have serious overtones and it could be argued that Ben was taking advantage of a seriously distressed and alcoholic woman, Mrs Robinson. Later on, Mrs Robinson claims that she was raped and although she wasn't, Benjamin's behaviour could be questioned.

Simon & Garfunkel were passed the rushes of the film and asked to supply the music. The production team placed 'Scarborough Fair' and other songs in the picture for the time being with the intention of replacing them. The music worked so well that there was no need for new material. As so often happens, accidents become innovations. Paul Simon said, 'Nobody had ever thought of taking old music and putting it on a soundtrack before.'

Simon had the riff for 'Mrs Robinson' but he was singing 'Mrs Roosevelt' to it. Mike Nichols said, 'Don't be ridiculous. We're making a movie here. It's "Mrs Robinson".'

'Mrs Robinson' is the only new song by Simon & Garfunkel in the film and even that is not complete. There are two short passages, one of which opens with a magnificent chord when Dustin Hoffman crosses a bridge. The song itself was written and recorded after the film had been completed.

The Graduate was a good film that had its finger on the pulse of modern America. Its themes included lack of communication, insincerity and the inanity of cocktail chatter. Mike Nichols could not have found more appropriate musicians, for these topics covered Paul Simon life's work.

The combination of music and story was perfect and despite the fact that the trailer gave away the plot, the film drew huge audiences and rave reviews. The new head of Columbia, Clive Davis, insisted on a soundtrack album for *The Graduate*. Paul Simon said no, the songs were on existing albums. Davis disagreed: he had seen the film – it was going to be massive and there had to be a souvenir album. He agreed to put their name only in small print on the cover to avoid it looking like a new Simon & Garfunkel album.

Davis had a brainwave for the new album, *Bookends*: put in a poster and charge one dollar extra. It worked well but both Simon and Garfunkel thought this a hard-nosed business strategy that they opposed. In his book Davis says, 'I didn't detect any gratitude for my efforts to make Paul and Artie superstars.'

When the souvenir album from *The Graduate* was released, it took all of five minutes to top the US album charts, and yet it adds nothing to Simon & Garfunkel's oeuvre. Comparatively little Simon & Garfunkel music is present and much of the LP is incidental music written by Dave Grusin. Although Grusin's music works in context, it sounds wrong next to Simon's songs. In short, this was not a record for Simon & Garfunkel fans but more for those who wanted a keepsake of the film. The release of films on video was still some years away.

What little there is of Simon & Garfunkel can be heard elsewhere. 'Mrs Robinson' and 'The Big Bright Green Pleasure Machine' are only snippets and there are only four full-length tracks by the duo: 'April Come She Will', 'Scarborough Fair' and two versions of 'The Sound of Silence', one acoustic, one electric. There isn't even a picture of the duo on the cover – unless you think that is Art Garfunkel's leg on display. That famous picture was parodied for the film, *Percy*, which had music from the Kinks.

Nevertheless, the soundtrack album from *The Graduate* topped the US album chart for nine weeks, being replaced by Simon and Garfunkel's next album, *Bookends*, and it remained on the listings for a year. In the UK, *The Graduate* made No. 3 and stayed on the charts for over seventy weeks.

At last 'Scarborough Fair/Canticle' was released as a US single, making No. 11. It should have gone higher but it was already on two hit albums. The song was credited to Paul Simon and Art Garfunkel and published by Lorna Music, which is fair enough as it was way out of copyright, but shouldn't Martin Carthy have been credited for his arrangement? Martin Carthy had one of the UK's Rottweilers, the manager and promoter Jeff Kruger, fight his cause.

Jeff Kruger told me, and you have to remember this is someone who never had any self-doubts, he was always right, '"Scarborough Fair" was an old British song and there had been a relatively new recording by Martin Carthy, and we published that song and that recording. My partner Hal Shaper said that Simon and Garfunkel were coming to the office and I played them Martin's recording. They said that they were going to record it and I was very pleased because I was sure they would make it a worldwide hit.

When they released it, they put it down as their arrangement of a traditional song and they claimed the copyright. They put it in *The Graduate*, which was going to open with a royal premiere the following Thursday week. I wasn't standing for that but their British publisher said there was nothing he could do. I said that I would put out an injunction to stop the release of the record and the film until my rights were acknowledged. United Artists must have spoken to Simon and Garfunkel as their manager sent me a first class air ticket to New York. Simon and Garfunkel were okay at the meeting but their lawyer called me every insulting thing it was possible to call me. After an hour or so, I said to them, "You may believe the rubbish that your lawyers are telling you but the bottom line is this, unlike in America, your celebrity will not protect you. When you go into the witness box, the first question that my QC will ask you is, 'Do you normally steal songs from poor British writers?' That is the reality of it. You heard the song in my office, you got the music from my publishing firm, and you stole it. One of two things can happen: you acknowledge us as the publisher and pay us the royalties or I will sell you the copyright", and it was the latter that we did. We lifted the injunction and I walked out of there with a lot of money for my publishing company, and the hatred of the lawyer who stopped me getting UK tours with a lot of major artists, but you have to protect what you believe to be right.'

In turn, Martin Carthy had seen the song in Ewan MacColl and Peggy Seeger's *The Singing Island*, so who really knows who deserved the money? Still, Martin Carthy was able to pay off his mortgage. Martin Carthy says today, 'You shouldn't feel sorry for me because of "Scarborough Fair" although I felt sorry for myself at the time. It was never my song. It was there for anybody to do. The only thing I resented is that Paul Simon implied he had written it when in fact he had taken enormous pains to learn it. I wrote the words down for him and I just think that his way of promoting the song wasn't entirely honourable, but it's tough bananas, isn't it? It's ridiculous to suggest that had it not been for Paul Simon, I would have had a hit with "Scarborough Fair". I wouldn't have had a hit because, leaving aside the question of whether people would have bought my version, I wouldn't allow Fontana to issue a single of it. I don't believe that my version would have made me $20m or whatever or that I would have got to do the music for *The Graduate*.'

Simon and Garfunkel developed 'Mrs Robinson' into a complete song. It was very catchy, featuring very rhythmic guitars and congas, and far less complex than most of Simon's work, being a two-chord tune. The outstanding lyrics were largely in blank verse. Simon was proud of them, telling *Melody Maker* in 1971, '"Mrs Robinson" was the first time that Jesus was mentioned in a popular song. Nobody had said "Jesus" before. People thought it was a word that you wouldn't say in pop music. On the radio they wouldn't play it; they'd find it blasphemous.'

Far from being profane, Simon thought the lyrics funny, although they sang them straight. There was a sardonic humour which gave the song a sting in its tail. There was a bewildering reaction when they appeared on *The Andy Williams Show*. The audience laughed loudly through it all and I have never understood why. Was somebody in the wings holding up a sign saying, 'LAUGH'? True, the song is amusing, but this is as though they were the new Marx brothers.

There is the much-quoted line about the baseball star, Joe DiMaggio, who was Marilyn Monroe's former husband. In 1970, June Southworth in the magazine *Rave* called it an 'incredible line' and continued, 'One line and it summed up the whole middle-class, middle-age of America, looking for its lost youth, and the heroes like Joe DiMaggio who went with it.' Said Paul Simon, 'It's an interesting line for a song that has nothing to do with Joe DiMaggio.' Indeed. Simon had planned to use Mickey Mantle's name in the song but that didn't scan. As it happens, Mickey Mantle had been in the US charts in 1956 as Teresa Brewer had recorded the novelty hit 'I Love Mickey' with him. Joe DiMaggio didn't get it. He asked Simon, 'What does that song mean? I haven't disappeared. I'm doing ads for Mr Coffee.'

Everybody fell for 'Mrs Robinson'. It soared up the American charts to become their second No. 1, replacing the disco favourite 'Tighten Up' from Archie Bell & the Drells. Three weeks later, they were replaced by Herb Alpert with a Burt Bacharach and Hal David song, 'This Guy's in Love with You'. In the UK it reached No. 4 but then was followed by an EP of four songs from *The Graduate*, which made No. 9.

Even rock critic Nik Cohn mellowed, writing in *Queen*, 'It hurts me badly to praise anything by these two – who have turned out what for me have been a series of baddies – but it's an irresistible hummable melody line and even the words have bite.'

There was tough competition for the Record of the Year at the Grammys: 'Mrs Robinson' (Simon & Garfunkel), 'Hey Jude' (the Beatles), 'Harper Valley PTA' (Jeannie C. Riley), 'Honey' (Bobby Goldsboro) and 'Wichita Lineman' (Glen Campbell) – all five being familiar oldies today. My personal preference would be for 'Wichita Lineman', which is a highly unusual Jimmy Webb composition, but the voters went for 'Mrs Robinson'. Simon was surprised; he had been certain he would lose to 'Hey Jude'.

In 1968, Simon was a guest on the double album *The Live Adventures of Mike Bloomfield and Al Kooper,* two musicians associated with Bob Dylan going electric. He joins them for harmonies on the final verse of 'The 59th Street Bridge Song (Feelin' Groovy)'.

Early in 1968, the New York writers Barry Mann and Cynthia Weil had fun at Simon and Garfunkel's expense, writing 'The Young Electric Psychedelic Hippie Flippy Folk and Funky Philosophic Turned-on Groovy 12-String Band'. Barry Mann's single couldn't match up to his magnificent title but it was a fun record. Mann who wrote and performed 'Who Put the Bomp' had an ear for pop satire but this was overblown.

In March 1968 they returned to the UK for further concerts, the first one being in Manchester. Garfunkel was out of sorts, complaining that the driver should go faster than thirty miles an hour and detaching Paul's guitar lead in Edinburgh so they couldn't do an encore. The following day he fell ill and returned to the States suffering from exhaustion. The remaining dates at the Royal Albert Hall and the Birmingham Odeon were rescheduled for May.

Al Stewart, who had known Paul Simon in London, met up with him in April 1968: 'I was 19 and I used to follow him round and Paul was 22 which was like a grown-up to me. I was the annoying teenager who carried his guitar case and went out for sandwiches when they were needed and got lumbered with the silly jobs. I was still doing it in 1968. I went to New York and he enlisted me as a roadie for a gig in Cornell University and so I think it took me a long time to stop carrying Paul Simon's guitar case, both literally and figuratively.'

Paul Simon gave some press interviews, staying in the Hilton Hotel with a 'Jesus Saves' T-shirt and saying how much he liked the Hollies. Well, sort of. 'They spent a lot of time at our recording sessions picking things up, watching the way we work. It obviously affected their own style.' He told the press that he had split up with Kathy and he had felt so bad that he had not been able to write anything for six months. Then came the *Bookends* album.

Bookends seemed destined for great heights and they had put so much into it. They worked in collaboration with Roy Halee, but this time with no outside producers. Simon, who could lose friends with his interviews, said the following about producers to *Record Mirror* in 1971: 'If someone is good, they know what they want and they can

The age of the train for Simon & Garfunkel, 1968 (Harry Goodwin)

do it themselves. And if they're not good and you as the producer add the element that's good, then what is it? You're just adding yourself to somebody and you might as well do it yourself. I don't think there's any need for producers anymore. All you need are engineers who know what's happening with the sound and then you go out and play.'

So Simon felt that they only needed Roy Halee, who had strong opinions but knew where to draw the line. Halee said, 'The producer calls the shots and wears many hats. An engineer's only function is sound. A lot of engineers get into trouble by crossing the line. The producer's role is the sound, the artist, the arrangement and the songs. He's the captain of the ship, or should be.'

Paul's strong opinions about producers were coloured by his time at Columbia. He added, 'Bob Johnston was a producer assigned to us by Columbia when Tom Wilson quit. I don't know why they put him on our production – he was an extremely overrated man. He used to fall asleep at our sessions. Bob Johnston never said anything. I don't know what he was there for. He just wanted to know whether anybody wanted a chicken sandwich or not.'

In interviews about his role as a producer, Bob Johnston stated that the producer should deliberately take a back seat if the artist knows what he is doing. This is what he did with Simon & Garfunkel and it seems harsh to be criticised for it. On *Nashville Skyline*, Bob Dylan asks Bob Johnston, 'Is it rolling, Bob?' Johnston let Johnny Cash record in prisons and he produced Leonard Cohen, who said, rather more charitably, 'It wasn't just a matter of turning on the machines. He created an atmosphere in the studio that invited you to do your best, stretch out, do another take – an atmosphere that was free from judgment, free from criticism, full of invitation, full of affirmation.'

Prior to the new generation of pop stars, most successful artists were obliged to record a Christmas album. Simon and Garfunkel were thinking along those lines as they recorded 'Star Carol' (known from Tennessee Ernie Ford) and an a cappella 'Comfort and Joy' in April 1967. They were not released at the time, but if Simon and Garfunkel had followed it though, it would have been a folky Christmas with magical harmonies.

The new album, *Bookends,* was all their own work, but its playing time didn't stretch to thirty minutes. Paul told Penny Valentine in *Disc*, 'I had the idea for this album immediately after the previous one. A common theme for an album is becoming popular in America. Ours starts with a track, "Save the Life of My Child", and goes on from there. Lyrically, I think it far better than anything we have done before.'

The theme of ageing only applies to the top side of the album. The second side comprises largely of singles although 'A Hazy Shade of Winter' encompasses the themes of the *Bookends* suite. Art said, 'The Beatles made *Rubber Soul* and moved onto *Revolver* and *Sgt Pepper,* which were not just collections of songs but the album as an art form. We were terribly impressed, and that shone a light on the path that led to *Bookends.*'

There are seven tracks in the *Bookends* suite, although it is not a song for each of the seven ages of man. The delicate 'Bookends Theme' is punctuated by a thunderous chord and the twosome plunge into 'Save the Life of My Child'. The so-called child is probably in his late teens and is about to kill himself by jumping from a high building. The atmosphere is tense and confused. The police officer's words are drowned in the chaos and then we suddenly hear the group singing the opening lines of 'The Sound of Silence', an early example of sampling. You have to listen hard to catch that, but it is after the second chorus. This was the fifth out of six albums to include 'The Sound of Silence' in some way. The production is extremely tight with good use of a Moog synthesizer and if you think that producing records is easy, then listen to the cover version from Mighty Howard which Pye released. You'll hear how badly the sounds are balanced and yet they had Paul Simon's blueprint to work from.

'Save the Life of My Child' is among their best tracks but whether something so deliberately chaotic appeals to you is a matter of taste. As for the ending, we are told that the boy flew away, an identical ending to another 1968 song, 'Rambling On' from Procol Harum, although written independently. In Simon's song, both the police and the crowd talk as though jumping off ledges was commonplace, and possibly the song is about the effects of hallucinogenic drugs, which is certainly the case with 'Rambling On'.

There is a brilliant song called 'America' in *West Side Story* in which the Puerto Ricans sarcastically weigh up their integration into American life and culture. In his 'America', written in blank verse, Paul Simon is wondering what is happening to his country. He is showing Kathy America. They have boarded a Greyhound and while they are admiring the scenery, Simon feels that he has lost his identity and so he too is looking for America. When he finally gives vent to his feelings, Kathy is sleeping and doesn't hear him. He realises that he is not alone as everybody is searching for America. The Nice did a workout on the *West Side Story* song, while another prog band, Yes, recorded a highly original, ten-minute workout of 'America' for the Atlantic sample, *The New Age of Atlantic*, in 1975.

Paul Simon says that the journey never happened: 'I think it's very 1968, about a generation of kids who have just started to travel the country. The girl is Kathy, my girlfriend in England, but we never actually took a trip like that. None of those events actually occurred to me in my life. In many ways, this is a song with no physical roots.'

This quest is also expressed in the last verse of 'Mrs Robinson' and in 'Papa Hobo' (1972). The crux of the matter was summarised by Jack Nicholson in *Easy Rider*: 'You know this used to be a hell of a good country. I can't understand what's gone wrong with it.' We are shown breath-taking American scenery and yet Wyatt (Peter Fonda) and Billy (Dennis Hopper) only find ugliness when they enter the towns.

The next song, 'Overs', is about the death of love, but the opening line is also a coda for 'America'. The singer gives many reasons for leaving, although he never actually leaves. He always stops to think it through and decides to stay. You could argue that it is about how too much travel can do your head in.

From middle age, we move to old age for 'Voices of Old People', which is what it says. The liner note explains, 'Art Garfunkel recorded old people in various locations in New York and Los Angeles over a period of several months. These voices were taken from those tapes. We wish to thank the United Home for Aged Hebrews and the Californian Home for the Aged at Reseda for their cooperation.'

But could Art have been arrested? 'We wanted to tape old people and have their sentiments as part of the theme in *Bookends*. I went to old age homes where I brought the mic out and sat down and talked about things. I also eavesdropped in Central Park. I would take a long shotgun mic and hide it under my shoulder inside a loaf of French bread and pick up on conversations.'

Many voices differing in sex, pitch, accent and delivery have been packed into a two-minute collage. It is an unexpected track but it works well the first time at least and each voice is full of conviction and character. Someone, presumably the matron, tries to liven up the proceedings by asking, 'Are you happy?' There is no reply. Paul commented, 'I liked "Voices of Old People" and I loved what Artie and Roy did with the stereo mix of those voices, the way one fades in and one fades out.'

The phrases and the moods are echoed in the closing songs, 'Old Friends' and 'Bookends Theme'. In these tracks, Simon displays his observations about growing old. He opens quietly and the simile he uses about the old men sitting like bookends is so powerful that it was deservedly used for the album's title. The song drifts off on a lovely sad melody, although at one stage it is replaced by wild, confused music. The sound of cellos accompanies Art Garfunkel as he asks if we can imagine ourselves in the same position. The conclusion is that all that the elderly possess are their reminiscences. The song would have a new application for Simon & Garfunkel's reunion shows.

There are no joys of living on this suite. The album is more dark than light, more death than life. On consecutive tracks, Paul Simon has told us that there is no future for youth, America, love or old age. There is little hope.

There are only five songs on the second side but once again there are no duds. Unfortunately, though, all but one of them had been used before. Alan Paramor, his UK music publisher, explained, 'The reason that *Bookends* had one side made up of previously released singles was simply that Paul Simon has not had the time to write new material. He is not the kind of writer who can force ideas.'

It would take even longer now that Simon was changing his approach to songwriting. There was a more deliberate fusion of lyric and melody, with the words being chosen as much for their sound as their content.

In May 1970, Simon spoke to Loraine Alterman of *Rolling Stone* about his working practices: 'I write sound and meaning simultaneously now. I used to write meaning first. I'd say what it is I want to say and say it in words. Then I set that with the melody. I don't like that so much. That period came to an end with "The Dangling Conversation". You say something specifically. Then I came to realise that you can do it another way. You don't have to do it that way. Then I went just straight sounds. Now I try to write simultaneously, sounds fit the melody — the right vocal sound, the word as it sounds right with this melody. At the same time you write the meaning. It's just a skill that you learn by practicing.' Maybe this led to his songs being more direct and conversational.

There is a folky blues song, 'Groundhog', that Simon wrote around this time but discarded. It has a hypnotic line, 'Morning is the best time of the day' which could easily have become popular. He put down a demo, which is on YouTube, but he did not take it further and the song was recorded by Peter Yarrow of Peter, Paul and Mary in 1973 for his solo album, *That's Enough for Me*.

Bookends was released two years before *Abbey Road*, and like *Abbey Road*, one side was a suite of songs. The Columbia press release called it 'a unique understanding of the soul of the young city-dweller'. Dean Friedman would go along with that: 'The *Bookends* album contains a lot of my favourite songs. I used to work at the Palisades Amusement Park, a place with carnival rides and Ferris wheels. I used to give away those little purple bulls whose heads would move back and forth and I gave out change in the penny arcade. I would come home late at night and I would put the speakers from the turntable on either side of the piano and I would put my head in-between those speakers and I would listen to *Bookends*.'

The only previously unrecorded song on side two was 'Punky's Dilemma', which had its first airing at the Monterey Festival. It had been intended for the scene in *The Graduate* where Dustin Hoffman is floating in the pool but Mike Nichols didn't go for it. The whimsical song is a cross between 'Feelin' Groovy', anything by Donovan and those lovely, lolloping songs which John Sebastian wrote for the Lovin' Spoonful. Unfortunately, its very light-heartedness goes against it as it tends to be overlooked. Put the album on and it's a pleasant surprise. The song is not as innocuous as its lyric suggests. Note the reference to draft dodging, and the rhythm of 'Old Roger, draft dodger' was later developed in '50 Ways to Leave Your Lover'. Lois Lane recorded a cover for the UK but the lyric had to be changed to get airplay. Simon had mentioned Kellogg's Cornflakes and such product placement was a no-no for the BBC. Instead, she sang, 'Wish I was a golden cornflake.'

However, a more grotesque amendment was round the corner. This was Frank Sinatra's 'Mrs Robinson'. Burt Bacharach describes the feeling: 'Sinatra has done a couple of our songs and sadly, I've been let down by what I've heard. He's so great and when you hear that Sinatra has recorded one of your songs and it is going to be on his next album, you think, "Fantastic, oh golly, I can hardly wait!" and then it doesn't work.'

Bacharach was complaining about changes in tempo, but his songs were treated with respect and not recast like 'Mrs Robinson'. I don't know how this came to be recorded but you can imagine the conversation...

Producer: 'Frank, you should do something for the kids, you know, one of their songs.'

Frank: 'Like what?'

'Something from *The Graduate*. How about "Mrs Robinson"?'

'That one about the broad, okay, we can make that swing, but hold on, that's the one with "Jesus" in it, isn't it?'

'Yeah, but...'

'No buts. I'm a good Catholic boy and I don't sing "Jesus". Cole Porter didn't write "Jesus". Lorenz Hart didn't write "Jesus". Jesus, who does this guy think he is?'

'Okay, Frank, we'll change it. I'll call Sammy.'

As a result, Sammy Cahn rewrote the lyric and added a few bits of his own. Frank now sings 'Jilly loves you more than you will know', a reference to his favourite restaurant owner, Jilly Rizzo. He mentions the PTA and adds his standard schtick like 'ding ding ding'.

It's super-kitsch and I'm sure that Simon didn't okay the way Sinatra did his thing.

Ding ding ding.

CHAPTER 7

See How They Shine

All of a sudden Simon & Garfunkel were everywhere, the hottest names in popular music. It was surprising, as no one would have called them charismatic. We recall the famous week in April 1964 when the Beatles held all five places at the top of the US charts. Now, in June 1968, Simon and Garfunkel had the top three albums – *The Graduate* at the top followed by *Bookends* and *Parsley, Sage, Rosemary and Thyme*. *Sounds of Silence* was still finding a new audience at No. 27 and even *Wednesday Morning 3am* was picking up attention at No. 163. Although it had nothing to do with Paul, a top-selling single was 'Simon Says' by the 1910 Fruitgum Company.

The Graduate was breaking box-office records and every film company wanted Paul Simon's services: 'I was inundated with requests to supply movie scores. Write the title song for this or write the music for some real inane, bullshit youth movie, I'm sure you know the thing... unrest on the campus.'

Simon stayed firm, saying in 1971, 'I loved *The Graduate* but I wouldn't really want to write the music to someone else's film again.' He turned down *Midnight Cowboy*, saying that he 'didn't want to look like Dustin Hoffman's songwriter.' He turned down writing for Dustin's Broadway play, *Jimmy Shine*, and John Sebastian wrote the score instead, the show running for a respectable 150 performances.

Midnight Cowboy, with its theme of loneliness in New York City, would have been perfect for Simon. Indeed, Simon, who rarely admits mistakes, may have regretted this as there is a nodding reference to the film on the back of *Bridge Over Troubled Water*. The photograph shows Art as Joe Buck with Paul trailing behind as Ratso Rizzi.

On the whole, though, Simon was right. Many of the films in the wake of *The Graduate* were better left alone. They were routine sub-*Graduates* and they ended up with sub-Simon scores. Examples of the new wave, anti-establishment movies included *Goodbye, Columbus* (Richard Benjamin and Ali McGraw), *Wild in the Streets* (Richard Pryor) and *Candy* (Marlon Brando and Ringo Starr).

There was not a follow-up to *The Graduate* itself although the ending left the story open. Many years later Buck Henry appeared in Robert Altman's satire on Hollywood, *The Player* (1992), making a comic pitch for *Graduate 2*.

Paul Simon did change his mind for *Brother Sun, Sister Moon*, a film about St Francis of Assisi, as Paul was to write the lyrics for Leonard Bernstein's music. Bernstein told the press that he was going to teach Simon a few things about composition – not sure how well that would have gone down. Although this did not materialise, Simon did see Bernstein and contributed a few words to his 1971 oratorio, *Mass*. This line is Simon's, 'Half the people are stoned and the other half are waiting for the next election.'

The director was to be Franco Zeffirelli who had made *The Taming of the Shrew* and *Romeo and Juliet*, art-house films which became commercial successes. Despite his track record, he had difficulty in obtaining finance and the project was shelved. Eventually, Zeffirelli revived the idea and shot the film with European money and a score from Donovan, who said, 'What interested me about St Francis was how he changed the music of the church from boring chants about Latin paradoxes to melodies about flowers, minstrels' ballads.' How convenient that he should be an early day Donovan, and Donovan did a good job of writing Donovan songs, but the film gathered little interest in 1973.

Month followed month and there was nothing fresh from Paul Simon. Simon & Garfunkel performed sell-out concerts and their reputation grew, but their repertoire was predictable. They added 'That Silver Haired Daddy of Mine', associated with Gene Autry but included on the Everly Brothers' *Songs Our Daddy Taught Us* (1958).

The music industry is highly competitive and, back then, artists made at least one album a year. You have to admire Simon's cool as well as credit Columbia for not pressurising him into releasing more albums. Simon may have felt guilty over the slow work-rate, as he told *Rolling Stone* this odd tale about Garfunkel – or was it a joke? 'Artie used to go into record stores and ask if they had the new Simon & Garfunkel album, even if he knew there was no album coming out. He'd just look in to see if maybe it would be there. It would be a surprise to him.' It certainly would.

In March 1969 Art and Mort Lewis were talking on a street corner in New York when twenty-three-year-old Linda Grossman walked by. She was an attractive brunette from Tennessee with a degree in architecture. Garfunkel said, as you do, 'Will you marry me?' Embarrassed by this, she crossed the street. Garfunkel followed her into a deli, apologised for his behaviour and invited her to a recording session for 'The Boxer' that evening. She became Art's girlfriend and later his wife.

Then in April 1969 a bearded Simon introduced us to 'The Boxer', saying the single had been recorded in several venues. The basic track was cut in Nashville, the end voices and the horns in St Paul's Church, New York, and the strings in Columbia's studios, New York. You hear the pedal steel and piccolo together and yet one was played in Nashville and the other in New York. Also Simon and Garfunkel could be exacting to work with – while making 'The Boxer', they and Roy Halee had a sprint across a car park, which Simon won.

Simon denied Bob Johnston's assertion that they had taken over 100 hours of studio-time to make a five-minute single. 'That's not true at all. It was nowhere near that long,' he said and then added disparagingly, 'Bob Johnston would have no way of knowing.' Johnston no longer produced Simon & Garfunkel and the production credit is to the duo themselves and Roy Halee.

If we hear 'The Boxer' today the lyrics sound crystal clear but there were problems in 1969. Simon told *Rolling Stone*, "'The Boxer' has a lot to do with sound and a lot of people said that they couldn't hear the lyrics. That came from the fact that the lyrics went from one word to another and it was hard to separate them. The end of one sound went into the beginning of the next.'

'The Boxer' was a superb example of Simon's new approach to songwriting where the sound was all-embracing. We have a quiet, melancholy start and it climaxes with fantastic, frenetic repetition, which owed something to 'Hey Jude'. In the midst of it were the lyrics. On the surface the song was about a boxer seeking his fortune in New York. Even though he had bad luck, he is a fighter by nature.

The lyric was both a metaphor and deeply personal. Simon told Roy Carr of the *New Musical Express*, 'I would say that "The Boxer" was autobiographical, but it surprised me. When we recorded it, someone said, "Hey, that song's about you" and I said, "No, it's not about me. It's about a guy who…" and as I was saying it, I thought, "Hey, what am I saying? This song is about me and I'm not even admitting it."'

Simon thought that 'The Boxer' was worth the effort. 'I am very pleased with it. It's one of my favourites of all Simon & Garfunkel records. It's a very personal song and it's hard to imagine any other interpretation.' He said that in 1971 and he couldn't say that now. There have been many versions of 'The Boxer', notably from Bob Dylan on his *Self Portrait* album, Waylon Jennings, Emmylou Harris, Joan Baez, Neil Diamond and Mumford & Sons. In 2014 Ben Howard sang a sorrowful version on *The Dermot O'Leary Show* on BBC Radio 2, which showed it worked fine with voice, guitar, cello and a bit of whistling.

Indeed, it was mooted that Dylan's life lay behind the song. Certainly there are parallels but Simon dismissed this. Bob Johnston had produced Dylan's recording and he was the first to play the cover version to Simon. 'It was fine... it was original,' said Simon. 'Like anything Dylan does, it has its own thing. He did it differently and I didn't think anyone could do that. Dylan's version makes me smile.' Is that damning it with backhanded praise?

On the back of 'The Boxer' was the bright and breezy 'Baby Driver', which shows that Simon could be capricious. Whereas 'The Boxer' was a narrative, this was a rock'n'roll pastiche with a witty lyric and a good dance beat, something not often said about Simon & Garfunkel.

The music critic Robert Christgau asserted that Paul Simon's good taste held him back. There may be something in that. The famed TV producer Jack Good said that rock'n'roll was all about bad taste. 'Baby Driver' could be Simon's response. The car is a sexual metaphor, hence the title and the line about feeling your engine. Everything is in the mix: Beach Boy harmonies, bottleneck guitar, raunchy saxophones and car sounds, not to mention the racing commentary.

While the songwriting Paul Simon was baby-driving, the real life Paul Simon was getting married. He and Peggy Harper married in the summer of 1969 and she is mentioned by name in 'Run That Body Down' (1972), but by then he had already dedicated his most famous song, 'Bridge Over Troubled Water', to her.

Richard Meltzer in *Rolling Stone* called the song 'the biggest metaphor bonanza of all time.' It was the logical follow-up to 'The 59th Street Bridge Song' and Meltzer continued that 'he probably decided that somewhere along the line he was gonna sit right down and write an epic testimonial to bridges in general and in particular to the metaphorical functions they perform.' Sarcastic or what?

Meltzer pointed out that Simon was fighting a losing battle as the metaphor was not only archaic but also bridges were far from safe. 'Did you see that photo of the bridge in Pakistan after the flood did it in?'

During his time in England, Paul Simon had played Bickleigh in east Devon. The story goes that Simon had stood on Bickleigh Bridge and watched the waters rising in the River Exe. Residents claimed that this was the inspiration for the song. Nice try, but Paul Simon was inspired by a 1959 gospel record about the raising of Lazarus, 'Oh Mary Don't You Weep' from the Swan Silvertones. During the Baptist hymn, Rev Claude Jeter, says, 'I'll be your bridge over deep water if you trust in my name.' The Swan Silvertones are a great gospel group with a depth of feeling and intensity in all they do. Their version of 'The Lord's Prayer' is electrifying. They recorded prolifically for King, Specialty and Vee Jay from the end of the war to 1965, when Jeter became a full-time minister. His falsetto is amazing and some of the tenor singing on the King records is by Solomon Womack, who was Bobby Womack's uncle.

When Simon was writing his new song, he had to break off for the birthday party of their lawyer Michael Tannen in Manhattan. He arrived late and told the partygoers, 'I've just written my "Yesterday"' and sang it for them. He told Artie, 'This is for you', but Artie said, 'I can't sing gospel well.'

Trivia point: Larry Knechtel played solos on four hit records on four different instruments. There is the piano on 'Bridge Over Troubled Water', bass on the Byrds' 'Mr Tambourine Man', harmonica on Dean Martin's 'Houston' and being the guitar man on Bread's 'Guitar Man'. He had also raised cattle and prospected for gold (and found it).

Paul's demo for 'Bridge Over Troubled Water' is low-key and the song with a few lyrical changes would have worked in that setting. However, he saw it as a bravura performance for Art Garfunkel. When Art worked it through with Larry Knechtel, he could see how Larry's flourishes could lead into a third verse. Simon came up with the 'Sail on silver girl' verse surprisingly quickly and he always felt that it didn't quite fit the rest of the song.

Rolling Stone reported that 'The silver girl who sails on in "Bridge Over Troubled Water" is a hypodermic needle, at least in the mind of a newspaper editor in Monroe, Iowa, who tried to keep the song out of the local high school's graduation ceremonies... The editor said she was particularly troubled over that "ease your mind" business.' The silver girl was resolved by *Disc*. Paul and Peggy were staying with Art and Linda in Blue Jay Way, Los Angeles in a house mentioned in song

Simon and Garfunkel, 1968 (CBS Records)

by George Harrison. Peggy had noticed a few grey hairs, hence the line.

The song has a strong gospel feel and Simon considered recording it with Booker T. & the MG's. In the end he employed his usual musicians and the resulting record is outstanding, not only for Art's vocal but also for Larry's piano playing. Larry received a special credit and often joined the duo in concert for that number.

In 1973 Art Garfunkel told *Rolling Stone* that the arrangement for 'Bridge Over Troubled Water' had been inspired by 'Ol' Man River' from the Righteous Brothers. Like that record, Simon had a growing accompaniment for the song right up to the last line where he suddenly pulled out all the stops.

When Simon asked Jimmie Haskell to write a string arrangement based on Art and Larry's demo, he didn't catch the words and wrote 'Like a Pitcher of Water' at the top. Paul was amused and has the music framed in his office. Pitcher of water or not, Jimmie Haskell won a Grammy for his arrangement.

When Simon first played it to David Clayton-Thomas of Blood, Sweat & Tears, he was unimpressed, one of the few musicians not to rave over it. Simon himself was very pleased with 'Bridge Over Troubled Water' and was quick to praise Art's contribution. 'It was Artie singing on that one. Artie sang that song, I think, very soulfully. Not black soul. He sang it from his heart and it sounded real.' He has called it 'astounding, a virtuoso performance'.

Around the same time, the Beatles released a new Paul McCartney composition, another song of consolation, 'Let It Be', written in a time of turbulence and instability. 'Bridge' kept 'Let It Be' off the top of the UK charts but it was replaced by 'Let It Be' in the US. 'I couldn't believe McCartney did that,' said Paul Simon. 'They are very similar songs, certainly in instrumentation, in their general musical feel, and lyrically too. They're both hopeful songs and restful, peaceful songs. He must have written it about the same time that I wrote mine and he gave it to Aretha Franklin, which is funny because when I wrote "Bridge", I said, "Boy, I bet Aretha could do a good job on this song." It's one of those weird things and it has happened simultaneously.'

The cover versions of 'Bridge Over Troubled Water' included soul treatments from Aretha Franklin, King Curtis and Merry Clayton, not to mention the Tamla-Motown artists – Jackson 5, the Miracles, the Supremes and Stevie Wonder. There were country stylings from Buck Owens and Chet Atkins and dramatic fireworks from Roy Orbison and

Shirley Bassey.

'Elvis Presley's version of "Bridge" was the same arrangement as ours,' said Simon. 'They copied the bass line. Aretha's version is tremendous, the best I've heard except Artie's.' If Simon didn't rate Presley's cover too highly, it's lucky he didn't catch him in cabaret where Presley used its opening line as a gag to refer to the height of his guitarist, Charlie Hodge.

Dave Marsh from *Rolling Stone* wrote of 'Aretha's ability to replenish the meaning of "Bridge" after it had been reduced to cliché by Art Garfunkel's oversung rendition.' But Art was not so keen: 'I'm not a fan of Aretha's rhythm and blues version. I thought I topped them all. I'm sorry if that sounds inflated. The song's brilliant, it should be possible for someone to do another great version, but it was a hell of a tour de force when I went from so soft to so strong at the end.'

Simon spoke of cover versions to the *New Musical Express* in 1971: 'There are people who haven't made good attempts simply because they haven't got the goods to do a good job on anything or because they didn't have enough time. I mean, there are more bad records than good ones, so the majority of covers won't be good, but I'm pleased when somebody takes the trouble to do it well.'

The title has also been parodied and the comedy folk singer Trevor Crozier recorded 'Trouble Over Bridgwater' in 1977. That was also the title of an album by Half Man Half Biscuit in 2000.

In terms of the Great American Songbook, 'Bridge Over Troubled Water' is in the Premier League. Not only was it a hit single but it was also the title track of the new Simon & Garfunkel album. At one stage 'Bridge Over Troubled Water' was topping the singles and albums charts in both Britain and America. In the US, the single topped the charts for six weeks and the album for ten. In the UK, the single replaced Lee Marvin at the top for three weeks – Lee Marvin and Art Garfunkel are at the two extremities of popular singing – and it was at the top of the album charts for forty-one weeks, a record only surpassed by the soundtracks for *South Pacific* (115 weeks) and *The Sound of Music* (seventy weeks).

Around 1970, it was thought for about five minutes that Quadraphonic sound would be the next thing. Simon & Garfunkel's albums were issued in Quad (though who had the equipment to play them?) and there were three newly recorded tribute albums for the Quad market by Caravelli & His Magnificent Strings, the Jim Nambara

Quartet, and Shiro Michi. It was soon phased out and *There Goes Rhymin' Simon* was one of the last albums issued in Quad.

One reason why the *Bridge Over Troubled Water* album took so long was the inaccessibility of Art Garfunkel. Mike Nichols had cast him as Captain Nately in the film of Joseph Heller's novel, *Catch-22*. The film ran behind schedule and although Garfunkel did not have a large role, he was involved for long periods of time.

The film concerns American bomber crews in Italy. Yossarian (Alan Arkin) wants to get out of flying on the grounds of insanity. However, the fact that he doesn't want to fly only shows that he is sane, hence the Catch-22 of the title. It was an anti-war film at a time when the big films were *Patton* and *The Green Berets*, but it was outclassed by the huge success of *M*A*S*H*.

Unlike *The Graduate*, *Catch-22* had a big budget ($15m) and the cast included Alan Arkin, Anthony Perkins and Orson Welles. Welles had considered filming the book himself but, as always, he had difficulty in raising finance. With so many subplots and a large cast of characters, this was an extremely difficult novel to film and today it would be made as a TV series. It is a lengthy book with a profusion, not to say a confusion, of characters. The humour stems from black comedy, which is notoriously difficult to pitch right. Indeed, it is hard to raise laughs when you see somebody's entrails spilling out in front of the camera.

Buck Henry wrote a good script, playing Lt. Col. Korn himself, the thinker who is prepared to let others take the credit so they are blamed if things go wrong. Nichols had offered Paul the role of Dunbar, a soldier who is intent on keeping out of conflict, but the length of the film dictated that several characters had to be dropped, Dunbar being one of them.

The fresh-faced Art Garfunkel plays the film's innocent. Whilst other characters are losing their cool or planning black-market operations, the naïve and idealistic Captain Nately pursues a romance with an Italian prostitute. Stationed in Rome, he meets an old man and their conversation is reminiscent of *Bookends*. Nately tells the old man that he will be twenty in January. The old man answers, 'If you live.' And he doesn't, being unwittingly killed as a consequence of Milo Minderbinder's black racketeering. Luckily, Garfunkel was around long enough to pick up good notices and Mike Nichols offered him a starring role in his next project, *Carnal Knowledge*.

Mort Lewis, knowing how films overran, wanted a catch-22 to talk

Garfunkel out of the film. Garfunkel was resilient and from January 1969, he was filming on an airfield on Guaymas, Mexico. For five months. Garfunkel rarely smiles on screen and Nichols commented, 'He just couldn't get cheerful.' To rehearse new songs, Simon had to fly to Mexico, and the actor, Bob Balaban, recalled an all-night session in Garfunkel's hotel room where they worked on 'The Boxer'.

While he was hanging around on a film set, Art began his project of reading the books an educated man should read. The first book was by Rousseau. He put a sticker on each one he completed and once the internet was in operation, he put the list on his website, which he keeps up to date. We're up to 1,227 by the end of December 2015 and that is a biography of Chet Baker, *Deep In A Dream*, by James Gavin. There could have been a diversion to play Woodstock but Mort Lewis felt there were enough problems meeting existing obligations so no, thank you.

In November 1969 Simon & Garfunkel performed their first concert dates in a year, a short tour prior to the release of the *Bridge Over Troubled Water* album. They sang some songs on their own but mostly they worked with a backing band of killer musicians, – Larry Knechtel, Fred Carter, Jr, Joe Osborn and Hal Blaine. They looked a little uncomfortable: Garfunkel stood still while Simon gyrated. They tried new songs with 'Bridge Over Troubled Water' getting standing ovations. They did 'Song for the Asking' with Paul on lead and Art the harmonies. On the album, it was just Simon at his most vulnerable.

'The last tour we used the guys who played on the records: drums, guitar, bass, piano,' Paul Simon told *Rolling Stone* in 1970. 'It worked out badly. First of all we came out on stage with the band, and people would yell, "Get that band off, we just want to hear you." I would say, "Oh, that riff is so old, you said that about Dylan. That's four years ago, so what are you talking about? Everybody has a band. We're the only ones around without a band."' Still, it was economically favourable that audiences preferred them that way.

One venue was Carnegie Hall on 28 November 1969. The ticket demand was so great that Mort Lewis wanted them to do two shows in one night. As they only performed for seventy minutes in concert, this was no hardship but he knew that Simon and Garfunkel's starting position would be no. However, he had a bargaining tool. Simon had requested a lot of freebies for friends and relations and he told him that he couldn't have them if they were only doing one show.

Arthur Garfunkel in *Catch-22* (Paramount Pictures)

The following night the show hit Boston. Garfunkel, who was becoming increasingly eccentric, chose to hitchhike rather than fly. He did make the show. Another time, Simon and Lewis passed Art in their limousine and gave him a 'screw you' gesture. A concert album was not released at the time but more recently, *Live 1969,* was issued by Starbucks.

In September 1969 Paul Simon purchased an out-of-town property, a Dutch farmhouse in seventy acres outside New Hope, Pennsylvania for $200,000. He also owned a property on the East River, while Garfunkel lived in hotels. Garfunkel was worried about Simon's relationship with Peggy, not because he disapproved but because he felt that they might lose their manager, Mort Lewis, but Mort was unconcerned.

By now they were playing large venues and Simon did become anxious about performing. Dustin Hoffman had introduced Paul to another actor, Elliott Gould, who in turn recommended his therapist.

You might have thought that it would be Garfunkel with the anxieties. Fans would often ask one of them, 'Do you write the words or the music?' No problem for Simon, but one for Garfunkel. Somewhere along the way Simon would credit him with the arrangements, which was obviously incorrect. This persisted for years including an extraordinary faux pas on *The Old Grey Whistle Test,* but more of this later.

For all their success, Simon and Garfunkel had planned *Bridge Over Troubled Water* as their swansong. 'We said something to the effect, we'll finish the album and that will be it,' said Simon. 'We didn't plan to do anything together after that. I would do an album by myself and Artie would work on the movie, *Carnal Knowledge.*'

By and large, the album had been made while Art was filming *Catch-22* and he added his vocals whenever he was around. 'We were tired and we fought,' admitted Paul. 'We even fought over the twelfth song, finally saying "fuck it" and leaving it at that.'

When Richard Nixon was elected in January 1969, Paul Simon broke down in tears. His unissued song, 'Cuba Si, Nixon No', was unheard for many years but has since become a bonus track. It is a new lyric to a Chuck Berry-styled riff similar to 'Roll Over Beethoven' and was sung solo by Paul in concert. It mocked the new president and gave support to the Cuban regime and possibly Garfunkel felt that this might impede sales. On the other hand, it could have been sour grapes, as Simon did not favour Art's suggestion of Bach's 'Feuilles-Oh'.

As well as the album, Simon and Garfunkel agreed on a TV special for the Bell Telephone Company, the intention being that one would support the other. As a frustrated executive told *Advertising Age*, 'We bought an entertainment show and they delivered their own social and political views.'

Simon and Garfunkel worked with the actor and writer Charles Grodin (Capt Aarfy Aardvark in *Catch-22*) and the director was Robert Drew, who made documentaries about social issues. They wanted to show how America was split into two with bad housing and poor social benefits and why so many were protesting. Paul Simon revealed, 'We decided to do a show about America rather than duets with Glen Campbell and dance numbers. Bell wanted to use it as recruitment for the Bell Telephone Company. They didn't know that we were planning a show which had something to do with real life. They thought it would have to do with TV. We had a film sequence with the Kennedys and Martin Luther King while we sang "Bridge Over Troubled Water", and they objected to that. We said, "Why?" and they replied that they were all Democrats – there's no Republicans in there.'

Bell wanted to drop the project but Columbia talked them round. A few weeks later, Simon told *Rolling Stone*, 'One of the most frustrating things I ever did was to work for hours and hours on that television special and then hear somebody put it down in the worst possible terms. They vilified the show. There was no talk of whether we did it artfully or not. They just couldn't bear to look at King, couldn't bear to look at the Kennedys, couldn't bear to look at Chavez. They said they didn't want the Woodstock footage in there, no footage of Woodstock, no footage of Vietnam, they said they could live with the Lone Ranger. If we wanted to keep that in, it's all right.'

In the end, the show was sold to Alberto-Culver, manufacturer of hair products, for $50,000. CBS put it on air and it was beaten in the ratings by a dancing-on-ice special, so what's new?

There were eleven tracks on the *Bridge Over Troubled Water* LP, one of which was a revival of the Everly Brothers' 'Bye Bye Love'. Of the others, four had been issued on two singles and Simon said he was not too happy with three tracks ('Why Don't You Write Me', 'Keep the Customer Satisfied' and 'So Long, Frank Lloyd Wright'.) All this suggests that Simon had held little back and the two years had not been prolific, but the album contained a wide variety of sounds. He said of the finished product, 'Tempos were different. Instrumentation was different. I think that's good. I enjoy that.'

Paul Simon, 1971 (CBS Records)

For all its variety, the album was by no means a miscellany and every track worked well in its own right. It was a stronger album than *Bookends* but part of its increased sales was because the songs were more upbeat.

The album opens with 'Bridge Over Troubled Water' and moves into 'El Condor Pasa', now better known as 'If I Could'. This was said to be an arrangement of an eighteenth-century Peruvian melody by Los Incas and this interest in world music led to the *Graceland* album. Simon recorded his lyric over the existing track by Los Incas. His words had the same charm as 'Scarborough Fair', and the lyric made the comparisons that you find in ye olde English folk songs. Simon would rather be a sparrow than a snail, a hammer than a nail, and a forest than a street. This was a Top 20 single in the US but it wasn't released as a single in the UK, leaving the way clear for Julie Felix, whose cover version made the Top 20.

There are numerous versions of 'El Condor Pasa' including a strange distorted one from Yma Sumac, whose wide vocal range made the *Guinness Book of Records*. Although she comes from the Incas, she performs it with a rock backing and displays her octaves several times over through multi-tracking. The song is missing, believed lost.

Unfortunately for Simon, 'El Condor Pasa' was not an eighteenth-century melody after all. It was written by Daniel Alomía Robles from Peru in about 1929. Robles died in 1942 and his son was to sue for royalties, which Simon settled out of court.

All this was in the future. By way of thanks, Simon offered to produce a solo album by Urubamba, which featured two members of Los Incas. Urubamba is the name of a river which flows past the Inca city of Machu Picchu. There was a single of 'El Eco', which was released by Columbia.

The third track on the first side was the ultra-catchy 'Cecilia' which reached No. 4 as a US single. Strangely, it flopped as a 45 in the UK, but it was not what audiences expected from Simon & Garfunkel, sounding more like Dave Dee, Dozy, Beaky, Mick & Tich. The rhythm was recorded in a living room with Paul, his brother Eddie (banging rhythm on a piano bench) and Art all contributing, and it sounded so infectious that it was kept on the record. It is witty and funny but the song was not a UK singles hit until Suggs recorded it in 1996. 'Cecilia' is the patron saint of music but that could be coincidence.

This was followed by the B-side of 'Bridge Over Troubled Water',

'Keep the Customer Satisfied'. Simon is taking a familiar expression and making a good song out of it. It is the story of a salesman who is hustled from state to state. It's a great song about life on the road with the chorus stating what a relief it is to be home. Among the covers, there is an unexpected big band treatment from Buddy Rich with horns blaring out.

The first side ends with the gentle bossa nova 'So Long, Frank Lloyd Wright', and Paul would later be entranced by the music of Brazil. It is a strange song as much about the famous architect as 'Mrs Robinson' was about a baseball player, but Simon does have this knack of finding the right name or phrase to put in a lyric.

Actually, Garfunkel had suggested that Frank Lloyd Wright would be a good subject. Difficulties arose when he was asked to sing it. Paul Simon told Penny Valentine of *Sounds*, '"So Long" was a source of intense battles, and I eventually left the studio and walked out because Artie wouldn't do it the way I wanted and he insisted on doing it his way. I insisted on doing it straight, and that was it. I mean, my choice was either to roll right over him and say, "Absolutely not. If you're not going to do it this way, then you are not going to do it at all"... and I couldn't say that, or to walk right out of the studio, which I did. I said, "Okay. I wash my hands of this whole thing. Do it any way you want."'

In the fadeout ending of that song where Art is singing 'So long, so long', Paul and Roy Halee add a 'So long already, Artie'. It was a telling joke that was soon to come true.

Ignore the fact that the song is called 'So Long, Frank Lloyd Wright'. It is really about the breakup of Simon & Garfunkel. You can say the same of 'Why Don't You Write Me', 'The Only Living Boy in New York' and 'Song for the Asking'. Simon was obsessed about the partnership falling apart. His main collaborator on the album had been the patient and cooperative Roy Halee.

We turn the record over for 'The Boxer' and 'Baby Driver', and then there is a trilogy comprising 'The Only Living Boy in New York', 'Why Don't You Write Me' and 'Bye Bye Love'. The first word of 'The Only Living Boy in New York' refers back to Art's days as Tom Graph and is about Art making *Catch-22* in Rome. The track is mostly sung by Paul but they sang 'aaahs' over and over together using an echo chamber and mixed the compressed results down for the record. Bob Dylan visited them in the studio while they were doing this and such technicalities were alien to him.

In 1970 Bob Dylan recorded 'The Boxer' for his own album, *Self Portrait*, and possibly the song was about him and his problems with Columbia. He changed one word: 'Every glove that's laid him down' became 'Every blow that's laid him down'. Dylan scholar Michael Gray says, 'We actually see the boxer better. We comprehend that outside the ring as well as inside it, his life is a series of defeats.' Dylan didn't record any more of Simon's songs, although he did sing 'Homeward Bound' and 'A Hazy Shade of Winter' in concert for a few gigs in the early 90s. Dylan recorded his own song about a boxer, 'Hurricane', in 1975

Simon normally took care to have original song titles but 'Why Don't You Write Me' revived the title of a doo-wop song he would have known from the Jacks. Simon's song works well enough but it is unimaginative by his standards. He told *Sounds*, 'I wasn't satisfied with it and I did it two or three times but I never liked it at all. I couldn't figure out what I was doing wrong. I'd recorded it in the wrong place. I should have recorded it in Kingston, Jamaica.' Simon wasn't to repeat this mistake as he went to Jamaica for 'Mother and Child Reunion' on his next album. Although fine in its own right, 'Cecilia' could have been recorded with a reggae beat.

With the talent and versatility of his studio musicians, you might suppose that it would have been easy for him to record songs any way he wanted, but he would disagree. He told *Disc*, 'Certain musicians will be perfect for certain things. But they could still be fine musicians and yet not be able to play something else. I mean, I can sing a certain kind of song very well, but if you booked me to sing "In the Midnight Hour", I wouldn't be the right guy.'

Simon and Garfunkel are naturals when it comes to the Everly Brothers' songbook and proved it when they revived the Everlys' first hit, 'Bye Bye Love'. Recorded in concert, it retained the drive and urgency of the original but their harmonies are somewhat lost amidst the handclapping. It comes over as a novelty and even more so when you learn the background story.

Simon told *Rolling Stone*, '"Bye Bye Love" was recorded in Ames, Iowa, mostly because of our fascination with handclapping. We went out and we said, "Now listen. You have to handclap on the rhythm; you can't fall behind like every other audience because we want the sound of 8,000 people handclapping. It's going to be a great backbeat." And it was. We did it twice. We sang and said, "No, too ragged, we've got to do it again." And that's why.'

You can't blame them for leaving the sound of 8,000 people applauding on the album, and that applause neatly segues into the final track, 'Song for the Asking'. The song creeps in on us and in a way, that's appropriate as the lyric all but apologises for being there. Simon keeps its length down although he could have spun it out with repetition. It is good listening and Simon whispers the lyric, and there is much more of Simon than Garfunkel on the album.

Despite his reservations, Simon thought it their best album, telling *Rolling Stone*, 'I certainly don't know why it should have been so much bigger than the others. I didn't know when I made it that it was going to be that much bigger. I guess it has a very broad appeal. That's the only reason I can think of. A lot of people who may never have bought albums before or never heard of Simon and Garfunkel got into it. We didn't even know if "Bridge" was going to be a big single. We talked about it and I said I thought it might be a little bit too long.'

Each album had done better than the previous one but *Bridge Over Troubled Water* surpassed expectations, having astonishing sales in Europe. The total sales are now over 25 million and it regularly features on lists of the best albums of all time.

CHAPTER 8

Everything Put Together Falls Apart

Although Simon and Garfunkel did not plan any more records together, they worked in concert whenever Garfunkel was available. Simon enjoyed performing. 'There's pleasure in doing a good show,' he told *Record Mirror* in 1971. 'If you do a good performance and everything is right and people like it, then you feel you're part of the whole rhythm of the evening. You're a part of the audience and the audience is a part of you and we've all entertained ourselves. That's great. The drag of performing is when you do it too often.'

But performing was taking its toll and it was clear that they would soon stop appearing together. Simon told the *New Musical Express* in 1971, 'I was not so much bored with performing as bored with what I was doing. We were singing the required Simon & Garfunkel hits which realistically we had to do. We couldn't say, "We won't sing 'Bridge' again" as people want to hear it and if we're going out on stage, we've got to do it.'

Paul Simon discussed his problem with fellow artists. 'I was talking to Dylan about going out on the road. It gets boring to me because they want to hear "The Sound of Silence". He said, "Well, I'd like to see you and if I came to see you, I'd want you to see you sing 'The Sound of Silence' and 'Scarborough Fair'."' As Dylan rarely played his hits as they had been recorded, there was some hypocrisy in what he was saying, but no doubt it was delivered with his knowing half-smile.

Possibly Art's presence amounted to more than just turning up to sing the songs. Wally Whyton certainly thought so: 'Art's part of the set-up is much stronger than most people realise. Art is an arranger. He has an arranger's mind and he knows how to get the best out of Paul's material. Without Art's influence, Simon might not be the star he is today.' Interesting thoughts, but hardly backed up by the album credits.

Simon said that such thoughts were nonsense. 'Anyone who knows

Joseph E. Levine Presents
A Mike Nichols Film
CARNAL KNOWLEDGE
An Avco Embassy Release

COLOR BY TECHNICOLOR

anything would know that this was a fabrication,' he told *Rolling Stone* in 1972. 'How can one guy write the songs and another guy do the arranging. Musically, it was not a creative team. Art is a singer and I am a writer, musician and singer. We didn't work together on a creative level and prepare the songs. I did that.'

Garfunkel had by far the more distinctive name. To be known by your surname implies a certain gravitas and status (Beethoven, Mozart, Gershwin, Lennon, Dylan, Springsteen) but that could never happen with Simon. Undoubtedly Garfunkel possessed the easier name for promoting new product, and the question was, would Paul Simon continue to be the star he was without Garfunkel? We had to wait for the answer as Paul pursued other interests.

Paul Simon's friend, David Oppenheim, was now in charge of arts education at New York University and he posted a notice in January 1970: 'Paul Simon of Simon & Garfunkel has offered to teach a course in how to write and record a popular song. Only those who are already writing and have music and lyrics to show Mr Simon should apply.' The course would run on Tuesday evenings from February to May.

Sixty-nine students applied and Simon held auditions for his pupils. Ron Maxwell and Joe Turrin, who had written a rock opera, *Barricades*, auditioned and were surprised that Simon couldn't read music. In turn, Simon thought they were too advanced for his class.

Eighteen-year-old Maggie Roche and her younger sister Terre were working clubs in Greenwich Village and knew Dave Van Ronk. His wife Terri told them of Simon's classes. They attended an audition and saw Simon arriving on his own. He heard their songs and said that they could join and not even pay. He told them that they had enough talent to win local contests but that they were not ready professionally.

There were fifteen students in Simon's class and he was always casually dressed in baseball cap and jeans. It was a two way street: one student told Simon of a new folk singer he had seen, James Taylor, who was sensational. Simon checked him out and agreed. He told one student, Melissa Manchester, that she had been listening to too much Laura Nyro and Joni Mitchell. He advised, 'Say what you have to say as simply as possible and then leave before they have a chance to figure you out.'

Although Simon couldn't read music, he explained the circle of fifths to them and told them about working in thirds for harmonies like the Everly Brothers. He said that nails had to be a certain length for fingerpicking.

He would tell the wannabe songwriters of the pitfalls in making records and how to correct them. He explained, 'That's what happened to most of the San Franciscan groups in the early days. Fine live groups but they didn't know anything about the recording studio and they couldn't figure out why their records were bad. They had to learn the whole thing and they had to learn it while they were making their albums.'

Simon took the best of the students' songs and then recorded them at Columbia's studios. The course was very successful – well, the Roches and Melissa Manchester came from it. Simon enjoyed it very much, saying, 'I like talking about songwriting.'

Simon brought in Isaac Stern and Al Kooper as guest speakers but not Art Garfunkel, who was on a long holiday with Linda Grossman. They went to Tangier, Gibraltar and London, often hitchhiking. They rented a house in Oban, Argyllshire. He posed with sheep for the *Oban Times* and said he loved stone walls, green hills, long rambling walks and chatting with strangers.

While Simon was teaching and Garfunkel was travelling, the album, *Bridge Over Troubled Water*, was released. What group today would be permitted to do that? Nevertheless, the album sold a million copies within a week. Some concert dates were planned including five European dates in London, Copenhagen, Paris, Amsterdam and another in London over a fortnight. Except for Larry Knechtel, there would be no other musicians, but it would be a semi-holiday as they would have Linda and Peggy, two girls from Tennessee, with them. Garfunkel insisted that they stayed at the Amsterdam Hilton like John and Yoko.

Simon and Garfunkel returned to the Royal Albert Hall in April 1970. The demand for tickets was enormous and some had been touted at fifty pounds. They sang their hits but Simon noticed a difference. 'It wasn't like the audience of old friends who had been at the Royal Albert Hall before. They just seemed to be people who wanted to see a chart-topping act.'

Reviewing the concert for *The Times*, Miles Kington wrote, 'My one criticism on Saturday was that they badly mismanaged their encores; there is no sight more depressing than squads of dumpy girls half-heartedly invading a stage.'

The concerts went well: they even managed 'Fakin' It' with just a guitar. At the Royal Albert Hall, they sang two songs from *Songs Our Daddy Taught Us* – 'Lightning Express' and 'That Silver Haired Daddy of Mine'. Miles Kington wrote, 'Some hate Simon and Garfunkel because their music has no guts, because it is a middle class look at life, because it slips too easily from idiom to idiom.'

Miles Kingston considered their music gutless, but Garfunkel had made a film which broke social boundaries. With a title like *Carnal Knowledge*, the film had to be a send-up and it was. Mike Nichols was again directing and he worked from a brilliant funny/sad script from the cartoonist Jules Feiffer, the original title being *True Confessions*. Arthur (not 'Art', and he was similarly listed for the *Bridge* album) played someone with romantic ideals and he helped select the music for the film.

We start in the mid-1940s with two college students, the brash Jonathan (Jack Nicholson, and like Dustin Hoffman in *The Graduate*, looking too old) and the mild-mannered Sandy (Arthur Garfunkel) who are both determined to get laid. They make it with the same girl, Susan (Candice Bergen), and there is one splendid moment where Art introduces the condom to the big screen. Sandy marries Susan while Jonathan continues in his quest to find the Great Ball-buster of All Time. He finds her in the well-proportioned Bobbie (Ann-Margret) while Sandy has switched to Cindy (Cynthia O'Neal). As Cindy and Bobbie move away, Sandy and Jonathan become disillusioned and the film becomes serious. In a pitiful epilogue, Sandy grows long hair, acquires a hippy girlfriend and says, 'I've found out who I am', while Jonathan visits hookers for sexual excitement. Art had good notices, although John Weightman in *Encounter*, describing him as 'ugly and sensitive', was more hurtful than any criticism of his acting.

Jonathan and Sandy are two friends who are tough on each other, so shades of Simon & Garfunkel there. In reality, Garfunkel got on well with Jack Nicholson and they hosted a stoned viewing of *Lawrence of Arabia* in Vancouver. Art took the cast to a show featuring Joni Mitchell, Phil Ochs and James Taylor.

Carnal Knowledge was a far cry from anything Art had done before and it wasn't long before a reporter – Lon Goddard of *Record Mirror* – wanted to know if Simon had seen Garfunkel's movies. He replied, 'Sure, I went with Artie. *Catch-22* was a big disappointment for me but he was fine in his role. *Carnal Knowledge* is a good film – not a great one, but a good one and again Artie did very well.'

Writers looking back on the early 70s sometimes wonder why the Beatles split up: why couldn't they have done their own things for a couple of years and then met up again? The answer is that no one had thought of a temporary break at that time, but that is what Simon and Garfunkel did. They had not ruled out working together, and Simon said, 'We're still good friends. We just have different interests, that's all. There was never anything legal binding us… I don't think that Artie wants a full-time career in acting. I think he'll take parts that come along if they're good, but he'll keep singing.'

Although Art was a good actor, there were plenty of actors around and yet there were few singers with a voice as distinctive as his. There was no reason why he shouldn't operate in both fields – after all, Frank Sinatra, Dean Martin and Elvis Presley had done that for years, and Kris Kristofferson was writing songs, recording albums and making films as though he had accepted some frenzied deadline.

In July they recorded a couple of other songs from that Everlys' album, 'Barbara Allen' and 'Roving Gambler', in New York. Simon sang lead on a Scottish ballad, 'Rose of Aberdeen'. It's lovely, but this was made for their own entertainment rather than some specific purpose. As Simon once said, 'I could sing these songs forever.'

But maybe not with Garfunkel. On 17 July 1970 Simon and Garfunkel played two shows at Forest Hills open-air stadium for a total audience of 28,000. They were paid $50,000 for their day's work. They included the Bronx doo-wop hit 'A Teenager in Love', made famous by Dion and the Belmonts, and they combined 'Cecilia' with 'Bye Bye Love'. They closed with 'Old Friends' and they agreed that this would be their final show, although they didn't tell the audience or Mort Lewis. Just a few miles away at Downing Stadium on Randall's Island, there was a huge New York Pop festival with Jimi Hendrix, Grand Funk Railroad, Steppenwolf, John Sebastian and Jethro Tull.

On 6 August 1970, Peter Yarrow of the then-splintering Peter, Paul & Mary had organised a show to raise money for the anti-war movement. The Summer Festival for Peace was at Shea Stadium with Creedence Clearwater Revival, Miles Davis, Big Brother and the Holding Company, and Paul Simon solo. It was the first time that music stars had got together for a large-scale political event. Garfunkel didn't want to do it and Simon did it solo without consulting Lewis. Only 15,000 turned up, a huge audience but less than 30% capacity.

Their TV special notwithstanding, Simon was viewed as safe and old-fashioned. They started booing when Simon sang 'Scarborough Fair'. Ellen Willis said in *The New Yorker*, 'I hate most of his lyrics; his

Simon and Garfunkel at the Royal Albert Hall, 1970 (New Musical Express)

alienation, like the word itself, is an old-fashioned sentimental liberal bore.'

Simon judged a song contest in Rio de Janeiro and he came to the UK to resolve his publishing. The company that administered his catalogue had been taken over by Granada, who sold him their interest so that he would have complete control of his work. He said, 'There's nothing wrong; just that they're my songs and I have a personal attachment to them.'

Roy Halee's talents were appreciated by Columbia and in December 1970 he was asked to run their new studio in San Francisco. Meanwhile, Garfunkel had started teaching mathematics at Litchfield Prep School in Connecticut and was learning harpsichord. He and Simon met up with the Carpenters, Paul McCartney and Marvin Gaye at the Grammys in March 1971 but the duo hardly looked at each other. For a TV performance, Art Garfunkel found a new duet partner, the weather-beaten Harry Dean Stanton and they sang 'All I Have to Do Is Dream'. Art appeared in a TV play, with Gene Wilder, *Acts of Love and Other Comedies*.

By late 1971, Simon had got round to a new album, his first solo recordings since *The Paul Simon Songbook*. He gave interviews while he was in the UK and he said that the album would simply be called *Paul Simon*. It had already been nine months in the making and he warned us against expecting too much: 'I can't follow *Bridge* and I don't want to have to follow it. I hope I won't get a feeling of disappointment for inevitably, what I do is going to be compared against that.' At the moment, he was very happy with what he was doing.

The solo album was becoming a new marketing concept with bands breaking up and solo projects being initiated – Simon & Garfunkel, the Beatles, the Mamas & the Papas, Diana Ross & the Supremes, Crosby Stills Nash & Young, and the Monkees. John Sebastian of the Lovin' Spoonful had been the unexpected hit at Woodstock, and all four Beatles had gone solo. Paul McCartney said of *John Lennon/Plastic Ono Band*, 'The album knocked me out. It's the first time I've heard his pain.'

But Simon preferred the throaty voice and brilliant slide guitar of Ry Cooder, who had just released his first album, *Ry Cooder*, in December 1970. 'Nothing killed me as much as the Ry Cooder album. The Lennon LP is all right but Cooder is funkier.'

For all that, the John Lennon album is one of Paul Simon's points of reference. Lennon was pioneering introspective, highly personal rock music. In their different ways, Marvin Gaye, Barbra Streisand and Don Everly had followed his example and looked inside themselves for their own albums. Paul Simon was going this way but without Lennon's rants or self-indulgence. Perhaps to make his point, this new album had none of the lushness of *Bridge Over Troubled Water.*

Although Dylan's sales were nothing like as substantial as Simon and Garfunkel's, Simon knew that Dylan gathered more respect, and his appearance at Shea had brought that home. He wanted to make a solo album where he would not have to defer to a musical partner. Clive Davis supported him but felt that he was unlikely to sell as many records as just Paul Simon.

The success of *Bridge* had worked in Simon's favour. Having had such a major success, he could record individual tracks wherever he thought fit. Since then there have been many globetrotting albums but *Paul Simon* was the first. He told *Sounds*, 'I wrote the songs and I thought I'd like to do this with Los Incas or with Stéphane Grappelli and so I'll go over to Paris.' As a result, tracks were recorded in France and Jamaica as well as New York and San Francisco. Columbia used the diversity as a sales pitch:

Simon and... Stéphane Grappelli
Guitarist Jerry Hahn
Pianist Larry Knechtel
A reggae band from Kingston, Jamaica
A couple of Brazilian guys (!)
A few Puerto-Rican percussionists
(But not Art Garfunkel)
And he's got into a whole lot of new things –
without losing any of the brilliance
of 'Bridge Over Troubled Water'.

This is a strange ad for several reasons. Firstly, it treats the whole thing as a novelty. Secondly, the exclamation mark is theirs, not mine. Thirdly, they are pushing the record by drawing attention to the very ingredient that is missing – Art Garfunkel. Fourthly, they're inviting comparisons to 'Bridge Over Troubled Water' even though they know this is something very different.

It's worth commenting on the lack of Garfunkel: was he needed? At first, Simon said, 'I don't know. They're different songs, a little funkier and harder.' By the time the album was released, Simon said, 'Artie could have sung any of the songs on the album.' He described the change in recording practices, telling *Sounds,* 'I did find it a little strange at first, not asking for an opinion and having his presence there, but after that initial feeling, I found it perfectly comfortable. Easier in a way because there were no conflicting opinions.'

Simon told *Rolling Stone,* 'Since I don't write well enough to orchestrate for strings, it means that I have to use an arranger and that moves it one step away. Consequently I have no interest in strings because they are not me – they have nothing to do with me. If it's a great string part, then somebody else wrote a great string part. Here, I'm playing on almost all the cuts or else I know the people who are playing on them.'

Simon & Garfunkel never went for lavish cover art and indeed, their covers are amongst the dullest of the 60s. Simon's new solo album was a close-up of his face with the hood up on his parka, but nevertheless, it has become a familiar image.

Despite the fact that several tracks were recorded around the world, this is still a New York album with Paul Simon writing about himself and his neighbourhood. The comparison would be with Woody Allen, who makes New York films no matter where he is working.

The album itself opens energetically with 'Mother and Child Reunion', a song he recorded at the Dynamic Sounds Studios in Kingston, Jamaica. He had wanted to go where Jimmy Cliff had recorded 'Vietnam'. He told *Melody Maker,* 'I like reggae. I listen to Jimmy Cliff, Desmond Dekker, Byron Lee – I send over to England for all those *Chartbusters* albums. I like 'em! I get off on it. So I say to myself, "I love it so much, I'm gonna go to Kingston, Jamaica." I'm happy because I am playing with some different musicians and it turns me on.'

The rhythm is so catchy that you almost forget the lyric. The title comes from a dish of chicken and eggs that was on the menu at a Chinese restaurant. However, Simon is singing about a death in the family. Despite his sadness, he looks forward to the reunion, even contemplating suicide. He told Robert Christgau for *Cheetah,* 'Last summer we had a dog that was run over and killed. I felt this loss – one minute there, next minute gone – and my first thought was, "Oh man, what if that was Peggy? What if somebody like that died?"'

The song is carried along by a pulsating rhythm and was an obvious single. It became an international hit, though not on the scale of 'Bridge Over Troubled Water' (US 4, UK 5, Ireland 15, Germany 23) and a few months later the musicians he used were in the UK, this time backing Johnny Nash under the name Sons of the Jungle. In 2000, the song was used to good effect in *The Sopranos* (Series 2, Episode 2) to highlight the differences between Tony and his mother.

The next track is 'Duncan' and as soon we hear the first line, we know we are into something good. Lincoln Duncan is brooding in his motel room and he recalls various incidents in his life. The goings-on next door remind him of his first sexual encounter and he talks of making it with a female preacher. The Latin American sound comes from Los Incas, and overall, it is reminiscent of 'The Boxer'. If it had had something similar to the 'lie-lie-lie' chant, it could have been a big single.

At least two critics (Jon Landau in *Rolling Stone* and Tony Palmer in the *Observer*) used the title of the third song, the bluesy 'Everything Put Together Falls Apart', to summarise the album but it was good work. This particular track is decent enough but the song is unexceptional by Simon's standards. Its message is that you should control the drugs you take or they will be controlling you.

We retain that mood for 'Run That Body Down' but here the lyric, melody and presentation are better. Simon's doctor has warned him not to do too much and he passes this message on, first to his wife and then to all of us. There's some gentle humour in his asides and some lovely crooning in the 'What's wrong, sweet boy?' section. This track is a tour de force and part of its strength could be attributed to Simon following medical advice and giving up smoking. He said, 'It's easier to sing. My range went up; it's easier to hold a note.' Even so, Simon can sound strained in the higher register, something Garfunkel could have done with ease.

Continuing with the blues, there is the melancholic 'Armistice Day', which completes the first side. The concept of contrasting love and war is hardly new, but it is a good song. Simon considered it the weakest song on the album. He had written it in 1968, preferring to use the former name Armistice Day instead of the current Veterans Day.

The second side opens joyously with 'Me and Julio Down by the Schoolyard', which updates 'Wake Up Little Susie'. There's a section in that song about what Susie's mother would do if she finds they've been

Paul Simon, 1973 (CBS Records)

out all night. Here she has and this time, the couple hasn't just slept through a dull movie.

There is a powerful backing from guitar and drums, beautifully engineered to cover the changes in tempo and volume. The words gush out and Simon tells an elaborate story with economy and humour. The girl's parents are instrumental in having him arrested, but a 'radical priest' secures his release. The saga makes the newspapers and the protagonist cannot return home. It sounds more like a film pitch than a song and it is remarkable how much is crammed into three minutes. What's more, there are excellent thumbnail caricatures along the way.

For the enhanced version of the album, Paul Simon's original voice and guitar demo for 'Me and Julio' has been added. It includes some wordless vocals as he hadn't completed the lyric. There is an early take of 'Duncan' with a slightly different melody and a different story, this time about a man who lost his job, more akin to Gordon Lightfoot's style than his own.

The finished take of 'Me and Julio Down by the Schoolyard' shows how the Everly Brothers could have updated their sound for the 70s. Indeed, the toughest competition that Simon & Garfunkel could have had in the late 60s would have been the Everly Brothers if they had been on top of their game and hadn't let it slide.

The Everlys' influence on Simon and Garfunkel and indeed the whole of popular music is enormous. Bob Dylan has said, 'We owe these guys everything. They started it all', and that is hardly overstatement. Dylan paid homage by recording 'Let It Be Me' and 'Take a Message to Mary', while Simon and Garfunkel cut 'Bye Bye Love' around the same time.

The Everly Brothers fell from grace largely through brotherly bickering which led to them going through the motions and recording mediocre material indifferently. Eventually, they saw what was going wrong and made *Roots* (1968), and two superb singles in the same year, 'Lord of the Manor', the quirkiest of quirky songs, and 'Empty Boxes', which sounds like Simon & Garfunkel. By then it was too late and although they made two fine albums for RCA, *Stories We Could Tell* (1972) and *Pass the Chicken & Listen* (1973), not many people were listening.

When Simon was working with Puerto Rican musicians, he wanted them to play on 'Me and Julio'. That didn't work out but he asked them to play something of their own. He enjoyed how the conga player,

Victor Montanez, was playing *dunk dunka dokka dunk dunka dokka dunk*. He made a tape loop and wrote 'Peace Like a River'. It has similar intentions to Ed McCurdy's folk song 'Last Night I Had the Strangest Dream' but is not as obvious. It is an underrated Simon composition, but it was on the soundtrack of the Maggie Smith film, *My Old Lady*, and in 2015 it was revived beautifully by the former lead singer of the Persuasions, Jerry Lawson, for the opening track of his album, *Just a Mortal Man*.

We're back to bluesy sounds for 'Papa Hobo', which features unusual harmonium effects from Larry Knechtel. Simon plays a hobo in Detroit who is determined to make something of his life. It begins with a good joke and continues with Simon justifying his intentions. Detroit is famous for manufacturing cars but the singer does not want to work on an assembly line. Ironically, he needs a car to make his getaway and he performs the song as he is thumbing a ride.

To help him on his way, 'Hobo's Blues' is travelling music, a much-publicised collaboration between Paul Simon and Stéphane Grappelli. It's very short (just eighty seconds) but wholly delightful. Lesser performers would have turned this into a ten-minute jam, but Simon knows that less is more. He knows when to take a back seat: the violinist is in front while he stands in for Django Reinhardt.

'Paranoia Blues' is a collaboration with Stefan Grossman, the singer/ songwriter who established a following through such albums as *The Ragtime Cowboy Jew*. Simon wanted to feature his bottleneck guitar playing and the result, 'Paranoia Blues', is another song about honesty and we move from the difficulties of living in Detroit to the difficulties of living in New York. The city is full of greed and Simon even has his meal stolen in a restaurant. Hal Blaine plays drums and Simon adds further percussion. Stefan watched Simon at work with his engineer, Roy Halee: 'When these two have a song, they get it done well. When Dylan is in the studio, he gets three takes done and that's it, but Paul keeps at it and takes a lot of trouble.'

Donald 'Duck' Dunn of Booker T. & the MG's would agree. He helped Paul record 'Congratulations', the final track on the album, which involved many takes. Paul scrapped them all and redid it with Larry Knechtel. It was worth Simon's perseverance as it is neatly concludes the album.

On this side of the album, Paul had been travelling. The singer is shown as dissatisfied with life in Detroit and New York and even when he is content, as in 'Me and Julio', he is forced out of town by circumstance. This time he is a little more positive in his search for America.

In 'Overs' on *Bookends,* a man didn't have the guts to leave his wife. On this album, in 'Congratulations', he leaves, and it's a wonderfully ironic title. Simon is melancholic about his society spawning so many divorces and his voice breaks with sadness for the final question, asking whether peaceful co-existence is possible. Simon wasn't perturbed about the pessimism of so many of his songs. 'I love my own music,' he admitted to *Time.* 'I can sit and play the guitar all night and I love it because it's me and I'm making it all up.'

Paul Simon was a No. 1 album in the UK (replacing Neil Young's *Harvest*) and No. 4 in the US. Columbia released a story which I like to think is accurate. 'This is one of the albums that President Nixon took with him on a trip to China. Chairman Mao (who is the most important poet in the eastern world) was reportedly knocked out.'

As Simon did not share Nixon's Republican views, he appeared at fundraising concerts for Senator George McGovern. One was at Shea Stadium in August 1971. 'It embarrassed me to be at Shea Stadium,' he told *Sounds.* 'I felt stupid. The sound system was bad. The artistic side becomes unimportant: you're just somebody who can raise money. We went to the biggest of venues and people were charged the highest of prices.'

Nevertheless, he was back there in April 1972 for a concert also featuring Joni Mitchell, Phil Ochs and James Taylor. This extract from *The Cleveland Scene* indicates that the sound was probably worse: 'Paul Simon started with "Me and Julio Down by the Schoolyard" followed by "Congratulations". He made a few short pleas for silence, had a few choice words for the police and the ushers, and, finally realising the hopelessness of the situation, he gave up. No more unfamiliar songs, no more fancy guitar work. He half-heartedly strummed half a dozen of his hits and walked off. It was sad. It was Paul Simon doing a mediocre imitation of Paul Simon.'

Paul was, nevertheless, fundraising at Madison Square Garden on 14 June 1972, this time reunited with Art Garfunkel. *Rolling Stone* reported, 'When Simon and Garfunkel came out, they looked as if they hadn't spoken in 12 years. Dressed in jeans and baggy sweaters, they stood at their mikes looking straight ahead like two commuters clutching adjacent straps on the morning train.'

Such reports hardly sounded encouraging but Simon and Garfunkel did consider touring again. As Paul told Roy Carr in *New Musical Express*, 'Certainly I'll do solo concerts, but I wouldn't rule out singing with Artie again. There's no animosity there and no rigidity either. The difficulty was structuring everything into Simon & Garfunkel. That was impossible.'

Columbia must have been sorry that the group split up and would have welcomed another album from the duo. In its place they put out *Simon and Garfunkel's Greatest Hits,* which was partly issued to combat bootleggers who were releasing their own compilations.

The album is unusual in that Columbia chose some of the songs in concert performances. They were the first official live recordings of Simon & Garfunkel's hits to be released. They chose 'Bridge Over Troubled Water', 'For Emily, Whenever I May Find Her', 'Homeward Bound', 'Kathy's Song' and 'The 59th Street Bridge Song (Feelin' Groovy)', though it's hard to tell as both 'Bridge' and 'Kathy's Song' open with applause and end with none. I suspect that Simon himself had some hand in the compilation as some of the songs that he had second thoughts about ('A Hazy Shade of Winter', 'The Dangling Conversation') are omitted in favour of 'Kathy's Song' and 'America'.

With a bizarre flourish, 'America' was released as the group's next single although it had been available on *Bookends* for four years. It only made No. 97 on the US Hot 100 but it climbed to No. 25 in the UK, thereby justifying its release. It was primarily a platform for the album. Maybe some were not aware that it was an old track as Ed Stewart heralded it as their great comeback single on the BBC's *Junior Choice*. The album itself made No. 5 on the US album chart and hung around for five months, but it went to No. 2 in the UK and remained on the listings for over five years, thus keeping the Simon & Garfunkel flame alive.

Although Art Garfunkel had no new film commitments, the projected plan for a Simon & Garfunkel tour evaporated. Sharing backing vocals on a few of Simon's solo gigs was Carly Simon (no relation) who had been friendly with them for some time. When she released her sardonic masterpiece 'You're So Vain' there was much speculation as to whom the song was addressed: Warren Beatty, Mick Jagger, Kris Kristofferson and record mogul David Geffen were all contenders. In 2015, Carly Simon admitted that the first verse was about Warren Beatty, but she didn't say anything about the rest.

Simon could have been a contender himself when he came out with such choice quotes as this, said to *Rolling Stone* in July 1972: 'Many times on stage, though, when I'd be sitting off to the side and Larry Knechtel would be playing the piano and Artie would be singing "Bridge", people would stomp and cheer when it was over and I would think, "That's my song, man. Thank you very much. I wrote that song."'

CHAPTER 9

Give Us Those Nice Bright Colours

Early in 1973 Simon reported that he planned to write his autobiography, but this never happened, although *The Songs of Paul Simon* was published by Michael Joseph. This contained many illustrations and the sheet music of most of his recorded songs. The pictures covered Simon's career with Garfunkel very effectively both as Simon & Garfunkel and as Tom and Jerry, but his UK folk club days were ignored as was the LP, *The Paul Simon Songbook*. Simon's own commentary was too short and said nothing new. The most significant comment from Simon was that his next songs would be better.

When Paul Simon visited London, he said that he was putting the finishing touches to a new album and arranging concert dates to tie in with its release. Simon acknowledged that the market had changed considerably with the rise of teenybop sensations including the Osmonds, the Jackson 5, Marc Bolan and David Cassidy. He told *Melody Maker*, 'To 14 year olds I'm sure the music is interesting, but if you've been listening to rock'n'roll for 16 years as I have, it's boring.'

He couldn't even raise enthusiasm for the singer/songwriters who were around. 'What's wrong is the emphasis that came in the 60s on the singer/songwriter, and I contributed to that. Nobody's content anymore to be just a songwriter or a singer. A good songwriter like Jimmy Webb or Paul Williams feels compelled to go out and be an artist and they're so mediocre. If you have a record by a really good group like Poco who aren't top notch songwriters, then they never reach their potential.'

But what about Elton John? 'I appreciate that Elton John makes a good record but I am not interested in it. I don't mean that in any offensive way. He's good. He might be the best in the world at making records as far as I'm concerned. They all sound so good and full. I just couldn't care less. I've been doing it for too long.'

In May 1973 Columbia issued Paul Simon's new album, *There*

Goes Rhymin' Simon. As might be expected, Simon had not followed contemporary trends, but had produced an album which was a logical extension to his previous one but also superior.

After the gospel-sounding 'Bridge Over Troubled Water' single, it was logical to find Simon whooping it up with gospel groups. Simon told the UK press, 'I like hearing oldies. Some are good and some are bad but everybody is nostalgic about their teenage years. I wonder if those kids who were born in 1955 like it – they probably don't. But do you know what I find interesting? The music that was the precursor of rock'n'roll which is gospel quartets reached its popularity before I was born, late 30s and then through the 40s. I love that music. I mean quartets like the Swan Silvertones and the Dixie Hummingbirds, and that's why I use those groups on the record.'

The Dixie Hummingbirds liked picking up early on the last note to give them an urgency. A rehearsal was recorded with them moving around and this was better than something more formal where they stood in the front of the microphones.

This time the lyrics were interwoven with the music and the music often shunned the obvious in favour of something more surprising. Simon told *Sounds*, 'The biggest influence lately on my music is that two years ago I went back to study the classical guitar. I learned more about harmony and orchestration and now I find it easier – I can change keys when I want to and I know more about musical options than I did in the past. I don't just have to Travis pick in the key of G.'

Paul's good-natured approach runs over into the cover illustration by Milton Glaser, which is a collage that represents each song. Such an approach would not have worked for *The Paul Simon Songbook*.

As with the previous album, Simon was ready to travel in order to work with the right musicians in the right studios. Simon struck lucky here: 'I called up Al Bell at Stax Records and asked him who played on the Staple Singers' "I'll Take You There". He told me about these guys in Muscle Shoals.'

Simon arranged a three-day session at the studio in Alabama. His intention was to record 'Take Me to the Mardi Gras' but to his astonishment, it was finished on the first day. Having two days to spare, he used the musicians to cut 'Kodachrome', 'One Man's Ceiling Is Another Man's Floor', 'Was a Sunny Day' and 'St Judy's Comet'. The songs for the album had taken him six months to write and here he was cutting five of them in three days. Once he was back in New York, he would work on the mixes and it would be six months before he had a product that he wanted to release. He said, 'An album in less than 18 months for me is lightning.'

William Bender wrote in *Time* magazine, 'Simon's second album since his breakup with Art Garfunkel testifies anew to a major talent that simply will not stop growing. By now a pop composer with no superiors and few equals, Simon, 31, manages to distil a diversity of pop styles into an original blend, yet remarkably enough, never losing the original force or point, whether it be rock, gospel, folk, soul, jazz or even hymnody.'

Nowhere is this diversity better illustrated than in the opener, 'Kodachrome', where Simon uses rock'n'roll riffs for one of the most uplifting and joyful tracks you are ever likely to hear. He had started the song as 'Going Home' but decided it was trite and changed it to 'Kodachrome', a celebration of colour film. You're carried along by the song's buoyancy with the *Melody Maker* reviewer comparing it to winning the pools.

Simon's energetic vocal is only one component of this clean-sounding rock'n'roll which includes glissandos from Barry Beckett that are worthy of Jerry Lee Lewis himself. Everything is so tight that it is hard to credit that this was only recorded because Simon had finished 'Take Me to the Mardi Gras' ahead of schedule. By the end the pace quickens to that of a whirlwind but you have to hear it yourself – and play it loud.

There are plenty of successful songs about photographs – 'Photograph' (Ringo Starr), 'Pictures of Lily' (the Who), 'Eight by Ten' (Bill Anderson, Ken Dodd), 'People Take Pictures of Each Other' (the Kinks) 'Wishing (If I Had a Photograph of You)' (A Flock of Seagulls) and 'My Camera Never Lies' (Bucks Fizz) – and 'Kodachrome' is one of the snappiest. The song is more about memories (schooldays and old girlfriends) than the pictures themselves, and he pays homage to 'You Are My Sunshine' when he pleads for his pictures not to be taken away. Note how strategically Simon places the word 'crap' in the opening verse – the word hardly matters now but it was not heard in popular songs in 1973 and did restrict airplay.

But there was another reason why airplay would be restricted in the UK and why indeed it was not released as a single. 'Kodachrome' is the registered trademark of Eastman Kodak for its colour film and so the BBC would be breaking its charter by advertising. An occasional outing escaped the net, notably on *The Old Grey Whistle Test*. Around the same time, Dr Hook's 'The Cover of Rolling Stone' was banned by the BBC for the same reason.

In 'Kodachrome', Simon reflects on his lack of education, so the song does not apply to himself. On the second track, 'Tenderness', he is accompanied by the Dixie Hummingbirds with Cornell Dupree on guitar and he recreates the magical doo-wop sounds of the Flamingos and the Spaniels. The ending is delightful as the bass meanders away on its own. The horn arrangement is by New Orleans musician Allen Toussaint, best known for soul hits with Lee Dorsey, Ernie K-Doe and Irma Thomas.

Oddly, 'Tenderness' is the only track that Simon made with the engineer Roy Halee. He had made 'Me and Julio Down by the Schoolyard' with Phil Ramone and he chose to work with him on this new album. There might have been a conflict of interest as Halee was working with Garfunkel and the change brought something different to this album.

'Take Me to the Mardi Gras' evokes the feeling of a fiesta extremely well. By the end of the song, Simon has reached the Mardi Gras and there is an atmospheric fade-out from the Onward Brass Band capturing the creole jazz of New Orleans. They came to the studio in their uniforms. Simon is not so much entering the spirit of the music as sounding like a city boy who would like to see its magic. Rev Claude Jeter, the former lead singer of the Swan Silvertones, sings a bridge about the coming of the Kingdom. He sings in high falsetto very effectively, a part that earlier would have gone to Art Garfunkel.

A song to his wife Peggy, 'Something So Right' is a slow ballad about how he is trying to slow down. Simon compares his shyness to the Great Wall of China – still, that's his problem, not mine. The arrangement is from Quincy Jones and, according to Simon, 'he made it a city love song with jazz overtones'. Simon recorded it live in the studio with a band 'just like Sinatra would have done'. It would have been perfect for Garfunkel or, for that matter, Sinatra if he was behaving himself.

Side one is completed by 'One Man's Ceiling Is Another Man's Floor', another of Simon's songs about living in New York City and about the paranoia of high-rise apartments. Some residents hold a mysterious meeting and the singer feels edgy and uneasy. Simon's vocal creates tension and is uncharacteristically harsh at times.

The pressures of living today continue on the second side with

'American Tune'. The singer is homesick for America, although it's a far cry from those straightforward homesick songs about someone in a foreign land wishing he were home. Simon refers to the Pilgrim Fathers and sees how their ideals have been destroyed by modern America. Their heritage has been so abused that he even dreams of the Statue of Liberty leaving the country. Simon has found the America he was seeking on *Bookends* but he doesn't like what he sees. It's a moving song with a performance to match and yet Paul Simon told *Sounds* in 1973, 'I love New York. I'm very happy here.'

The melody is enhanced by a beautiful string arrangement from Del Newman, which gives the track a hymnal quality. Indeed, Simon had based his melody on a Lutheran hymn which was also used by Bach in *St Matthew Passion,* namely the aria, 'O Sacred Heart Sore Wounded'. It is not an American tune at all and certainly not Paul Simon's.

The words have a similar feel and message too.

> *We come in the age's most uncertain hour and sing an American tune.*
>
> *To hold me that I quail not in death's most fearful hour.*

The first line is Paul Simon, the second Robert Bridges.

'In those days if you were working with an unknown they would give you a month to finish the whole thing, but the top people could spent three years making an album,' recalls the arranger Del Newman. 'There was an enormous orchestra for "American Tune". Paul had given me a guide vocal and guitar. It is a lovely tune, a beautiful tune, and he wanted a string orchestra and I could really get my teeth into that. I was asked to do the arrangement for an orchestra, to be recorded four or five days later. When I left the studio, they had been working about an hour on a little harmonium, and the bass player hadn't even got his upright out of the case. I had heard one or two verses of the song and I thought, "Fantastic". Two and a half hours later when I left, Paul was still going over the chords with this pianist. I came back for the session four days later and the bass player told me that he hadn't even got his bass out of the case. They still only had the guide vocal and guitar. Paul put Grady Tate on drums who is one of the greatest drummers in America and he's so far back in the mix he might as well have not been there, and all you really have is the guitar and my strings. The cost of those strings would have been my complete budget for an album if I'd been working with an unknown.'

Neither Phil Ramone nor Paul himself were completely happy with the vocal. Phil suggested that he went jogging to open up his lungs. Simon returned an hour later and cut a perfect take.

'American Tune' has not been covered as much as I would have thought but Curtis Stigers cut a vulnerable, world-weary voice and piano version in 2007. It is a pity that Ray Charles never cut this tune. In 2004 Simon and Garfunkel included it on their reunion tour and Art said, 'Wish I could have gotten to this song before the two of us split. I adore this song.' They performed a serious and very moving version of the song.

The West Indian rhythms return for 'Was a Sunny Day', but this is more calypso than reggae. The staccato verses are ideal for Simon's clipped vocal and he is joined on the chorus by Maggie and Terre Roche, the two girls who had attended his songwriting course. Later, with sister Suzzy, they had a following with a succession of quirky albums as the Roches.

Del Newman could have worked with them. 'Paul Samwell-Smith used to produce Cat Stevens and he was a lovely man who had been a bass player and he introduced me to two sisters who had come over from America and were protégés of Paul Simon. I was invited to dinner and they were going to make an album. Paul hadn't told me that this was why I had been invited to dinner. I don't like being taken for granted. We had a lovely meal and these two girls were saying to me, "We want you to do this" and "We want you to do that" and I said, "What are we talking about here?" Paul said, "I am sorry, Del, I am going to produce this record with them and I would like you to write the arrangements." I found them so arrogant and I said, "I am afraid that you have got the wrong person." I thanked them for the meal and I just walked away.'

Paul was one of the producers and played guitar on Maggie and Terre Roche's first album, *Seductive Reasoning*. They used many of the same musicians as Simon had on *There Goes Rhymin' Simon* and also worked in Muscle Shoals. It can be viewed as the lesser-known companion to that album.

'Was a Sunny Day' is an effortless, easy on the ear song about a young girl losing her innocence, though there is a reference to the Cadillacs' 1955 doo-wop record, 'Speedoo'. It's a lightweight song, short on detail, but the track is enhanced by the Latin American percussionist,

Airto Moreira, associated with Antônio Carlos Jobim.

'Learn How to Fall' is a reflective song in a similar mood to 'Peace Like a River'. Musically, you think that you can predict how it will run, but there's a sudden chord change and we're on a different course. The political content is introduced ever so gently in the final verse. Simon's guitar work is up there with the best of John Fahey.

'American Tune' ends with Simon trying to get some rest and it could be considered a lullaby to himself. On 'St Judy's Comet', he is singing a lullaby for his infant son, Harper. The lyric has a jokey edge although the reference to himself as his son's famous daddy seems heavy-handed. This was falling in with other singer/songwriters who were writing songs for their offspring – Tom Paxton, James Taylor, Paul McCartney, Loudon Wainwright III and Donovan. Maybe it's the genes but many of these children ended up as performers themselves.

If Simon is a 'famous daddy' on 'St Judy's Comet', he dreams of being president in 'Loves Me Like a Rock', the album's final cut. The verse is oddly prophetic in the light of Watergate. The Dixie Hummingbirds convey a gospel feel but it has a secular lyric. Simon supplies a rugged vocal, but he's got too much control to let go completely. The demo for 'Loves Me Like a Rock' sounds more wistful than the record and includes an additional verse about the congregation singing.

As James Davis didn't want to be in a whisky-drinking gospel group, he started up the Dixie Hummingbirds in 1928. He found a great lead singer in Ira Rucker. They became one of the most famous gospel groups and they resisted offers to switch to rhythm and blues. They were also to record their own version of 'Loves Me Like a Rock'.

With few blemishes, *There Goes Rhymin' Simon* was a great album and Simon's most consistent to date. What's more, he wasn't standing still but exploring new possibilities. A comparison can be made with John Lennon: both their first solo albums were stark but then their second ones had a fuller, more commercial sound.

The demos from the album include an early version of 'Something So Right', including the line, 'I'm just a travelling man, eating up my travelling time.' The acoustic demo for 'Take Me to the Mardi Gras' is very good indeed and there is an unfinished demo for 'American Tune'.

Art Garfunkel had been fine in *Carnal Knowledge*, but film companies weren't flooding him with offers. The only news had been his wedding to Linda Grossman at her family home in Nashville in October 1972 with Paul Simon attending. He returned to recording again the follow year.

The press had a night of long knives when Art Garfunkel released *Angel Clare* in September 1973. It was cruelly slated for being a collection of pop songs with no cerebral material to get into. Many thought that it proved conclusively that Paul Simon had been the heavy talent in the duo.

Well, of course he was. That Simon had been the mainspring had been apparent since the first records in 1965 and we didn't need the new album to tell us that. But – and it's a big but – Art Garfunkel had a beautiful, delicate voice and he knew how to use it intelligently. His voice contrasted with Simon's own and Garfunkel's sound often sweetened the bite of Simon's bitter lyrics.

Art chose songs by contemporary writers which would showcase his voice to the best advantage. Among the writers were Jimmy Webb, Carole King and Randy Newman but no Paul Simon. These were classy writers and there was no loss in quality through Simon not being involved. I was very pleasantly surprised when I played this album again in 2015; I hadn't heard it in full for thirty years and thought it was a superlative MOR record, although that might be damning it with faint praise. Angel Clare, a character in Thomas Hardy's *Tess of the D'Urbervilles*, was a perfect title, two words which convey Garfunkel's sound. His multi-layered voice with the children's choir on Osibisa's 'Woyaya' could not be more celestial.

The album is technically perfect and the engineering and production was by Ron Halee, who knew his voice and its capabilities. They took enormous pains to get it right and Garfunkel has said that eighty per cent of his time was spent in mixing the instrumental tracks. They sometimes used the clever trick of 'The Only Living Boy in New York' of taking a very full production and mixing it down.

As a sound picture, there are no complaints and a much wider audience was deserved on the tracks which used Garfunkel's voice primarily as an instrument, for example, the merging of 'Feuilles-Oh' and 'Do Space Men Pass Dead Souls on Their Way to the Moon?' The first is a Haitian folk song, written in French, about a mother trying to save the life of her child. Paul hated it and their treatment of it, but he had gone along with it to be sure it wouldn't work: it was later a bonus track on a Simon & Garfunkel set. The second has the bizarre composing credit of J. S. Bach and Linda Grossman, not to mention a remarkable title. The overall effect is like the Swingle Singers.

Randy Newman's homage to his father, 'Old Man', could be a companion to 'Old Friends/Bookends', but it is brilliant in its own right, and is much tougher than Simon's. A man is visiting his dying father and the song concludes:

> Won't be no God to comfort you,
>
> You taught me not to believe that lie.

Jimmy Webb had an impressive portfolio of songs, almost as good as Simon's – 'By the Time I Get to Phoenix', 'Wichita Lineman', 'MacArthur Park' and 'Up, Up and Away' – but he relied on others to perform his material. Indeed, in 2015, two of his main channels, Linda Ronstadt and Glen Campbell, were no longer performing and so maybe he will be working with Garfunkel again. Webb does make his own albums but his voice is a songwriter's voice rather than a singer's voice and he needs great voices for some of those songs.

In 1973, Jimmy Webb gave Art Garfunkel two songs for *Angel Clare*. I would have had 'All I Know' down as the first cut on the album, as the opening lines are so unusual.

> I bruise you, you bruise me,
>
> We both bruise too easily.

The rest of the lyric doesn't match this compelling start but it is still good and it was a US hit single, reaching a respectable No. 9, and topping the new AOR listings. The other song was 'Another Lullaby', good enough but intentionally somnambulistic.

A radical reworking of Van Morrison's 'I Shall Sing' turns it into a cheerful little folk song – hardly Van Morrison at all – but it works well, although it is rather slight. There is lovely passage where Garfunkel sings a counter melody to himself. It was a US single but stalled at No. 38.

The third single, 'Traveling Boy', missed the charts completely. This was a good but not great song from Paul Williams and Roger Nichols, who wrote for the Carpenters.

Then there are the folk songs; 'Barbara Allen' and 'Down in the Willow Garden' are both beautiful performances. 'Barbara Allen' has a lovely mixture of flutes, accordion and strings and he is joined by Paul Simon for the final verse. Art is so intent on the sound that he has overlooked that they are grim and violent songs and he sounds too pallid to be the murderer on 'Down in the Willow Garden', which comes with Jerry Garcia's guitar. Both songs were on the Everly Brothers' *Songs Our Daddy Taught Us*.

Albert Hammond, who had written 'The Air That I Breathe', 'The Free Electric Band' and, it must be said, 'Gimme Dat Ding', wrote one of the best tracks on the album, 'Mary Was an Only Child'.

Art Garfunkel released a fine single of a Tim Moore song, 'Second Avenue', which was not included on the album. His version and Tim Moore's original were released simultaneously and he made No. 34 in the US, while Moore's original was No. 58. It is a moving song of lost love, containing personal details, and I prefer Garfunkel's lush orchestral recording, although there is not much in it. It has not been served well on reissue as a shortened version has been used. Check out Garfunkel's single at just over four minutes. I am amazed that neither Art Garfunkel nor Tim Moore's record companies thought that this song was worthy of major promotion. Even today the song could be a major hit for someone.

Angel Clare was released in September 1973 and Art only made one appearance to promote it. He appeared without Simon at the Columbia Records sales convention in October where he sang 'Bridge Over Troubled Water' to an audience which included Paul Simon. Still, it was a successful album, making No. 5 in the US and No. 14 in the UK.

An individual assessment of Garfunkel's place in Simon & Garfunkel was written by Bob Edmands and published in *Cream* in May 1973. He said, 'On the sleeve of their *Greatest Hits* album, they've got that self-satisfied look of average hip millionaires right down to the hand-faded Levi's. How come they threw it all away.' He added, 'Mr Garfunkel's ego seems to have swelled with a pride in his own talents from the earliest days of their collaboration.'

Earlier we printed Art's comments on 'He Was My Brother' and Edmands thinks it a miracle that Art 'didn't get his face punched at that stage in their relationship'. Edmands sees Garfunkel spoiling Simon's songs by insisting on top-heavy accompaniments and his insistence on being on the creative side is manifest in 'Voices of Old People', a track which Edmands assumes Simon hates as much as he does. 'Simon should really have told his junior partner where to get off.' This may contain some truth but Simon doesn't hold back in interviews and he has never criticised this track.

Here's how Simon reacted in 1972 when *Rolling Stone* suggested he could never be as successful as he was with Simon & Garfunkel. 'Yeah, like Dean Martin and Jerry Lewis. Don't tell me that, that I'll never be bigger than... How do you know what I'll do? I don't even know what I'm going to be doing in the next decade of my life. It could be my greatest time of work. Maybe I'm finished. Maybe I'm not going to do my thing until I'm 50. People will say then, "Funny thing was, in his youth he sang with a group. He sang popular songs in the 60s." Fans of "rock and roll", in quotes, may remember the duo Simon & Garfunkel. That's how I figure it.'

To promote *There Goes Rhymin' Simon*, Paul arranged a series of concerts in June 1973, starting with three days at Carnegie Hall and ending at the Royal Albert Hall. The shows featured Simon in concert with Urubamba and the Jessy Dixon Singers. Urubamba were four South American musicians who play flutes, percussion and charango. Two were with Los Incas and Simon used Urubamba on stage for 'El Condor Pasa', 'Duncan' and 'The Boxer'.

Simon had heard the Jessy Dixon Singers at the 1972 Newport Jazz Festival and they joined him for 'Bridge Over Troubled Water', 'Loves Me Like a Rock' and 'The Sound of Silence'. They performed a spirited 'Jesus Is the Answer' in their own spot. Ian Hoare, reviewing the concert at the Royal Albert Hall for *Let It Rock* wrote, 'The crunch came when he allowed the Jessy Dixon Singers to do a couple of numbers on their own. It didn't matter that they were saying, "Jesus is the answer, there is no other"; they were bursting at the seams with music that expressed a sense of human potential in comparison with which everything Paul Simon has ever done seemed bleached, placid and sterile.'

Ian Hoare had been at the press conference. 'He struck me as an arrogant, sulky, pompous little sod, repeatedly comparing himself with Dylan and apparently taking himself 100% seriously as a purveyor of potentially world-saving observations. More to the point, he was a pedestrian guitarist and had a wet, weedy voice, which sounded exactly like it was – the voice of a would-be pop star of the early-60s breed.' So you lose some, you wince some.

The seven-minute version of 'Bridge Over Troubled Water' indicates how slowly they took the song. Paul in concert sounded more American than on his studio recordings and he frequently used a half-talking, half-speaking approach to his material, particularly on 'The Sound of Silence'.

The concerts led to the album *Live Rhymin'* and possibly one reason for the release was so he could lay claim to 'Bridge Over Troubled Water' and some others for himself. 'The Boxer' was now performed with an additional final verse,

Live Rhymin' is generous on playing time but aside from introducing the musicians, his only announcement on the album is to tell the audience, 'Let's hope that we continue to live.' The album made No. 33 on the US album charts and was not on the UK charts, but then live albums are not usually big sellers.

There is considerably more speech on the bootleg *Simply Simon*, unofficially released after he played Los Angeles in November 1973. The recording is not as clear as an official release but it is worth catching for Paul's comments. When someone requests 'Papa Hobo', he says, 'I could play "Papa Hobo" if I could remember the changes, which I can't.' He adds a choppy rhythm to 'Was a Sunny Day' and runs the song into 'Cecilia'. His 'Kodachrome' is excellent and he receives six bursts of applause and three of laughter during the performance, although the audience must have known the jokes already.

One track, 'Death in Santa Cruz' is not a new Simon song but an Urubamba instrumental. It was featured on Urubamba's own album, which Simon produced in 1973. He also produced Maggie and Terre Roche but their single 'If You Emptied Out All Your Pockets, You Could Not Make the Change' was not released in the UK. Following Paul's songwriting classes in New York, he had presented a talk on the history of rock'n'roll with Clive Davis. Many anecdotes from the Davis/Simon/Columbia days are quoted in Davis' own book. *Rolling Stone* carried a further one shortly before Davis was ousted from the label: 'Simon strode into the conference room in the midst of a meeting. Davis was pleasantly surprised. Then Simon slammed a book onto the table in front of the president telling him, "You need to read this book more than anyone I know." Davis glanced at the volume, *The Life of Krishna*, as Simon spun round. "Wait, stay," urged Davis. Simon continued out through the door.'

The same issue of *Rolling Stone* contained this quote from Paul: 'Once in a while when I turn on the radio in the car, the lyrics I hear are really banal. Toast – when I hear Carole King, I think of toast. Carly Simon is an exception. The rest of the stuff is either attempts to be campy or it's madness and destruction type of rock'n'roll or it's "Let's boogie again like we did in the 50s."'

Another exception must surely be Peter Yarrow and his much neglected album, *That's Enough for Me*. Yarrow had sold 35m records as part of Peter, Paul & Mary, but his solo outings had fallen flat. In an effort to get moving again, he enlisted expert help and Paul wrote and produced 'Groundhog', which includes Paul Butterfield with Levon Helm and Garth Hudson from the Band among the musicians. It's a gentle, reflective song in the 'Papa Hobo' tradition and you can imagine Simon performing it himself.

Yarrow had been influenced by Simon's cosmopolitan approach to record-making. His songs were recorded in Alabama, New York, Louisiana, Jamaica and London. He used the Jessy Dixon singers and had David Bedford write an intriguing arrangement for 'Old Father Time'. It's the Paul Simon record that he never made and is certainly more adventurous than Yarrow's recordings as part of 'two beards and a blonde'.

CHAPTER 10

Still Crazy

Paul and Art's differences in tastes had been noticeable in their solo work. Paul considered *Angel Clare* 'too sweet'. He said, 'I told Art that I want to write an odd piece of nastiness for his next album.' That nastiness was 'My Little Town', an evocative study of childhood and about how difficult it can be to revisit the past:

Nothing but the dead and the dying,

Back in my little town.

That much-repeated line is highly effective and the whole lyric is short but tightly packed with images. Art loved the song and asked Paul to sing with him. They sounded as fresh as ever and for a change Art goes for the lower harmonies. It was produced with Phil Ramone who was producing Paul's new album.

Phil Ramone had been born in South Africa in 1934 and was a violin prodigy, playing before the future Queen Elizabeth. The family moved to New York and he studied at Juilliard but he preferred jazz. He was the recording engineer on 'The Girl from Ipanema' (Astrud Gilberto) and 'It's My Party' (Lesley Gore) and he worked on the films *Midnight Cowboy* and *Flashdance* (marrying Karen Kamon from the cast). At one stage he was working with Billy Joel, Chicago and Paul Simon at the same time and the back cover photograph for *The Stranger* shows him with Billy Joel's band. He was an optimistic, upbeat guy – and needed to be.

'My Little Town' restored the duo to the US Top 10 (No. 9) but, despite much radio play, it was not a UK hit. It was included on both their solo albums, *Breakaway* (Art Garfunkel) and *Still Crazy After All These Years* (Paul Simon), which were released side-by-side in October

1975. As the albums only had ten tracks apiece, they contained an A-side, a B-side and a mean side.

That track aside, *Breakaway* was produced by Richard Perry, an adventurous producer whose credits included Tiny Tim, Ella Fitzgerald, Fats Domino, Captain Beefheart, Harry Nilsson and Carly Simon. By skilful production, he had produced Ringo Starr's highly infectious album, *Ringo* and brought out the best in his voice, and it was a cosmic leap from Ringo Starr to Art Garfunkel. His plan was to 'make a romantic album for the 70s', a sentiment Garfunkel wholly embraced, but that meant an album of superior MOR music.

Art was cool and calm and loved a fragility in the songs he chose, whereas Richard was a volcano of nervous energy. The combination worked and they especially succeeded with 'I Only Have Eyes for You'. The song had been written by Harry Warren and Al Dubin for a Busby Berkeley extravaganza, *Dames* (1934), starring Joan Blondell. Dick Powell sang the song in the film but it was a hit for Ben Selvin and later recorded by Frank Sinatra. There have been numerous versions but Art's was based on the Flamingos' doo-wop revival in 1959. It's a beautiful production but I wish Art had repeated the Flamingos' 'doo-wop-she-bop' refrains. It had been one of the few doo-wop records to mention the word itself.

Art visited the UK to promote 'I Only Have Eyes for You' on *Top of the Pops* and he was a model of diplomacy at the press conference at the Savoy Hotel. He wouldn't be drawn into opinions on either the Bay City Rollers (the current fad) or Paul Simon and most reporters got their copy by writing about his beautiful girlfriend, Laurie Bird, who had played opposite James Taylor (the driver) and Dennis Wilson of the Beach Boys (the mechanic) in the cult film *Two-Lane Blacktop*, released in 1971.

Art told of his plans to tour with a small group in 1976, of how he was writing poetry and 'noodling on the keyboard', and how he wanted to produce Stephen Bishop and possibly cut his own album of Bishop's songs. Bishop wrote two songs on *Breakaway*, 'Looking for the Right One' and 'The Same Old Tears On a New Background', which were good but not great ballads. Still, it did lead to him securing his own recording deal. My main complaint about his songs, and also Steve Eaton's 'Rag Doll', is that they were not compelling enough. Some think that Garfunkel's work as a whole is like that but you only have to hear the vitality as he bursts into the chorus of Stevie Wonder's 'I Believe

(When I Fall in Love It Will be Forever)' to know it is not always so.

Garfunkel's energy is evident on the title song by Gallagher and Lyle. It integrates Garfunkel's voice with Steve Cropper's guitar, Bill Payne's synthesiser and the harmonies of David Crosby, Graham Nash, Bruce Johnston and Toni Tennille. It is most infectious and reminiscent of the Beach Boys who had recorded a different song called 'Break Away'. Bruce Johnston was a Beach Boy and his classic composition 'Disney Girls' is neatly placed next to this track. It is a less jaded and more idyllic view of adolescence than 'My Little Town'. As the song says, fantasy worlds and Disney girls are coming back.

An intriguing songwriting combination is that of Albert Hammond with Hal David, a lyricist in search of a partner since his break-up with Burt Bacharach. The song '99 Miles from L.A.' is very good, rather like a pop version of Antônio Carlos Jobim. Jobim's own South American rhythms can be heard on 'Waters of March'. Garfunkel loves lists and so the lyric grabbed his attention:

A mile, a must, a thrust, a bump,

It's a girl, it's a rhyme, it's a cold, it's the mumps.

Make what you will of that or take Art's explanation, broadcast on Radio 1: 'Don't take it for granted that there is such a thing as a chair. A chair, that's great, wherever did it come from? Just a few short years ago you came into the world and you saw all these things. As a child your eyes were wide open at the mystery of all the things that make up our civilisation and in truth, you've never really grasped how magical, how fabulous and how busy it all is. You've gotten cool about it but you've never really gotten cool about it because it's still terrifically wonderful daily. That song is just about enjoying all these things, it's celebrating a night, a point, a grain, a bee, a buzzard, a trap, a gun, a death. And it makes a kind of fabulous swirl in the end which is what I'm looking for. To me, it's like Fellini.' Convinced?

The album made No. 7 on both the UK and US album charts but the single of 'I Only Have Eyes for You' was a UK No. 1, replacing David Essex's 'Hold Me Close', but only lasting two weeks as David Bowie was flying high with his reissued 'Space Oddity'. The single of 'I Only Have Eyes for You' made No. 18 in the US and 'Break Away' floundered at No. 39.

It was a sound commercial move to release Simon's and Garfunkel's albums simultaneously, although having a press photograph of Garfunkel smoking a cigar and holding up Simon's LP was still crazy. Artistically it was not the best move for Garfunkel as it demonstrated what everybody knew – that Simon had the heavy talent.

Although Simon and Garfunkel's new albums were so different, Antônio Carlos Jobim provided a common link. Paul told Radio 1 DJ Stuart Grundy, 'I noticed that in a lot of Jobim's songs, he uses every note of the chromatic scale. I've started doing this and it's like a game I play. I feel I have to do it and I'm involved in a score of possibilities for a melody line.'

Jobim recorded for CTI and another of their musicians, Bob James, was playing on *Still Crazy After All These Years*. He plays electric piano on two cuts and arranges the title track and 'I Do It for Your Love'. He brings a Jobim feel to the latter and 'Still Crazy After All These Years' has similarities with 'American Tune', a track from the last studio album, also featuring Bob James.

A jazz feeling underscores the album. Paul himself did some arranging and he had been studying under jazz musicians Chuck Israels and David Sorin Collyer. The saxophonist Phil Woods, who had played with Charlie Parker, contributes a coda to 'Have a Good Time'. Said Simon, 'We told him to play anything he wanted as long as it was in the key of B flat. Two or three takes and it was over.' Thirty seconds of bebop. Dave Matthews, best known for his work with James Brown, arranged the horns on 'Have a Good Time'.

By now Paul and Peggy had divorced and Paul had dropped his manager as he had stopped touring. He had a sixteen-month-old son, Harper, and he was going to look after him. Although Paul had not intended to write personally about his marriage, that is how the songs fell into place. He came out of the shower one morning and said, 'I'm still crazy after all these years', realising he had a highly original title. Indeed, the phrase has passed into the language as 'Still... after all these years' or 'Still crazy after all these...' In 1998 a British Spinal Tap film, *Still Crazy*, was made about a reformed rock band with Jimmy Nail, Billy Connolly and Stephen Rea. In 2015 Bob Harris' revamped autobiography was called *Still Whispering After All These Years*.

The film *Las Vegas Nights* was issued in 1941 and featured the Tommy Dorsey Orchestra with Frank Sinatra. They sang a new Frank

Art Garfunkel, 1975 (CBS Records)

Paul Simon, 1975 (CBS Records)

Loesser song, 'Dolores', with witty but irritating rhymes. It sounded very dated but it was the inspiration for '50 Ways to Leave Your Lover'. Whereas that was playful nonsense, Paul Simon's song is much better constructed. It features Simon with backing vocals from Patti Austin, Phoebe Snow and Valerie Simpson.

Although it is humorous, '50 Ways to Leave Your Lover' can be seen as a commentary on divorce. The song came out of a play session with Harper, and Paul developed it with a Rhythm Ace drum machine. The final version with drumming from Steve Gadd is superb as he played a rhythm that is as distinctive as anything on *Graceland*. He didn't get a songwriting credit for it: 'he was just doing his job,' said Simon.

There are many instrumental highlights on the album, notably Michael Brecker's saxophone on 'Some Folks' Lives Roll Easy'. There is a magical accordion on 'I'd Do It for Your Love', a wonderful song for Peggy relating to happier times. The combination of three instruments in 'Night Game' adds a dimension to what would otherwise be a fairly ordinary song.

For all this instrumentation, the album is bleak and is not bursting with the joie de vivre of some of *Rhymin' Simon*. You have the impression that whatever colouring has been added to Simon's songs has been well considered and that every instrument is there for a purpose.

A major exception to this laidback feeling is the rip-roaring 'Gone At Last', a furiously-paced gospel song with Phoebe Snow and the Jessy Dixon Singers. Simon had recorded a slower version with Bette Midler but it didn't work. Phil Ramone was working independently with Phoebe Snow and he suggested that Paul try it with her. She gives a great performance, concluding with a staggeringly high note. Overall though the song is not as strong as 'Loves Me Like a Rock'. Among the outtakes is a less frenzied version with Paul Simon, the Jessy Dixon Singers and percussion, which also works.

Jessy Dixon organised the Chicago Community Choir who are featured on 'Silent Eyes'. The song, taken at a mournful pace, has a disturbing lyric about the quandaries around Jerusalem.

In 'My Little Town' the adolescent Simon felt secure knowing that 'God keeps an eye on us all', but the more adult Simon is disillusioned. The middle section of 'Some Folks' Lives Roll Easy' is unnerving and the album's gloom is heralded by the title cut which finds him contemplating suicide: 'I fear I'll do some damage one fine day.'

The humorous touches in 'Have a Good Time' are ironic and the kindness he experiences in 'You're Kind' is at variance with everything else he knows:

Why you don't treat me like

The other humans do?

Although the record is not a concept album, the songs fit well together. They represent different aspects of the same experience, namely the breakup of his marriage. The music is cleverly varied, from the gentle shuffle rhythm of 'You're Kind' to the vitality of 'Gone At Last', from the lightness of '50 Ways to Leave Your Lover' to the fire of 'My Little Town'. Special credit goes to Phil Ramone: everything is sharp and clear and the balance is perfect.

Rolling Stone critic Dave Marsh said, '"My Little Town" is Simon & Garfunkel's final studio duet and with the exception of "The Boxer", the best rock track they ever created. Simon takes the lead, using Garfunkel's eerie wimp tenor to add an edgy thrill; the arrangement is heavy with brass, percussion, and thunderous bass chords from a grand piano. As a statement of Self-Importance (Simon's perpetual theme), it's tops.'

He added, 'Simon may have waited his entire career to create "My Little Town", which is an equally perfect expression of self-importance's companion: the revenge motif. Though the mill town detail tries to hide it, "My Little Town" is a portrait of the middle-class Forest Hills, New York neighbourhood where Paul and Art grew up.'

Paul submitted 'Still Crazy After all These Years' and 'Have a Good Time' to the Warren Beatty movie *Shampoo*, although the songs were not used. Indeed there is so little of his music on the soundtrack that you wonder why his credit is there.

The single of 'Gone At Last' made No. 23 on the US charts and 'Still Crazy After All These Years' No. 40, but the big one was '50 Ways To Leave Your Lover', which was Simon's first solo US No. 1, replacing the Ohio Players' 'Love Rollercoaster' at the top and staying there for three weeks. In the UK, the only hit single from the album was '50 Ways' but even then it only reached No. 23. The British public preferred 'I Only Have Eyes for You' to '50 Ways to Leave Your Lover' and in America, it was the other way round.

In the UK, '50 Ways' is such a golden oldie that most people would assume that it went higher, but then 'Scarborough Fair' was never a single. It has also been a minor US country hit for both Bob Yarbrough (though his name was misspelled on the single as 'Yarborough') and Sonny Curtis. The *Still Crazy* album topped the US chart, replacing Elton John's *Rock of the Westies,* and was No. 6 in the UK.

In 2005 Paul Simon and Herbie Hancock recorded a new arrangement of 'I Do It for Your Love', changing it to a minor key and giving it a modern jazz treatment which worked very well.

When Simon appeared at the London Palladium in 1976, someone threw a request on stage. 'Read it,' shouted the audience. It said, 'Will you play some different songs – not just pre-arranged ones?' Simon said, 'How rude, would it suffice if I re-arranged the pre-arranged songs?' An awkward moment had passed but there was a lack of spontaneity and Simon seemed somewhat distant. Penny Valentine said that he 'delivers his songs in an invisible box', which was very perceptive.

CHAPTER 11

Trick or Treat

Although Simon and Garfunkel had come together for 'My Little Town', their relationship was strained and they had little interest in working as Simon & Garfunkel. When Paul was the guest host of the American TV show *Saturday Night Live,* he invited Art to join him. Catch it on YouTube and you will find their fifteen minutes together enthralling for all the wrong reasons. Firstly, it was the land that fashion forgot. Simon, with ear-covering hair and moustache, wearing an old-fashioned jacket with key pocket and patches and faded jeans, was an art teacher on a day out, while Garfunkel, with his frizzled hair, wearing a cowboy shirt and worn-out jeans, looked like someone you would cross the street to avoid. If they had consulted a style advisor, they would be due a full refund.

Simon introduced Garfunkel, who walked through the audience and sat on the stool next to him, unclear where to put his legs. As he was sorting himself out, Simon said, 'So, Artie, you've come crawling back.' This was unscripted as you could sense Garfunkel wondering about the best response, which was possibly to throw a punch. They performed a decent version of 'The Boxer' and Simon remarked that it was good to be back again, but followed it with a remark that Garfunkel's movie career was over. 'Scarborough Fair' followed and then Simon put his guitar down and they stood for 'My Little Town' with Garfunkel reading from the autocue. Well, he could have been reading a newspaper for all the effort he put into it. Simon said, 'I have to give him his solo number' and Garfunkel sang 'I Only Have Eyes for You'.

It's bizarre but a year later Simon was back on *Saturday Night Live* with George Harrison and they performed charming versions of 'Here Comes the Sun' and 'Homeward Bound' and looked comfortable together. Although not filmed, Art Garfunkel, Kinky Friedman and Bob Dylan sang Barbra Streisand's 'People' at a Hollywood party.

Simon enjoyed collaborating with others, but not necessarily with Garfunkel. David Sanborn, the saxophonist from the Paul Butterfield Blues Band, made an album, *Sanborn*, in 1976 which was produced by Phil Ramone. Paul and Phoebe Snow sang on the slow groover 'Smile', not an oldie but a new song from Simon. In 1977 he co-produced an album of covers for the CBS album, *Libby Titus*, a singer with a really good voice and a stimulating choice of boyfriends – Levon Helm and Dr John.

As his brother, Eddie Simon, was running the Guitar Study Centre in New York, Paul gave the students a talk about 'American Tune' and Art spoke about harmony.

Paul Simon was friendly with the producer of *Saturday Night Live*, Lorne Michaels and in 1976 he was asked to send up his own image as 'Mr Alienation' by dressing as a turkey on their Thanksgiving show and singing 'Still Crazy After All These Years'. It is both funny ha ha and funny peculiar and you couldn't imagine Van Morrison being talked into something like that.

Paul Simon had much in common with Woody Allen in that they wryly commented on the life of New Yorkers, and Simon was given the role of Tony Lacey, a record producer, in his 1977 film, *Annie Hall*. Lacey, an exiled New Yorker, lives in a lavish house in Los Angeles that was once owned by Charlie Chaplin and Nelson Eddy and he is insincere and deceiving with a cocaine spoon dangling from his neck. He invites Annie Hall (Diane Keaton) to a party, neatly contrasting with Allen's ungainly hero, the Jewish comedian Alvy Singer. Shelley Duvall was cast as a pretentious rock critic, and she and Simon had a relationship whilst filming. At the time, Paul was living a few blocks from his former wife, Peggy, and his main interest was in building an art collection.

For Christmas 1977 Columbia released *Greatest Hits, Etc* to show that Simon had amassed a solid body of hits without Garfunkel. There were twelve previous tracks – three from *Paul Simon*, five from *Rhymin'*, four from *Crazy*, with the *Etc* representing two new ones – 'Slip Slidin' Away' and 'Stranded In a Limousine'. The album went Top 20 in the US and Top 10 in the UK, but the single 'Slip Slidin' Away' was much bigger in the US, making the Top 10.

'Slip Slidin' Away' is a superb song, about the incontestable path towards death but also about an unhappy marriage and divorce. The four verses are exceptionally strong, as good as anything Simon has written, and he said, 'I always felt it should be shorter but I didn't know which verses to take out.' It works very well and has the Oak Ridge Boys supplying background harmonies.

'Stranded in the Limousine' has a fabulous rhythm and a deliberately rushed vocal from Paul Simon, but the song is light on detail. Who is this 'mean individual' who leaves his car at the traffic lights?

In 1978 Simon met his new flame, the actress Carrie Fisher. Carrie was the daughter of singers Eddie Fisher and Debbie Reynolds, who had divorced in 1959 when she was three. Her first movie role, to show how things move in circles, was in *Shampoo*.

It was smart of Art Garfunkel to ask Jimmy Webb to write him an album of songs. Jimmy decided on a theme of obsessive romance and the songs would be lushly orchestrated and employ the Muscle Shoals musicians, Paul Desmond's saxophone, Jimmy Webb's piano, and Irish folk band the Chieftains. A number of disparate elements came together to make a very fine album, which was produced by Art.

The LP was called *Watermark* and Webb wrote ten of the twelve tracks. Some were songs that had been used previously ('Paper Chase' by Richard Harris, 'Marionette' and 'All My Love's Laughter' by Webb himself) but most were new. The cover photograph was taken by Laurie Bird. The title track is a lovely song about a girl who is like a watermark, never there but never gone. The classic track is 'Crying In My Sleep' about a man trying to forget his lover.

The two outside tracks are the traditional 'She Moved Through the Fair', performed with the Chieftains, and '(What a) Wonderful World', a fun version of Sam Cooke's hit with Art, James Taylor and Paul Simon, with a new verse and produced by Phil Ramone. *Watermark* was a US Top 20 album and this track was a US Top 20 single. Talking of James Taylor and Jackson Browne, Art said, 'You could say those artists are the children of my sound, yeah. We were folkies – softer, more thoughtful – goosebumps with melodies.'

And what about the rabbits?

Richard Adams wrote his first book, *Watership Down* (1972), while he was working at the Department of the Environment. It depicted a colony of rabbits, which was forced to move from their warren by building developments. Unlike many children's books, Adams did not endow them with human characteristics and took great pains to treat life in the warren seriously: in short, they behaved like rabbits, admittedly rabbits who were talking and scheming.

There was much speculation as to how the book could be filmed and, after several years in the making, an animated film was released in 1979. John Hurt's voice was used for Hazel and Richard Briers' for Fiver, while Joss Ackland was the Black Rabbit and Sir Ralph Richardson the Chief. Mike Batt, whose CV included the Wombles, desperately wanted to write the score, but the work went to Angela Morley (previously known as Wally Stott) and Malcolm Williamson. Mike Batt kept submitting ideas for songs. 'Even "Bright Eyes" wasn't going to be used,' he says, 'but then "Over the Rainbow" was almost taken out of *The Wizard of Oz*. I had two songs that were dropped, so I then recorded "Run like the Wind" with Barbara Dickson and "Losing Your Way In the Rain" with Colin Blunstone.'

Mike Batt told the producers that Art Garfunkel would be ideal for 'Bright Eyes' and, he says, 'within a week, there he was, in my home in Surbiton, doing a routine for the song.' The track was recorded in 1976, but it could not be released until the animated film was ready and that took three years.

Although 'Bright Eyes' was a UK No. 1 for six weeks in April/May 1979, it didn't impress Richard Adams. 'I was watching *Wogan* and he asked Richard Adams what he thought of the film,' says Mike Batt, 'He said, "I hated 'Bright Eyes.'" He based his dislike on the assumption that it was wrong factually. He said it was about a dead rabbit – well, if he read his own book, he'd realise that the song is sung and thought by Fiver at a time when he thinks Hazel is dead. The whole point is that the other rabbit thought he was dead.'

In total contrast to 'Bright Eyes', Art lent his harmonies to 'A Junkie's Lament', a 1976 song which was written and recorded by James Taylor, clearly from personal experience. The stark track closes, unexpectedly, with thirty seconds of celestial harmonies.

Quickly following *Watermark*, Art was recording his next album, *Fate for Breakfast,* this time produced by Louie Shelton. 'Bright Eyes' was added for the UK release, but the packaging was different in many territories. Six different photographs of Art having breakfast were used for the various issues: there you are, a record collector's dream.

Art is back with Larry Knechtel on piano for one of his greatest performances, 'Miss You Nights', although hardly anyone knows it. The song by Dave Townsend had been recorded by Cliff Richard and been a minor UK hit. Garfunkel's version is so strong that it should have been released as a single and promoted heavily. Instead, Columbia went with 'Since I Don't Have You', another revival of a doo-wop hit, albeit without the Skyliners' harmonies. The track is very good but not as strong as 'I Only Have Eyes for You'.

The infectious oldie 'Oh How Happy' with a double-tracked Garfunkel works well and should have been released as a single but I've no strong feelings about the rest of the album. They follow the style of the romantic ballads that Garfunkel does well but the songs are only so-so – 'In a Little While', 'And I Know', 'Finally Found a Reason', 'Beyond the Tears', 'When Someone Doesn't Want You', 'Take Me Away' and Stephen Bishop's 'Sail On a Rainbow'.

In 1978 the Canadian singer/songwriter Dan Hill toured with Art Garfunkel; he had had one huge success with 'Sometimes When We Touch'. He was to be signed to Columbia once Paul had left and possibly they thought he was the replacement but there was only one Top 10 record with him, 'Can't We Try' (1987). Roy Halee sometimes worked with him, and Roy was also producing Blood, Sweat & Tears and Laura Nyro.

The film director Nicolas Roag was known for his strange, disoriented films – *Performance* with James Fox and Mick Jagger, *Don't Look Now* with Julie Christie and Donald Sutherland, and *The Man Who Fell to Earth* with David Bowie. The erotic thriller *Bad Timing* was another for Roag's gallery.

Art Garfunkel was cast as the lead actor in *Bad Timing*. He was living in New York with Laurie Bird, who had played Paul Simon's girlfriend in *Annie Hall*. In June 1979, while Art was away, she took an overdose and died in their apartment. Art became withdrawn and he said, 'I was stunned to have lost Laurie. I kept my love for her even though she was gone. I read her diaries over and over.' He played classical music and read philosophy and rarely went out. His poems about her are included in his collection, *Still Water*, which was published in 1989. The poems are very affectionate but are more like musings than poetry.

In the light of that tragic event, *Bad Timing* was incredibly bad timing. Art Garfunkel played psychoanalyst Dr Alex Linden who works for the CIA and is obsessed with Milena Flaherty (Theresa Russell). The film is set in Vienna and she has a husband in Poland, Stefan Vognic, played by Denholm Elliott. Everything goes wrong and Alex finds Milena comatose after taking an overdose. He calls for an ambulance and rapes her before it arrives. A detective tries to find out what happened but drops the charges when Milena survives. For all its art house pretentiousness, *Bad Timing* is rubbish – an unpleasant film with disagreeable characters. Watching it today, it seems an endless commercial for cigarettes.

In 1977 Lorne Michaels produced *The Paul Simon Special* for US TV which gently mocked the idea of making a special with Charles Grodin as the director Chuck and guest appearances from Lily Tomlin and Chevy Chase. Art Garfunkel joined in for 'Old Friends/Bookends' and the Jessy Dixon Singers were featured on 'Loves Me Like a Rock'. At the end, Chuck encouraged them to plan a reunion tour because 'The sound of the two of you together is so much better than either of you can sound alone.' Charles Grodin won an Emmy for his script and then became a CBS News commentator. He fought injustice, helped the homeless and fought for drug offenders to be released. When he was sixty he returned to acting and often plays old men in feature films.

In 1978 Paul Simon appeared in the spoof Beatles' film, *All You Need Is Cash*, starring Eric Idle and Neil Innes. He denied that the Rutles had had any effect on his career at all. But had Simon inspired the real Beatles? While Simon was with Clive Davis in a coffee shop, John Lennon and Yoko came in and Lennon praised his solo work.

Simon had not made an album since *Still Crazy After All These Years* and Clive Davis told him it was time for something new. Simon said that he would make an album of covers, but that was unacceptable to Davis. 'Whyever not?' said Simon, 'That's what Artie does.' But no, a Paul Simon album had to feature new material.

Simon had other gripes with Columbia. He accused them of bad or fraudulent accounting, leading to him being underpaid. He claimed poor promotion on his single 'Stranded in a Limousine', which was never a hit song.

Reluctant to deal with Columbia anymore, Paul Simon bought himself out of his contract for $1.5m and moved to Warner Brothers. The deal was reported as $10m for three albums but there are so many clauses and sub-clauses in these contracts that you can't say with certainty what any of them are worth. As it happens, Warner would be getting one of the greatest albums ever made but all that was down the line. What Simon liked about the deal was the ability to be able to pitch a movie to them.

Paul Simon was a singer, guitarist, composer, concert performer, record producer and innovator, anything but a one-trick pony, but that was the title of his next project, a feature-length film. Paul Simon did not want to drift too far from his own life – he wanted to set his film in New York and people it with characters that he understood. Indeed, the closest comparison to *One-Trick Pony* would not be another rock movie but Woody Allen's *Stardust Memories*. There are touches of Allen's humour in the script, but not enough. When someone says 'Hare Krishna' to Simon, he responds 'Harry Chapin' and when he calls his wife he says, 'I'm not dead, I'm in Cleveland.'

In a sense, he was dealing with his alter ego. He wondered what would have happened if he had had a couple of hits in the 60s, say, 'The Sound of Silence' and 'Homeward Bound' but then faded away. This film was about the singer/guitarist Jonah Levin, who scored with a folky hit about Vietnam, 'Soft Parachutes', and continued with club dates through the 70s. He hears the B-52's at a club and realises that the scene is changing.

Jonah Levin is going through a divorce and he refers to his ex-wife (Blair Brown) and his ex-dog but not his ex-son (played by seven-year-old Harper) with whom he plays baseball. He wants to get his marriage back but at the same time he has affairs with a waitress and with a record executive's wife. His wife thinks he should give up his childish dreams: 'You've wanted to be Elvis Presley since you were thirteen years old, and he didn't do too well himself.'

Simon delivers his lines dolefully and he is too inhibited to let go in any of the scenes. Indeed, thinking of the film as a whole, everybody is too polite. Dustin Hoffman could have played the part with ease and both Gary Busey and Richard Dreyfuss were considered, However, Simon was not keen on his songs being sung or mimed by somebody else and Warner Brothers wanted a Paul Simon album to sell. Hence, with a little reluctance, Paul had to star in the film he had written. He had strong control as the executive producer Michael Tannen was also his business manager.

Now we come to the music, which is both the film's biggest strength and its biggest weakness. Theoretically, Simon had to write songs for his character which would be passable but lack commercial potential. Instead, Simon was writing to the best of his ability and in most cases and unlike most music films, the songs were performed in their entirety without cutaways to further the plot. What's more, he assembled a wonderful band – Richard Tee, Eric Gale, Steve Gadd, Tony Levin – and they are his road band in the film. It is unlikely that somebody this good would be performing songs of this quality with such a strong band

and not getting the recognition he deserved.

We only hear a shortened version of 'Soft Parachutes' during a 60s revival concert and it is the weakest song on offer and certainly not one which would have established Jonah.

Indeed, when Paul Simon is auditioning new songs for a bunch of disinterested record executives, the inclination is to stand up and shout, 'I'll sign him.' In the end, they take him, largely because Walter Fox's wife likes him. Fox (Rip Torn) tells Steve Kunelian (Lou Reed) to produce him and Kunelian adds his own orchestration to 'Ace in the Hole' which so disgusts Jonah that he returns to the studio at night and destroys the tape. End of film. Yes, that's right, the end of the film – a feeble ending for a full-length film.

The film includes some guest appearances, and Sam & Dave steal the show with a spirited 'Soul Man'. The Lovin' Spoonful reunite for 'Do You Believe in Magic?' and Tiny Tim wanders around aimlessly.

One-Trick Pony cost $7m but it fared poorly at the US box office. Although Simon did an American and European tour with musicians from the film and performed some of the songs, he wasn't into promotion. Indeed, it never had a UK release, but the album made the UK Top 20. The tour went well and he was joined by Carrie Fisher on stage in Fort Worth for his birthday and together they sang 'Bye Bye Love'.

He toured Europe in November 1980 with a set based around *One Trick Pony*, which no one would have seen, and a four-piece horn section, three of whom had worked with the Band. Garfunkel came on stage in Paris. At the end of the first half at the Hammersmith Odeon, he asked for requests and someone shouted, 'Buy me a drink' and Simon said, 'I'll buy everyone a drink.' True to his word, Simon bought the interval drinks which cost him £1,000.

He was unlikely to have bought Annie Nightingale a drink after an interview on *The Old Grey Whistle Test*. Anne wondered how he was writing songs, now that Garfunkel had gone. He replied, 'We never wrote any songs together. I wrote all the songs. Not wishing to sound immodest but Art only sang them with me.'

'Is this generally known?' asked Nightingale, feeling that she had the scoop of the decade.

'I guess everyone knew but you,' said Simon.

At the Hammersmith Odeon, someone shouted out, 'Where's Annie Nightingale?'

The album sold strongly in the US, making No. 12 on the charts, with the highly rhythmic 'Late In the Evening' reaching No. 6 and the title song also making the Top 40. Another song, the yearning 'Long, Long Day' was performed by Simon on *The Muppet Show*. He performed with Harper on *Sesame Street*.

The outtakes from *One-Trick Pony* include 'All Because of You', which became 'Oh, Marion' and 'Spiral Highway' which became 'How The Heart Approaches What It Yearns'.

Art Garfunkel was also touring and he appeared with Chieftains in Dublin and had both Paul Simon and Jimmy Webb join him at Carnegie Hall. Garfunkel had a new girlfriend, Penny Marshall, and his 1981 album *Scissors Cut* was dedicated to Laurie Bird with her photograph on the back cover.

I thought that the title might refer to a new hairstyle but no, it is a reference to the childhood game and is an excellent love song from Jimmy Webb. Webb wrote the remarkable 'In Cars', which had been on his own album, *Angel Heart*. It is about the importance of cars in adolescent life. The opening line is 'Went to school in cars', which didn't happen much in the UK. The harmonies on this track are exceptional, which include Paul Simon's, and it sounds like the Beach Boys at their best. The track ends with a snatch of Garfunkel singing 'Girl from the North Country', the new lyric Bob Dylan had put to 'Scarborough Fair'.

Webb had written the music for the animated film *The Last Unicorn*, featuring the voices of Jeff Bridges and Mia Farrow, and Art recorded the plaintive song 'That's All I've Got To Say' to close the album.

The arranger Del Newman has mixed feelings about the album. 'Art Garfunkel rang me and said, "Del, how much do you charge?" He felt that there were people in the States ripping him off so he was trying to collate what was going on. I was going to New York to do his next album. I had written three arrangements but he was rude to me on the phone. He said, "I am tired of people ripping me off" and he slammed the phone down. I thought, "Right, I have already written these arrangements and the orchestra has been booked in New York, and so nobody is going to get these arrangements until I get paid." CBS rang me and said, "Put them in Air Freight will you, Del?" I said, "No, you will have to pay me in advance." I knew that if he didn't have the arrangements, he would still have to pay the orchestra. He rang back and said that I could go to CBS in London and get my money. I took them to CBS, but they hadn't heard anything about it. I explained the situation and they asked me to take a cheque. I said, "No, I want ready money please." I had to sit in the office for several hours with my arrangements, adamant that I wasn't going to leave until I got paid. I got my money and Art didn't want me to go over and conduct. Later he sent me a letter from New York apologising for the telephone call and saying, "The London players would have been better." It was nice of him to do that as he was saying sorry. A lot of people would have left it. I had a great respect for him over that.'

The hit single from the album, albeit No. 61, was 'A Heart in New York', by the Scottish songwriters Benny Gallagher and Graham Lyle, which contains many cultural references and a clip of the Yankees crowd.

Clifford T. Ward was a most underrated UK songwriter and so I am always glad to see his work on albums. 'Up in the World' had been recorded by Ward himself and then Cliff Richard. It's a beautiful performance from Art Garfunkel and although it's short, you are drawn into the story.

The US version of this album included 'Bright Eyes' somewhat late in the day, and in the UK, it was replaced by an Eric Kaz song, 'The Romance'.

Paul Simon was saddened by the lukewarm reception given to *One-Trick Pony*, and in the UK the sales were outstripped by *The Simon and Garfunkel Collection*, which went to No. 4 and was on the album chart for eighty weeks.

In the summer of 1981 Paul Simon was approached by the Parks Commissioner of New York about the possibility of a free concert at Central Park, during which they would raise funds through T-shirts and fast food. Paul liked the idea of 'a neighbourhood concert' as he called it and he asked Garfunkel if he wanted to join him for some of their successes. They soon realised that it didn't feel right that Paul should be an opening act for Simon & Garfunkel, or vice versa, and they decided to do the whole concert together with occasional solo spots ('Still Crazy After All These Years', 'A Heart in New York' where crowds cheered the reference to Central Park). They were told that the sound could not go beyond eighty-five decibels but Paul Simon's first words were 'Turn it up, Phil.'

Because of calcium deposits in his hand, Paul could not carry the concert with just his guitar and anyway he felt more comfortable with a band. Garfunkel was less sure but Paul pointed out that he needed an electric piano for 'Still Crazy' and horns for 'Late In the Evening'. Art had to sing 'Me and Julio', 'Kodachrome' and 'Late In the Evening' for the first time. The arrangements were clever and 'Kodachrome' merged into Chuck Berry's 'Maybelline'. They sang the Everly Brothers' 'Wake Up Little Susie'. The best moment was the merger of their voices and the changes in lead vocals on 'American Tune'.

Half a million people came to the park on 19 September 1981 and the applause on the live album is so long that you wonder when the first song 'Mrs Robinson' is going to start. Paul performed a new song, 'The Late Great Johnny Ace', which linked the gun deaths of three Johnnys – Ace, Kennedy and Lennon, but was also a love song to rock'n'roll. Someone rushed the barricades and said, 'I need to talk to you', which was a scary moment although it was soon resolved. They were singing only a few hundred yards from where John Lennon had been shot. Indeed, Simon had been in the Dakota building from time to time as he dropped Harper off to play with his friend, Sean Lennon. The TV film was directed by Michael Lindsay-Hogg, who had directed the Beatles' *Let It Be*, so he knew something about squabbling groups.

The success of the double album and the popularity of the film encouraged Simon and Garfunkel to perform more concerts. They did European dates in June 1982 and I saw them at Wembley Stadium, or at least, I think I did. These were the days before big screens and I was so far away that I can't say for certain whether I saw them or not. They could have been the lookalikes from the cover of *The Simon and Garfunkel Collection*, as I'd wager that is not them.

The seats weren't numbered and the gates opened at 4 p.m. for a concert billed to start at 7 p.m. Our seats were a long way from the stage and as the show started at 8.15 p.m. (no opening act), there was a good sale of food, drinks, T-shirts and programmes. The sound system was fine: it sounded like Simon and Garfunkel but it could have been a record. How stadium concerts have changed. Their set was much the same as Central Park but with the understandable addition of 'Bright Eyes'. They closed with 'All I Have to Do Is Dream' and 'Late In the Evening'. It struck me that this was the biggest gathering of people who had my book on Paul Simon.

Since Paul had found his first marriage and divorce painful, he didn't want to remarry. He lived with Carrie Fisher and she persuaded him to marry her in 1983. Paul was unsure but as they watched baseball at Yankee Stadium, he was in such a good mood that he said okay. Five days later they were married. Billy Joel gave Paul and Carrie a jukebox stacked with great records for a wedding present.

Simon and Garfunkel had decided to make a new album together and Paul had the songs, the ones that would constitute *Hearts and Bones*, but by the time it was released in 1983, he had removed Art's vocals. The album had four producers (Paul Simon, Russ Titelman, Roy Halee, Lenny Waronker) but no Art Garfunkel. Paul was in control, as it were, but his reason for deleting Art is unclear – Art said that Simon felt that his voice would take the focus away from the songs and that the songs were too personal for two voices. Art retaliated with 'I understand the emotions. I am a singer.'

This was not a commercial album. Paul Simon was over forty and getting divorced for the second time, and the songs, more directly personal than usual, are about that. He is having trouble with his hands and the album even starts with the words, 'My hands can't touch a guitar string', hardly a sentiment to give purchasers confidence.

Simon only plays on six of the eleven tracks, but the musicianship is a tour de force. There are the jazz musicians, vibraphonist Mike Mainieri and saxophonist Mark Rivera (also known for his work with Billy Joel), some Chic touches from Nile Rodgers and the redoubtable Steve Gadd on drums. What's not to like?

'Train In the Distance' is about his first marriage and his son Harper. The train in the distance is a strong image and he spells it out by saying that the idea that life could be better is 'woven indelibly' into our hearts and our bones. What a wonderful choice of words. The song contains a much-quoted Simon phrase, 'negotiations and love songs.' Several songs are revealing about his stormy marriage with Carrie Fisher. She was half-Jewish and Simon has the amusing phrase about 'one and one half wandering Jews'. The title song is blisteringly honest about their relationship.

Simon had told a therapist that there was no point in him writing songs anymore. The therapist said his songs were loved by millions and he had a duty to continue. This led to his two-part 'Think Too Much', in effect two different songs with a related theme. In one he is laughing at himself and in the other he is taking it seriously, probably proof, if any was needed, that he was thinking too much. Simon said that the two songs reflected how often he changed his mind, another example being the lyric of 'Outrageous' on *Surprise*.

Paul Simon worked on 'Cars Are Cars' after contributing to 'In

Cars' with Art Garfunkel. He is making the point that although there are many different makes and models of cars, they are, when it comes down to it, just cars whereas people are all different. The bridge is about that red Impala that burst into flames.

Paul saw a photograph in a book, reproduced on the inner sleeve, and its caption led to the song, 'Rene and Georgette Magritte With Their Dog After the War'. Alone in their hotel room, they play doo-wop records. The groups that are mentioned – the Penguins and the Moonglows – didn't get going until the mid-50s but that is hardly the point. Magritte was the father of surrealism and so why should any song about him make sense? The track is a delightful waltz, enhanced by background harmonies from the Harptones. Paul is singing in an unusual key for him and possibly this arrangement had been intended for Art.

Not everything is serious or the result of thinking too much. One day Paul was just playing Sam Cooke's 'Bring It on Home to Me' and he started changing the chords. He arrived at a new melody to which he wrote a lyric about songwriting, 'Song about the Moon'.

The album concludes with a studio version of 'The Late Great Johnny Ace'. The song is enhanced by Marin Alsop's violin and the closing section is orchestrated by the minimalist composer, Philip Glass.

Columbia had funded a recording of a four-hour opera by Philip Glass called *Akhnaten*. Part of the deal was that he should team up with rock lyricists for a more commercial enterprise. He was given lyrics by Paul Simon, Suzanne Vega, David Byrne (Talking Heads) and Laurie Anderson which he set to music. The result was *Songs from Liquid Days* with vocalists including Linda Ronstadt and the Roches.

Glass told Simon, 'Your music is classical. It will be heard as long as people listen to music.'

'You think so?' said Simon, somewhat surprised.

'I think so,' said Glass.

The songs by and large are about living in New York. Simon wrote 'Changing Opinion' about a man who hears a hum in his room. What is it – is it an electric hum, the hum of a refrigerator, the hum of our parents' voices from long ago, or the hum of changing opinion. It takes ten minutes to deliver this profundity in which Bernard Fowler, who regularly works with the Rolling Stones, sings Simon's words.

Two songs were dropped from *Hearts and Bones*. One, 'Shelter of Your Arms', was incomplete, but had potential. Simon liked 'Citizen of the Planet', which was a plea for nuclear disarmament, but felt that the song was too direct for him. It sounds like an early 60s folk song for the Clancy Brothers. Simon thought of passing it to a committed folk group but then it got lost. Simon and Garfunkel's version was added to the double live CD *Old Friends* in 2004.

The public had been expecting a new album from Simon & Garfunkel and it didn't happen, so some might say there was a backlash over this album. I don't think that is the case. These weren't hit songs and, as Simon remarked, he could hardly complain that he hadn't had hit singles when he was writing about surrealism. Warner Brothers must have been hoping for some return on their investment but nevertheless, this is a superb album and one of his best.

In December 1983 Art Garfunkel and Amy Grant appeared at a charity concert at the Royal Festival Hall. It was for Jimmy Webb's cantata, mostly for children's voices, *The Animals' Christmas*. It was very well received and was broadcast on the BBC on Christmas Day and later issued as an album.

In April 1984, Carrie and Paul announced that they were splitting up after eight months of marriage, although the album *Hearts and Bones* had made it abundantly clear. Carrie went into a clinic for drug rehabilitation. She remained friendly with Paul and they were often seen together in the late 80s.

At the end of 1984 Bob Geldof assembled an all-star group, Band Aid, to make a charity single, 'Do They Know It's Christmas' to help famine relief in Ethiopia. It sold 3.5m copies in the UK and Michael Jackson and Lionel Richie then wrote 'We Are the World' for the USA for Africa. The recording took place after the Grammys in L.A. in January 1985 and a sign outside the studio instructed participants to leave their egos behind. Paul Simon had a spot next to Prince, but Prince didn't show. The single topped the US and UK charts. The comedian Ben Elton made the remark, 'You must know who Bob Dylan is. He's the one who can't sing in the 'We Are the World' video.'

This was followed by the huge Live Aid concert on 13 July 1985. Simon & Garfunkel were not invited but Paul was scheduled to harmonise with Bob Dylan which didn't bother Paul at all. He said, 'I can harmonise with anyone' and was happy for Bob to sing lead. In the end, Dylan worked with Keith Richards and Ronnie Wood, performing a ragged set, partly because they had been carousing. If Simon had been involved, there would have been some much-needed discipline.

Art cut a new single, 'Sometimes When I'm Dreaming', a fine performance of a romantic ballad written and beautifully orchestrated by Mike Batt, but it was no 'Bright Eyes'. The song was included on *The Art Garfunkel Album*, the first compilation of his solo work with some remixing to give a richer sound. It was a Top 20 album in the UK.

The producer of *Saturday Night Live*, Lorne Michaels, had asked Paul to give some advice to a young Norwegian singer/songwriter Heidi Berg. She was going to be in a TV talent series, *The New Show*. She told Paul that when she was going to record, she wanted the same accordion sound as a tape she had of South African musicians, *Gumboots: Accordion Jive Hits, Volume 2*. She lent Simon the tape. Some weeks later he invited her to a one-man show in Saratoga. He told her that he bought the rights to the tape and he was going to Africa to work with the band. She said, 'I didn't think you were my competitor', to which he apparently replied, 'You try and compete with me, little girl, and I'll cut you down.' In the notes for *Graceland*, Simon credited Berg as 'a friend who gave me a tape'.

CHAPTER 12

The Days of Miracle and Wonder

Louis Armstrong said all music was 'folk music' as he had never heard of animals making music. The same logic applies to 'world music'. It is generally used for songs sung in a foreign language that are not directly related to the main American genres – that is, the great American songbook of jazz, pop, rock or country. In other words, anything that sounds a bit different to western ears. World music is local music from somewhere else.

World music is a good phrase for media attention, but the music of Africa is so different from the music of India that it is pointless to bracket them together. The term has the feeling of authenticity but it was coined as a marketing tool by specialist American record companies in 1987 to define their products better. Sometimes it is called 'roots music' as much of it goes back to ancient cultures in Asia and Africa.

Long before the term was brought into use in the 1980s there were many examples of world music in western culture. In 1958 Elias & his Zig-Zag Jive Flutes made No. 2 on the UK charts with 'Tom Hark'. At the time it was regarded as a very catchy, novelty hit.

In 1960 Harry Belafonte recorded 'One More Dance' with Miriam Makeba on a live album from Carnegie Hall and the young singer from Johannesburg became well known to American audiences. She and Belafonte won a Grammy for their 1965 album, *An Evening with Belafonte/Makeba,* which featured South African tunes sung in tribal languages. Belafonte encouraged other African acts and he himself recorded many African songs. In 1967 Miriam Makeba had a US hit with 'Pata Pata', and the following year her husband, the trumpeter Hugh Masekela went to No. 1 in the US with 'Grazing In the Grass'.

In 1971 the drummer from Cream, Ginger Baker, worked with African musicians in Lagos and two years later, Paul McCartney was there recording *Band on the Run.* There is a slight African connection with the track 'Mamunia' but McCartney preferred to play drums himself rather than use African percussionists. Had he explored the local culture, *Graceland* might not have been such a groundbreaking album.

In 1973 the jazz saxophonist Manu Dibango, from Cameroon, made the US charts with 'Soul Makossa'. If you read James Brown's autobiography, you will read how he and Fela Kuti formed a mutual admiration society and had an influence on what the other was doing. There are examples of African rhythms in much of James Brown's work and the soul band Osibisa mixed the music of America and Africa. On *The Hissing of Summer Lawns* in 1975, Joni Mitchell wrote 'The Jungle Line' around some drums played by Burundi musicians in the 60s.

The most famous African chant is Solomon Linda's 'Mbube', often performed as 'Wimoweh' or 'The Lion Sleeps Tonight'. It took several decades for Linda's family to secure its copyright and hence the royalties to the song, which to this day is performed in *The Lion King*. Very often songwriters and musicians who adapt songs for western ears don't appreciate what they are doing. 'In the mighty jungle, the lion sleeps tonight' was written by a city boy; lions are nocturnal and live on the plains, not in the jungle.

So there were numerous examples of world music in western popular culture before Paul Simon's *Graceland* in 1986. The best-known examples surround Indian music in the mid-60s. Many groups used sitars on their records, notably the Beatles, the Rolling Stones, the Byrds and the Yardbirds, starting with 'Norwegian Wood' in 1965. Simon & Garfunkel were in on the act with 'Fakin' It'. In most cases, the Indian influences were being brought into western songs to add colouring to a group's sound.

One of the best examples is the Byrds' 'Eight Miles High'. Roger McGuinn says, 'We turned the Beatles on to Indian music. We were in a house in Beverly Hills. They had invited us up and we were passing guitars back and forth. We showed them some Ravi Shankar licks and they wondered what it was. We said it was Indian music and they really got into it after that. We turned them onto it! (laughs)'

With the best of intentions, Miriam Makeba recommended Roger McGuinn to take the Byrds to South Africa in 1968 so that they could see Third World poverty and oppression for themselves. Gram Parsons had joined the Byrds a few months earlier and was uncomfortable about this, leaving the band in London on the eve of their tour. Their roadie,

Carlos Bernal, took his place.

The United Nations had imposed a cultural and sporting boycott in South Africa until it abolished apartheid. Ironically, one of the first sportsmen to ignore the ban was a cricketer named, believe it or not, Geoffrey Boycott.

In a clever and manipulative move, Bophuthatswana had been declared an independent state by the South African government, although it was still part of South Africa to the rest of the world. They built a huge entertainments complex called Sun City with a 6,000-seat auditorium. It became a holiday resort for residents in Johannesburg.

Several British and American entertainers convinced themselves that it was okay to play Sun City. Among those who went were Frank Sinatra, Paul Anka, Rod Stewart, Linda Ronstadt, Chicago and Elton John, Sinatra being the first major star to play there. Frank maintained that playing Sun City was part of his campaign against apartheid, and he ignored that he was being used by the apartheid government. The performers were taking money out of Africa so perhaps were making the situation marginally worse. Said Paul Simon, somewhat ridiculously, 'To play Sun City would be like doing a concert in Nazi Germany at the height of the Holocaust.'

Simon turned down Sun City but he would not participate in a single organised by Little Steven on the ground that it mentioned names. It was credited to Artists United Against Apartheid and the performers included Bob Dylan, Bobby Womack, Lou Reed and the Temptations. In the end, the record didn't name names as other performers objected.

The first major star to embrace African dance rhythms was Peter Gabriel and he also sponsored the WOMAD (World of Music and Dance) Festival and gave benefit concerts for Amnesty International. He made records with Youssou N'dour from Senegal, who became an international star in his own right. Gabriel turned to South African politics with 'Biko' in 1980, and the Specials recorded 'Nelson Mandela' in 1984.

The Sex Pistols' manager Malcolm McLaren went to South Africa and he released a highly successful album, *Duck Rock*, in 1983 that had many influences but at its core it combined hip hop with mbaqanga (township jive). Simon was to say in defence of his own activities, 'Malcolm McLaren came over a year before we did, didn't pay anybody and took all the credit.'

Paul Simon had liked the *Gumboots* tape very much. The instruments

– accordion, electric guitar, bass and drums – were familiar to him and the music reminded him of some favourite acts from the 50s, notably the street sounds of New York. Despite all the hardships of living in South Africa, this was very happy music. It was an album of township jive from Soweto and Simon ordered another twenty albums of South African music. He listened to it during the summer and knew he had his next project.

The word 'gumboots' was a reference to the miners and railway workers who wore heavy boots and loved this music. He bought the rights to the 'Gumboots' track with the Boyoyo Boys and added his own voice and conversational lyrics. The new track was completed before Simon and Roy Halee went to South Africa in February 1985. Paul Simon thought it the weakest cut on *Graceland* but it was the one which had stirred his interest.

It set the template for the album. Most of the lyrics are precise, rapid-fire and conversational, as though you have met a man in a bar and he won't stop talking. Most of the time, Simon is writing about himself and his life in New York City. The opening line of 'Gumboots' goes 'I was walking down the street' is echoed in 'A man walks down the street' from 'You Can Call Me Al'. He talks about a man having a breakdown and, as so often on this album, you wonder if he had asked Woody Allen to help with the words. For example, the line 'Don't I know you from the cinematographers' party?' sounds more like Woody Allen than anything from South Africa.

There are enough indications on this album and elsewhere to suggest that in another life Simon could have been a stand-up Jewish comedian. Indeed, the big hit single from the album, 'You Can Call Me Al', was not promoted by a video of Simon working with African musicians but Simon doing a comic routine with Chevy Chase.

With the possible exception of 'The Boy in the Bubble', there were no overt political references; there were no pleas to free Nelson Mandela. Not only did Simon not mention politics in the songs, there was nothing in his accompanying sleeve note. Simon has been criticised for this, probably unfairly. If he had made an album with African musicians and used it to criticise the status quo, might he not have put them in jeopardy and at the very least, had the album banned in South Africa?

Nevertheless, Simon was cautious about going to South Africa. He told Harry Belafonte, who ran AAA (Artists and Athletes against

Apartheid), that he was not going to perform concerts in South Africa: he only intended to do studio work with the musicians. As they did not have much money, he would pay them double the New York scale and they would receive appropriate credits on anything that was released.

Belafonte had mixed feelings. He thought that Simon should discuss it with the ANC (African National Congress) but Simon did not want to get immersed in politics. He had the union for black musicians in South Africa approve his visit and this, he believed, resolved the issue. Many of his fellow musicians were uncomfortable with this, one likening him to a slave owner. In milder terms, Jerry Dammers from the Specials said, 'Who does he think he is? He's helping maybe thirty people and he is damaging the solidarity over sanctions.'

When Simon and Roy Halee set off for South Africa, they were pleasantly surprised to find that Ovation Studios was better equipped than they had expected. They had booked some of the musicians from *Gumboots* to work with them.

The group, Tau Ea Matsekha (the Lion of Matsetha) from Lesotho, played the rhythm tracks for what became 'The Boy in the Bubble' and 'Graceland'. Their bass player Bakithi Kumalo said, 'He fell in love with the music and that was good for everyone. It was fresh for us and fresh for Americans too. It was unbelievable for me as a South African to hear music in English and see how he put everything together.'

'The Boy in the Bubble' has a frenetic lyric which captured the unrest in the world. The first verse is about a bomb in a baby carriage which blows up some soldiers; the second verse turns to starvation in the desert; and the third the advances in medical technology. The song shows how we are drawn together by news reports and telephone calls. It was an unusual choice for a single, but it is rather like a township version of 'Subterranean Homesick Blues'.

While at Ovation, Simon worked with the band Stimela, and they recorded the basic track for 'Crazy Love, Vol II'. The lead guitar was played by Ray Phiri but soprano sax and guitar synth were added in New York. It's another song about divorce and the reason for the title, according to Simon, is because Van Morrison had recorded a song called 'Crazy Love', which had just been revived by Maxi Priest. As Paul Anka, Poco and the Allman Brothers Band had recorded different songs called 'Crazy Love' and indeed any number of people, perhaps this should have been 'Crazy Love, Vol 86'.

'I Know What I Know' was recorded with General M. D. Shirinda

& the Gaza Sisters. Simon added synclavier in New York and the synth drums have been overdone, although they make an impression. It's disjointed and it is the weakest track on the album.

After the visit to Johannesburg, Paul Simon invited a rhythm section to New York and he selected Ray Phiri (guitar), Bakithi Kumalo (bass) and Isaac Mtshali (drums). Their standard of musicianship was high and he could place them alongside key New York session men.

The best-known of these tracks and also the best is 'You Can Call Me Al', which includes a penny whistle solo, not recorded in South Africa, but played by Morris Goldberg, a white South African who had lived in New York for twenty years.

The origin of the title is said to be Simon going to a party in New York and the host mistakenly calling him Al when he left. This may have happened, but if so, it is an intriguing coincidence that the key song about the Depression, Bing Crosby's 'Brother, Can You Spare a Dime' from 1932, has Bing playing a hobo and singing:

Say, don't you remember when they called me Al,

It was Al all the time.

'You Can Call Me Al' is a comic song about a confused man in New York who finds salvation in Africa. He sees 'angels in the architecture'.

The three African musicians recorded the track for Simon's beautiful song, 'Under African Skies', which he then sang with Linda Ronstadt in Los Angeles. There is nothing musically wrong with having Ronstadt's wonderful voice on this track but was Simon doing this provocatively? She was, after all, one of the stars who had played Sun City. This is a beautiful song; talking about an African child, Simon wrote, 'Give her the wings to fly through harmony.'

They play too on 'Diamonds on the Soles of Her Shoes' with the percussion enhanced by other musicians including Youssou N'Dour, though Simon didn't ask him to sing. Still, Simon performed the song with Ladysmith Black Mambazo. This is a delightful song, very catchy and chastising someone who can't appreciate the value of what she has.

The singing group Ladysmith Black Mambazo had been formed by Joseph Shabalala in 1964 and they specialised in songs and harmonies from Zulu roots. They performed in a church close to Durban but their fame spread across Africa and then abroad. Simon had seen them on a

BBC documentary. He wanted to use them on his record and he sent Shabalala a demo of him singing 'Homeless', a song about exiles, and asked him to add a Zulu beginning and end. They met for the first time at the Abbey Road studios. It's a lovely a cappella track although it is hard to tell what Simon himself is doing as he takes few solo passages. There's a neat joke at the end as Shabalala adds a line in Zulu to say that Ladysmith Black Mambazo are the best singing group around. And indeed they are.

Simon did consider adding a string part and he recorded the Soweto String Quartet. Their contribution has been used as a bonus track on a special edition of *Graceland*.

The southern music, zydeco, had something in common with African music, mostly the prominence of the accordion and among the key practitioners were Rockin' Dopsie and the Twisters. Dopsie played the accordion upside down because he didn't know any better when he started. The group recorded for Sonet and Rounder and Simon was impressed with their work. He went to Crawley, Louisiana to record with them and 'That Was Your Mother' is a cheerful song about standing on a street corner and drinking wine in Lafayette.

Although they call themselves 'Just another band from East LA', Los Lobos were far more than that. Simon was taken with their 1985 album, *How Will the Wolf Survive*. He met them for a couple of days in Los Angeles and he wanted them to play traditional songs that he could perhaps turn round and reword. Maybe he was hoping for another 'La Bamba'. During the session, Cesar Rosas and David Hildago played a melody they were working on and Simon asked if he could add a lyric. The result was 'All Around the World Or the Myth of Fingerprints'.

When the *Graceland* record was released, Rosas and Hildago were surprised to find that the songwriting credit was 'Words and music by Paul Simon'. They complained about their lack of credit, which created ill feeling and the matter surely could have been resolved by listening to early practice tapes. The 2004 reissue of *Graceland* still says 'Words and music by Paul Simon'. Not to worry, Los Lobos hit the big time in 1987 with their soundtrack for the Ritchie Valens biopic, *La Bamba*.

So far I haven't mentioned the 'Graceland' track itself, the reason being that it cut across the whole of the recording sessions and taken by itself must be one of the most costly tracks ever produced. Only a major star with major record company backing could have indulged himself to this degree, although the time and the effort were worthwhile.

Just see how the dollars mount up. Paul and Roy Halee went to South Africa and developed a rhythm track. Simon only kept the drums which had a travelling rhythm that reminded him of Johnny Cash at Sun Records in Memphis. Back in the States, he isolated that drum part and asked Ray Phiri (guitar) and Bakithi Kumalo (bass) to augment it. He was surprised when Phiri went to a minor key as that was not generally heard in African music. When he asked why, Phiri said, 'Because that's the way you write.' Simon was happy with the result and then asked Demola Adepoju from King Sunny Adé's band to add pedal steel guitar, which was not incongruous as the instrument was heard in some African music.

While Simon had been making this track, he has been singing the words 'Graceland, Graceland' over certain sections. The word did not seem appropriate – what had Elvis Presley's mansion got to do with South Africa? – but when he was recording with Rockin' Dopsie in Louisiana, he thought he would visit Graceland and he took nine-year-old Harper with him

There the words took shape and Simon found himself continuing the theme of *Hearts and Bones*. He was reflecting on his marriage to Carrie Fisher and, once he had the lyric, he asked the Everly Brothers to add harmonies. They are down in the mix so you wouldn't know it was them.

This song contains some of Simon's greatest wordplay. He often has great first lines and is there anything more stunning than the Mississippi Delta shining like a National guitar? As he was walking past the American Museum of Natural History in New York, the line about a girl calling herself the human trampoline came to him – there was nothing significant about it, he just thought it was fun. He admitted, 'A lot of my lyric writing is instinctive. I don't know why "Losing love is like a window to your heart" came out the way it did. I can't tell anyone why it comes. It just comes.' Interestingly though, this line is attributed to Carrie in the song. In 1990 Salman Rushdie referred to the human trampoline line when reviewing *Vineland* by Thomas Pynchon.

Around the same time Carrie Fisher was writing a novel *Postcards from the Edge* about a female character making her way back after drug rehab. It is done in the form of a diary that is both harrowing and funny. It was made into a film by Columbia with Meryl Streep, Shirley MacLaine and Dennis Quaid with a theme song from Carly Simon.

Later Carrie wrote a memoir, *Wishful Drinking*. She said that they had argued on their honeymoon. They made each other laugh but 'the day-to-day living was more than he could take.' She said, 'We were both small. When we went to a party, I had to say to him, "Don't stand too close to me – people will think we're the salt and pepper pots."'

Straight after making his recording, Paul Simon thought that the song would suit Willie Nelson and sent it to him, asking him to cover it. Willie listened to it casually, thought it a song about Elvis and put it to one side. Some years later, he came to realise that the song was about the healing process after you've lost the one you love and he knew it would suit him. He agreed to cut it if Paul would play guitar and he included it on his album, *Across the Borderline*. Simon also plays guitar on 'American Tune' from the same album, and both versions are pure Willie.

So much had been spent on *Graceland* that Warner Brothers undertook a heavy publicity campaign to encourage heavy sales. It could have gone wrong as the album could have been boycotted, not only by fans but also by the record shops themselves. Paul McCartney commented, 'Everybody in all forms of art uses their influences as a turn-on. The difference with Paul Simon is that he does it very well. *Graceland* was in dangerous territory and he more than pulled it off.'

Graceland turned out to be a huge success, selling 7m copies over the first year. It reached No. 3 on the US album charts and No. 1 in the UK. It sold predominantly to white audiences in the States. Strangely, only one single made the US Top 40, 'You Can Call Me Al', and that stalled at No. 23. In the UK, 'You Can Call Me Al' was No. 4 and 'The Boy in the Bubble' No. 26.

The album did well in South Africa, helped by the popularity of the local musicians, and topped their charts for two months. As well as the videos, Simon performed 'Diamonds on the Soles of Her Shoes' with Ladysmith Black Mambazo and his Soweto rhythm section on *Saturday Night Live*.

The album won a Grammy for album of the year but 'Graceland' lost out to 'That's What Friends Are For' as the song of the year. In 1988 Simon produced an album for Ladysmith Black Mambazo called *Shaka Zulu*, which won a Grammy for the best traditional folk recording and sold 100,000 copies. He then made a second album with them, *Journey of Dreams*.

There were problems with the album, which was sometimes called *Disgraceland*. Paul Weller, Billy Bragg and Jerry Dammers amongst others called for a sincere apology from Simon for breaking the UN boycott. Simon was regarded as naïve and dubbed 'Simple Simon'.

All actions have consequences and Paul Simon remarked, 'I hoped the ANC are as happy as I am.' They weren't. Both the United Nations and the ANC criticised what Paul Simon had done and Simon found himself in discussions he could have done without. Indeed, he was mortified to be criticised in this way. Their opposition was lifted in January 1987.

Paul Simon took *Graceland* on the road for a tour which also featured Hugh Masekela and Miriam Makeba. Indeed, Simon was only on stage for half the time. He regarded himself as the producer of the show and in his opening remarks, he said, 'This evening is composed of music from South Africa.' Simon did not receive payments for the *Graceland* concerts and gave it to musicians and to charities. There were protests at some venues, notably in London at the Royal Albert Hall. The tour did not go to South Africa but they did perform in Zimbabwe.

Simon's performances had some idiosyncratic touches as doo-wop was never far away and he added 'Whispering Bells' to the end of 'Gumboots'. Ladysmith Black Mambazo were very well received. There were a very visual act – ten men dressed colourfully and identically, using hand and body movements to convey the meaning of their songs. Seven of them sang bass so it was a very distinctive sound.

In 1988 David Byrne of Talking Heads started his own label, Luaka Bop, and he introduced many records from Third World countries to western listeners. The label continues to this day.

Also in 1988, Harry Belafonte made *Paradise in Gazankulu* with South African musicians. He didn't go to South Africa himself – indeed, he would have been refused entry if he had – and he worked to backing tapes. The Belafonte LP included Rubén Blades' 'Muevete', and Blades had made his first English LP *Nothing But the Truth*, writing about death squads in Central America. We will be meeting him shortly.

CHAPTER 13

Lefty or Left Behind?

Art Garfunkel hadn't worked with Paul Simon since the reunion tour and since his voice had been taken off *Hearts and Bones*. Paul hadn't included him in his South African journey. Art's voice would have suited 'Under African Skies' but his choice of Linda Ronstadt produced a stunning track.

Art and Jimmy Webb had travelled to Tahiti and sailed around the Polynesian islands. Art took occasional jobs, playing a hard-drinking journalist in Washington for the film *Good to Go,* which was later remarketed as *Short Fuse.*

Art was seemingly unconcerned about making new music. He told *Melody Maker*, 'Paul's heartbeat is a lot faster than mine. He is more neurotic than I am and he needs to achieve more than I do. I can sit back and eat a peach and I don't have the urge to work that he does.'

Furthermore, Art didn't want the indignity of making an album which didn't sell while Paul was shifting millions of copies of *Graceland*. In 1988 he returned with *Lefty,* a baseball pose from his youth on the cover and the title referring to Art being left-handed. *Lefty* had some familiar components: a doo-wop revival, songs by Stephen Bishop and strings from Del Newman but the album was too soporific and didn't get out of second gear. Individually, the tracks are fine but it is too much to take, although when Nat King Cole recorded slow love ballads, I could listen forever.

By far the best track and the only one with commercial potential (although it wasn't pushed) was a revival of the Tymes' US No. 1 from 1963, 'So Much in Love'. The Philadelphia group had cut a definitive doo-wop side with sound effects from the sea, birdsong, finger snapping, immaculate harmonies and a lead singer, George Williams, who sounded like Johnny Mathis. The song had been revived by Timothy B. Schmit for *Fast Times at Ridgemont High* in 1982 and his single had made the

US charts, albeit stopping at No. 59.

Art's revival of 'When a Man Loves a Woman' shows what is wrong with the album. The original combines Percy Sledge's utterly soulful voice with a superb arrangement and it is pointless to do something different if you can't do it better. Art loses the distinctiveness of the song in a ponderous setting with flutes but he must have liked it himself as he performed it on *The Johnny Carson Show*. Would Percy Sledge have even recognised his song?

Everybody knows the final scene of *West Side Story* where Maria cradles the dying Tony but they still have the wherewithal to belt out 'I Have a Love', a beautiful ballad from Stephen Sondheim and Leonard Bernstein. Art Garfunkel and Leah Kunkel (sister of Mama Cass) revive the song here, but the song does not sound so great out of context.

'This Is the Moment' has the impressive songwriting credit of David Foster, Cynthia Weil, Linda Jenner and Ray Parker Jr and it is the love theme for the American graduation drama *St Elmo's Fire*, starring Demi Moore and Rob Lowe. It's a good performance from Art, who should have sung it in the film.

The British writer Peter Skellern offers 'I Wonder Why' (sung with Kenny Rankin) and the Stephen Bishop songs ('Slow Breakup', 'If Love Takes You Away') are disappointing: Bishop wrote 'King of Tonga' which contains some nice Latin rhythms but there's no clue as to what the song is about. Nick Holmes' 'The Promise' is laborious but 'Love Is the Only Chain' is a good song which finds Art with the original performers, Pam Rose and Mary Ann Kennedy. It has the feel of Fleetwood Mac.

Mike Batt had become entranced with Lewis Carroll's poem, 'The Hunting of the Snark'. I happened to be interviewing Mike at his house in 1985 when he received a fax from Sir John Gielgud agreeing to be the Narrator. Art Garfunkel was the Butcher and his main song was 'As Long As the Moon Can Shine' as well as three songs with Deniece Williams playing the Beaver. Art wasn't available for the TV concert filmed at the Royal Albert Hall in 1987 but the role was played very well by Justin Hayward.

Art performed at the White House for the Reagans and he did short tours, playing the Royal Albert Hall in 1988. He spoke between songs but never mentioned his former partner. His set included Randy Newman's 'Sad Song' and James Taylor's 'If I Keep My Heart Out of Sight'. Art sang 'Bridge Over Troubled Water' for the Prince's Trust at the London Palladium. He performed on a star bill with Billy Joel and Boz Scaggs at the Tokyo Dome.

Art was spending much of his time at home in New York, often writing personal poems and a collection, *Still Water*, appeared in 1989. Although it was no best seller, he was confident about his work as he includes poems in his stage act up to today and the individual poems from the book can be found on his website.

For a short while he was dating Penny Marshall, an actress and film director who was a friend of Carrie Fisher. Then in 1985 he was introduced to an actress and singer Kathryn (Kim) Cermak, and they married at the Brooklyn Botanic Gardens in September 1989.

Warner Brothers wanted to release their own greatest hits collection on Paul Simon and they put out *Negotiations and Love Songs, 1971–1986*, the title coming from his song, 'Train In the Distance'. It made the UK Top 20 albums, but it didn't contain anything new.

In 1987 Paul Simon was in the club Sounds of Brazil, in Greenwich Village, and he was talking to the jazz trumpeter Dizzy Gillespie and the Puerto Rican pianist Eddie Palmieri. They praised *Graceland* but told him that it shouldn't be a one-off: he had to continue the trail. They told him to follow the West African diaspora and see how drumming went to the Caribbean and then to Brazil and Cuba.

Simon visited Brazil with the producer Phil Ramone and talked to musicians. While they were dining in Salvador, they heard some drummers in the distance in a poor part of town. It was a large percussion group called Grupo Culteval Olodum and Simon wanted to record them in the street. Ramone set up his equipment and this became the heavy percussive sound which runs through 'The Obvious Child', the opening cut on *The Rhythm of the Saints*.

Once again, Simon shows his ingenuity by writing about his insecurities and throwing in a melodic reference to Eddie Cochran's 'Summertime Blues'. 'The Obvious Child' is Jesus, and Simon refers to 'the crosses in the ballpark', presumably a reference that Jesus stood for peace.

Several songs on *The Rhythm of the Saints* continue the theme of *Graceland*. Both 'The Coast' and 'Born at the Right Time' could have been on that album, and on the enhanced release of *Rhythm*, there is Simon's excellent voice-and-guitar demo for 'Born at the Right Time', but rather high-pitched for him. It is intriguing to hear the demo for 'Spirit Voices' as Simon's initial lyric included a reference to 'Graceland'.

'The Coast' is an excellent song about a group of musicians seeking shelter in a church. One of Simon's best songs, 'The Cool, Cool River' is about terrorism and the talking blues 'Can't Run But' is about Chernobyl. Despite the album's title, the songs don't have the bounce and the joyousness of *Graceland* and the overall theme is the practicality of faith in an immoral world.

Is it 'Proof' or is it 'Poof' or is it 'Proust'? If you know what I am talking about then you will have seen the colourful and funny video for the song with Paul, Chevy Chase and Steve Martin. It's an excellent song anyway, though lacking the commercial potential of 'You Can Call Me Al'. 'She Moves On' is a bittersweet song with an infectious rhythm about his marriage to Carrie Fisher, sung here with Charlotte Mbango.

There are close to 100 musicians on *The Rhythm of the Saints*. They include the blues guitarist J. J. Cale, Ringo Starr (name misspelt on the sleeve and playing guitar but it must be him) and Ladysmith Black Mambazo. Take 'Proof', which Roy Halee likened to the United Nations. The Cameroonian rhythm section was cut live in Paris, and Simon added some horn players. Back in New York he added a South African bass player, an American drummer and an accordion player from New Orleans. Then it went back to Brazil for more percussion. After that, the tape was taken to New York for female singers from Cameroon and a shaker player from New York, Ya Yo. After all that, Paul Simon put on his vocal.

The reviews for *The Rhythm of the Saints* were good but some critics saw it as *Graceland*-lite or *Graceland* Jr. None of them said that it was better. In the US, *The Rhythm of the Saints* went to No. 4 and was on the charts for twenty-six weeks. *The Rhythm of the Saints* was a No. 1 album in the UK and 'The Obvious Child' made No. 15.

Simon dropped one song, 'Thelma' from the album, feeling that listeners would be tired by the time they got to it. Enough was enough. He might be right but it was an attractive song about childbirth which deserved to be heard, perhaps with a softer arrangement. He recorded a duet of 'Vendedor de Sonhos (Dream Merchant)' with the Brazilian singer and composer Milton Nascimento, a song that Nascimento performed on TV with James Taylor.

I was half expecting Simon's next album to be made in Cuba as that would have been logical, but then he might have run into Ry Cooder. The interest in world music was intensifying and one could imagine a comedy sketch in which Paul Simon, Ry Cooder, David Byrne and Sting found themselves in the same location.

The singer and guitarist Ry Cooder has worked with many musical cultures. *Talking Timbuktu*, his 1994 album with Ali Farka Touré, is well known and three years later, he created a phenomenon by releasing *Buena Vista Social Club*, largely featuring elderly Cuban musicians. These musicians toured in various combinations in Britain and America and the original album, which sold three million, was followed by several others. Ry Cooder made a telling remark which could easily have been said by Paul Simon: 'The music is alive and is not just some museum we have stumbled upon.'

In 1989 Paul Simon was one of the collaborators on Joan Baez's album *Speaking of Dreams* and together they sang a delightful medley of 'Rambler Gambler' and 'Whispering Bells' with instrumentation similar to *Graceland*.

In August 1991 Simon gave his own solo Concert in the Park with a seventeen-piece band. Many of the old favourites were there but he had rearranged them to accommodate the African and South American musicians. This didn't always improve on the songs because 'America' was perfection anyway. They performed an extended version of 'Diamonds on the Soles of Her Shoes'. The following year Paul performed in the *MTV Unplugged* series, although he happened to be very plugged. The set included a strange, jazzy arrangement of 'Bridge Over Troubled Water'.

Both Paul and Art had cameo roles, as Simple Simon and Georgie Porgie, in a TV movie, *Mother Goose's Rock 'n' Rhyme,* which featured Shelley Duvall, Cyndi Lauper, Slim Jim Phantom, Van Dyke Parks and Debbie Harry. It's good to see Little Richard whooping it up but his song is nonsense, and the best thing about Paul Simon's performance is his snatch of Willie Nelson's 'On the Road Again'. I found it lamentable but then it was made for young children.

Art performed Randy Newman's 'Texas Girl at the Funeral of her Father' on *The Tonight Show*. He performed a graduation song, 'We'll Never Say Goodbye', for the film *Sing* and a beautiful choral version of 'O Come All Ye Faithful' for the multi-artists collection *Acoustic Christmas*. In June 1990, Art performed at an outdoor rally to promote democracy in Bulgaria with 1.4m people attending, said to be the largest live audience ever.

In 1994 it was me and Julio as Garfunkel and Iglesias performed the Everly Brothers' 'Let It Be Me' for Julio's album *Crazy*. The stilted

English of the Everlys' version was because it was a translation of a French song. Iglesias' European accent sounded right in context.

In 1997 Art with a male chorus sang Eric Idle's 'Always Look On the Bright Side' on the soundtrack for the Jack Nicholson film *As Good as it Gets*. In 1998 he was a narrating moose who sang a bit on the cartoon series *Arthur.*

In 1990 Simon and Garfunkel were inducted into the Rock and Roll Hall of Fame. They sang 'Bridge Over Troubled Water' and 'The Boxer' together. In 1992 he and Paul played a charity show at the Brooks Atkinson Theatre in New York to benefit the terminally ill. Another one-time duo, the comedians Mike Nichols and Elaine May, were on the bill.

Paul Simon's new relationship was with the singer and songwriter Edie Brickell (pronounced Bree-kell) from Oak Cliff, Texas. When she was a waitress in Dallas she had sung with the New Bohemians and things had taken off from there. Their 1988 album *Shooting Rubberbands at the Stars* was No. 4 in the States and they had a Top 10 single with 'What I Am'. Their second album, *Ghost of a Dog*, was a Top 40 album. They toured with Bob Dylan, Don Henley and the Grateful Dead, and appeared on *Saturday Night Live* which is where she met Paul Simon. They were married on 30 May 1992. Their first son, Adrian, was born later that year.

Simon and Halee co-produced a solo CD for Edie called *Picture Perfect Morning* in 1994 with a single of 'Good Times'. Simon played acoustic guitar on several tracks and guest musicians included Art and Cyril Neville, Dr John and Steve Gadd plus, strangely, the deep vocal tones of Barry White. The stellar musicians are framing the songs rather than overshadowing them.

In 1992 Simon and Garfunkel gave a series of twenty-one concerts at the Paramount Theatre in New York called *The Concert of a Lifetime*, which featured Phoebe Snow, the Mighty Clouds of Joy and Ladysmith Black Mambazo. By now Ladysmith were enjoying international success and had their own popularity through 'African Alphabet' and 'Put Down the Duckie' on *Sesame Street*. In the UK, in 1997, they were used to sell Heinz Baked Beans. In 1999 they recorded a beautiful, a cappella medley of 'Amazing Grace' and 'Nearer My God to Thee', arranged by Paul Simon with the group.

From now on, you might be in virgin territory. We have now covered all the Simon and Garfunkel tracks, both individually and collectively, that the public know. Both Simon and Garfunkel have recorded solo albums since 1990 but, until 2016 there have been no hit singles or hit albums to speak of. What has gone so dramatically wrong, and are there good tracks which should be recognised? What have Simon and Garfunkel being doing for the past twenty-five years?

Art was concentrating on family life; his son James Arthur was born in December 1990. He played a concert in Japan in 1992 and introduced James to the audience. Whether James wanted it or not, he was in the spotlight as he was pictured with Art on the cover of his next album. He presumably wanted it as he has often appeared with his father since then.

Garfunkel sang the theme for the TV series *Brooklyn Bridge*, which was written by Marvin Hamlisch and he then recorded Hoagy Carmichael's 'Two Sleepy People' for the baseball film *A League of Their Own*, with Tom Hanks and Madonna and directed by his old flame Penny Marshall. James Taylor and Billy Joel also recorded oldies for the soundtrack.

The director Jennifer Chambers Lynch made an erotic, surreal film, *Boxing Helena*, in 1993, which was on a par with anything her father David Lynch did. It tells of a surgeon who has fallen out with his girlfriend but then holds her captive by amputating her limbs. This is entertainment? Art Garfunkel had a small role as one of the other doctors in the film.

Garfunkel had already released a solo compilation and his new CD in 1993, *Up 'Til Now*, was a curious affair. The thirteen tracks included a comic recording of a radio promotion with Paul Simon for a concert tour. There is an outtake from *Scissors Cut*, 'One Less Holiday', written by Stephen Bishop; an early take of 'All I Know'; and a great live version of 'Skywriter' with Jimmy Webb from the Royal Albert Hall in 1988, a song that Webb had written about Garfunkel. Said Art, 'Jimmy wrote it with my life in mind, so it's autobiographical.' (No, it's biographical. This from a man who has read the dictionary.) 'I did it recently at the Royal Albert Hall and we recorded it there with Nicky Hopkins on piano. It is a really meaty, new Jimmy Webb song, very romantic with a lot about my private pain.'

The real gems are two tracks that Art recorded with James Taylor in March 1993, the Everly Brothers' sublime 'Crying In the Rain' and Tommy Edwards' 'It's All in the Game'. Paul Simon loved James Taylor as well, saying, 'With James Taylor, I think of his songs as part of the package – he has a very pleasant voice and he sings very well.'

So far I haven't mentioned *the walk*, really because I didn't want to bore the pants off you. This in a nutshell is it. In 1984 Art Garfunkel determined to walk across America. He started from New York and went through to Portland, Oregon, which is over 4,000 miles but he was doing it in 200-mile stages in twelve years. He talked to people along the way but he was not Bill Bryson: he never wrote a book or made a TV series about it, he did it for the pleasure of walking and the joy of getting to know America. Had Paul's song spurred him into action? He must have sung it many times as he walked along.

Art celebrated the end of the journey with two shows in the Registry Hall at Ellis Island, New York Harbor, condensed to an album called *Across America*. James Taylor joined him for 'Crying In the Rain' and Jimmy Webb for 'All I Know'. Art recorded his first Beatles song, 'I Will' from the White Album, and there is a new ballad from John Bucchino, 'Grateful' about being appreciative for what you've got. The CD ends with the doo-wop lullaby 'Goodnight, My Love'.

Synthesizers were used for strings and the cutbacks might have extended to Art's wardrobe. I know how the press makes fun of Jeremy Corbyn's wardrobe, but how could a major star go out in loose tie, shirt outside his jeans, and a waistcoat? Still, his hair was less eccentric than usual.

Most tellingly of all, Art sings 'Homeward Bound' but with a change in the lyric. He now says, 'All *his* words come back to me in shades of mediocrity.' Ouch! Who said that there were only fifty ways to leave your lover?

Art brought out Kim and James for 'Feelin' Groovy' which was well received on the night but it was ridiculous to put it on the CD. Considering how meticulous Garfunkel normally is about getting the sound right, it is odd that he succumbed to such self-indulgence.

Meanwhile Paul was working with one of his heroes from the 50s, Carl Perkins, and the result was a fascinating song, 'Rockabilly Music', written by both of them. It is a celebration of the 1950s but combined with the sound of *Graceland*, but then the title track of that album was about visiting Elvis's home. The musicians on the track included Harper Simon (guitar) and Stan Perkins (drums), two musical sons.

In 1997 Art released a whole album, dedicated to Kim and James, although it was called, somewhat confusingly, *Songs from a Parent to a Child*. The songs were chosen to take you through the course of a day. The family likeness between father and son is spooky and James is even dressed in white shirt, waistcoat and jeans. This time round James sings the first verse of Elvis Presley's 'Good Luck Charm'. In 2005 Kim made her cabaret debut in New York to a standing ovation, so watch this space.

The packaging and the concept of the album turned me off at the time and it was the first Garfunkel album that I hadn't pursued. However, I heard a BBC broadcast of a concert from the London Palladium and heard Garfunkel singing a remarkable song about genetics, 'The Things We've Handed Down', by Marc Cohn. The lyric is so perceptive and so original that I am surprised that this has not found as big an audience as 'Walking in Memphis'. Incidentally, Garfunkel thanked the audience for making it to the Palladium and not being misled by Garfunkel's restaurant next door.

The CD included yet another title from the Everly Brothers, 'Who's Gonna Shoe Your Pretty Little Feet?', James Taylor's 'Secret O' Life' and the Lovin' Spoonful's 'Daydream' with John Sebastian playing guitar and harmonica and whistling. There's a bit of Motown ('You're a Wonderful One' with Billy Preston and Merry Clayton), a bit of Disney ('Baby Mine' from *Dumbo*), some country (Mary Chapin Carpenter's 'Dreamland'), a hymn ('Morning Has Broken' in the Cat Stevens setting) and Jimmy Webb's arrangements of 'Lasso the Moon', first recorded by Steve Amerson, and a combination of 'The Lord's Prayer' with 'Now I Lay Me Down to Sleep'. It's not my sort of album but it's a good one.

CHAPTER 14

The Capeman

The Story

Abandoned by his father, Salvador Agron was born in Mayagüez, Puerto Rico on 24 April 1943. His mother Esmeralda worked in a poor house run by nuns, earning eight dollars a week, and he and his sister Aurea were raised there. He showed no interest in schoolwork.

When his mother remarried, the family came to New York but he was mocked at school for being illiterate and then sent to an institution for disturbed children. At night he would see demons in his room and he was always hearing voices.

His stepfather was abusive and he sought solace with his older sister who had moved to Manhattan. When he visited her he fell in with a street gang called the Vampires. He found a nurse's black cape and they called him the Capeman. When one of the Vampires was attacked by the Norsemen from Hell's Kitchen, Sal and his friend Tony Hernandez sought vengeance. On 30 August 1959, Sal borrowed a knife and off they went.

They made a mistake and attacked two innocent adolescents. Sal set to with his knife and killed them. Bystanders told the police of this boy with the black cape and red lining and in early September he was arrested. His guilt was never in question and he became the youngest criminal in New York to be sentenced to death. He said, 'I don't care if I burn. My mother could watch me.'

The president's wife, Eleanor Roosevelt, pleaded on his behalf and in 1962 Governor Nelson Rockefeller commuted his sentence to life imprisonment. He was locked up and he became a model prisoner. He learnt to read and write. He studied philosophy and he wrote poetry. In 1979 he was released on remand. He died at home on 22 April 1986 from a heart attack.

Can you look at that story and say this could be a hit musical? It's a tragic story with some redemption but where are the spots for the showstoppers? Furthermore, you are asking the audience to sympathise with a murderer. Maybe it would work as an arts centre musical but thinking in terms of a Broadway blockbuster was muddled thinking and ultimately madness.

The Musical

Simon remembered the newspaper stories very well and he saw how this could be a musical. He could explore his doo-wop heritage and he could incorporate Latin rhythms and gospel, thus making it a logical follow-up to *The Rhythm of the Saints*. It would be the third of his cross-cultural mixes.

While Simon had been working on *The Rhythm of the Saints*, he had been impressed by the work of the Caribbean poet Derek Walcott from St Lucia. He was a Nobel Prize winner with theatrical experience and Simon asked him if he would like to be involved. Starting in 1993 Simon spent many days at Walcott's home and they wrote over thirty songs for the show, as they wanted to explore many different angles. One song, 'Virgil', was from the point of view of a prison guard and Simon bought some gun magazines before he wrote the lyric.

They appreciated the main problem. How could they have a killer at the centre of the show, someone who couldn't possibly be sympathetic until he was redeemed? One possibility would be flashbacks, but they chose a curious route. Sal would be played at different ages by Latin American singer Marc Anthony and salsa star Rubén Blades. But how could an audience build any sympathy for a character if he kept morphing?

Simon enjoyed writing the musical but he hated securing the investment. Schmoozing wasn't for him but he had to do it and $7m was raised. When a backer pulled out, Simon increased his own investment to $2m but expenses escalated. The British stage designer Bob Crowley came up with some great ideas but the sets were way ahead of the budget and additional money had to be found. The final expenditure was $11m.

They chose a relatively new theatre, the Marquis, which had opened in 1986 with a short season by Shirley Bassey and could seat 1,500. Up to that point, the theatre had specialised in old-time musicals – *Me and My Girl*, *Man of La Mancha* and the baseball musical *Damn Yankees*, which marked the Broadway debut of Jerry Lewis.

If *The Capeman* was a hit, it could be in profit within six months. Simon had the veto for the cast and the creative team and he was to sack the first two directors. He then asked the choreographer Mark Morris, who had no Broadway experience, to direct. Hence, the three key figures – Simon, Walcott and Morris – had no first-hand experience of Broadway.

Simon determined that as these were his songs, he would record them and a cast album could follow later. The CD, *Songs from The Capeman*, was released in December 1997 and featured thirteen songs. Simon sang most of them and played several parts but he brought in three actors (Blades, Anthony and Ednita Nazario) in subsidiary roles. The result is confusing and anyone listening without the lyric sheet would be lost.

Individually, some songs are great, but on the whole they are narrative songs. Simon regarded 'Bernadette' as his best song since 'Graceland' and said it had been influenced by the Cleftones. It's very good but I prefer the fast and furious 'Quality' in which girls are discussing a teen idol. The mother's plea, 'Can I Forgive Him', takes us back to the folk songs that Simon was writing in the mid-60s. 'Trailways Bus' is about a journey through America, and the comparison with 'America' is inevitable.

The album had good reviews but the critics didn't see hit singles. If Simon had written a huge blockbuster ballad, it might have made a difference. On the other hand, it would have been out of character for someone to suddenly belt out a new 'Bridge Over Troubled Water', but that's the way musicals often are. Look at *West Side Story*, also set amongst the gangs of New York: is it really believable that they would have sung 'Tonight' and 'Somewhere' and that nobody spoke any bad language? Times had moved on but the language in *The Capeman* was as outlandish as gangsta rap and it wasn't right for Broadway musicals. In short, the show wasn't for coach parties and theatre groups.

The press was having a field day reporting on the production difficulties for *The Capeman*. Sid Bernstein, the promoter of the Beatles at Shea Stadium, was often in coffee shops around Broadway and he told me that the main problem was Simon's arrogance: highly experienced Broadway personalities were making suggestions and he was taking no notice. At one point, he held the entire production up for thirty minutes as he found the right spot to place a gourd player.

Simon wanted the show done his way and he overestimated his

power at the box office. He did consider joining the cast for a couple of the songs every night but that wasn't going to save the show and could make it look ridiculous. Simon said that he was taking 'a psychological beating, a gleeful pummelling' and he was defending his decisions at every opportunity. He told the press that this was not a happy 50s rock'n'roll musical like *Grease* or *Happy Days*.

To add to the problems, the victim's families objected to the deaths of their loved ones being used for entertainment. They could not be placated and in the previews and on opening night, the theatregoers had to walk through the protesters.

Opening on 29 January 1988, the *New York Times* said it was 'sadly inept' and that the music was 'a hopelessly confused drone'. Apparently, and I never knew this and find it hard to believe, theatregoers could buy tickets 'pending good reviews'. The reviews were bad and the New York papers had headlines like *The Capeman – Slip Slidin' Away*, so the attendances dropped to half full. *The Capeman* closed after sixty-nine performances on 28 March, which was not disastrous but nowhere near good enough. It had had four directors and the investors had lost $6.7m, a key investor being Paul himself. 'It was a privilege,' said Simon. 'I can afford it.' Although he never said so, I suspect that Simon saw this as his folk opera, his *Porgy and Bess*. Sorry, Paul, not even close.

The Aftermath

Sadly, *The Capeman* was not staged in the UK although a one-hour documentary, *The Roll of the Dice*, narrated by Michael Gambon, was shown on TV. The cast album never materialised. However, the original album has been enhanced with two superb bonus tracks. 'Born In Puerto Rico' is a new version of the song with an intense vocal from José Feliciano and 'Shoplifting Clothes' can be seen as the other side of the Coasters' doo-wop classic 'Shopping for Clothes'.

Two subsequent albums perhaps show the direction that Simon should have taken. The first was *New York Voices Sing the Songs of Paul Simon* (1997). His songs were reworked with considerable ingenuity into jazz arrangements. 'Me and Julio Down by the Schoolyard' was exceptional, with the group revelling in the many different rhythms and tempos. The misty 'I Do It for Your Love' featuring an accordion was very good.

In 1998 there was *The Paul Simon Album: Broadway Sings the Best of Paul Simon*. It was showy and brassy but illustrated how the songs could work for the big Broadway voices. In the midst of 'Kodachrome' and 'Homeward Bound', 'Bernadette' sounds fine. There is a hidden track on this CD – a rap version of '50 Ways to Leave Your Lover' and you'll be laughing as much as the girls are.

In 2010 *The Capeman* was produced in a new stripped-down form at the Public Theater in Central Park, New York. Derek Walcott was annoyed that much of his work had been cut but the *New York Times* gave it a good review.

In 2015 Ray Davies accepted an award for his Kinks musical, *Sunny Afternoon*, in the West End, astutely commenting that he had got it right the second time. The first time he had tried an original musical, which had flopped, but the new one with the old hits had become a West End favourite. Simon should have considered how his old songs could have been shoehorned into a show, now rather disparagingly called a jukebox musical. He would have discovered how a musical worked, probably netted a small fortune, and then decided the best way forward for *The Capeman*.

There has been no official Simon and Garfunkel musical yet but *The Simon and Garfunkel Story* has had success in London and in large regional theatres, especially when billed as part of the fiftieth anniversary celebration, whatever that might be. It toured large regional theatres in the UK early in 2016.

But for all that, Simon could have had a success with *The Capeman*. At the time, *The Capeman* was the most expensive musical to fail on Broadway but then came *Spider-Man* with music from U2. This had a disastrous time with major upsets in the production, but the theatre kept promoting it and eventually turned it around.

And here's the way to do it, my friends: here's the way to make millions. At the core of Simon and Garfunkel is this fascinating, troubled relationship between Simon and Garfunkel. Nearly all of Simon's songs on the *Bridge Over Troubled Water* album touch upon this. Therefore, you build the musical around the recreation of this album with a few flashbacks to Tom and Jerry and to Paul Simon on his own in London.

Of course there are fifty ways to find an audience and maybe a straightforward jukebox musical might work best. In *I Am a Rock Musical*, Simon could collaborate on new songs with Andrew Lloyd Webber: "Your words are too nice, Rice. Write me some gall, Paul."

CHAPTER 15

Simon and...

Roy Halee commented, '*The Capeman* was such a disaster that I thought Paul would be gone for a while but then before I knew it, he was back in the studio and out on the road with Bob Dylan.'

Paul Simon's ego was badly bruised after *The Capeman* had closed so dramatically. Maybe he had been hoping for a new life in the theatre but that was no longer possible. His new songs had not taken off with the public so what was there to do? The one sure-fire way to restore his bank balance and retain his popularity, the one thing he knew as well as the back of his hand, was to go on tour with his hits. He could have reached out to Garfunkel but that would have been too humiliating.

Simon did like the idea of a double-top though and, starting in June 1999, he and Bob Dylan toured North America together for thirty-eight high-priced concerts at large arenas. The tour was called Still Cranky After All These Years – sorry, I made that up. They alternated as to who would open and who would close, and they usually did four songs together 'The Sound of Silence', Dylan's 'Knockin' On Heaven's Door', and a rockabilly medley of 'I Walk the Line' and 'Blue Moon of Kentucky'. They tried 'Forever Young' once and dropped it and they sometimes sang 'That'll Be the Day' and 'The Wanderer' in a medley. For the second leg of the tour in September, they began with 'The Boxer'. One of the shows was Dylan's homecoming in Hibbing, Minnesota with a Ferris wheel behind them and 30,000 fans in front.

At the Hollywood Bowl, Simon opened with 'Bridge Over Troubled Water' but his only other song from the 60s was 'Mrs Robinson'. He introduced 'Trailways Bus' by saying, 'Here's a song from *The Capeman*, sometime referred to as *The Ill-Fated Capeman*.' The set was perfectly prepared and performed, but he allowed himself some scat singing on 'Diamonds on the Soles of Her Shoes'.

Dylan was mostly leaning towards the 60s, although often nobody knew what he was singing. The sign language interpreter at the Hollywood Bowl concert had a difficult job, but did the deaf people at Bob Dylan concerts in fact enjoy it more than the people who could hear?

The double bill with Bob Dylan came as a surprise because the general feeling was that Dylan and Simon had no time for each other. In terms of sales, Simon was the major success but in terms of credibility, Dylan was way out in front. It would have been ridiculous if Lennon had sung, 'I don't believe in Paul Simon.'

It's a question of perception. Dylan has a remarkable image – nobody really knows what he thinks and his song are seen as the antithesis of the Brill Building, that is, his songs are written with real passion and commitment. Simon is seen as someone who labours over his songs so long that the passion has been drained out of them. Although that is true of their approach to songwriting, there is no reason why a carefully polished song shouldn't retain its initial spirit, possibly even more so because the songwriter has such faith in it.

As it happens, Dylan is far more sociable than the press suggests, often working with other performers (Baez, Cash, Harrison, McGuinn, Costello and the Traveling Wilburys, for starters) but somehow retaining that reclusive image. Simon was less inclined to work with others as he demanded full rehearsals, but he definitely wanted to replenish his funds after *The Capeman*. There were no reports of rows or tensions between them and, to everyone's surprise, they got on well.

Apart from bootlegs, there was no live album following these concerts but both artists had released enough of them anyway. Simon did contribute to a charity album for the Rainforest Foundation, *Carnival*. He sang a new song, 'Ten Years', to praise the foundation which had been set up by Sting and his wife Trudie Styler some ten years earlier. Simon put in the sleeve note, 'I believe there is an urgent need for us all to do our utmost to look after our planet, for the sake of our children and our children's children. Time is running out.'

Although it was written for a specific purpose, 'Ten Years' is an exceptionally good song, which has been overlooked, not least by Simon himself. Maybe he thought it wouldn't work out of context but the same could be said of songs from *The Capeman*. The album is a little gem, also including Rubén Blades' own song 'No Voy a Dejarte Arder (I Will Not Let You Burn)', and James Taylor's 'I Bought Me a Cat' with the San Diego Symphony orchestra.

Simon came slowly to appreciate Sting's music. 'At first there was a little too much fashion in the Police for me. It was distracting, although I accept that good haircuts are fairly important for No. 1s.'

If I owned a record label and had limitless money, I would have invited some great, socially aware songwriters (Bob Dylan, Paul Simon, Joni Mitchell, Elvis Costello, Tom Waits, Ian Dury, Jarvis Cocker) to contribute songs for the new century. Nobody asked them and none of the artists did that individually. Still, why should they? When Britain's greatest living playwright, Harold Pinter, was asked to comment on the year 2000, he said, 'I have no millennium message to give to the fucking world.'

In 2000 Paul Simon's main activity was touring. He had become a relaxed and mature performer, confident that he had a very strong catalogue and that the audience loved the songs.

Art Garfunkel was enjoying family life so much that he even agreed to an 'at home' feature for *OK!* magazine. He sang a fine composition, 'If I Ever Say I'm Over You' with the theatre composer John Bucchino on piano for the album *Grateful – The Songs of John Bucchino*. He also sang 'Grateful' itself for a children's book and CD put together by Julie Andrews. He sang 'Morning Has Broken' with Diana Krall as guests of the Chieftains. He performed 'America the Beautiful' for his baseball team, the Philadelphia Phillies.

After punishing reviews for *The Capeman*, Simon was wary about throwing himself into the critical arena again, but he continued writing. He told the music journalist Bill Flanagan that he was writing every day. He might discard what he wrote but he wanted to keep the creativity flowing. Not many major songwriters thought this way and it is an extension of what he witnessed in the early 60s around the Brill Building.

The next Paul Simon album, *You're the One*, was recorded at the Hit Factory in New York City and with familiar musicians: Vincent Nguini (guitar), Bakithi Kumalo (bass) and Steve Gadd (drums). They laid down instrumental tracks and then Simon wrote his lyrics. The music was stylish and beautiful, rock music with African overtones and if Simon had not written any words, it could have been marketed as a New Age album.

By now Simon had a settled life with a new baby, but the contentment of family life is not apparent from his songs, and his cynicism is at variance with the New Age concept. He had retained his conversational singing style, first seen in *Graceland* and throughout *The Capeman*. Once again, he was singing more subtle melodies and not going for the big notes.

Half the songs had been completed before touring with Dylan and the album was finished at the start of 2000, being released in September. There was some unexpected publicity, though not really wanted, when Karen Schoemer, the rock critic of *US Weekly*, resigned because her editor, Jann Wenner (a friend of Simon's), refused to publish a poor review. She told the *New York Post*, 'I felt like I wasn't free to say what I thought. I'm not a publicist and I'm not paid to promote records.'

'You're the One' is a realistic love song from Paul Simon but with a surprisingly banal title. The song goes into several different rhythms, so it could never be a dance hit. The opening section with the reference to 'a waste of angels' is reminiscent of the 'Third World' line in 'You Can Call Me Al'.

Buddy Holly's rhythms are at the centre of 'Old' and the singer is namechecked. However, the song is not about Simon himself as he was not twelve when he first heard 'Peggy Sue', more like sixteen. It's an amusing song in that being old is nothing compared to the age of the universe, which is hardly an original thought. 'Look At That' includes a reference to the Marcels' 'Blue Moon'.

The best song is his narrative 'Darling Lorraine'. Frank from New York meets Lorraine and Paul Simon takes us through their relationship. It is often funny – 'What? You don't like the way I chew' – but it ends with her death.

'Señorita With a Necklace of Tears' is a song about writing a song and it would have been better if he had written a song about a señorita with a necklace of tears as that sounds a winning combination, like 'Diamonds on the Soles of her Shoes'. As it stands, it is a noodling composition with some good passages.

Mark Stewart added pedal steel and dobro to 'Pigs, Sheep and Wolves', which gives it a bluesy country feel. It starts as a children's story but it's hard to predict where this song is going and even harder to care. Even odder is 'Hurricane Eye' which ends with Paul Simon rewriting 'There Was an Old Woman Who Lived in a Shoe'. I don't mind someone being surreal but these songs seem pointless.

There is a good song, 'Love', about being grateful for what we have and the album ends with the contemplative 'Quiet' featuring organ, harp and a vintage Spanish instrument, a vihuela. The song is contemplating death and so is an appropriate closer.

You're the One was a good album but I was never drawn to it. It seems slight in comparison to *Rhymin' Simon*, *Still Crazy* or *Graceland*.

To give Simon some street cred, extracts from 'Diamonds on the Soles of her Shoes' were included in some dance remixes of Missy Elliott's 'Work It'.

Simon said that he would continue to tour, using the same musicians and doing some lesser-known songs. I caught the tour at the Summer Pops in Liverpool in July 2002. Top marks for Paul Simon, but very few for the audience. Close to me, a lady turned to a couple and said, 'I am not going to listen to you two arguing all night.' She called the security guards who evicted the bickering pair, ironically when Paul Simon was singing 'The Sound of Silence'. I wish they had removed the girls in front of me too, but I am too docile to complain. During the evening they went back and forth to the bar at least six times, were totally bladdered and one of them was constantly calling 'Paul, it's my birthday' as if this occasion would hold some significance for him. Keeping the bars open while performers are on stage is not a good idea, but it has now become standard practice.

The opening act, Menlo Park, was a hybrid band – Jagger/Bowie movements from the lead singer, Chris Taylor, and alt country, rock and Lee Hazlewood influences in the songs. They sounded interesting but it was hard to make out the lyrics, which were often about sexual perversions. One of the musicians was Harper Simon, who returned at the end of his father's set. Their biggest applause was for saying, 'Paul Simon's on next'.

Paul Simon presented a two-hour show with his twelve-piece band and said little. He introduced the musicians from time to time and said 'Thank you', but his only acknowledgement of Liverpool was, 'It's a long time since I've been here. This one is for you guys', before singing 'Homeward Bound'. He opened, quite surprisingly, with 'Bridge Over Troubled Water' and he didn't sing the final line, thereby avoiding the top notes.

I loved the smoky verses to '50 Ways to Leave Your Lover', the slow 'Slip Slidin' Away', the rhythms of 'Late In the Evening' and the various *Graceland* tracks including 'You Can Call Me Al'. The set moved very swiftly along and featured much of *You're the One*, indicating that this was the end of the tour to promote his last album. I thought he wasn't going to do many Simon & Garfunkel songs but then we had

'The Sound of Silence', 'Homeward Bound', 'I Am a Rock' and 'The Boxer' in quick succession. Among the songs he didn't perform were 'A Hazy Shade of Winter', 'America', 'Mother and Child Reunion' and 'Kodachrome'.

Without having to do anything, Simon & Garfunkel's past was brought into the present with the West End productions of *The Graduate*, written and directed by Terry Johnson. I saw it at a London matinée in 2001 and I was a little disappointed. Mind you, I saw a very unlikely performance. The actor playing Mr Robinson had an accident during the first half and he was replaced by another actor for the second, who in turn was replaced by somebody else. I reckon I have seen the only performance of *The Graduate* with three Mr Robinsons.

That was unfortunate and my main gripe was that the music was only used in snippets for scene changing, whereas it was such an integral part of the film. David Nicolle was fine as Benjamin Braddock but he was playing him more like Woody Allen than Dustin Hoffman. Linda Gray, who played Sue Ellen in *Dallas*, was a very good Mrs Robinson. Other Mrs Robinsons have been Kathleen Turner, Amanda Donohoe and Jerry Hall. The theatre was half full but the production was closing soon and going to Broadway with Kathleen Turner. The Broadway production ran for 400 performances and so was more to audiences' tastes than *The Capeman*.

It looked as though Simon had joined Garfunkel in making new albums that suffered from diminishing returns. Then something unexpected happened. In 2002 Garfunkel made the best solo album of his career, and what's more, he wrote half the songs. Well, let's not overdo this – he wrote one third of one half of the songs, but it was still a considerable achievement. After his book of poems, *Still Water*, he had moved onto songwriting, and autobiographical songs at that. 'Wishbone' contained specific references to Laurie Bird.

Art Garfunkel's album, *Everything Waits to Be Noticed* (Do you sense a message in the title?) was far superior to Paul Simon's *You're the One* and possibly the only thing that stopped it being a big seller was Art Garfunkel, as he had become unfashionable.

Billy Mann, Art's producer, had put him in touch with the Nashville songwriter Buddy Mondlock and the Los Angeles songwriter Maia Sharp, who were both fine singers and musicians. The result was a tremendous album of original songs with excellent harmonies, containing shades of Fleetwood Mac, the Mamas & the Papas, Manhattan Transfer and, naturally, Simon & Garfunkel, but with enough originality of its own. The arrangements are well thought out with the cellos and violins in 'Crossing Lines', which has some sudden, surprising chords like 'The Boxer'.

Jann Wenner's sleeve notes were over the top, but not too much. The opening track 'Bounce', written by Graham Lyle and Billy Mann, was both a fine opener and a good indication of what was to come as the harmonies bounce back and forth. It is a mixture of pop, jazz and choral singing.

The title song finds the G (as Jann Wenner calls him) sounding like Paul Simon, a bit like the way McCartney sounded like Lennon on 'Let Me Roll It'. He said of this song, 'It started as a poem when I was up all night with Paul and Beverley Martyn. We were maybe a little stoned, and in St James's Park, we saw 28 geese take off over the pond as if they had waited for us to notice. It was such a nice high.' It is a fine track and another one, 'The Kid', has shades of 'April Come She Will'.

The only cover on the album is 'Every Now and Then', a song that Buddy Mondlock had written with Garth Brooks for Garth's 1992 album, *The Chase*. Considering that Garth sold millions of copies of *The Chase*, it was an unnecessary song for Garfunkel to sing, but why not? It was Buddy's most successful composition.

The trio did concerts to promote the album and I caught them at the Philharmonic Hall in Liverpool. Buddy Mondlock did four songs but it was difficult to catch all the words. One song had been recorded by Nanci Griffith and he ended with the excellent 'No Choice'. Maia Sharp played keyboards, guitar and something that looked like a cross between a clarinet and a saxophone and again did four songs. She was most impressive, or rather would have been, if we had not suffered from some deafening percussion, which distorted the balance.

Art Garfunkel, dressed in blue shirt, blue jeans and black shoes, did eighteen songs – six from the Simon & Garfunkel days, four from his solo career, one from Paul Simon's ('American Tune') and five from the new album, plus a lovely version of Jesse Belvin's 'Goodnight, My Love' to end, followed by the repetition of 'War is not the answer' from 'What's Going On' by Marvin Gaye.

In view of America's foreign policy, he had apologised for being American. The audience was very responsive, especially when Paul Simon's name was mentioned, and for once at least, he was very favourably disposed towards him. At the Grammys, Simon had called him 'my past and perhaps future partner'.

In Nick Hornby mode, Art said that his favourite American songwriters were Bob Dylan, Randy Newman, James Taylor, Paul Simon and the best writer of romantic ballads, Jimmy Webb. He then sang 'All I Know'. He described how touchy Paul could be and said that Paul didn't care for 'Jesus loves you much more than you knew, woo, woo, woo' in "Mrs Robinson".' There was 'The Sound of Silence', 'Bridge Over Troubled Water' and 'If I Could', but I could have done without the long drum solo in 'Cecilia'. 'Kathy's Song' was a lesser-known choice and a very good one. Garfunkel did his No. 1's 'I Only Have Eyes for You' and 'Bright Eyes', and the songs from *Everything Wants to be Noticed* were presented excellently. He read the poems that inspired two of them, 'Perfect Moment' and 'The Thread', which are about life along Park Avenue. He came across as a very warm performer, which surprised me because I thought he would be aloof. Not a mention of his walk across Europe though.

CHAPTER 16

Surprises

Paul Simon was in a dilemma, feeling an old man in a young man's world. He said, 'In 2001, two things made me stop and ponder before I could write songs again: 9/11 and my sixtieth birthday. They both made me think, "What do you have to do now that needs to be said?"' He did not want to be an oldies act, simply doing reunions with Garfunkel. As he remarked, 'You can stay fixed in your timeframe like Fats Domino and Chuck Berry or you can be inventive to the end like Miles Davis and that's what I'm holding myself up to.'

But Simon felt that a harsh inner voice was preventing him from working. A psychiatrist told him to imagine the voice was comic and it would go away. Then you could put it under your shoe. This advice crops up in 'Sure Don't Feel Like Love' on his album *Surprise*. I'm English so I'm cynical. Randy Newman said that Simon was as much a critic as a songwriter which caused him to reject most of his own output. Better, he thought, to be simply a songwriter and let others judge. That sounds more like the root of the problem.

From time to time, Simon met and worked with Paul McCartney although they have never played on each other's records. In June 2001 both artists appeared at the Adopt-a-Minefield Gala at the Regent Beverly Wilshire Hotel in Los Angeles. After a set from Paul Simon, the host Jay Leno asked, 'Is the lad from Liverpool here yet?' McCartney performed his set and as a finale Simon joined him on stage for 'I've Just Seen a Face'.

In 2005 Paul McCartney rang the other Paul on his birthday to sing 'When I'm Sixty-Four' – yes, tacky but he couldn't resist it. In 2010 Paul Simon sang John Lennon's 'Hold On' at a tribute concert in Brooklyn.

Every year the Kennedy Center honours those who excel in the performing arts and Paul Simon was an honouree in 2002 with President George W. Bush in attendance. The opening speech by

Steve Martin was, and still is, hilarious. Instead of praising Simon, he has fun at his expense: his partnership with Garfunkel 'ended in an acrimonious split' and that with Sony Records 'ended in an acrimonious split'. Martin says that he has been friends with Simon for twenty-five years but that is ending tonight. It is very rare to see Simon laughing heartily in public, but he looks rather concerned when the music gets going, no doubt wishing he had a say in it. Alicia Keys destroys 'Bridge Over Troubled Water' with her histrionics; James Taylor and Alison Krauss should have worked out their harmonies for 'The Boxer' and John Mellencamp chose to combine 'Graceland' with 'Mrs Robinson'. Fortunately, the Dixie Hummingbirds are on hand for 'Loves Me Like A Rock'. President Bush told Paul Simon that he often listened to *Graceland* while he was jogging. You'd have thought that it might have improved Bush's decision making.

An offer from out of the blue inspired an excellent song. *The Wild Thornberrys* was a successful American TV cartoon series for Nickelodeon about a family coping with life in the wilds and it relayed messages about endangered species. It was made into a full-length feature, *The Wild Thornberrys Movie,* with familiar actors supplying the voices – Brenda Blethyn, Tim Curry, Rupert Everett. The soundtrack featured many leading world musicians including Sting, Peter Gabriel, Youssou N'Dour, Hugh Masekela and, naturally, Paul Simon. He wrote the beautiful and reassuring 'Father and Daughter'. The song fitted into the context of the film, especially with its *Graceland* accompaniment, but it was also about Paul's own relationship with his daughter, Lulu, who had been born in 1996.

The song was nominated for an Oscar in 2003 and Simon performed it at the ceremony. There were four other candidates: a new song, 'I Move On', for the film version of *Chicago*, 'Burn It Blue' from *Frida*; 'The Hands That Built America' by U2 from *Gangs of New York*; and 'Lose Yourself' by Eminem from his film, *8 Mile*. Although an unlikely Oscar song, 'Lose Yourself' was the winner.

Paul Simon made an exceptionally good video for the song, which included clips from the film. It was issued as a single and appeared on the soundtrack album and Simon must have liked it as three years later he included it on his next studio album, *Surprise.*

The speculation about Simon and Garfunkel getting back together was always news, but in Southport two lads saw a gap in the market and, with impressive wigs, launched themselves as The Sounds of Simon and

Garfunkel. I saw them a few times and enjoyed what they did. In 2004, I was even more impressed when I learnt they could get £3,000 for an appearance.

In 2002 Dustin Hoffman introduced Simon and Garfunkel at the Grammys where they received a lifetime achievement award. The acclaim was such that they decided to do some more concerts.

In 2004 Simon and Garfunkel were together for a reunion tour – their first tour together in twenty years. It was a golden and lucrative period for 60s bands to reform because their original fans were in their sixties with disposable income as their children had left home. They toured with the Everly Brothers, singing a couple of songs with them and allowing them a fifteen-minute spot, which was close to insulting them. It should have been something resembling equal time. To make matters worse, they sang their pastiche, 'Hey Schoolgirl' before they introduced them – the audience could have had another song from the real thing instead. But why were the Everlys on the bill? Were Simon and Garfunkel thinking, 'Well, if you think we argue, listen to these two.'

At one concert, Garfunkel referred to something that had gone wrong and Simon said, 'Wasn't my fault' to which Garfunkel retorted, 'I'm not touching this goldmine of comic material.'

The tickets were highly priced and Simon was now raking in the money from his catalogue. He owned the songs through Paul Simon Music but in 2004 he made a deal with Universal, who would look for suitable uses in films, TV and, most lucrative of all, commercials.

Simon met the experimental musician, Brian Eno, at a dinner party. Brian Peter George St John le Baptise de la Salle Eno, to give his splendid full name, had been a member of Roxy Music and he had provided electronic accompaniments for many musicians including David Bowie (*Low*), Talking Heads (*More Songs About Buildings and Food*) and U2 (*The Unforgettable Fire*). He had many albums of his own ambient electronica and they included *Here Come the Warm Jets* (1974) and *Music for Airports* (1978). Simon knew his work and wondered what he would make of his demos. He took some new songs to Eno's studio and he liked Eno's suggestions very much.

They made *Surprise* together and Eno is credited with 'sonic landscape', which introduced Simon to drum'n'bass. There are standard instruments as well as ambient electronica and 'Wartime Prayers' finds Eno adding his sounds alongside the Jessy Dixon Singers and Herbie

Hancock on piano. Simon and Eno wrote three tracks together including the meandering 'Another Galaxy', which sounds like part of a larger story and contains a great line about leaving home being the lesser crime.

On the album, Simon is reflecting on contemporary events, the meaning of faith and the importance of family life; he had a young family but his father had died in 1995 and his mother the following year. They are not protest songs as such, more sad reflections on the state of the world. 'How Can You Live In the Northeast?' is about religious factions and 'Wartime Prayers' about the invasion of Iraq: 'People hungry for the voice of God hear lunatics and liars.'

There is also humour amongst the barbed comments. In 'Outrageous', he says, 'It's outrageous to line your pockets off the misery of the poor' but then adds that it's outrageous that a rich man like himself should be complaining about this. The song ends with the line, 'Who's gonna love you when your looks are gone?'

It's back to religion for 'I Don't Believe' and he commented, 'I'm not religious at all. I agree with Richard Dawkins' suppositions about religion. I'm interested in God, but I'm not interested in religion as a path towards God. My interest in religion is that it doesn't annihilate me or my family.'

The title for the album came after Simon was amused by people saying, 'I can't believe this happened' or 'I can't believe this was so long ago'. He realised that we were continually being surprised hence *Surprise* for the album title. He had a pleasant surprise himself as it sold 30,000 copies in the first week of release in the US, although the sales fell away. The reviews were his best for some years, but the album was trying to be too smart and there was too much confusion in the lyrics. Contrast that with the clarity of the songs on *Bookends* or *Bridge Over Troubled Water.*

Simon did some dates to promote *Surprise* including some in the UK, where he met up with an old acquaintance. 'Paul Simon phoned me,' said Martin Carthy, 'and said he was doing three gigs at Hammersmith Apollo and did I fancy coming along. I could only make the last one and so I went and hung around until I could get a message through. People like Paul Simon and Bob Dylan assume that if they say, "Come down", everyone will say, "Gosh, it's Martin Carthy, let him in", but the reality is that you wait around for hours. I didn't mind and when I saw him, he said, "Would you like to do something with me?" It was

"Scarborough Fair" and he had Steve Gadd on drums, who is Dave Swarbrick's favourite drummer and so I was able to go back to Swarb and brag about it. It was great thing to have done that and Paul asked me if I was mad at him. I said, "Yes, I was but it was very stupid of me." I had just taught him something, hooray! That was how we were all learning things back them. We all learnt from Davey Graham. He is the one everybody has fed off for years.'

Since rock'n'roll began in the mid-50s, the performers of the day have dipped into the so-called Great American Songbook. Elvis Presley sang 'Blue Moon; Gene Vincent 'Over the Rainbow'; Little Richard 'Baby Face'; the Marcels 'Blue Moon'; Frank Ifield 'I Remember You'; Gerry & the Pacemakers 'You'll Never Walk Alone'; the Platters and Bryan Ferry 'Smoke Gets in Your Eyes', and hundreds more. Occasionally a contemporary artist released a whole album of standards, a famous example being Nilsson's *A Little Touch of Schmilsson in the Night*, a million-selling LP from 1973 with Frank Sinatra's arranger Gordon Jenkins.

In 2002 Rod Stewart upped the game by recording *It Had to Be You*, and it was so successful that it led to four more albums plus a Christmas one. Art heard Rod's first album and probably thought, 'I can do that and I know the man to produce me – Richard Perry.' At the same time, Richard Perry heard Rod's album and thought he could make one with Art. He had made *Breakaway* with Art in 1975, which had included 'I Only Have Eyes for You'.

Some Enchanted Evening (2007) is a good MOR album but Garfunkel is subdued, perhaps for romantic effect. The title song from *South Pacific* is normally belted out but Garfunkel takes it gently. The individual tracks work fine, but overall it needed more variety and energy to show that this is indeed an album by Art Garfunkel. In the notes, he acknowledges his debt to Chet Baker and Johnny Mathis.

Many of the great composers are represented including Harold Arlen ('Let's Fall in Love'), George Gershwin ('Someone to Watch Over Me' where Garfunkel sings 'handsome' instead of 'pretty' and loses the rhyme) and Irving Berlin's 'What'll I Do'. With the harmonica solo, there is nod to Frank Ifield in Johnny Mercer's 'I Remember You'. There is 'If I Loved You' from *Carousel* and 'I've Grown Accustomed to Her Face' from *My Fair Lady*. It is good to hear 'Life Is But a Dream' without the usual doo-wop accoutrements. Best of all are the two Latin arrangements, 'Quiet Night of Quiet Stars and 'You Stepped Out of a Dream'.

In 2008 Paul Simon starred alongside Crowded House and Joe Bonamassa at the Cornbury Musical Festival in Oxfordshire. In February 2009, Garfunkel was a surprise guest when Simon reopened the Beacon Theatre in New York and they sang 'Old Friends', 'The Sound of Silence' and 'The Boxer'. In October 2009 Simon joined David Crosby and Graham Nash at a concert for the Rock and Roll Hall of Fame where they sang 'Here Comes the Sun'.

In March 2010 Simon & Garfunkel announced a tour of the USA and Canada but the tour was cancelled in June because Garfunkel had a vocal cord paresis. Garfunkel stopped smoking but it took him over a year to recover his voice. Nevertheless, he enjoyed his time at home as he raised his two sons, James and Beau Daniel.

Surprisingly, he didn't use the time to write his autobiography, which had been talked about for years. A solo tour was announced but several dates had to be cancelled as his voice wasn't ready and he resumed touring in 2014, often with Tab Laven on acoustic guitar. He joined the so-called Black Simon & Garfunkel on *The Tonight Show* for 'Can't Feel My Face'.

In 2011/2, Paul Simon set about celebrating the twenty-fifth anniversary of *Graceland* with arena shows featuring twetnty-four supporting musicians and singers including Vincent Nguini and Bakithi Kumalo. A commemorative issue of *Graceland* was released and there was a documentary film, *Under African Skies*, made by Joe Berlinger.

A double CD of Simon's successes called *Songwriter* was issued in 2011 with thirty-two tracks, 140 minutes playing time, and a sleeve note from the painter Chuck Close. Simon sang the songs except for 'Bridge Over Troubled Water', which came from Aretha Franklin. Simon said that the song had fulfilled its destiny as she had treated it like a gospel hymn. He admired Johnny Cash's treatment, which was one of his final recordings. Said Simon, 'He didn't feel he was up to it but the fragility of his voice brings something extremely powerful.'

The CD may be in its final days but the reissues continue. In 2013 there was *The Complete Albums Collection,* but with same bonus tracks as the remastered CDs, and then the cut-down *Original Album Classics: Paul Simon,* which was five albums in a pack with bonus tracks.

In 2011 there was a new Paul Simon album, *So Beautiful or So What,* which marked a return to his original method of songwriting, and was produced with Phil Ramone. He would work out songs on his guitar and then bring in the musicians. Not that the songs themselves sounded too much like his earlier ones. He said that his prime influences were 1950s rock'n'roll and African music, and when he spoke to students in Florida, he said, 'Forty per cent of my music is based on "Mystery Train".' He had decided to make his album without bass as there was no bass on Bo Diddley's records. He used Vincent Nguini's guitar throughout and had Indian percussion.

The title song combines Miles Davis' title, 'So What' with a Bo Diddley-styled rhythm. Simon is cooking a chicken gumbo and telling his children a bedtime story but he wonders what life is all about – is he just a raindrop in a bucket? There's not much melody but it is an infectious groove. Following his tour with Bob Dylan, he realised that Bob's old bluesman voice would be ideal for a couple of verses. They shared the same manager, Jeff Kramer, which made negotiations easy. Bob agreed but didn't get round to it.

The songs were about his preoccupations – the meaning of life, the fact that he was going to die, the nature of God – but at the end of the day, his message was probably no deeper than a disco record: life is what you make it.

Bizarrely, and probably uniquely, Simon opened his album with a seasonal song, 'Getting Ready for Christmas Day'. Simon had found a wartime sermon from the Reverend J. M. Gates dating from 1941 on the *Goodbye, Babylon* box set. He samples this during the song and relates it to soldiers fighting in Iraq.

'The Afterlife' is a comic look at what happens when we die. Simon is waiting to receive attention but 'You gotta fill out a form first'. When he finally reaches God, all he can say is 'Be-bop-a-lula', which is akin to the secret of the universe in *The Hitchhiker's Guide to the Galaxy*. Simon's love for 50s rockabilly is in 'Love and Blessings', while the theme of 'The Afterlife' can be twinned with 'Love and Hard Times' in which God and Jesus revisit Earth but don't stay as they have further work to do. The song then turns into a love song for Edie.

Paul evolved another love song to Edie, 'Dazzling Blue', as he was driving from New York City to his home in New Canaan, Connecticut. It is a love song but, being Paul Simon, it posed the question 'What is love?' The title refers to Edie's favourite colour and the track has a great rhythm.

An old guy who saw action in Vietnam is working at the carwash in 'Rewrite', but his main interest is in finishing his screenplay. He is eliminating family trauma and substituting car chases and how the main character saves his children. Simon includes wildebeest sounds, which were recorded on a family holiday.

'Love Is Eternal Sacred Light' is a history of creation from the Big Bang to the final Big Bang ('the bomb in the marketplace', which echoes 'the bomb in the baby carriage' in 'The Boy in the Bubble'). Simon sings, rather tellingly, 'Some folks don't get it when I'm joking / Well, maybe someday they will.'

There is more reflection on mankind in 'Questions for the Angels', wondering how important we are. Simon sees Jay Z advertising clothes and wonders if it has all gone too far. If all human life were to disappear, would a zebra grazing in Africa miss us? As well as the nine songs, there is a folky instrumental, 'Amulet'. Simon hadn't intended it this way but he found the chords too complicated for lyrics.

When Paul Simon did a show with Diana Krall, he gave her an advance copy of his new CD. She took it home and played it to her husband, Elvis Costello. Elvis sent him a flattering email, which led to him writing the booklet note for the CD. Around the same time, Paul McCartney praised Simon's songwriting, saying that his lyrics had the economy, phrasing and rhythm of the best poetry.

In 2012 Simon issued a new 2CD/DVD set, *Live in New York City*, recorded at the 1,200 capacity in Webster Hall in Manhattan. It included some songs from *So Beautiful Or So What* but only two songs out of twenty relating to Simon & Garfunkel days – 'The Sound of Silence' and 'The Only Living Boy in New York'. In Memphis he added 'Mystery Train' and the instrumental 'Wheels' to the set list. The band played Bo Diddley's 'Pretty Thing' with drummer Jim Oblon singing and Paul Simon on harmonica. Another addition was 'Here Comes the Sun' and he would look upward with a 'Thank you, George'.

Edie Brickell was working as well, often writing songs with the comic actor and folk musician Steve Martin and recording with him. She occasionally appeared in concert with Paul Simon but usually to sing comic country songs such as 'You're the Reason Our Kids Are Ugly'. As it happens, they had three children – Adrian, Lulu and Gabriel.

Harper Simon meanwhile had suffered from depression and took drugs but he tried to keep his musical career on track. Edie made an album with Harper Simon as the Heavy Circles in 2008 as they had written several songs together and the additional musicians included Sean Lennon. The CD, simply called *The Heavy Circles,* was produced by Harper with Bryce Goggin and collected decent reviews.

In 2009 Harper released his first solo album, *Harper Simon*, again with Sean Lennon among the musicians and he had written 'Tennessee' with his father about his mother's background. Another song 'The Shine' was written with Carrie Fisher, and his dad then revised it. Musically and lyrically, the song has something of 'The Only Living Boy in New York' about it. Paul Simon plays on 'The Audit'.

The cover of the album was a series of sketches by Tracey Emin entitled *Get Ready for the Fuck of Your Life*. With a little push, this family could be up there with the Wainwrights. Indeed, in 2014, Paul and Edie were arrested by the police after a family argument. The matter was reported in the UK press, notably in a *Daily Mail* feature which contrasted Edie with his UK girlfriend of the 60s, Kathleen Chitty, who lived with her partner in a mountain village in Wales.

In 2012 the American resonator and lap steel guitarist Jerry Douglas made the highly acclaimed *Traveler* with some famous friends like Eric Clapton and Alison Krauss. The album was beautifully crafted and Douglas was joined by Mumford & Sons and Paul Simon for 'The Boxer'.

In 2013 Harper was back with *Division Street*, an album of all his own songs and with Benmont Tench on keyboards and Pete Thomas from the Attractions on drums. This was much more of a group setting, not unlike Talking Heads, but it wasn't as distinctive as *Harper Simon*. Harper's weekly talk show is on the internet and the links are on his website. He has yet to interview his father or his father's wives but TV doesn't get much worse than this. He is incompetent and the mistakes are retained. One guest, the screenwriter Buck Henry, seemed amazed that Harper even had a show, commenting, 'There's an animal escaped from the zoo up here.'

Simon had had an operation for carpal tunnel syndrome but he still had trouble with his hands and in playing the guitar, but he liked touring and he went out on a double-header with Sting. On their 2014 tour, Sting was performing 'Bridge Over Troubled Water' with Simon, much to Garfunkel's chagrin. O Sting, where is thy depth?

Meanwhile, Art Garfunkel was working with Jimmy Webb and he added his voice to the delicate 'Shattered' on Webb's 2013 album, *Still Within the Sound of My Voice*. Considering that Webb has been such a close friend of Garfunkel's it is surprising that he has come to songwriting rather late.

Art Garfunkel told *Rolling Stone*, 'Will I do another tour with Paul?

Well, that's quite doable. As far as this half is concerned, why not? But I've been in the same place for decades. This is where I was in 1971.' He then added, 'How can you walk away from this lucky place on top of the world, Paul? What's going on with you, you idiot? How could you let that go, jerk?'

In 2015 Garfunkel was on tour and played the Royal Albert Hall. He commented, 'I was once a little curly-haired boy and now I'm an old entertainer, but the heart is still young and the voice is back.' His son James joined him for an Everly Brothers song and at one stage Art looked into the wings and said, 'Come on out, Paul.'

In order to raise funds, the Lewisham and Greenwich NHS Choir combined 'Bridge Over Troubled Water' with Coldplay's similarly uplifting 'Fix You' for a charity single, 'A Bridge Over You' (eccentric title), for Christmas 2015. The pundits expected Justin Bieber to have the No. 1 but the Canadian star asked his fans to support the choir, who then had the Christmas No. 1, undoubtedly helped by a very touching video. It was a robust arrangement, being seventy-five per cent 'Bridge' and twenty-five per cent 'Fix You'. The good doctors and nurses had resuscitated 'Bridge Over Troubled Water'.

Also in 2015, the hard rock band Disturbed released their new album, *Immortalized,* which included a cover of 'The Sound of Silence'. The lead vocal by David Draiman was intense and angry, far harder than Simon & Garfunkel's original. It became the third single from the album and the video is heading for fifty million hits on YouTube, an astonishing achievement. Simon has said how much he enjoys the new version, which has given his song a new audience. Simon himself chose to perform 'The Sound Of Silence' at an event to mark the tenth anniversary of 9/11 rather than the requested 'Bridge Over Troubled Water'.

In April 2016 Art Garfunkel announced that a memoir incorporating his poetry would be published later in the year and it was clear from the extract that he is not settling for being the junior partner. As Simon was also working on a book with the noted Los Angeles music writer, Robert Kilburn, I wondered how the two very different musicians were going to view the same events. There were some similarities though, as they both supported Bernie Sanders for the Democratic nomination and allowed him to use 'America' as his campaign song. Sanders was the one who had the most to say about eliminating poverty in America.

As both Simon and Garfunkel would reach the age of seventy-five in 2016, it looked as though this could be a momentous year, but Paul Simon told *Rolling Stone* that he had had enough of his former partner and that they were no longer on speaking terms. There would be no more Simon & Garfunkel concerts but he has said that before. He said that audiences were coming to the concerts to hear 'You Can Call Me Al' rather than the Simon and Garfunkel hits, but I somehow doubt that.

You will have gathered from this book that the question is not 'When will Simon & Garfunkel reform?' but 'When will Simon & Garfunkel next reform?' Over the years, they have got together and split up several times.

One huge factor that is overlooked when bands reform is the split of the proceeds. It is highly unlikely that the income would be divided equally and, in this instance, Simon's management would argue that he is the one who can fill stadiums on his own and so his share of the take should be that much higher – possibly 70:30 and that is on top of songwriting royalties. Hence, the very event of a reunion is more likely to stoke the fire and make a problematic relationship even worse.

It is possible that either or both of Paul Simon's autobiography and Art Garfunkel's memoir could sour the water completely but, despite what Simon is currently saying, the good money is on a final reunion tour. Until the next one, that is, or until it is time for one of them to say, 'Hello darkness, my old friend'.

CHAPTER 17

The Fighter Still Remains

In 2015 Paul Simon had a new partner, the king of the white doo-wop singers, Dion from Dion and the Belmonts.

Paul Simon has said, 'Everybody's hometown has a big effect on their writing — the first things that you see and hear and love.' That obviously applies to Simon himself and it can be seen in Dion, who lives in Florida but is drawn back to his adolescence in the Bronx for his songs. The tattooed stud in his 1961 hit 'The Wanderer' was someone he envied from afar. Paul Simon and Dion knew each other well and Simon was delighted to be a temporary Belmont along with Lou Reed in 2009 when Dion performed 'A Teenager in Love' at the Rock and Roll Hall of Fame.

In 2015 Paul Simon got together with Dion for an homage to their home city, 'New York Is My Home'. Simon is largely doing back-up vocals although he does take the lead in the bridge. Their voices work extremely well together and the words are strong, with Dion nearing his vintage best when he sings about his girl in the Bronx. The video is entertaining with Dion, at the age of seventy-six, still looking good and ultra-cool, but Simon looks like Eric Burdon in need of a tailor.

Dion told me, 'Paul and I have been friends for a long time. When I wrote it, I saw it as a love song for the city of my birth. He's from Queens and I'm from the Bronx. We are both at home in New York and he is great with harmonies amongst his other gifts. He loved the song and we worked on it together. He put a unique, very distinctive touch to it.'

It is a great track, especially as they both have such recognisable voices. 'Yeah, and even his gift for the window dressings is very distinctive,' continued Dion. 'We had a good time and we did a video in Manhattan among the cobblestones.'

Dion also comments on Paul's generosity of spirit. 'I was at his apartment when there was a terrible downturn in this country, financially and economically, and Paul wanted to do something special for the city and he put together a great concert in Central Park and he did some charity work at Madison Square Garden and it was off the Richter Scale for me, it was, whoa, really touching New York with an empathetic hand.'

The song did well on download and became the title song for Dion's new album in 2016. Paul Simon used the track as one of five bonus cuts on his new album, *Stranger to Stranger*.

Meanwhile, Steve Martin and Edie Brickell released their second album, *So Familiar*, and they had also written a bluegrass musical, *Bright Star*, which was tested in various cities and moved to Broadway in March 2016. Edie must have been apprehensive after the mauling received by her husband's musical, *The Capeman*, but an Americana musical from two proven songwriters had potential and if Steve Martin doesn't know what works on stage, then who does? The reviews were mixed, the general feeling being that the plot was creaky but the music was good. Meanwhile, Paul's former wife, Carrie Fisher, was not only starring in the new *Star Wars* film but also featured on a UK postage stamp.

Simon was in the UK in April 2016 to announce *Stranger to Stranger*, which was being released in June, and to perform one of the tracks, 'Wristband', on the BBC programme, *Later... with Jools Holland*. It was an impressive performance, held together by Danny Thompson's double bass. Being Paul Simon, the lyric covered fronting a band, meeting St Peter at the Golden Gate, and world poverty as the children are born without wristbands. I was expecting a verse about being a hospital patient too but that never came.

We all know Jools Holland is a hopeless interviewer (deliberately so, I think) and the conversation didn't work well as Simon was hesitant on basic facts about his career, even asking if the Seekers were Australian. He seemed doddery – or perhaps suffering from jet lag – but he did make the interesting observation that 'everything was better in 1964'.

Fortunately, Simon was more coherent elsewhere. He said the new album was about 'getting you to hear something in a new way. It's about making music that sounds old and new at the same time; music with a sense of mystery.' He added that, 'Sound is the theme of this album as much as the subjects of the individual songs. If people get that, I'll be pleased. The right song at the right time can live for generations.'

The album was produced by Simon and Roy Halee and they were willing to experiment. Simon was intrigued by Harry Partch, a classical composer who devised instruments to fit his own tunings. Simon and Halee studied his devices at Montclair State University in New Jersey and used them for 'Insomniac's Lullaby'.

'Wristband' is a very good example of their approach to sound: it is doo-wop street harmonies with a touch of African rhythms, and yet it sounds completely new. Its inspiration surely stems from 2012 when Simon was a guest on the US show *Late Night with Jimmy Fallon*. He was backed by the cast of the hit musical *Stomp*, who clap and bang metal and plastic waste bins for a brilliant percussive sound. They provided the accompaniment for 'Cecilia' but it was unfortunate that he sang it with Fallon himself whose leaden vocals weighed it down. Nevertheless, it was an excellent invigorating sound.

Simon performed excellent versions of 'Wristband' and 'Duncan' on *A Prairie Home Companion* with the musicians including Chris Thile and Sarah Jarosz and these performances were included as bonus tracks on the album. Another bonus track was Simon's theme song for Louis CK's TV series *Horace and Pete*, but the lyric is little more than a fragment. Released at the same time, but not on the *Stranger* CD, was Simon performing 'The Boxer' with Joan Baez and Richard Thompson on Joan's 2CD/DVD set of the New York concert to celebrate her 75th birthday.

Stranger to Stranger's sound also involved the Italian electronic dance music artist Clap! Clap!, the project of Italian music producer, C. Crisci, and several flamenco musicians.

The new album seemed especially encouraging as Bob Dylan released at a new album at the same time, *Fallen Angels*. This contained no new material. Indeed, Bob was continuing his quest to record the Frank Sinatra songbook, but had he given up on writing songs?

Paul Simon went on an extensive US tour to promote *Stranger to Stranger*, which started at the New Orleans Jazz & Heritage Festival on 29 April and then went to the Beale Street Music Festival in Memphis, the Ryman Auditorium in Nashville, the Hollywood Bowl, the Greek Theater in Berkeley and ended in home territory at the Forest Hills Tennis Stadium on 1 July.

Simon has also spoken to students at Yale and other universities from time to time. His most interesting piece of advice is that you shouldn't bother with a song unless you can see yourself working on it six months from now. As his song said, everything is neatly planned.

So in June 2016, Paul Simon's new album, *Stranger to Stranger*, was released. I'd heard a few tracks beforehand, mostly the bonus cuts, but I hadn't heard them in context. When I first played it, I was impressed – very impressed. Naturally, I would have liked him to have written a great MOR ballad to show he could still do it, but 'Wristband' is ideal for those large arena events where everybody has to wear a wristband.

You can argue incidentally that the deluxe edition is effectively the regular one. This album became the No. 1 best-seller in the week of release with most people purchasing the deluxe edition (fifty-three minutes) over the standard (thirty-seven minutes), the difference in price being £2. The standard version was at No. 3 in Amazon's Top 100. Why didn't Concord simply release one edition of sixteen tracks and be done with it?

That hooded man Bob Dylan was recently seen at the back of a folk club and when asked what he was doing, he said, 'I'm learning'. Let's hope that he adopts the same attitude towards Paul Simon's album. It is remarkable creativity from someone who is well past retirement age. In terms of quality, I wouldn't put this album much below *Graceland,* and it was released, in the UK at any rate, with a similar amount of publicity, which shows that the record company had faith in it.

Stranger to Stranger contains more surprises that the Brian Eno collaboration *Surprise.* The pun in the title has to be deliberate. The album is produced by 'Paul Simon and his old partner, Roy Halee'. Halee, who was eighty-two at the time of release, was well up to the challenge, but note that odd billing – was it a snide dig at Garfunkel? There might be another dig too when he sings, 'Could you imagine us falling in love again?' in the title song; the phrase 'Can you imagine us' is in 'Old Friends'.

Simon is in excellent voice but is favouring the conversational delivery of recent years and he is playing acoustic or electric guitar on most cuts. The album opens with an eerie sound that he created on an Indian instrument, the gopichand, to add a gothic setting for 'The Werewolf'.

This time Simon was hooked on flamenco rhythms. He hadn't wanted to make a flamenco album but much of the percussion is derived from that music. Its influence is especially noticeable on 'The Riverbank' and there is flamenco dancing itself on 'Stranger to Stranger'.

Outside of live albums, I don't think I have heard an album with so much hand clapping. You don't need expensive instruments and it works especially well on 'The Riverbank'. The percussion from Clap! Clap! is featured on 'Wristband' and 'Street Angel', and as he had been introduced to this musician via a CD enjoyed by his son, Adrian, it will be interesting to watch Adrian's musical development. The CD booklet includes a photograph of Harry Partch's numbered chamber bowls which are played with mallets and they add a disturbing sound to 'Insomniac's Lullaby'. A regular drum kit is played by Jim Obion, a long-time friend currently in his road band.

The album, even with the bonus tracks, works as a continuous whole and I love the way that thoughts and sounds weave in and out. The short instrumental pieces – 'The Clock', 'In the Garden of Edie' and 'Guitar Piece 3' – may not stand up on their own but they enhance the feel of the album and give us a respite from often impenetrable lyrics. There is no way that this album could be viewed as easy listening.

The little reminders of the past work so well – the nod of the head to the Impressions' 'Amen' in 'Proof of Love'; the famous opening line of 'Stardust', 'Sometimes I wonder' in 'Horace and Pete'; the voices of the Golden Gate Quartet going backwards and forwards during 'Insomniac's Lullaby'. All this is brilliantly merged with contemporary sounds. Fairly recently, Paul McCartney worked with Kanye West but Macca's contribution was imperceptible; that would never happen with Simon, whose own voice never gets lost in what he is doing.

The lyrics are similarly hyper, as though he is a child with Attention Deficit Disorder and can't wait to get to the next thought. This has a disadvantage as Simon is not able to explore stories or characters. Although one of the bonus cuts, a concert version of 'Duncan', fits seamlessly into the album, it does have a character-based narrative and it makes me realise what we are missing. The same can be said of Dion's 'New York Is My Home', a sentiment Simon lovingly endorses, which closes the album. Note, incidentally, Dion's reference to insomnia – even his song addresses one of Simon's themes.

The scattergun effect is apparent from the start. The first verse of the first song is about a wife in Milwaukee who kills her husband with a sushi knife. What's it all about? Is this a genuine case and was Simon fascinated by the choice of murder weapon? It's intriguing, but Simon has moved on with the brilliant line, 'Most obits are mixed reviews'. He tells us that life is a lottery and most people lose – he has clearly won – and this is followed by an attack on the wealthy and the misuse of public funds. After all of this we are only halfway through the first track, which also tells us that the werewolf is coming.

Simon's most memorable line is 'Where have you gone, Joe

DiMaggio?' and here we have a song about a black baseball player, Cool Papa Bell of the St Louis Stars, who in the 1920s was considered the fastest man alive. A cigarette card for the centre fielder is reproduced in the CD booklet. Once again though, Simon veers from his subject matter and ends up musing on life itself.

Simon appears to have gone out of his way not to write awesome melodies on *Stranger to Stranger* but the rhythms are enticing and as long as you're not expecting another *Bridge Over Troubled Water*, this is a very satisfying album. There is a feeling that we are privy to the inner workings of Simon's mind, but even he is confused by his thoughts. 'Street Angel' harks back to his love of 'Earth Angel' and Simon is talking about writing his "rhymes for the universities". Two songs later, the street angel is 'In a Parade' and diagnosed as a schizophrenic. These lyrics should have come with an explanatory booklet.

Since he was a child, Paul Simon has suffered from nightmares, and as their frequency increased, Edie recommended John of God, a faith healer in Brazil who had helped her. He wasn't cured but the nightmares became less frequent. This had led to a song with a clever oxymoron in its title, 'Insomniac's Lullaby'.

The album is not mournful but 'The Riverbank' was inspired after Simon attended a meeting for wounded veterans in the Walter Reed National Military Medical Centre in Bethesda, Maryland and played at the funeral of a teacher who had been killed in a school shooting in New Town, Connecticut.

The reviews for *Stranger to Stranger* were exceptionally good. The critics enjoyed playing with Simon's previous song titles to come up with lines like 'Not hazy after all these years' and 'Still hungry after all these years'. No one seemed to appreciate that the original title, 'Still Crazy After All These Years', worked best. That line sums up Paul Simon, and judging by the final line of 'Cool Papa Bell', he is 'never gonna stop', but he can't talk now, he's in a parade.

Meanwhile, Art Garfunkel played extensive dates in 2016, coming to the UK for Hampton Court Palace and Glastonbury. He said on stage at Hampton Court, "I say some stupid things about him to the press from time-to-time but it's like a marriage, it waxes and it wanes." This, I suppose, gives us some insight into Mr Garfunkel's home life. He concluded, "This is my dear, dear friend whom I have known since I was eleven. He's enriched my life."

So, if there's to be a reunion, the ball is now in Simon's court.

Bibliography

Fisher, Carrie, *Wishful Drinking* (Simon & Schuster, 2008).

Humphries, Patrick, *The Boy in the Bubble* (New English Library, 1988).

Kingston, Victoria, *Simon and Garfunkel: The Definitive Biography* (Sidgwick & Jackson, 1996).

Leigh, Spencer, *Paul Simon – Now and Then* (Raven, 1973).

Luftig, Stacey (Ed.) *The Paul Simon Companion* (Omnibus Press, 1997).

Ramone, Phil, *Making Records: The Scenes Behind the Music* (Hyperion, 2007).

Simon, Paul, *Lyrics 1964–2008* (Simon & Schuster, 2008).

Zollo, Paul, *Songwriters on Songwriting* (Da Capo Press, 1997).

Discography

BEFORE SIMON & GARFUNKEL (1957–1963)
Singles

Hey Schoolgirl / Dancin' Wild – Tom & Jerry (US Big 613 & King 5167, 1957) (US 49)

True or False / Teenage Fool – True Taylor (Paul Simon) (US Big 614, 1958)

Our Song / Two Teenagers – Tom and Jerry (US Big 616, 1958)

That's My Story / Don't Say Goodbye – Tom and Jerry (US Big 618 & Hunt 319, 1958)

Baby Talk / Two Teenagers – Tom and Jerry (US Big 621, 1959)

Baby Talk – Tom and Jerry (US Bell 120, UK Gala 806, 1959) (US B-side I'm Gonna Get Married by Ronnie Lawrence: UK B-side Thank You Pretty Baby by Paul Sheldon) (Photograph of Tom and Jerry on Gala 45 is definitely not Simon and Garfunkel)

The Shape I'm In / Ya Ya – Johnny Restivo (Paul Simon, guitar) (US RCA 47-7559, UK RCA 1143, 1959) (US 80)

Lookin' at You / I'm Lonesome – Tom and Jerry (US Ember 1094 in 1959, UK Pye International 7N 25202 in 1963) (*Record Collector* values this UK single at £90.)

Loneliness / Annabelle – Jerry Landis (Paul Simon) (US MGM 12822, 1959)

Just to Be with You / Ask Me Why – Jerry Landis (US Chance 102, issued on both black and blue vinyl, 1959)

Beat Love / Dream Alone – Artie Garr (Art Garfunkel) (US Warwick 515, 1960)

Shy / Just A Boy – Jerry Landis (US Warwick 552, 1960)

All Through the Night / (I Begin) To Think Again of You – Mystics (Paul Simon: second tenor and arrangement on A-side; Paul Simon, harmony singing on B-side) (US Laurie 3047, 1960)

I'd Like to Be (The Lipstick on Your Lips) / Just A Boy – Jerry Landis (Paul Simon) (US Warwick 588, 1960)

Play Me a Sad Song / It Means a Lot to Them – Jerry Landis (US Warwick 619, 1961)

I Wish I Weren't in Love / I'm Lonely – Jerry Landis (US Canadian-American 130, 1961). (This is the rarest pre-S&G single: mint copies worth over £100.)

Motorcycle / I Don't Believe Them – Tico & the Triumphs (Paul Simon, lead singer) (US Madison 169 & Amy 835, 1961) (US 99)

Private World / Forgive Me – Artie Garr (Art Garfunkel) (US Octavia 8002, 1962)

Wildflower / Express Train – Tico & the Triumphs (Paul Simon, lead singer) (US Amy 845, 1962)

Get Up and Do the Wobble / Cry Little Boy Cry – Tico & the Triumphs (Paul Simon, lead singer) (US Amy 860, 1962)

Tick Tock / Please Don't Tell Her – Ritchie Cordell (Paul Simon, backing vocals) (US Rori 707, 1962)

Surrender, Please Surrender / Fightin' Mad – Tom and Jerry (US ABC-Paramount 45-10363, 1962) (Probably a different Tom and Jerry)

The Lone Teen Ranger / Lisa – Jerry Landis (Paul Simon) (US Amy 875, 1962) (US 97)

Cards of Love / Noise – Tico & the Triumphs (Paul Simon, lead singer) (US Amy 876, 1963)

I Wrote You a Letter / Play Me a Sad Song /– Dotty Daniels (US Amy 885, 1963) (B-side written by Paul and Eddie Simon: Paul Simon arranged and produced both sides)

That's My Story / Tijuana Blues – Tom and Jerry (US ABC-Paramount 10788, 1966: B-side not issued before)

In addition, there are around twenty demos of songs, often written by Paul Simon, which have appeared on subsequent CD releases:

Aeroplane of Silver Steel / An Angel Cries / Back Seat Driver / Bigger And Better Things / Bingo / A Charmed Life / A Different Kind of Love /

Dreams Can Come True / Educated Fool / Flame / Forever and After / A Frame Without a Picture / A Good Foundation for Love / I Want You in My Stocking / Just a Kid / Let's Make Pictures / Lighthouse Point (2 takes) / Make a Wish / North Wind / One Way Love / Rock'n'Roll Skaters' Waltz / Simon Says / Sleepy Sleepy Baby / That Forever Kind Of Love / That's How I Feel / Up and Down the Stairs / When You Come Back to School / Wow Cha Cha Cha

Although Simon & Garfunkel have performed 'Hey Schoolgirl' on stage, they have never authorised collections of these old recordings. They took legal action over *Simon and Garfunkel* (US Sears 435, UK Allegro 836, 1967), which led to it being withdrawn.

In 1993 two Italian CDs were released: *Tom & Jerry Their Greatest Hits, Vols 1 & 2,* each with twenty-two tracks. In 2012 Jasmine released *Two Teenagers,* a twenty-six-track CD (UK Jasmine JASCD 231) which is an exceptionally good attempt by Bob Fisher at resolving what was Simon, what was Garfunkel and what was somebody else.

Now, in 2016, all records issued prior to 1963 are out of copyright in the UK so any company can issue them.

THE SIMON & GARFUNKEL YEARS (1964–1970)

He Was My Brother / Carlos Dominguez – The Voice of Paul Kane (US) and Jerry Landis (UK) (Paul Simon) (US Tribute 128, UK Oriole CB 1930, 1964) (If you should see a copy with Paul Simon's name on the label – beware, it's a fake.)

Wednesday Morning 3am LP – Simon & Garfunkel (US Columbia 9049, 1964; UK CBS 63370, 1968) (US 30, 1968: UK 24, 1968)

You Can Tell the World / Last Night I Had the Strangest Dream / Bleecker Street / Sparrow / Benedictus / The Sound of Silence / He Was My Brother/ Peggy-O / Go Tell It on the Mountain / The Sun Is Burning / The Times They Are A-Changin' / Wednesday Morning 3am

The Paul Simon Songbook LP – Paul Simon (UK CBS 62579, 1965)

I Am a Rock / Leaves That Are Green / A Church Is Burning / April Come She Will / The Sound of Silence / Patterns / A Most Peculiar Man / He was My Brother / Kathy's Song / The Side of a Hill / A Simple Desultory Philippic (Or How I Was Lyndon Johnson'd into Submission) / Flowers Never Bend With the Rainfall

I Am a Rock / Leaves That Are Green – Paul Simon (UK CBS 201797)

Wednesday Morning 3am EP – Simon & Garfunkel (UK CBS EP 6053, 1965)

Bleecker Street / Sparrow / Wednesday Morning 3am / The Sound of Silence

The Sound of Silence / We're Got a Groovey Thing Goin' – Simon & Garfunkel (US Columbia 43396, UK CBS 202020, 1965) (US No. 1 for two weeks). Some US DJ copies have the electric 'Sounds' on one side and the acoustic on the other – a nice rarity.

Jackson C. Frank LP – Jackson C. Frank (UK Columbia 33X 1788, 1965)

Album and single (Blues Run the Game, Columbia DB 7795) produced by Simon. There have been various UK reissues, often with non-Simon related tracks but the whole of his output with Simon – fifteen tracks – is on the Castle CD CMRCD 366 issued in 2001.

I Am A Rock EP – Simon & Garfunkel (UK CBS EP 6074, 1966) (UK EP charts, No. 4)

I Am a Rock / Flowers Never Bend With the Rainfall / The Sound of Silence / Blessed

Homeward Bound / Leaves That Are Green – Simon & Garfunkel US Columbia 43511, UK CBS 202045, 19665) (US No. 5, UK No. 9)

Sounds Of Silence LP – Simon & Garfunkel (US Columbia 9269, UK CBS 62690, 1966) (US 21, UK 13)

The Sound of Silence / Leaves That Are Green / Blessed / Kathy's Song / Somewhere They Can't Find Me / Anji / Homeward Bound / Richard Cory / A Most Peculiar Man / April Come She Will / We've Got a Groovey Thing Goin' / I Am a Rock. (The US version of this LP does not include Homeward Bound.)

I Am a Rock / Flowers Never Bend With the Rainfall – Simon & Garfunkel (US Columbia 43617, UK CBS 202303, 1966) (US 3, UK 17)

The Dangling Conversation / The Big Bright Green Pleasure Machine – Simon & Garfunkel (US Columbia 43728, UK CBS 202285, 1966) (US 25)

Parsley, Sage, Rosemary and Thyme LP – Simon & Garfunkel (Columbia 9363, CBS 62860, 1966) (US 4, UK 13)

Scarborough Fair – Canticle / Patterns / Cloudy / The Big Bright Green Pleasure Machine / The 59th Street Bridge Song (Feelin' Groovy) / The

Dangling Conversation / Flowers Never Bend With the Rainfall / A Simple Desultory Philippic (Or How I Was Robert McNamara'd into Submission) / For Emily, Whenever I May Find Her / A Poem on the Underground Wall / Seven O'Clock News – Silent Night

A Hazy Shade of Winter / For Emily, Whenever I May Find Her – Simon & Garfunkel (US Columbia 43873, UK CBS 202378, 1966) (US 13)

At the Zoo / The 59th Street Bridge Song – Simon & Garfunkel (US Columbia 44046, UK CBS 202608, 1966 (US 16)

Feelin' Groovy EP – Simon & Garfunkel (UK CBS EP 6360, 1967)

The 59th Street Bridge Song (Feelin' Groovy) / The Big Bright Green Pleasure Machine / Homeward Bound / A Hazy Shade of Winter

Fakin' It / You Don't Know Where Your Interest Lies – Simon & Garfunkel (US Columbia 44232, UK CBS 2911, 1967) (US 23)

Scarborough Fair / April Come She Will – Simon & Garfunkel (US Columbia 44465, UK CBS 3317, 1968) (US 11)

Bookends LP – Simon & Garfunkel (US Columbia 9529, UK CBS 63101, 1968) (US No. 1 for seven weeks, UK No. 1 for six weeks)

Bookends Theme / Save the Life of My Child / America / Overs / Voices of Old People / Old Friends / Bookends Theme / Fakin' It / Punky's Dilemma / Mrs Robinson / A Hazy Shade of Winter / At the Zoo (Fakin' It is a remixed, slightly faster version of the single)

The Graduate LP – Simon & Garfunkel (US Columbia 3180, UK CBS 70042, 1968) (US No. 1 for nine weeks, UK No. 3)

Sounds of Silence (two versions) / Mrs Robinson (two versions) / Scarborough Fair – Canticle (two versions) / April Come She Will / The Big Bright Green Pleasure Machine. Neither version of Mrs Robinson is the hit version.

(Music composed and arranged by Dave Grusin) The Singleman's Party / Sunporch Cha-Cha-Cha / On the Strip / The Folks / The Great Effect / Whew

Mrs Robinson / Old Friends – Bookends Theme – Simon & Garfunkel (US Columbia 44511, UK CBS 3443, 1968) (US No. 1 for three weeks, UK No. 4)

Mrs Robinson EP – Simon & Garfunkel (UK CBS EP 6400, 1968) (UK singles chart No. 9) EPs were dropped from the singles charts from February 1969 and so the EP was only on the charts for five weeks.

Mrs Robinson / April Come She Will / Scarborough Fair – Canticle / Sounds of Silence

The Boxer / Baby Driver – Simon & Garfunkel (US Columbia 44785, UK CBS 4162, 1969) (US No. 7, UK No. 6)

The Live Adventures of Mike Bloomfield and Al Kooper 2LP (US CBS PG 6, UK CBS 66216, 1969) (US No. 18)

Simon joins them for an extended version of 'The 59th Street Bridge Song', which really is feelin' groovy.

Bridge Over Troubled Water LP – Simon & Garfunkel (US Columbia 9914, UK CBS 63699, 1970) (US No. 1 for ten weeks, UK No. 1 for thirty-five weeks)

Bridge Over Troubled Water / El Condor Pasa (If I Could) / Cecilia / Keep The Customer Satisfied / So Long, Frank Lloyd Wright / The Boxer / Baby Driver / The Only Living Boy in New York / Why Don't You Write Me / Bye Bye Love / Song for the Asking

Bridge Over Troubled Water / Keep the Customer Satisfied – Simon & Garfunkel (US Columbia 45079, UK CBS 4790, 1970) (US No. 1 for six weeks, UK No. 1 for three weeks)

Sounds of Silence / The 59th Street Bridge Song – Simon & Garfunkel (UK CBS 5172, 1970)

Cecilia / The Only Living Boy in New York – Simon & Garfunkel (US Columbia 45133, UK CBS 4916,) (US No. 4) UK catalogue number shows that this was held back.

El Condor Pasa (If I Could) / Why Don't You Write Me – Simon & Garfunkel (US Columbia 45237, 1970) (US No. 18)

THE SOLO YEARS (1971–2016)

Paul Simon LP – Paul Simon (US Columbia 30750, UK CBS 7964, 1972) (US No. 4, UK No. 1 for five weeks)

Mother and Child Reunion / Duncan / Everything Put Together Falls Apart / Run That Body Down / Armistice Day / Me and Julio Down by the Schoolyard / Peace Like a River / Papa Hobo / Hobo's Blues / Paranoia Blues / Congratulations

Mother and Child Reunion / Paranoia Blues – Paul Simon (Columbia 45547, CBS 7793, 1972) (US No. 4, UK No. 5)

Me and Julio Down by the Schoolyard / Congratulations – Paul Simon

(US Columbia 45585, UK CBS 7964, 1972) (US No. 22, UK No. 15)

Greatest Hits LP– Simon & Garfunkel (US Columbia 31350, UK CBS 69003, 1972) (US No. 5, UK No. 2)

Nine studio recordings together with five unreleased live performances – For Emily, Whenever I May Find Her / The 59th Street Bridge Song (Feelin' Groovy) / Homeward Bound / Bridge Over Troubled Water / Kathy's Song

America / For Emily, Whenever I May Find Her – Simon & Garfunkel US Columbia 45663, UK CBS 8336) (US No. 97, UK No. 25) Did as well on the US charts as The Lone Teen Ranger.

Mrs Robinson / Bookends Theme – Simon & Garfunkel (UK CBS Hall of Fame Series, CBS 1159, 1973)

There Goes Rhymin' Simon LP – Paul Simon (US Columbia 32280, UK CBS 69035, 1973) (US No. 2, UK No. 4)

Kodachrome / Tenderness / Take Me to the Mardi Gras / Something So Right / One Man's Ceiling Is Another Man's Floor / American Tune / Was a Sunny Day / Learn How to Fall / St Judy's Comet / Loves Me Like a Rock

Kodachrome / Take Me to the Mardi Gras – Paul Simon (US Columbia 45859, UK CBS 1578, 1973) (US No. 2 for Kodachrome, UK No. 7 for Mardi Gras)

Loves Me Like a Rock / Learn How to Fall – Paul Simon (US Columbia 45907, UK CBS 1700, 1973) (US No. 2, UK No. 39)

All I Know / Mary Was an Only Child – Art Garfunkel (US Columbia 45926, UK CBS 1777, 1973) (US No. 9) (The original US single was simply issued under the name 'Garfunkel')

Angel Clare LP – Art Garfunkel (US Columbia KC 31474, UK CBS 69021, 1973) (US No. 5, UK No. 14)

Traveling Boy / Down in the Willow Garden / I Shall Sing / Old Man / Feuilles-Oh / Do Space Men Pass Dead Souls on Their Way to the Moon / All I Know / Mary Was an Only Child / Woyaya / Barbara Allen / Another Lullaby

American Tune / One Man's Ceiling Is Another Man's Floor – Paul Simon (US Columbia 45900, UK CBS 1979, 1973) (US No. 35)

I Shall Sing / Feuilles-Oh – Art Garfunkel (US Columbia 45983, UK CBS 2013, 1974) (US No. 38)

Live Rhymin' LP – Paul Simon (US Columbia 32855, UK CBS 69059, 1974) (US No. 33)

Me and Julio Down by the Schoolyard / Homeward Bound / American Tune / El Condor Pasa (If I Could) / Duncan / The Boxer / Mother and Child Reunion / The Sound of Silence / Jesus is the Answer (Jessy Dixon Singers) / Bridge Over Troubled Water / Loves Me Like a Rock / America

The Sound of Silence / Mother and Child Reunion – Paul Simon (UK CBS 2349, 1974) From *Live Rhymin'* album

Second Avenue / Woyaya – Art Garfunkel (US Columbia 10020, UK CBS 2672, 1974) (US No. 34)

Traveling Boy / Old Man – Art Garfunkel (UK CBS 2318, 1974)

Something So Right / Tenderness – Paul Simon (UK CBS 2822, 1975)

Seductive Reasoning LP – Maggie & Terre Roche (US Columbia 33232) Simon produced and played guitar.

I Only Have Eyes for You / Lookin' for the Right One – Art Garfunkel (UK Columbia 10190, UK CBS 3575, 1975) (US No. 18, UK No. 1 for two weeks)

Gone At Last / Tenderness – Paul Simon (US Columbia 10197, UK CBS 3594, 1975) (US 23) A-side with Phoebe Snow

Breakaway LP – Art Garfunkel (US Columbia PC 33700, UK CBS 86002,) (US No. 7, UK No. 7)

I Believe (When I Fall in Love It Will Be Forever) / Rag Doll / Breakaway / Disney Girls / Waters of March / My Little Town (with Paul Simon) / I Only Have Eyes for You / Lookin' for the Right One / 99 Miles From LA / The Same Old Tears on a New Background

My Little Town (Simon & Garfunkel) / You're Kind (Paul Simon) / Rag Doll (Art Garfunkel) (US Columbia 10230, UK CBS 3712, 1975) (US No. 9)

Still Crazy After All These Years LP – Paul Simon (US Columbia 33540, UK CBS 86001, 1975) (US No. 1 for one week, UK No. 6)

Still Crazy After All These Years / My Little Town (with Art Garfunkel) / I'd Do It for Your Love / 50 Ways To Leave Your Lover / Night Game / Gone At Last (with Phoebe Snow) / Some Folks' Lives Roll Easy / Have a Good Time / You're Kind / Silent Eyes

50 Ways to Leave Your Lover / Some Folks' Lives Roll Easy – Paul Simon

(US Columbia 10270, CBS 3887, 1976) (US No. 1 for three weeks, UK No. 23)

In The Pocket LP – James Taylor (US Warner BS 2912, UK Warner K 56197, 1976)

Art adds harmonies to 'A Junkie's Lament'.

Still Crazy After All These Years / Silent Eyes – Paul Simon (US Columbia 10332, 1976) (US No. 40)

Breakaway / The Same Old Tears on a New Background – Art Garfunkel (US Columbia 10273, 1976) (US No. 39)

I Believe (When I Fall in Love It Will Be Forever) / Waters of March – Art Garfunkel (US, CBS 4348, 1976)

Sanborn – David Sanborn (US Warner BS 2957, UK Warner 925150 2, 1976)

Solo album from saxophonist includes new Simon song 'Smile' with vocals from Paul Simon and Phoebe Snow. Album produced by Phil Ramone.

We Are Going / Second Avenue – Art Garfunkel (CBS 4778, 1976)

Crying In My Sleep / Mr Shuck 'N' Jive – Art Garfunkel (CBS 5683, 1977)

Libby Titus LP (US Columbia 34152, 1977)

Four producers on this album (Phil Ramone, Paul Simon, Carly Simon and Robbie Robertson). Musicians include members of the Band and Libby was the partner of Levon Helm and, as it happens, mother of Amy. If seeking this album, be aware that there is a different album also called *Libby Titus*.

Greatest Hits, Etc LP – Paul Simon (US, Columbia 35032, UK CBS 10007, 1977) (US No. 18, UK No. 6)

Twelve previously issued tracks plus Slip Slidin' Away and Stranded in a Limousine.

Slip Slidin' Away / Something So Right – Paul Simon (US Columbia 10630, UK CBS 5770, 1977) (US No. 5, UK No. 36)

Watermark LP – Art Garfunkel (US Columbia JC 34975, UK CBS 86054, 1978) (US No. 19, UK No. 25)

Crying In My Sleep / Marionette / Shine It on Me / Watermark / Saturday Suit / All My Love's Laughter / (What a) Wonderful World (with James Taylor and Paul Simon) / Mr Shuck 'N' Jive / Paper Chase / She Moved

Through the Fair / Someone Else / Wooden Planes

Stranded in a Limousine / Have a Good Time – Paul Simon (UK CBS 6290, 1978)

Marionette / All My Love's Laughter – Art Garfunkel (UK CBS 6325)

(What A) Wonderful World / Wooden Planes – Art Garfunkel (with James Taylor and Paul Simon on A-side) (US Columbia 10676, 1978) (US No. 17)

Fate for Breakfast LP – Art Garfunkel (US Columbia JC 35780, UK CBS 86082, 1979) (UK No. 2)

In a Little While / Since I Don't Have You / And I Know / Sail On a Rainbow / Miss You Nights / Bright Eyes / Finally Found a Reason / Beyond the Tears / Oh How Happy / When Someone Doesn't Want You / Take Me Away

Bright Eyes / Keehar's Theme – Art Garfunkel (UK CBS 6947, 1979) (UK No. 1 for six weeks) (B side by Angela Morley)

Since I Don't Have You/ And I Know – Art Garfunkel (US Columbia 3-10999, UK CBS 7371, 1979) (US No. 53, UK No. 38)

One-Trick Pony LP – Paul Simon (US Warner 3472, UK Warner K 56846, 1980) (US No. 12, UK No. 17)

Late In the Evening / That's Why God Made the Movies / One-Trick Pony / How The Heart Approaches What It Yearns / Oh, Marion / Ace in the Hole / Nobody / Jonah / God Bless the Absentee / Long, Long Day

Late In the Evening / How the Heart Approaches What It Yearns – Paul Simon (US Warner 49511, UK Warner K 17666, 1980) (US No. 6, UK No. 58)

The Complete Collection (US TV-promoted 5LP set covering both solo and duo releases, 1980)

One-Trick Pony / Long, Long Day – Paul Simon (US Warner 49601, UK Warner K 17715, 1980) (US No. 40)

Oh, Marion / God Bless the Absentee – Paul Simon (US Warner 49675, UK Warner K17745, 1981)

The Simon and Garfunkel Collection LP (UK CBS 10029, 1981) (UK No. 4)

A Heart in New York / Is This Love – Art Garfunkel (US Columbia 18-0237, UK CBS 222861, 1981) (US No. 66)

Scissors Cut / So Easy to Begin – Art Garfunkel (US Columbia 4674, CBS A1708, 1981)

Scissors Cut LP – Art Garfunkel (US Columbia 37392, UK CBS 85259, 1981) (UK No. 51)

Scissors Cut / A Heart in New York / Up in the World / Hang On In / So Easy To Begin / Can't Turn My Heart Away / The French Waltz / The Romance / In Cars / That's All I've Got to Say / (US only) Bright Eyes instead of The Romance

The Concert In Central Park 2LP – Simon & Garfunkel (US Warner BSK 3654, UK Geffen GEF 96008, 1982 but recorded in New York on 19 September 1981) (US No. 6, UK No. 6)

Mrs Robinson / Homeward Bound / America / Me and Julio Down by the Schoolyard / Scarborough Fair / April Come She Will / Wake Up Little Susie / Still Crazy After All These Years / American Tune / Late In the Evening / Slip Slidin' Away / A Heart in New York / The Late Great Johnny Ace / Kodachrome – Maybelline / Bridge Over Troubled Water / 50 Ways To Leave Your Lover / The Boxer / Old Friends / The 59th Street Bridge Song (Feelin' Groovy) / The Sounds of Silence

Late In The Evening / Me and Julio Down By The Schoolyard (US Geffen GEFA 4298)

Mrs Robinson / Late In the Evening – Simon & Garfunkel (UK Geffen 2221, 1982)

Wake Up Little Susie / The Boxer – Simon & Garfunkel (US Warner 50053, UK Geffen GEF 2287, 1982) (US No. 27)

Hearts and Bones LP – Paul Simon (US Warner 23942, UK Warner K 92-3942-1, 1983) (US No. 35, UK No. 34)

Allergies / Hearts and Bones / When Numbers Get Serious / Think Too Much (b) / Song About the Moon / Think Too Much (a) / Train In the Distance / Rene and Georgette Magritte With Their Dog After the War / Cars Are Cars / The Late Great Johnny Ace

Allergies / Think Too Much – Paul Simon (US Warner 92 94537, UK Warner W 9453, 1983)

When Numbers Get Serious / The Late Great Johnny Ace – Paul Simon (UK Warner SAM 180, 1983)

Hearts and Bones / Think Too Much – Paul Simon (Warner SAM 186, 1983)

The Art Garfunkel Album LP (UK CBS 10046, 1984) (UK No. 12)

The first compilation of his solo work with some remixing.

Sometimes When I'm Dreaming / Scissors Cut – Art Garfunkel (CBS A4674, 1984)

We Are the World – USA For Africa (US Columbia 04839, UK CBS USAID 1, 1985) (US No. 1 for four weeks, UK No. 1 for two weeks)

Charity single for famine relief in Africa. Simon is the third soloist and part of the massed choir.

The Hunting of the Snark – Mike Batt & Cast (UK Adventure SNARK 1, 1986)

Art Garfunkel is the Butcher. His solo is As Long as the Moon Can Shine and he sings The Beaver's Lesson and A Delicate Combination with Deniece Williams, who is the Beaver. They both sing The Escapade with Julian Lennon, who is the Baker. The CD was reissued on Dramatico DRAM CD 0030 in 2010, the package including a DVD of the concert version at Royal Albert Hall, which did not involve Art Garfunkel.

Songs from Liquid Days LP – Philip Glass Ensemble (CBS FM 39564, 1986)

Philip Glass and Paul Simon wrote Changing Opinion

Graceland LP/CD – Paul Simon (US Warner 2-25447, UK Warner WX 52 925 447 1, 1986) (US No. 3, UK No. 1 for six weeks)

The Boy in the Bubble / Graceland / I Know What I Know / Gumboots / Diamonds on the Soles of Her Shoe / You Can Call Me Al / Under African Skies / Homeless / Crazy Love Vol. 2 / That Was Your Mother / All Around The World Or the Myth of Fingerprints (2004 reissue on Columbia Legacy 88697842502 includes three alternative versions)

You Can Call Me Al / Gumboots – Paul Simon (US Warner 28667, UK Warner W 8667, 1986) (US No. 23, UK No. 4)

The Boy in the Bubble (remix) / Hearts And Bones – Paul Simon (US Warner 928 6097, UK Warner W 8509, 1986) (UK No. 26)

The Animals' Christmas LP – Art Garfunkel and Amy Grant (US Columbia FC 40212, UK CBS 26704, 1986)

The Annunciation / The Creatures of the Field / Just A Simple Little Tune / The Decree / Incredible Phat / The Friendly Beasts / The Song of the Camels / Words from an Old Spanish Carol / Carol of the Birds / The Frog / Herod / Wild Geese

Carol of the Birds / The Dance – Art Garfunkel and Amy Grant (US Columbia 06590, 1986)

Graceland / Crazy Love Vol II – Paul Simon (US Warner 7 27903, UK Warner WB 8349, 1987) Also on twelve-inch single with the Late Great Johnny Ace. (UK Warner WT 8349, 1987) (You might be expecting a chart entry for Graceland but it was released too late – everybody who wanted it had bought the album.)

Under African Skies / I Know What I Know – Paul Simon (UK Warner WB 8221, 1987)

Lefty CD – Art Garfunkel (US CBS CK 40942, UK CBS 460694 2, 1988)

This Is the Moment / I Have a Love / So Much in Love / Slow Breakup / Love Is the Only Chain / When a Man Loves a Woman / I Wonder Why / King of Tonga / If Love Takes You Away / The Promise

When a Man Loves a Woman / King of Tonga – Art Garfunkel (UK CBS 5516327, 1988)

So Much in Love / King of Tonga – Art Garfunkel (US Columbia 07711, 1988)

This is the Moment / Slow Breakup – Art Garfunkel (US Columbia 07949, 1988)

When a Man Loves a Woman / I Have a Love – Art Garfunkel (US Columbia 08511, 1988)

Negotiations and Love Songs, 1971–1986 CD – Paul Simon (Warner WX 223, 1988) (UK No. 17) Compilation

Speaking of Dreams CD – Joan Baez (US Gold Castle D2-71324, UK Virgin CDVGC 12, 1989)

Joan Baez and Paul Simon perform a medley of Rambler Gambler and Whispering Bells

The Rhythm of the Saints CD – Paul Simon (US Warner 26098 UK Warner WX 340, 1990) (US No. 4, US No. 1 for three weeks)

The Obvious Child / Can't Run But / The Coast / Proof / Further to Fly / She Moves On / Born at the Right Time / The Cool, Cool River / Spirit Voices / The Rhythm of the Saints

The Obvious Child / Further to Fly / You Can Call Me Al – Paul Simon (UK Warner W 9549, 1990) (US No. 92, UK No. 15)

The Definitive Simon & Garfunkel (UK Columbia MOODCD 21, 1991)

(UK No. 8) Compilation

A Hazy Shade of Winter / Silent Night – Seven O'Clock News – Simon & Garfunkel (UK Columbia 65765370, reissue 1991) (UK No. 30, both sides listed but how many people bought it for Silent Night?)

Paul Simon's Concert in the Park 2CD – August 15, 1991 (UK Warner WX 448, 1991) (UK No. 60)

The Obvious Child / The Boy in the Bubble / She Moves On / Kodachrome / Born at the Right Time / Train In the Distance / Me and Julio Down by the Schoolyard / I Know What I Know / The Cool, Cool River / Bridge Over Troubled Water / Proof / The Coast / Graceland / You Can Call Me Al / Still Crazy After All These Years / Loves Me Like a Rock / Diamonds on the Soles of Her Shoes / Hearts And Bones / Late In the Evening / America / The Boxer / Cecilia / The Sound of Silence

The Boxer / Cecilia – Simon & Garfunkel (UK Columbia 6578067, reissue 1992) (UK No. 75)

Up 'Til Now CD – Art Garfunkel (1993) Compilation but with some alternative versions and a mock interview The Breakup with Paul Simon.

The Paul Simon Anthology (Warner, 1993)

Tracks include Thelma

Picture Perfect Morning CD – Edie Brickell (US Geffen GED 24715, 1994)

Produced by Simon and Roy Halee, Simon plays guitar on several tracks.

Something So Right – Annie Lennox featuring Paul Simon (RCA 74321 332392, 1995) (UK No. 44)

Across The Borderline CD – Willie Nelson (US Columbia CK 52752, 1993, UK CBS 4729422)

American Tune and Graceland with Paul Simon on guitar. Graceland co-produced by Paul Simon and Roy Halee.

Across America CD – Art Garfunkel (US Hybrid 7243 8 42655 2 6, UK Virgin VTCD 113, 1996) (UK No. 35)

A Heart in New York / Crying In the Rain (with James Taylor) / Scarborough Fair / A Poem on the Underground Wall / I Only Have Eyes For You / Homeward Bound / All I Know / Bright Eyes / El Condor Pasa (If I Could) / Bridge Over Troubled Water / Mrs Robinson / The 59th Street Bridge Song (Feelin' Groovy) / I Will / April Come She Will / The Sound Of Silence / Grateful / Goodnight, My Love

Go Cat Go! CD – Carl Perkins (US Dinosaur 76401 84508 2, 1996)

Rockabilly Music is written by Paul and Carl, features both of them along with Harper Simon and Stan Perkins.

Songs from The Capeman CD – Paul Simon (US Warner 9362 46814 2, 1997)

Adios Hermanos / Born in Puerto Rico / Satin Summer Nights / Bernadette / The Vampires / Quality / Can I Forgive Him / Sunday Afternoon / Killer Wants To Go To College (2 parts) / Time Is an Ocean / Virgil / Trailways Bus

Old Friends 3CD – Simon & Garfunkel (Columbia Legacy 3CK 64780, 1997) Compilation of forty-four original recordings with another fifteen previously unreleased tracks including demos, live shows and studio work.

Carnival! CD (US RCA 74321 447692, 1997)

Simon performs his own song, Ten Years.

Songs from a Parent to a Child CD – Art Garfunkel (UK Sony Wonder LK 67674, 1997)

Who's Gonna Shoe Your Pretty Little Feet? (2 versions) / Morning Has Broken / Daydream / Baby Mine / Secret O' Life / The Things We've Handed Down / You're a Wonderful One / Good Luck Charm / I Will / Lasso the Moon / Dreamland / The Lord's Prayer – Now I Lay Me Down to Sleep

Shining Like A National Guitar CD – Paul Simon (Warner 9362477212, 2000) (UK No. 6) Compilation

The Very Best of Simon and Garfunkel – Tales from New York CD (Columbia SONYTV 81 CD, 2000) (UK No. 8)

Grateful – The Songs Of John Bucchino CD (US RCA B0004SBV2, 2000)

Art Garfunkel performs If I Ever Say I'm Over You with Bucchino

You're The One CD – Paul Simon (US Warner 9362 47844 2, 2000) (UK No. 20)

That's Where I Belong / Darling Lorraine / Old / You're The One / The Teacher / Look At That / Senorita with a Necklace of Tears / Love / Pigs, Sheep And Wolves / Hurricane Eye / Quiet

Live From New York City 1967 CD – Simon & Garfunkel (Columbia Legacy 508067-2, 2002)

He Was My Brother / Leaves That Are Green / Sparrow / Homeward Bound / You Don't Know Where Your Interest Lies / A Most Peculiar Man / The 59th Street Bridge Song (Feelin' Groovy) / The Dangling Conversation / Richard Cory / A Hazy Shade of Winter / Benedictus / Blessed / A Poem on the Underground Wall / Anji / I Am a Rock / The Sound of Silence / For Emily, Whenever I May Find Her /A Church Is Burning / Wednesday Morning 3am

Everything Waits to Be Noticed CD– Art Garfunkel with Maia Sharp and Buddy Mondlock (UK Manhattan 7243 5 40990 2 1, 2002)

Bounce / The Thread / The Kid / Crossing Lines / Everything Waits to Be Noticed / Young And Free / Perfect Moment / Turn, Don't Turn Away / Wishbone / How Did You Know / What I Love About Rain / Every Now And Then /Another Only One

The Essential Simon and Garfunkel CD (UK Columbia 5134702, 2003) (UK No. 25) Compilation

Old Friends – Live on Stage 2CD – Simon & Garfunkel (Sony 519173 2, 2004) (UK No. 61)

CD1: Old Friends – Bookends / A Hazy Shade of Winter / I Am a Rock / America / At the Zoo / Baby Driver / Kathy's Song / Hey, Schoolgirl / Bye Bye Love (with Everly Brothers) / Scarborough Fair / Homeward Bound / The Sound Of Silence

CD2: Mrs Robinson / Slip Slidin' Away / El Condor Pasa (If I Could) / The Only Living Boy in New York / American Tune / My Little Town / Bridge Over Troubled Water / Cecilia / The Boxer / Leaves That Are Green / (bonus track) Citizen of the Planet

Surprise CD – Paul Simon (Warner 9362 49982 2, 2006)

How Can You Live In the Northeast? / Everything About It Is a Love Song / Outrageous / Sure Don't Feel Like Love / Wartime Prayers / Beautiful / I Don't Believe / Another Galaxy / Once Upon a Time Thee Was an Ocean / That's Me / Father and Daughter

Father and Daughter – Paul Simon (UK Warner W 719CD, 2006) (UK No. 31)

Radioplay single – That's Me – Paul Simon

Some Enchanted Evening – Art Garfunkel (US Atco 8122 74851 2 2, 2007)

I Remember You / Someone To Watch Over Me / Let's Fall In Love / I'm Glad There Is You / Quiet Nights of Quiet Stars (Corcovado) / Easy

Living / I've Grown Accustomed To Her Face / You Stepped Out Of A Dream / Some Enchanted Evening / It Could Happen To You / Life Is But a Dream / What'll I Do / If I Loved You

Live 1969 – Simon & Garfunkel (US Starbucks Entertainment – Opus Collection, 2008)

An LP was intended in 1970 but then dropped. This was the first release of an 'in concert' album covering several venues from November 1969.

Harper Simon CD – Harper Simon (US Tulsi 945.A171.022, 2009)

Paul Simon co-wrote three songs and plays on The Audit

This Better Be Good – Paul Simon (US Starbucks Entertainment – Opus Collection, 2009)

Although this compilation was only available at Starbucks, it still made No. 60 on the US album chart. The CD came with a download code for a new track on *iTunes*, Questions for the Angels. It was released in 2011 on Simon's next studio album.

Bridge Over Troubled Water 2CD & DVD (Columbia Legacy 88697828292, 2011)

CD1 is the standard album. CD 2 is a concert from 1969 and the DVD features the *Songs of America* TV special from 1969 and *The Harmony Game*, a documentary film about the making of the album. The repertoire of the concert CD is:

Homeward Bound / At The Zoo / The 59th Street Bridge Song (Feelin' Groovy) / Song for the Asking / For Emily, Whenever I May Find Her / Scarborough Fair / Mrs Robinson / The Boxer / Why Don't You Write Me / So Long, Frank Lloyd Wright / That Silver Haired Daddy of Mine / Bridge Over Troubled Water/ The Sound of Silence / I Am a Rock / Old Friends – Bookends Theme / Leaves That Are Green / Kathy's Song

So Beautiful Or So What CD – Paul Simon (US Hear 0888072328143, UK Decca, 2011)

Getting Ready for Christmas Day / The Afterlife / Dazzling Blue / Rewrite / Love and Hard Times / Love Is Eternal Sacred Light / Amulet / Questions for the Angels / Love and Blessings / So Beautiful Or So What

Radioplay single – So Beautiful Or So What

The Traveler CD – Jerry Douglas (US E One B005DZMQ0Y, UK Membran B0085GOCGS, 2012)

Paul Simon and Mumford & Sons join Jerry Douglas for The Boxer

Live in New York City – Paul Simon 2CD & DVD package (Decca B008UTV658, 2012)

CD1: The Obvious Child / Dazzling Blue / 50 Ways to Leave Your Lover / So Beautiful Or So What / Mother and Child Reunion / That Was Your Mother / Hearts and Bones / Crazy Love, Vol II / Slip Slidin' Away / Rewrite

CD2: The Boy in the Bubble / The Only Living Boy in New York / The Afterlife / Diamonds On the Soles of Her Shoes / Gumboots / The Sound of Silence / Kodachrome / Gone At Last / Late In the Evening / Still Crazy After All These Years

Still Within The Sound Of Your Voice CD – Jimmy Webb (E One 23795, 2013)

Garfunkel joins Webb for Shattered

The Complete Albums Collection 14CD – Paul Simon (Sony 2013)

Perfect for the beginner who wants everything and retailing at around forty pounds.

The Complete Albums Collection 12 CD – Simon & Garfunkel (Sony 2014)

All the original albums with live concerts which have been issued before. No bonus tracks. These albums have been reissued many times, but all the albums here are without the bonus tracks, which is a bit of a cheat when the cost is around forty pounds. Impossible to read the lyrics or the notes on the back of the sleeves now they have been reduced to CD size.

New York Is My Home CD – Dion (US Instant, 2016)

Paul Simon harmonises on the title track, which had made available on download in 2015.

Stranger to Stranger CD – Paul Simon (US Virgin Deluxe B01DWK0634, 2016: vinyl does not have bonus tracks)

The Werewolf / Wristband / The Clock / Street Angel / Stranger to Stranger / In A Parade / Proof of Love / In the Garden of Edie / The Riverbank / Cool Papa Bell / Insomniac's Lullaby.

Bonus tracks: Horace and Pete / Duncan and Wristband (both from *The Prairie Home Companion*) / Guitar Piece 3 / New York Is My Home (lead vocal: Dion)

UNDER THE COVERS
Tribute albums

Instrumental Versions of Simon and Garfunkel LP – Don Costa (Fontana, 1968)

Bridge Over Troubled Water LP – Paul Desmond (A&M, 1970)

Simon and Garfunkel's Greatest Hits LP – Caravelli and his Magnificent Strings (CBS, 1970)

Strings for Pleasure Play Simon and Garfunkel LP (Music For Pleasure, 1970)

Simon and Garfunkel History LP – Jim Nambara Quarter (US CBS, 1971)

Simon and Garfunkel Songbook LP – Shiro Michi (US CBS, 1971)

Alan Caddy Orchestra and Singers Pay Tribute To Simon and Garfunkel LP (UK Avenue, 1971)

The Piccadilly Pops Orchestra Plays the Simon and Garfunkel Songbook LP (UK Concord, 1971)

Portrait of Simon and Garfunkel LP – Mike Batt Orchestra (UK DJM Silverline, 1972)

The Paul Simon Songbook CD – Various Artists (UK Connoisseur, 1992)

The Paul Simon Album: Broadway Sings CD – Various Artists (US Varese Sarabande, 1998)

Notable cover versions

America – First Aid Kit, Razorlight, Yes (US No. 46, 1972) ('I don't really know the other versions,' says Art Garfunkel. 'I thought I hit a nice upper high suspension at the end and I like that.')

American Tune – Eva Cassidy, Willie Nelson, Gretchen Peters (as a response to 9/11), Starland Vocal Band, Curtis Stigers, Allen Toussaint

The Boxer – Chet Atkins, Joan Baez, Paul Butterfield Blues Band, Neil Diamond, Jerry Douglas (with Mumford & Sons and Paul Simon), Bob Dylan, Emmylou Harris, Ben Howard, Waylon Jennings

The Boy In The Bubble – Blue Aeroplanes, Peter Gabriel

Bridge Over Troubled Water – Chet Atkins, John Barrowman, Shirley Bassey, Cilla Black, Alfie Boe, Susan Boyle, Glen Campbell, Johnny Cash, Eva Cassidy, Merry Clayton, Linda Clifford (UK No. 28, 1979), Judy

Collins, Perry Como, King Curtis, Roberta Flack, Aretha Franklin (US No. 6, 1971), Davey Graham, Lewisham and Greenwich NHS Choir (UK No. 1, 2015), Senator J. Ervin Jr (hoping to catch some votes), Gladys Knight and the Pips, Jackson 5, Tom Jones, Annie Lennox, Barry Manilow, Bill Medley, Nana Mouskouri, Aaron Neville, Willie Nelson, Roy Orbison, Buck Owens, PJB featuring Hannah and her Sisters ((UK No. 21, 1991), Elvis Presley, Smokey Robinson and the Miracles, Demis Roussos, Shadows, Supremes, Bobby Womack, Stevie Wonder

Carlos Dominguez – Val Doonican, Tom O'Connor

Cloudy – Richard Anthony, Cyrkle, Cliff Richard, Seekers

The Dangling Conversation – Joan Baez

El Condor Pasa (If I Could) – Chet Atkins, Perry Como, Placido Domingo, Julie Felix (UK No. 19, 1970), James Galway, Yma Sumac, Andy Williams

The 59th Street Bridge Song (Feelin' Groovy) – Mike Bloomfield and Al Kooper, Val Doonican, Harper's Bizarre (US No. 13, 1967: UK No. 34, 1967), Johnny Mathis, Seekers

50 Ways to Leave Your Lover – Sonny Curtis, Miley Cyrus

For Emily, Whenever I May Find Her – David Essex, Rick Nelson, Johnny Rivers

Graceland – Big Daddy, Willie Nelson

Groundhog – Peter Yarrow (Simon's demo on YouTube)

A Hazy Shade of Winter – Bangles (US No. 2, 1987; UK No. 11, 1988), Simon James (guitar instrumental)

Homeward Bound – Beau Brummels, Cher, Glen Campbell, Davey Graham, Burl Ives, Jermaine Jackson, Waylon Jennings & Willie Nelson, Jack Jones, Quiet Five (UK No. 44, 1966), Cliff Richard, Sandie Shaw, Mel Tormé

I Am a Rock – Coolies, Hollies

I Do It For Your Love – Bill Evans, Herbie Hancock

I Wish You Could Be Here – Richard Anthony (No known version by Simon), Cyrkle (US No. 70, 1967)

Keep the Customer Satisfied – Marsha Hunt (UK No. 41, 1970), Gary Puckett and the Union Gap, Buddy Rich Big Band, Robson and Jerome

Kodachrome – Christiane Noll

Late In The Evening – Eva Cassidy, Tom Jones

Loves Me Like A Rock – Dixie Hummingbirds, Oak Ridge Boys

Me and Julio Down by the Schoolyard – Boston Pops

Mrs Robinson – Booker T. & the MG's (US No. 37, 1969), Davey Graham, Yank Lawson, Lemonheads (UK No. 19, 1992), Hank Marvin, Billy Paul, Frank Sinatra

Most Peculiar Man, A – Harvey Andrews

Mother and Child Reunion – David Cassidy, Randy California, Pioneers, Uniques

Old Friends – Four Freshmen

Peace Like a River – Joe Henderson, Jerry Lawson

Punky's Dilemma – Barbra Streisand, Lois Lane

Red Rubber Ball – Cilla Black, Cyrkle (US No. 2, 1966), Seekers

Richard Cory – Animals, Them

St Judy's Comet – Mickey Dolenz, Kenny Loggins

Scarborough Fair – Harry Belafonte, Sarah Brightman, Marianne Faithfull, Kenneth McKellar, Sergio Mendes & Brasil '66 (US No. 16, 1968), Andy Williams

Slip Sliding Away – Persuasions

Someday, One Day – Seekers (UK No. 11, 1966) (No known version by Simon)

Song for the Asking – Mary Travers

The Sound of Silence – Bachelors (UK No. 3, 1966), Dickies, Disturbed (at the time of going to press their official music video on YouTube had received over 80 million hits!), Barney Kessel, Peaches & Herb (US No. 100, 1966), Ventures

Still Crazy After All These Years – Carpenters, Ray Charles, Rosemary Clooney, Lacy J Dalton, Amanda McBroom, Willie Nelson

Stranded in a Limousine – Michelle Shocked

Still Crazy After All These Years – Amanda McBroom

Was A Sunday Day – Paul Desmond (modern jazz saxophonist)

Index

Dubin, Al 128
Dubliners, The 20
Duck Rock (album) 153
'Duncan' 107, 109, 124, 196, 198
Dunn, Donald 'Duck' 110
Dupree, Cornell 117
Duvall, Shelley 137, 165
Dylan, Bob 16–17, 19, 30–2, 40, 43, 47, 50, 54–5, 61, 64, 71, 73, 82, 88, 94–5, 97, 105, 109, 110, 136, 144, 149, 153, 166, 175–6, 178, 182, 189, 196, 197
'Earth Angel' 4, 22
'Easy Living'
Easy Rider (film) 74
Eaton, Steve 128
Edmands, Bob 123
'Educated Fool' 13
Edwards, Sherman 11
Edwards, Tommy 167
'Eight By Ten' 116
'Eight Miles High' 152
'El Condor Pasa (If I Could)' 93, 124
'El Eco' 93
Elias & his Zig-Zag Jive Flutes 151
Elliott, Denholm 140
Elliott, Missy 179
Elliott, Ramblin' Jack 40
Elton, Ben 149
Emin, Tracey 191
'Empty Boxes' 109
Eno, Brian 185
Essex, David 129
'Eve of Destruction' 59
Everly Brothers, The 4, 5, 7, 16, 22, 55, 62, 79, 99, 105, 109,

158, 166–7, 169, 185, 192
'Every Now And Then' 181
'Everything Put Together Falls Apart' 107
'Everything Waits to be Noticed' 180–1
Everything Waits to be Noticed (album) 180–2
'Express Train' 12
Fairport Convention 44
'Fakin' It' 65–6, 100
Fallon, Jimmy 196
Fariña, Richard 16
Fate for Breakfast (album) 139
'Father and Daughter' 188
'Feelin' Groovy' – See '59th Street Bridge Song'
Feiffer, Jules 101
Feliciano, Jose 173
Felix, Julie 93
'Feuilles-Oh' 90, 121, 133–4
'50 Ways To Leave Your Lover' 77, 174
'59th Street Bridge Song (Feelin' Groovy), The' 60, 62–65, 71, 76, 112
'Fightin' Mad' 8
'Finally Found a Reason' 140
Fisher, Archie 43
Fisher, Carrie 138, 143, 146–7, 149, 158, 163–4, 191, 195
Fisher, Eddie 138
Fitzgerald, Ella 128
Five To Ten (BBC) 28–29
'Fix You' 192
'Flame' 13
Flamingos, The 117, 128
Flashdance (film) 127
'Flip, Flop and Fly' 3
Flock of Seagulls, A 116

Gielgud, Sir John 162
Gilberto, Astrud 127
Gillespie, Dizzy 163
'Girl for Me, The' 5
'Girl from Ipanema, The' 127
'Girl from the North Country'
32, 144
Glaser, Milton 115
Glass, Philip 148
Goodman, Andrew 16
'Go Tell It on the Mountain'
20–21
Goddard, Lon 9, 101
Goldberg, Morris 156
Golden Gate Quartet, The 198
Goldsboro, Bobby 70
'Gone at Last' 133–4
'Good Luck Charm' 169
'Good Times' 166
Good to Go (film) 161
Goodman, Dick 11
Goodbye, Columbus (film) 79
'Goodnight My Love' 168, 181
Goss, Curly 27
Gould, Elliott 90
'Graceland' 155, 158–9, 168,
184
Graceland (album) 10, 133,
150, 152–160
Graduate, The (album) 68, 78,
93, 163–5
Graduate, The (film) 66–70, 76,
78–9, 180
Graham, Davey 23–24, 187
Granada Television 63
Grant, Amy 149
Grappelli, Stéphane, 105, 110
'Grateful' 168, 177
Grateful Dead, The 64, 166

Gray, Michael 95
'Grazing in the Grass' 151
Greatest Hits (1972 album) 112
Greatest Hits, Etc (1977 album)
137
Green, Colin 38
'Greenfields' 13
Grodin, Charles 141
Grossman, Albert 59
Grossman, Linda 81, 85, 100,
110, 120–1
Grossman, Stefan 24
'Groundhog' 76
Grundy, Stuart 130
Grupo Culteval Olodum 163
Grusin, Dave
'Guitar Man' 83
'Guitar Piece 3'
'Gumboots' 154, 160
Gumboots (album) 150, 153–5
Guthrie, Woody 15, 22, 31

Hahn, Jerry 105
Halee, Roy 19, 56, 72, 81, 94,
104, 110, 117, 121, 140, 147,
154, 164, 166, 175, 196, 197
Half Man Half Biscuit 86
Hamlisch, Marvin 167
Hammond, Albert 123, 129
Hancock, Herbie 135
Hanks, Tom 167
Hardy, Thomas 121
Harper, Peggy 50, 82, 85, 90,
100, 107, 117, 130, 137
Harper, Roy 34, 44
Harper's Bizarre 63
'Harper Valley PTA' 70
Harptones, The 148
Harris, Bob 130